BY JOSH MALERMAN

GOBLIN

GOBLIN

A NOVEL IN SIX NOVELLAS

JOSH MALERMAN

 NEW YORK

Copyright © 2017 by Josh Malerman

All rights reserved.

Published in the United States by Del Rey, an imprint of Random House, a division of Penguin Random House LLC, New York.

DEL REY is a registered trademark and the CIRCLE colophon is a trademark of Penguin Random House LLC.

Originally published in paperback in the United States by Earthling Publications, in 2017.

LIBRARY OF CONGRESS CATALOGING-IN-PUBLICATION DATA
Names: Malerman, Josh, author.
Title: Goblin: a novel in six novellas / Josh Malerman.
Description: New York: Del Rey, [2021] | "Originally published in paperback in the United Stations by Earthling Publications, in 2017"
Identifiers: LCCN 2020036061 (print) | LCCN 2020036062 (ebook) |
ISBN 9780593237809 (hardcover; acid-free paper) |
ISBN 9780593237816 (ebook)
Subjects: LCGFT: Novellas.
Classification: LCC PS3613.A43535 G63 2021 (print) |
LCC PS3613.A43535 (ebook) | DDC 813/.6—dc23
LC record available at https://lccn.loc.gov/2020036061
LC ebook record available at https://lccn.loc.gov/2020036062

Printed in Canada on acid-free paper

Illustration by Deena Warner

randomhousebooks.com

1 2 3 4 5 6 7 8 9

First Edition

Book design by Edwin Vazquez

From East Lansing to New York, a wedding, a New Year's Eve, and an acid test come to mind. But those are only landmarks on a gorgeous drive. And when the person you're traveling with points left as often as right, you start to realize it's the actual act of seeing, not the sights.

This is for Matt Sekedat.

CONTENTS

GOBLIN

PROLOGUE: WELCOME

1

If Tom hadn't left his sweater in his locker, if he hadn't gone back to get it, and if he hadn't passed the main office on the way, the whole dark night might've been avoided.

"Hold up a minute, Tommy. Got one more run for you."

Dammit. Tom had a fun night planned ahead. A great one. Pizza, beer, old movies, feet on the table, and the open prairie of the living room to himself.

"Where to, Jerry?"

Before his boss even said the city name, Tom knew he'd scratch his evening plans. He never said no to Jerry.

"Goblin."

Goblin?

"Jeez, Jerry. Goblin's what . . . an hour away? I haven't been to Goblin in something close to . . . thirty years."

To Goblin might've been an hour's drive, but there and back would make it two.

"I know it," Jerry said, making his most sympathetic face. Cigar smoke rose from the ashtray on his desk and curled about his big belly. "And I'm gonna give you triple for the run. The recipient gave us some extra. Wants it done his way. Very specific."

"Triple? Wow. What is it, Jerry?"

Jerry shrugged and looked to a stack of papers.

"It's a pain in the ass is what it is. Obsessive instructions. And he wants it delivered at midnight. No kidding. Maybe there's a party going on or who knows . . . but I'd send you with a carload of uncuffed prisoners for this kind of money. There's a whole list of demands attached to the crate."

"Crate?"

"Box."

Tom removed his yellow ball cap and ran greasy fingers through his greasy hair. Triple. That added up to $1.20 a *mile*. What with Goblin hanging at least seventy miles north (and maybe even more, Tom would certainly check), not to mention the seventy back, he stood to make a cool hundred sixty-eight dollars on a last-minute run. Tom could drop the box off at midnight and be in front of his TV by two in the morning. Hell, he could drink all day from there.

"Just follow the directions to a T, Tommy. The fella already made good on his money. Now it's just up to us not to mess it up."

The union had the drivers going at eighteen an hour or taking forty cents on the mile. Most of the guys opted for the hourly because most of the guys factored in the dreaded *long wait* upon delivery. But Tom had been driving for sixteen years and he knew this guy there and that guy here and by the time the option was granted he'd had his routes down pat. And if there was an unexpected delay? Well, that was okay, too. Tom loved to count the miles. He wasn't about to give that small distraction up.

"You know, Jerry," Tom said, smiling, "I kissed my first girl up in Goblin. Alice Pratt. She bit clean through my lower lip."

Tom pulled his lip out for Jerry to see.

"Jeez. That's something, Tommy. Maybe you could look her up."

Tommy once knew Goblin. His mother had taken him there three summers in a row. His eleventh, his twelfth, and his thirteenth birthdays. Three summers spent swimming in Goblin's deep lakes, not to mention the ice-cold Blackwater River, on whose banks Tom's mouth was ambushed by Alice after she fooled him into thinking he was getting a kiss without a bite. He'd played games in the West Fields, walked through Perish Park. Still standing in Jerry's office, he had detailed memories of passing The Hedges on the east side and driving between the two giant topiaries framing the highway coming in from the south. He recalled the savage tour of the slaughterhouse and the pleasant one of the Hardy Carroll Goblin Zoo. He recalled the owls, too; postcards and photos of the owls, keepsakes his mother had purchased downtown.

Tom smiled. A hundred sixty-eight dollars was a lot of money to revisit his youth. A place he remembered enjoying, if he remembered it right.

"It's already ten fifteen," Jerry said. "You better get moving if you're gonna reach Goblin by midnight."

Goblin.

"Thanks, Jerry. I'm on it. Thanks for the gig."

"Thank *you*, Tommy. I was planning on making the run myself before you showed up." He took a long pull on the cigar, then pointed at Tom with it. "The box is already on the lift. You're gonna need that. It's heavy as hell. And remember"—he held up his hands like *it's my job to say it more than once*—"make sure you follow those directions."

2

The box was easy to see from across the warehouse. It was tall, taller than Tom. When he climbed the lift and tried to move it, the resistance told him he didn't have much of a chance without some help.

"Delivering lead?" He removed his cap again and wiped his hairline dry.

He wasn't even sure how Jerry got the thing where it was.

Crossing the warehouse again, he started the smaller truck and backed it up. Then he got out and started the lift.

It made a nasty squawking sound Tom had never heard it make before.

"Sucker's testing the lift."

By the time the machine got it level with the truck, it looked to Tom like the gears were going to fold in on themselves. He climbed up into the truck, took the power dolly, and rolled its lip under the box.

Before trying to move it, Tom spotted the instructions, nailed to the wood.

DELIVER TO:
DEAN CRAWFORD
726 ROLLING HILLS DRIVE, ROLLING HILLS
GOBLIN, MI
48929

CONTENT: ONE BOX, 8 FT. X 3 FT. 110 LBS.

"You're more than a hundred and ten pounds, buddy."
He read on:

SPECIAL: DO NOT DELIVER BEFORE MIDNIGHT
(12 AM)—

RECIPIENT WILL NOT BE HOME TO RECEIVE
BEFORE MIDNIGHT—

DO NOT DELIVER PAST 12:30 AM—RECIPIENT WILL
NOT BE HOME TO RECEIVE AFTER 12:30 AM. IF
RECIPIENT IS NOT HOME (OR DOES NOT ANSWER
THE DOOR) BETWEEN 12 AND 12:30 OR IF DRIVER
MISSES THIS WINDOW OF TIME, DESTROY
CONTENTS OF BOX.

"Wait. What the fuck?"

Here Jerry wrote in pen:

Customer is real serious about this . . . no typo. Destroy box if you can't reach him.

There was more:

DO NOT ATTEMPT TO OPEN BOX BEFORE
DELIVERY—MAKE SURE BOX IS SECURE—
CUSTOMER WILL NOT RECEIVE BOX IF ATTEMPT
TO OPEN IS EVIDENT.

Tom shook his head. Triple the money or not, this was a weird gig.

DELIVER BOX ALONE—DO NOT LOAD ON TRUCK
WITH OTHER ITEMS—MAKE SURE BOX IS ALONE IN
TRUCK—DO NOT GET IN THE REAR OF TRUCK WITH
BOX AND TRUCK DOOR CLOSED.

"Okay," Tom said. "Now you're telling me shit I learned six-teen years ago, buddy. Think I'm gonna lock myself in?"

DO NOT STOP TO CHECK ON BOX—ONCE BACK
DOOR IS SECURE DO NOT OPEN UNTIL YOU HAVE
ARRIVED AT 726 ROLLING HILLS DR., ROLLING
HILLS, GOBLIN, MI.

And *this:*

IF BOX SHOULD FALL OR ANY NOISE THAT
INDICATES AS MUCH SHOULD OCCUR,
DO NOT ATTEMPT TO CHECK ON BOX—
KEEP DRIVING TO DESTINATION.

Tom grunted.

"Well, I ain't gonna let it fall, buddy."

There was one more instruction, followed by another note from Jerry in pen:

DO NOT COMMUNICATE TO OTHER DRIVERS
WHERE YOU ARE DELIVERING BOX TO—
RECIPIENT WANTS STRICT ANONYMITY AND
INSISTS ON DISCRETION.

So don't go yapping on the CB!

Tom let out a long dull whistle. He'd been given some pretty far-out orders before but never—not once—had he been in-structed to *destroy* a package if no one was there to get it. He'd had to bring a few back, of course, and sometimes they had you drop it off somewhere else, but never this.

"Goblin and back," he said. "Come on."

He tried to move the box by way of the dolly, but it simply wouldn't budge.

"One hundred and ten pounds, my ass."

He found that if he sort of knelt and put his shoulder into it, if he put all his weight into the middle and lower part . . . the box slid. And he was sweating when he finally got it against the wall. He had to take a second before wrapping the straps around the box and securing them to the truck wall. Then he secured the power dolly to the opposite wall.

"I won't be seeing you until Goblin. And we're both better for it!"

He got down from the truck and pulled the rope, slamming the door closed. After locking it, he walked to the cabin and stopped at the driver's-side mirror.

He looked at himself.

"You haven't been to Goblin in thirty years." Then he smiled. "Think you'll recognize the city? Think the city will recognize *you?*"

He heard a sound like a hammer falling a short distance to the ground. He looked over his shoulder, deep into the warehouse, then climbed into the cabin at last.

"Don't let mysterious boxes freak you out, Tommy," he told himself. "And don't follow directions from people who don't know any better than you do."

3

He started the drive on edge but didn't really know it. He'd made it out of the lot by ten fifty-two and the map told him Goblin was actually seventy-two miles away. Cool: $172.80. And sixteen years of driving trucks had given him an excellent sense of timing, if nothing else. He popped in a cassette tape, smoked the butt end of a cigarette he'd hidden in the ashtray, and figured he'd reach Goblin by eleven forty-five. At an average of eighty miles an hour for seventy-two miles, with some give or take here and there, he ought to pass between the topiaries at *exactly* eleven forty-five ... giving him some time to drive the additional twelve miles from the city gates to 726 Rolling Hills Drive.

Destroy contents of box.

Tom rolled the window down partway and thought he could smell a storm coming. What was with the loony-tunes instructions? Seriously. Was he delivering something illegal? Sounded like it. He knew a bunch of drivers who sniffed cocaine to stay awake—hell, there were even guys blowing lines for full three-hour runs—but he ran a pretty clean ship himself. After sixteen years of successfully avoiding all the seedy shit, he wasn't interested in transporting drugs no matter how good the money. It wasn't *that* good.

He knew a guy back when he started driving, a grizzly sort named Wernor Mount, who got *ten years* for driving a hundred and something pounds of—

110 lbs.

Come on. Could the unfathomably heavy box be a hundred and ten pounds of ... *drugs?* Tom didn't think so. He didn't want to think so and he actually didn't believe that was the case. Jerry *must* have gone over all that with this Dean Crawford of 726 Rolling Hills Drive ... right? Jerry didn't want that happening any more than Tom did. And Jerry certainly didn't want a driver-in-the-dark saying,

I had no idea what was in it. Jerry just told me to get it to Goblin by midnight.

Not even for triple the money. No way.

But *Tom* was getting triple. How much was Jerry making on this delivery? Would it be beneath Jerry to pocket a few grand for a sideshow like this? Maybe. Maybe Jerry and this guy Crawford worked it out that they'd get an innocent bystander (a *patsy*) to move the goods. Get the illegal stuff into the hands of someone who honestly knew nothing and couldn't point any fingers.

Destroy contents of box? Truthfully? This was nuts.

He turned the radio up. Rolled the window down. Definitely smelled a storm.

4

At eleven seventeen Tom thought he heard something like a giggle come from directly behind his seat.

He turned quick to check on it but the driver's seat was flush against the cabin wall and Tom knew nothing could fit behind him.

Maybe it was the tires. Maybe it was the radio.

The CB suddenly piped up static and Tom jumped in his seat.

"Is Tomcat out there?"

Someone was trying to reach him. Someone had seen him out on the road and was phoning in.

He reached for the CB and stopped.

The instructions told him not to tell anybody where he was going. What would he say? Should he lie?

"Tomcat . . . it's Beartrap here . . . thought I saw you out there . . . was I wrong?"

Tom felt a sudden surge of shame, as if he'd been spotted transporting something illegal.

Answer the CB, Tom thought. *The instructions just said not to mention 726 Rolling Hills . . . Goblin . . .*

Beartrap was an old friend. A fellow road dog.

Answer the CB. Come on.

"Tomcat?"

He picked it up.

"Hey, old Bear . . . Tomcat indeed. You saw me right."

There was no response from Beartrap. Only static. Tom turned the volume up, but all it did was give him more static.

"Hey, old Bear . . . repeat . . . that was handsome Tomcat you saw on the road."

Still no response. Only static.

Tom hung it back up.

"Well, Beartrap," he said to nobody. "Let's hope it isn't drugs. Let's hope it's a shitty piece of art that couldn't hurt a fly if it fell on it."

5

If there was a fly in the back, the box might've fallen on it.

At eleven twenty-nine Tom heard a thud so loud he was sure it had to be the tires. He gripped the wheel and braced himself, already accepting the fact that he might not get the package to Goblin on time.

But it wasn't a wheel. And he hadn't hit anything. And nothing had hit him.

So, what then? What then other than the box falling on its side in the truck?

6

*O*nce back door is secure do not open until you have arrived at 726 Rolling Hills . . .

Call it habit or professionalism or just plain interest but Tom didn't care about this particular instruction. If the box fell, the box fell. And it was his job to see that what he delivered was in the same shape coming as going.

"And how will *Dean Crawford* know the difference?"

He looked at himself in the driver's-side mirror and saw he looked a little wiry, gaunt, crazy.

The box was getting to him. The instructions were driving him nuts.

He pulled the truck to the side of the highway, let her idle in park, and got out. He hadn't had to use his wipers on the drive so he was surprised to feel drops of rain upon his face and hands.

He walked to the truck back with the key out and ready.

Then he did something he hadn't planned on doing at all.

Rather than opening the back, he put his ear to the closed door and listened. And the silence inside was somehow convincing enough for him to head back to the cabin.

"Sounds like it's upright," he said, turning on the wipers and putting the truck in drive.

Then he drove.

7

"Jerry?"

"Yeah, Tommy. You in Goblin already?"

Tom liked the feel of the CB in his hand. Like he was still connected to Jerry, to his job, to his life.

"Not yet."

"Everything all right?"

"Sure. It's just—"

"Just what, Tommy?"

"Just nothing. Just wanted to thank you again for the gig. Hell of a gig."

"You getting emotional on me?"

"Suppose I sort of am."

"Don't mention it. You deserve all the big runs anyway. You're the best driver we got and you know it. You gonna look up that Alice girl?"

"Who?"

"First kiss. The biter."

"Oh . . . Alice Pratt." Tom laughed. It felt really good to laugh. How could he be transporting something illegal and laughing at the same time? Didn't seem possible. "I think I'll leave her be."

"All right, well. CB me after the delivery."

8

With every mile the truck swallowed, Tom felt like the box was getting lighter. Not that the truck was easier to handle, no, but like the pressure of following those instructions was lessening.

Less time spent with a rule was less time to break it.

He thought he might ask Mr. Crawford what it was when he got there. Maybe it was like a riddle.

What's sealed and heavy and might smell like a storm and might giggle and you can't approach it under any circumstances?

The sort of brainteaser that pins you down before it tells you the answer and *all at once* you understand it so clearly that it's shameful you didn't figure it out on your own.

"He'd better be home," Tom said.

Then he had a vision of himself in a stranger's driveway, busting up the contents of a mystery box. Because of Alice Pratt he imagined this driveway on the banks of the Blackwater River, the pieces taken by the cold flowing water.

"He'd better be home."

Was it a gift for a mistress? The secrecy, the small window to deliver, the hush money.

A Pontiac Sunbird pulled up next to him, and through its window Tom saw two young men pointing to the back of the truck.

"What?" Tom mouthed.

Through the falling rain, the men became more animated.

"The back of your truck!" Tom heard, before the faces with their open mouths vanished into the rain ahead.

"Did the back open up?"

Tom looked in the driver's-side mirror. He saw no swinging door. He took his foot off the gas, then pressed it hard. No swinging door.

He didn't want to admit what was so obvious about the sudden road encounter:

They looked scared.

Scared for themselves.

"What's on my truck?" Tom asked the otherwise empty cabin.

Keep driving to destination—Do not stop to check on box—

He looked at the clock.

Eleven thirty-eight.

He was seven miles from Goblin.

He had time to stop. He had time to do his job.

9

Tom pulled the truck to the side of the road, the front tires in matching puddles of rain. He grabbed the flashlight from the glove compartment. The short walk from the door to the rear of the truck went too quickly, it seemed, and he was facing the closed door before he wanted to.

What am I delivering to Goblin?

But the hollering from the Sunbird turned out to be just what Tom expected it was: a lot of fuss over nothing. What else but a burned-out taillight?

Tom smiled. He looked up to the back door.

"He's not gonna know if you open the damn door, buddy."

He placed his hand on the lock. Would this be the first time he ever willingly defied instructions on a delivery? Tom wanted to say no, of course not, but he couldn't think of another time he had.

He unlocked the door.

"You see?" he said. "No fireworks. No bomb going off. No sudden police lights, either."

The door screeched unoiled when he pushed it up.

And there it was! Lying on its side! The big box *did* tip over!

But . . . no.

Tom turned the flashlight on it and saw it was just the power dolly. He must've done a poor job securing it. The box itself stood exactly as he'd last seen it. Strapped in five times over.

He climbed up into the back of the truck. The rain came down hard against the metal roof and echoed in the rectangular chamber.

Tom stepped on something gooey and slipped and fell on his ass.

WHUMP!

On the floor now, he saw movement, a thousand insects, crawling at the base of the box. But when he trained his light on it, there were none.

"Fuckin' hell," Tom said. "I've got the heebie jeeb—"

"*Drive.*"

A voice. Unquestionably a voice. The echo of its one word lingered, round and round in Tom's ear.

Then movement indeed. A shadow, a shape, just beyond the box, someone crouched behind it.

"Hey!" Tom yelled. "Is someone in there?"

He couldn't believe the words that came out of his mouth.

"*Driiiiiiiive.*"

Headlights from the road painted just enough of the inside of the truck for Tom to see the shoulder of a silhouette, a pair of white eyes.

He felt tears swell up in his own. He thought he was going to piss himself. He wanted badly to be home, on that couch, eating pizza, pounding beers. He wanted help. He wanted someone to pull him out of this situation.

But it was his own feet . . . his own legs . . . that took him to the edge of the truck bed. The rain didn't "wake him up." He wasn't asleep. It crashed against him like it would a windowpane. A flowerpot. A stone.

Numb in this way, Tom leapt from the back and pulled the door down quickly.

The box was still strapped in, wasn't it? It hadn't been opened. Had it?

So why did it feel like the owner of that voice had not sneaked into the truck at all? That, rather, Tom had dollied him inside himself?

He hurried back to the cabin and got behind the wheel.

He merged.

He drove.

At eleven forty-five he reached the Goblin city limits. Both hands were trembling white piles of dust on the wheel.

Tom didn't know who the two leviathan topiaries were that greeted him, but they were George Carroll, Goblin's founding father, and Jonathan Trachtenbroit, the man who brought all the owls so many years ago and who was later strangled on Pride Hill, strangled by the ancestor of the very man who trimmed these bushes. Lit from below with giant floodlights, the pair were as intimidating a welcoming committee as Tom had ever seen.

Why did you drive? Why didn't you run? Why did you listen to that voice?

As he entered the city, he couldn't answer these questions other than to imagine himself abandoning the truck and being tracked forever by whatever was inside it.

"I got a better question than *why*," Tom said, wide-eyed and shaking as the traffic increased, as the landmarks and cityscape came into view through the rain-obscured windshield of the truck. "*What* have I brought to Goblin tonight, Tommy my man? *What?*"

But whatever it was, its white eyes must still shine in the back and the echo of its timeless voice must still be back there, too.

Tom was too late. He knew that, whatever was back there, he was too late in keeping it from Goblin.

He wondered when it began, this unforeseen route, hidden in the bigger route of delivering a package. Was it when Jerry called him into his office? When he agreed to make the run?

Or was it long before then, sixteen years ago, when he applied for the driver's job in the first place?

Or maybe it went even further back than that. To the day Goblin itself was discovered, growing ever since, until one rainy evening Tom forgot his sweater and passed the office on his way to retrieving it.

"Too late," Tom said, too afraid to turn back, too afraid to defy whatever was back there. "You've already delivered it."

He felt shameful. Like he'd delivered something illegal after all. Something dark enough to eclipse the legends of the city and to cast shadows over the stories of the people who lived there.

He'd made $86.40 so far but was no longer sure of his chances to spend it.

A MAN IN SLICES

1

R ichard stood outside Charles's house with a heavy rain crashing against his face. A rain so thick that, earlier tonight, Charles appeared to *vanish,* after exiting Richard's car, like he'd stepped through a wet curtain. The pair had had a decidedly weird night, or rather *Richard* was the one who suffered the strange; Charles's night must have been something more . . . liberating.

They'd spent many hours parked downtown, at the corner of Lily and Neptune, as all that Goblin rain came furious against the windshield. The wipers of Richard's Dodge Dart remained asleep, and the water poured down the glass like at the car wash on Samhattan Street. Charles unloaded some things he didn't feel like keeping secret anymore. Richard, the good friend, had listened. And now, long after Charles stepped through that curtain (and Richard was left with the story), Richard stood under that very rain, staring into the eyes of the life-sized topiary of Charles himself. It was one of Wayne Sherman's finest, most Gobliners agreed. But Richard wasn't thinking of the fabled proprietor of The Hedges. Rather, he weighed whether or not he had to turn his old friend in to the Goblin Police. He could phone Mayor Blackwater directly. That felt right, somehow. The mayor's tie to this city went further back than any bond between its citizens ever could.

Charles, he thought. *Oh boy, Charles.*

Richard could defend Charles all he wanted (and how he had!). He could argue that everybody, even a monster, needed a friend (and how he was!). He could preach that Charles had never meant anybody any harm. That his friend lived without a governor, outside the social constructs that crippled so many. And yet being free was not necessarily being happy. And Richard would never be able to hide the fact that he knew his friend was troubled.

He'd always known it.

Tonight Richard wore his green slicker, the rain coming down so heavy it molded the plastic to his upper body, making him look something like a topiary himself. He looked into the eyes of that Sherman work of art and saw the same vacancy that he noted in the eyes of the actual man he'd just been with. Did Wayne Sherman recognize this in Charles? When he lifted his shears to clip the leaves, did Charles's vacancy burn in his mind like it burned in Richard's now? Perhaps every topiary, marble statue, and plaster casting ever rendered had something of that same void.

The void that Charles was.

Richard closed his eyes and when he opened them, the bush statue remained. Charles in nature. Charles's nature.

Richard thought back.

Charles wasn't the only kid Richard's mom advised her son to steer clear of, but it struck him as extra meaningful when, after seeing Charles the eleven-year-old for the first time, she leaned in and said,

"You must try to avoid that one, Richard."

It was clear to everyone who met him that Charles was something problematic. Not the manic, destructive hell-raiser or the conniving and enervated bully that unnerved so many adults, but the sort that even *those* types of kids stayed away from. From the start, Charles was different in a different way.

And Richard became his only friend.

You've put me in a spot, Charles, Richard thought, staring into the deep-green eyes of that Sherman topiary.

Even by Goblin standards the rain was fantastic, punishing, and Richard thought back, attempting to isolate Charles's history in a jar, the history he'd witnessed himself, growing up in Goblin, through the years.

There were scenes . . .

High school parties where girls pulled Richard aside to ask him what was wrong with his friend.

Times at Charles's house when Richard saw real and raw fear in the eyes of Charles's own parents.

Times when Richard was just as afraid.

Was there a singular moment, a beat or a bump, that could act as a finger and point to the story Charles had just unloaded in the car? Should Richard have seen this story coming?

Staring into the dark-green, leafy eyes of the false man before him, Richard thought hard about the real one.

Yes, he knew, there were scenes. . . .

2

The day Charles moved to Goblin, Richard's doorbell rang and his mom, looking through the living room window, flashed Richard a concerned expression.

But Richard was curious. A new friend? Richard, a shy book-worm, could use all the friends he could get.

Richard answered the door himself.

"I'm here to introduce myself," Charles said.

"Okay, so who are you?"

"I'm Charles Ridnour. I live in the green house . . . there."

He pointed up the street. Richard knew the house.

"I'm Richard Robin," Richard said.

"Well," Charles said, "our names should keep us close together even if our interests don't. Roll call. Lockers. You know."

Richard liked him right away. Charles was nothing like the other boys from Goblin: the kids who tried so hard to stay cool. The kids who made more jokes than they did observations. The world felt youthful, open, and Richard noted a spark of inner electricity. Maybe the odd new neighbor could show him odd new things.

"I'm interested in the Blackwater River," Charles said, without a qualifier. But Richard understood it was an invitation.

"Hang on."

After closing the door, Richard asked his mom if he could show Charles the river.

"Be back in two hours," she said. Then she pointed at him, her way of underscoring a rule.

Though he was far from high school, Richard grabbed his Goblin Marauders sweatshirt and joined Charles outside.

"I'll show you around."

"You'll show me the Blackwater River?"

"No," Richard said, already heading up the street. "I'll show you *Goblin*."

And so he did. And how fresh Goblin looked to Richard then! Through the eyes of a new friend! How new the very street he lived on! Even the STOP sign shone bright red in the afternoon sun.

This is Goblin, Charles! My hometown. And now your hometown, too. Isn't it something? Isn't it magic?

"Coach Snow used to live there," Richard said, pointing to the last house in the neighborhood before reaching Christmas Road.

"What does he coach?"

"What *did* he coach. Track and field. But the guy met a nasty end, they say. Found in pieces in a well."

So many legends, so many yarns. Richard could feel the swell of the city building within him. Its history, its characters, its soul.

And much of that soul could be found in the rain.

"It's a fact that there's sixty percent more rain in Goblin than any city within a hundred miles. Some people say it's the original sixty settlers, crying from up there." Richard pointed to the blue sky.

"What happened to the settlers that they would cry?" Charles had asked.

Richard could feel Goblin working its magic on the newcomer already.

"Ambushed by natives. Dad says they had it coming. I don't doubt it."

As the boys walked up Christmas, as the very tops of the buildings of downtown came into view, Richard told Charles about how the sun set a full minute before all the neighboring towns because Hardy Carroll (the legendary unruly son of Goblin's founder) lost a bet and, too afraid to ask his father for the money, agreed to pay in *daylight*. How the paved roads were all so bumpy because the city's construction crews decided not to wait for the protestors to get out of the way. How the North Woods harbored Great Owls, Goblin's very own endangered species.

"Off limits," Richard said. "Protected by the police. And you don't want to mess around with the Goblin Police. They're . . . *spooky*."

"It sounds like a lot of Goblin is spooky."

"See the cemetery over that way?" Richard pointed to a crowded lot. Stones very close together.

"Yes."

"In Goblin the dead are buried standing up."

Charles's eyes grew wide. The image associated with this information was crystal clear, Richard knew, as it was for him when he learned it, too.

What pride Richard felt, painting this detailed picture of his hometown for a new friend to view!

"You see that great brown building, Charles? With the white windows?"

"Yes."

"That's Goblin General. Where I was born."

Richard told Charles how the hospital was once quarantined when it was discovered that an RN had contracted leprosy. How no one was allowed to leave, for fear of contaminating the city at large, and how all two hundred and twelve people inside gradually deteriorated, peeling to pieces, before all of them died and Goblin sanitation removed what remained with mops.

"And the one with the sort of crisscross design is where my mom works."

Richard told Charles how there used to be a drive-in theater. How the theater got shut down because too many kids were sneaking up on hilltops or climbing trees to watch R-rated movies.

"That's how I saw movies for years. From Pride Hill in Perish Park."

Perish Park, what a place! Where every winter people reenacted the death of Jonathan Trachtenbroit, who was strangled by a political rival, Henry Sherman.

"One time," Richard said, "some bad people set fire to many trees in Perish Park. People were worried the whole square would go up. But that's crazy . . . what with all the rain."

Charles stopped walking. He pointed to the city's modest sky-line. "Are you taking me *there*?"

"You mean downtown? Yes."

Charles smiled. "Take me, Richard. Tell me everything."

With a heart full of happiness, Richard did. He'd never met anybody exactly like Charles. Nobody who spoke like him, moved like him, stared at the skyline like he just had. And yet, even that day, that first day, Richard detected something swimming deeper within his new friend. Something dark and formless that could be seen only under certain conditions, under certain light.

But that first day Richard didn't care. Like the kid who hears that smoking the plants found in the North Woods can lead to a life of debauchery and trouble with the Goblin Police, Richard decided that, whatever was swimming in Charles, whatever would eventually surface and show itself, Richard would chance seeing it for a day like this.

3

For all his newfound extroversion, Richard was nervous about being downtown once they got there. How overwhelming it all seemed without Mom! And he hadn't told her he was coming here. But Charles seemed to drink it all in. The grown-up men and women walking the streets in their suits and dresses. The bums, buses, street vendors, and storefronts. The magic shop, the zoo, the stores with souvenirs, all of which featured mini-Shermans, topiaries in the shape of every known name a tourist might have.

And the Goblin Police, in their pale-gray uniforms, patrolling the city streets in that sluggish way that marked them.

"They move like . . . the dead," Charles said.

Richard opted not to talk about them at all. They passed a sign that read KEEP GOBLIN PRISTINE! TOSS YOUR TRASH HERE! Richard pointed out dog walkers, coffee stands, the proprietors who invited you in with a few words, and the people handing out flyers concerning shows coming to town.

"A circus!" Charles said. "Wow!"

But both boys were more interested in other things.

"What's *that*?" Charles asked, indicating a purple-painted theater ahead.

Richard followed Charles's finger to The Milky Way.

"It's the adult theater," Richard said. "Mom gets mad at me for just looking at it."

The way his mom put it, Richard imagined a horde of drooling, hairy men within, their pants at their ankles. The marquee read (to the point):

XXX

"Let's sneak inside," Richard said suddenly. His stomach dropped at his own suggestion. But the thrill of a new friend, and one who seemed so strangely open, overwhelmed him.

"Do you mean it?"

"I do."

The obedience to youth took hold of them and the pair started through the theater's gravel lot before they had any real courage or conviction behind them. Their hesitant steps became an excited trot and they raced to the purple brick side, out of view of the foggy glass ticket booth where an ancient woman smoked long cigarettes.

There was a small side door.

"Open it," Richard said.

"Me?"

"Come on."

"It must be locked."

"Oh, Charles. I'll do it."

Then Charles pointed to something in the bushes. "Look," he said. "A key."

The two crouched and Richard pulled the bushes apart, and they saw, yes, a wooden key in the dirt.

"That looks two hundred years old," Richard said. Neither touched it.

"It's a toy," Charles said. "It's—"

But Richard was already up and pushing the door.

It opened without resistance.

"Holy crap," Richard said.

"Holy crap, indeed."

Charles left the key in the bushes, got up, and met Richard at the open door.

They stared down a long and dark hallway. And from deep within they heard the sounds of women moaning.

The far-off look that would dominate Charles's face as an adult appeared for the first time for Richard to see. It was as if that deeper thing within Charles had swum to the top after all, and had taken charge of things.

Charles stepped into the hall first. Richard followed.

Their eyes adjusted quickly and the red EXIT sign illuminated just enough footing to lead them deeper. They crept silently, their shoes soft on the carpet, holding their breath. They both paused at the sound of slapping. A palm against a skin.

"This is weird," Richard whispered. "Maybe we should scram."

But that deeper Charles, the dark formless swimmer, remained.

"I wanna see this," he said. "And so do you."

When they reached the end of the hall (the moaning now as

loud as the tanks in the war movies), Richard saw that they had been walking along the other side of the wall where the movie was projected. Peeking around the corner he saw it glowed, but the light of the projector blinded him for all else.

"We're going to have to crawl in," Charles whispered. "Or they'll see us."

"They?"

"The men in here."

Crouched now, they could see the faces seated in the dark, smoky theater. Half a dozen men, well spaced out, stared intently at the screen.

Richard spotted a woman out there, too.

Charles crawled deeper into the room and Richard followed. The screen was behind them now. And it wasn't until they reached the curtains at the theater's entrance that they turned to see what all the sound was about.

They sat, cross-legged, and watched. Two new friends, strangers only hours ago.

A woman lay on her stomach on a bed while a man did what looked like push-ups above her.

"Oh," Charles said. "I know what this is."

"What is it?"

"This is love. My mother told me that when a man attaches himself to a woman it's called 'love.'"

Richard considered this. "It looks more like exercise to me."

Charles laughed and, years later, standing before a Wayne Sherman topiary of Charles himself, as a Goblin rain soaked him to his marrow, Richard couldn't remember another time Charles had laughed again.

You seemed so normal to me then. I know we were young, but . . . should I have been able to see it then? Would a different boy . . . a different guide to Goblin . . . have noticed and maybe known what to do with you? Did I fail you as a friend? That's impossible . . . right? I was the only friend you had. We both know that.

After the two sneaked out of the theater, they explored the rest of Goblin as Richard knew it. They walked across the stone bridge over the Blackwater River, drank from the fountain in the Nash Museum, peed in the toilets in the lobby of the Woodruff, played pinball in Goblin Games, rolled dice at Master of the Multiverse, fed found pizza crust to the pigeons, tossed dimes in the pond at Perish Park, and rode the bus. They got off near The Milky Way and took Christmas back home, walking the smaller streets Charles now knew one time over and Richard now knew one time better. The streets that would get them to their homes, where they would tell their respective mothers what a terribly dull time they'd had down at the Blackwater River. They'd eat dinner at their separate homes, too, and crawl into their warm, made beds.

And almost immediately after the lights were turned off in his room, Richard thought of Charles.

He needs me.

Unsure exactly what it meant, he fell asleep and dreamed of what he'd seen on that giant screen. Dreamed that the woman *enjoyed* the love the man gave her.

It would be four months before young Richard would see the side of Charles that older Richard was now, in the rain, trying so hard to piece together. And still, now, the thought

he needs me

was as confusing as it was when it first came, unbidden and frightening, too big for a young boy to make sense of. Only the need Charles had for Richard would change, like the extreme seasons of the city they called home, the city they explored together.

It used to be you needed a friend, Richard thought, his slicker pasted to his body. *But now you need an alibi. And if I provide for you like I once did . . . if I give you what you need . . . what will you need next from me, Charles? What will you need next?*

4

That first summer the two were sent together to swim camp. Camp Tanawanna was a big step for Richard's mother, but by then the boys were playing every day and there was no doubting their bond. She agreed, at Richard's behest, with less convincing than he'd anticipated.

And yet Mom continued to give her son a cautionary glance whenever Charles came up.

Camp Tanawanna was built on a massive black lake the campers called Lake Goodbye because it looked like anyone who entered it might vanish. Big pines lined the cove used as the swimming area, and the shadows these woods cast rendered the water tar-like to look at. Lake Goodbye.

Big, sharp rocks littered the small semicircle of sand the counselors called a beach, and the path to get there wasn't much smoother. The water was invaded by a series of battered wooden docks in the shape of an H. The younger kids would use the bottom half of that H. Even in such shallow water it looked like a tar pit, and every time Richard walked past it he imagined the eight- and nine-year-olds stuck in it, trying desperately to free their arms and legs. The older kids (at eleven, Richard and Charles were considered such) would use the top half, where the bottom really dropped off and, if you wanted to, it looked like you could swim forever and out . . . leaving Camp Tanawanna behind. But the camp was already seventeen miles from Goblin, and part of Richard wanted to hug these docks forever. Who knew what swam beneath the dark surface? Who knew what called these depths home?

But the only real monster on Lake Goodbye was the trouble brewing in young Charles's mind.

How dark the waters were!

On the first day, before jumping in, the campers were instructed to pair off. The counselors explained that every twenty minutes a whistle would blow and the "buddies" would team up. Richard, aware of the counselors' indifference to the campers, imagined them shoving him and the others in . . . one by one. He nearly expected to feel the clammy hand of a counselor on his back as he was tossed, then submerged, then stuck in all that dark water.

As Charles knelt on the dock and touched the surface with a finger, Richard could hear the counselors yelling at him.

It's okay, Richard! It's natural! Keep your head up . . . don't panic! until he felt something bloated and puffed beneath his feet . . . something like a rubbery limb.

It's all the children that didn't make it . . . that's all . . . the ones that couldn't swim. They're all below you now, Richard . . . in piles . . . a thousand kids who couldn't handle it . . . a thousand kids who got too tired . . .

But of course the counselors didn't shove him in. And at the first command to jump, Charles dove first . . . alone.

And even the counselors could see how good a swimmer he was.

Richard frowned. He'd been hoping the two could struggle together. But while Richard was still psyching himself up to leap in, Charles was already swimming laps. And by the time Richard was in the water, cold and shivering, his view of his "buddy'" was obscured by the others, treading water beside him.

More playing. More splashing. By then the counselors were talking and flirting, stoned on the dock. Birds called to one another from the big woods. Boats passed farther out on the lake, bringing small waves like toys for the kids to play with.

Richard joined a breath-holding contest with two strangers. He was a little anxious, a little out of step, a little alone. It seemed like everyone else had a friend. And all the chaos concerned him. Hadn't his mom told him that "an anxious swimmer is a swimmer in danger"? Hadn't she said worry could cause the muscles to tighten? And that, if you weren't careful, you could end up sinking to the bottom of a lake?

Cracking these thoughts in half, severing the screams from the cheers, the sound of water crashing, and the distant motors, too (a discordant symphony of frenzied youth set free) . . . in the center of all that *noise,* from the docks, the whistle blew.

The activity subsided slowly and, tasting the lake on his lips, Richard looked to the height of that rickety H, then to the base of the pines, as far as the water could go.

And he had no idea where Charles was.

"Buuuuuuuddy call!"

But this was impossible because it *had* to be. Charles couldn't rightly go missing in a lake. Not the way he swam. And yet, as kids locked hands and headed for the dock, Charles simply wasn't there. He really wasn't there.

And with every pair who reached the dock, there was that much more empty water surrounding Richard.

Still treading, alone now, he thought of the counselors calling Charles's mom.

We're sorry, Mrs. Ridnour . . . we know you thought this whole camp thing a good idea but, as it turned out, your little Charles up and vanished and we couldn't find him. Not for a few hours anyway. The county deputy came and rolled up his pant legs and went after him personally. Yes . . . found him at the bottom of the lake . . . seems he got a little tangled up in all that seaweed.

Turned his skin green. It's a wonder Deputy Johns could even differentiate. Oh, and one more thing: Your neighbor's kid, Richard? He was supposed to be watching him.

"Charles!"

Richard's voice traveled, unimpeded, to the pines.

"Where's your buddy, kid?"

A counselor stood on the edge of the dock, looking down at him.

This was really happening.

"Come on, kid. Don't fuck around. Where's your buddy?"

But Richard didn't know where his buddy was.

"This isn't funny," the counselor said. "You know that, right? You know this isn't a freakin' joke, right?"

Richard started crying. He couldn't help it. And his tears fell to the surface of the lake.

Then Richard saw the moment of comprehension, when it registered with the counselors that this was real.

They all jumped in at once.

None of the campers spoke as the counselors dove deep, came up, and dove deep again.

Some of them watched Richard.

That kid lost track of his buddy.

The counselors started to panic.

They started to yell at one another.

"Where's that kid? WHERE THE FUCK IS THAT KID?"

They went under for long stretches. Too long. Richard saw their feet swallowed by the dark water. When two came up, three more went down. They were getting tired. Those who treaded at the surface breathed heavy. Waiting.

A girl counselor started to cry.

"Where is he? Dan? Did we do something wrong? *Dan?*"

Dan didn't have any answers. None of them did. Seventeen years old . . . camp counselors . . . supposed to be watching these kids . . .

"*Dan?* What's happening? Have we done something wrong? Where is he?" Her voice shook. The campers began trembling on the dock.

Richard, still in the water, clung to the side of that dock and watched the desperate counselors in a daze.

Time was ticking. Two then three minutes is a long time to be expected to hold your breath. And survive . . .

Under again. Up.

The counselors were obviously exhausted. Richard could tell.

Three and a half minutes passed. Richard climbed out.

A counselor came up and turned to Richard, praying the whereabouts of the missing kid might be there somewhere in his buddy's face.

Under again. Up.

"You . . . you . . . you can't go this long," the girl cried. "You can't do it. A human being needs to—"

Under again Up.

"You'd *die.* You can't . . . a person has to . . ."

Under again. Up.

"Dan?"

Four minutes had passed.

"Dan?"

"*What?*"

"People have to breathe, Dan. He—he's dead."

It was a long time before the counselors quit. One by one they gave in. One by one they lifted themselves onto the dock.

Nobody spoke. Lips trembled, but nobody said a word.

And then . . .

The sound of something emerging from water, and out from the left tip of that great H, Charles pulled himself onto the dock.

"Oh!" the girl shrieked. "Oh my *God* you're okay!" She was smiling, hysterical, but most of the counselors remained on their knees. Stone-faced.

It was clear Charles had been hiding.

"Where were you?" one asked. He rose to his full height, dwarfing Charles beneath him.

Charles was as blank-faced as ever.

"Hey kid, where the *fuck* were you?"

And then it broke.

Noise. Yelling. Crying.

"I'm gonna break your fucking skull."

The counselor raised a fist.

Another reached out and stopped him.

"The kid is a *motherfucking psycho!*"

"Then bring him to the office, man," the second counselor said. "But don't do this."

Charles started to cry. He cried the same way Richard would see him cry nineteen years later, in Richard's Dodge Dart, at the corner of Lily and Neptune in downtown Goblin.

"Get this piece of shit out of here," the first counselor said. Then, to Charles, "You're a piece of shit and we're sending you home."

The second counselor led him quietly through the other campers. Richard, dripping on the battered dock, watched Charles pass with confusion.

In that moment, watching Charles pass, understanding what Charles had done, Richard understood clearly every suspicion his mother held.

The campers were ushered solemnly back to shore. The day

couldn't go on. They took the path back to their cabins and were instructed to play games.

Later that night, just when Richard heard the first heavy breathing of his bunkmates falling asleep, Charles returned.

He knelt by Richard's bed.

"It was fascinating," he said. Like he knew Richard was awake. Despite the dark. Like he knew Richard was up, worrying about him.

"What was?" Richard asked, still so confused.

"Watching people try so hard to save your life."

Richard was quiet.

"They're making me leave, of course. Sending me home."

Richard was quiet.

Then Charles was up and noiselessly shuffling to his own bed.

Richard heard him snoring before long, and he understood that, despite the horrific energy, the fear, surrounding the incident, Charles had seen it differently. While everyone else was scared, weighing life and death, Charles was simply clutching a wooden dock, watching.

It was fascinating.

A silent handshake occurred deep within Richard's mind. One hand belonged to himself, clearheaded, young. The other belonged to someone he might become, someone who understood that, if he were to walk away from Charles now, Charles would never find another friend to look out for him.

Falling asleep, Richard shook hands. And in doing so, agreed to stay.

5

"**A**re you inside the house?" Richard asked the green statue. "Did you come home after leaving my car? I thought you might come home."

Earlier this night, the night Charles unloaded, Richard was at home, reading a psychology magazine on the couch. Charles called. He sounded anxious. He was stuttering . . . muttering . . . mumbling. Richard was alarmed. He'd never heard his old friend quite so . . . *emotive.* It sounded like Charles was going to open up, emotionally, really for the first time, and Richard wasn't sure he was prepared to hear it.

Suddenly, holding the phone, he wished there was no swimmer in Charles at all, no depth to be plunged. No explanation.

But Richard, always the lone friend, always shaking hands, agreed to meet up.

They agreed upon downtown (Charles said, "I really need to talk to you, Richard. In person. I'll take the bus. Lily and Neptune?") and both arrived at the intersection just as the real rain dropped.

Richard didn't know what to expect. With Charles it could have been anything. And he hadn't given him any hints to go on. ("I'll tell you everything when you get there, okay?") But in the backest of his heart, Richard knew that whatever it was, it wasn't good. The truth was, the tone of voice he'd heard over the phone was brand new to him. He hadn't recognized it.

This was somehow the most fearful part.

Charles, huddled up in his jacket beneath the small pink awning over the front door of Goblin Games, came out of the shadows the second Richard pulled up. For a moment Charles the man was beside Charles the shadow, cast by the lamppost, distorted by rain, and Richard had difficulty telling the difference. Which was coming to get in his car?

"Thank you," Charles said. He ran a wet hand through his wet hair. "Let's just stay here. In the car."

"What's this about, Charles?"

Charles faced his friend, wide-eyed. Richard tried to locate him in there, but struggled.

"I think I'm in trouble, Richard. I think I've done something wrong. Something very very wrong."

6

Later, standing before the topiary, outside Charles's house, Richard thought back some more. Just a little more. Sifting through the shadows of their history, looking in the corners for clues.

By the time the pair were sixteen years old, Charles had folded enough sheets at Soap's Hope (a Goblin staple; a Laundromat well known for criminal break-ins and poetry meetings, too) to cover the city's jarring green skyline. He'd saved up money, too, enough to buy himself a dented brown Oldsmobile. On that very day, the Ridnours invited Richard to join them for dinner in the lobby of the Woodruff. They took Richard out to eat annually by then, a thank-you, Richard imagined, for his service, for being their son's only friend. Charles suggested they ride downtown in his new car.

Charles was in good spirits on the drive.

"I'm thinking of going into statistics," he said.

They took Christmas south, the same road they'd walked five years ago, the day Richard introduced Charles to Goblin. Showed him the landmarks. The hot spots. The municipal buildings, too.

Gravel kicked up from the tires into the border of thick trees lining the road. The North Woods were north of them, but the rogue evergreens could be found this way, too.

"Statistics," Richard echoed. "That sounds like the perfect thing for you."

He imagined his odd friend occupied by crunching numbers. Perhaps there was a match in there.

A yellow Lab trotted out of the woods, onto the road ahead.

Richard turned to Charles, to point it out, but the look on his friend's face stopped him.

Charles had seen it, no doubt, but rather than show any concern his eyes lit up.

Richard thought of the things people whispered in the halls of Goblin High. They were juniors now and Charles had long become the butt end of a hundred thousand weirdo-jokes. And yet not many told them to his face.

"Hey," Charles said. "I think we can get him."

Richard looked to the dog.

"Get him, Charles?"

Charles slammed his foot down on the gas. The Oldsmobile roared to joyful life, as if it'd been waiting for just this moment since its last owner left it dented and alone so many years ago.

The dog stopped in the middle of Christmas. It looked up at the coming car.

Richard wanted to think his friend was joking. But the idea wasn't going down easy.

He's going to do this, Richard. He's going to do this!

"Charles. Come on."

"We're gonna get him, Richard."

In the shadows of the trees, his eyes went black.

Richard estimated they were fifty yards from the dog. He could see it was old now. But wise or not, the dog remained, sniffing at pebbles, its tail lolling in the sun's slanted, cracked rays.

At twenty-five yards Richard lifted a hand. As if he might grab the wheel and turn it.

"Charles!"

He thought he was too late. He had to be. Either the dog moved now or they were going to get him, indeed.

Richard's stomach dropped. His throat tightened. He placed a hand on the wheel.

"Charles!"

But they were on top of him now. There wasn't enough time for him to move. Charles let out a deep, almost orgasmic, breath of air as the car lifted.

Richard heard the crunch beneath them.

"Oh my God, Charles . . . Charles, what the fuck did you do?"

The car glided, slowly, with Charles's foot off the gas.

"Death," Charles said. "Is *so* striking."

As the Oldsmobile came to a natural stop at the foot of a gravel hill, Richard felt sick. The violence of it . . . the reality of it . . . the fact that he'd only put his hand on the wheel but had not turned it. It felt as if he'd assisted Charles somehow, helped aim the car.

Charles put the car in park and turned the engine off. Dust from Christmas settled like small storm clouds by the doors.

Birds sang in the trees. Richard imagined one of Goblin's Great Owls. An endangered species.

But not more endangered than that dog.

Breathing hard, Charles turned to face his friend. "Let's go look at it."

"No. I wanna go home."

"Home?" Charles looked ahead. "This is Goblin, Richard. You *are* home."

He got out of the car. Richard watched him in the side mirror. Saw it as Charles walked with his hands in his pant pockets. He made such an innocent profile in the glass, but Richard imagined the slow-moving, zombielike Goblin Police approaching him all the same.

How wrong was this? Richard wondered. Exactly how wrong? *Murder* wrong?

He saw Charles looking right and left, over his shoulder, up ahead. Hope rose in Richard's chest.

He got out of the car.

"Can't find it?" he asked.

Charles turned to face him, and the disappointment Richard saw was enough to tell him never to speak to this man again. They were only sixteen years old. Richard could do it. Could get out right now. College was a year away. He could leave the state, leave the country, slowly but surely never speak to Charles again.

"I don't get it," Charles said. "He's not here."

By the time Richard reached him, hope was past rising, it was afloat.

"He's gotta be in the woods," Richard said. He spoke to himself. But when he searched the scant trees lining the woods, he saw no body.

There was no blood in the dirt, either. No mark. No sign that they had hit anything at all.

Richard was electric with exhalation as he searched the woods more deeply. No broken sticks. No fur. No blood.

No dog.

He returned to the car. Charles was kneeling at the grille.

"I don't understand," Charles said, his brow darkening in step with the Goblin sky above. He looked up at Richard. "Not a nick."

Richard checked for himself to make sure.

"What a shame," Richard said. And by then the hope he felt had turned to joy. "Looks like he got away."

Charles frowned at the grille of his new used car for a beat before he broke out into a deep, rich smile.

"Well, holy shit. *Good for him.*" He stood up. "We gotta go." He looked at his watch. "Mom and Dad are waiting." Then, as Richard rose, too, as both of them scanned the dirt road once more, Charles added, "I'm gonna order the meatloaf. You?"

7

Scenes like these . . . litter on the green Goblin topiary of Richard's life . . .

To his deep relief, the pair graduated from Goblin High and went to different colleges after all. Both would return home for the holidays (Charles went to school near Goblin and still lived with his parents, Richard was downstate), and never at any of these reunions did Charles ever mention so much as a *crush*. The more Richard thought about it, the more he loved and lost, the more he saw, in relief, how little Charles seemed to speak of women. For this, when he first heard news that Charles had found himself a girlfriend, when Mrs. Ridnour told him so, Richard shamefully wondered what type of woman could feel comfortable entering Charles's world. If *he* himself had partially glimpsed the inner workings of Charles's mind, what intimate view would a woman have? Charles wasn't the kind of man to hide his colors. He wouldn't have known what they looked like to begin with.

Richard couldn't stop marveling at the concept. And what he discovered was that he felt vindicated by the news. All those nights he'd fought to ignore what the other kids at Goblin High thought of his friend; all those nights he'd wished (painfully) for Charles

to make another friend; all the times he'd backed him . . . spiritu-
ally . . . sending some faith his friend's way for no reason other
than a deep, unfounded obligation to do so. And now! Charles
had a *girlfriend*. Charles Ridnour, a man whom women avoided on
sight, on instinct, despite his not having spoken to them at all.
Richard had long been fearful of introducing his love interests to
Charles. It seemed like a strike against him, a reason for a woman
to turn away. And yet . . . still . . . the *faith*. Richard had never been
able to extricate that silent, unseen handshake, the deal he'd made
within himself in a cabin at swim camp so long ago.

Flashes! Slices! Richard, standing before the topiary of Charles,
the rain making masks of his own face, recalled standing in the
bleachers at a Marauders home game . . . those bleachers packed
with manic students . . . waving green-and-purple flags . . . the
smell of hot dogs and pretzels and the shampoo of all the pretty
girls . . . the great floodlights illuminating the big game on the
field . . . Charles below, beating a bass drum in that great Goblin
band. Brianne Stockton leaned over to Richard and said, "Isn't
that your friend Charles?"

Your friend Charles.

Nobody else's friend Charles.

Flashes! Slices! Richard coming home from college to find a note
taped to his door:

I'm in town. At the library. Meet me?
　　　　—Charles

And how Richard walked the streets of downtown to greet his
lonely friend. How they'd gone out that night and drank more
than they'd planned. Richard threw up on the walk home and
Charles talked as if ten people were vying for speaking space
within him.

There was a girl . . . at the bar . . . a girl Richard had his eye on . . . a girl Richard found the nerve to talk to . . . a girl who got so creeped out by Charles that she came right out and told Richard she didn't want to be around his friend. How Richard had flamed inside, how he shoved her back against a wall.

Why? Because she was cruel enough to say what he himself would not? Or was it perhaps because she threatened his *duty* to Charles. His role. His lot.

The two stumbled home and when he woke, Richard found another note:

Wonderful night. Thank you, friend.

And now, by some providence, by unseen fingers knitting impossible collages in the sky, Charles had gotten himself a girlfriend. *Scary* Charles. The guy who had blown it for him (or brought him inexplicably to blow it for himself) so many times. Charles had met someone. Incredible. Unreal. *Vindicating.* It didn't matter that Richard didn't see or hear from Charles in the four months between hearing about her and getting the strange hushed call from Charles tonight. It didn't matter at all. Richard held it like a precious baby bird. Charles having a girlfriend meant Charles was that much closer to having met a second friend.

And perhaps, Richard mused, his work here was done.

8

Okay, Richard thought, still looking into the eyes of that Sherman topiary. *Let's go back. Just a little this time. Hardly any at all. To tonight. Earlier tonight. When you got in the car and told me you might have done something very very wrong. How I had no doubt that you had. How I had never doubted this day was coming, always, en route . . .*

9

"Wat is it, Charles?"
The two had been sitting long enough for the rain on the windshield to become a second pane of glass, a layer of distortion, of cover. Richard was nervous.

Confessing something is different from telling someone something, Richard thought. *Remember when he told you how he let that hamster rot? How he didn't want the hamster his father got him and how he put it in the basement with a blanket over the cage and walked away? How he went about his business up-stairs for days while that animal suffered then starved then rotted away a floor below? If this is any worse than that—*

"Don't worry, Richard," Charles said. "I didn't kill anybody."

Richard shifted uncomfortably in his seat. Again he imagined those long-limbed, slow-moving Goblin Police in their sickly gray uniforms.

Come out! We have reason to believe there is a man about to confess a crime in there! It's our job to hear it, our job to document it, our job to—

But it was *Richard's* job. And it always had been.

The rain came hard against the car.

And suddenly Richard understood that he *wanted* Charles to confess something. Something terrible. He'd stretched his soul so far for Charles, too far, and perhaps a crime would be closure after all.

Just east of them, the black gates of Perish Park jutted high above the surrounding trees. The rain changed shape, from a thousand pinpricks to thick tar-like drops that made hollow thuds against the windshield. A light from an apartment above kept things visible, but it was very dark.

Richard turned in his seat to face his friend.

"So . . . what's up, Charles?"

"Do you remember when we sneaked into The Milky Way?" Charles asked. "Remember how, when you pushed on the door . . . it just opened?"

"Yes."

"That happens in this story, too."

Charles met Andi at a wedding. This much Richard already knew. Everything else that followed was new to him.

10

It was a little surprising for Charles when he opened a fancy letter and saw that Gordon Dixie, an old family friend, was marrying a girl named Jane and that they would be filled with joy if he would attend.

"He didn't have to do that, Richard. I was very excited about this."

But he was late for the wedding. He was late because his pants wouldn't dry and they were still damp when he left the house. He showed up fifteen minutes into the ceremony and waited outside.

Through the many windows of the chapel he was able to watch the proceedings within. The sun was strong above him and he had to shield his eyes against the glass to get a better look. He could make out Gordon at the altar. The families on either side of the aisle. And just inside of that window, enough in view for him to make out her entire profile, sat Andi.

"A living drawing," Charles said. "As if she'd been painted into the scene. And as if that had been done for me to see. And me alone."

11

The reception was at the Woodruff, the very hotel where Richard had annually dined with the Ridnours. Richard could see the top of its neon red letters from here, at the corner of Lily and Neptune.

Andi was on the back porch having a cigarette. Charles followed her outside.

"I'm Charles," he said, extending a hand. "And I've been watching you all night."

"Ah," Andi said. "I felt . . . *something.*"

"You're the most beautiful woman I have ever seen. I'm not a liar."

Now, in the car, Richard asked, "You said all that, Charles?"

"Yes. Why? Do you think I came on too strong?"

"No, no. It's great."

Charles and Andi talked outside for a long time. She was from St. Paul and was returning to Minnesota the next afternoon. Charles wasn't upset by this. He'd never had a girlfriend before and the idea of "space" didn't frighten him.

Andi, it turned out, felt the same way.

She did return to St. Paul the next day, and Charles continued living the life he'd been living. He lived in an apartment off Farraline. He worked at the Transistor Planet downtown. Two weeks after the night of the wedding, Andi made it clear where she stood by signing *your girlfriend* at the bottom of a letter. Charles couldn't stop reading the two words.

"It was amazing," he said, sitting in the passenger seat, staring at the wall of falling rain before them. "But as good as that moment was, that's how bad it became."

Richard shifted in his seat.

Oh shit. Here it is. The confession.

And the feeling that followed (the one that demanded he become Charles's friend so long ago) was exhausting. He didn't want that responsibility tonight. This was to be the night the swimmer living inside Charles broke the surface and Richard could finally say, *Okay . . . it's official. I'm off the clock.*

"She wanted me to prove my love, Richard. That's what happened. She wanted me to prove it."

Richard took a deep breath and held it. "A lot of girls want that," he said.

Charles stared deep into the rain. "Andi asked for a toe."

"A what?"

"She told me that the greatest symbol of true love is self-sacrifice. That our love could be legendary. Bigger than Van Gogh's. She wanted a toe."

"Hold on," Richard said, hardly able to make sense of what Charles had just said. "She . . . she asked you to send one of your body parts through the mail?"

"Yes."

"And you didn't think this was—"

"I love Andi, Richard. Do you know what they say about couples who meet at weddings? That they have a ninety percent chance of getting married themselves."

"Charles . . ."

"Andi wanted a toe. I sent her one."

12

"What did you expect me to do?" Charles asked, turning to face Richard, desperation in his eyes. "Send her one of *mine*?"

Richard was stunned.

"Wh—what do you mean?"

"Andi lives in St. Paul. How would she know if it was mine or not? She wouldn't. Not for a while anyway. I'm not a liar, Richard, but my own toe. I just couldn't do it. I tried."

He did.

The day he got her call, he sat with it for an hour before he rushed to his apartment bathroom. He removed his shoe and then his sock and sat down on the edge of the closed toilet seat. The idea of doing it sounded possible. But sitting with it . . . looking at it . . . *touching* it . . . everything changed. He became very aware of how delicate human flesh can feel. After an hour of staring, he rose and went downstairs. He sat in front of the muted television and sank deep into the couch.

He thought of Andi. He thought of true love.

Her letters, her feminine penmanship, rose to the surface of his mind's eye. Her turns of phrase spun before him. Her voice came through those letters as clearly as when they last spoke . . . when, with the gentility of a drawing room hostess, she had asked him for his toe.

I will do this. He sprang to his feet.

He entered the bathroom with renewed vigor. He'd cut off his toe. His baby toe. One clip of the shears. Like Wayne Sherman trimming The Hedges at Goblin's eastern border.

It was nothing. A single motion.

True love. Legendary love.

From under the sink he removed a pair of scissors and sat down in the bathtub. No water. Just space. Space to work. Space for one quick motion.

He set the twin blades on the two sides of his baby toe.

Andi, he thought. *This is for you.*

He squeezed gently, the edges starting to pinch his skin. A little harder now . . . a little harder now . . . a little—

"Then I was struck with a vision," he told Richard in the idling Dart. "As if something much more powerful than myself was leading the way."

"What'd you do?" Richard asked, amazed at his own ability to ask a question.

"You ever been to the morgue, Richard?"

13

"I didn't have much of a plan, Richard. I rightly assumed the front doors would be locked. But there's a dark alley there along the side of the building. Trash cans, too. I shudder to think of what they've put in there. But I suppose I'm no cleaner than a trash can in the alley of a morgue. And there was a door in the bricks back there. An open one."

The hinges cried for oil as the door swung inward. Charles faced a small set of concrete stairs leading up to the first floor.

"Up there it was all offices. Frosted glass and nameplates. As if I had broken into a detective agency. I was very worried some-body might be working late so I tiptoed the length of the hall, to the other side of the building. I was lucky, I suppose. There wasn't a sound in the place. Not even the sound of a ceiling fan. A phone. A computer humming, at rest. You know . . . I don't think they have a security guard at the Goblin City Morgue. Isn't that odd?

Of all the places to leave unattended. The zoo has a guard. The cemetery has a guard. Even Wayne Sherman's cousin watches The Hedges for him at night. But the morgue? Nobody. No eyes and ears. No mouth, either, to call out to me, to ask me what I was doing, to put a stop to it before it began.

"The door to where they keep the bodies is at the far north end of the first-floor hallway. I found it easily. And can you imagine? *Me* walking through the morgue with a pair of scissors in my hand close to midnight? I hardly recognized myself. Stepping through that door I began searching my history, *our* history, Richard, for a sign. A point in time that might suggest, yes, one day I'd be illegally inside the Goblin City Morgue, with a mind to steal something other than money. But I didn't find any sign. No chain of events so far as I could see. Know what? I think love is a very powerful thing, Richard. I really do."

The door had a sign upon it, a man with a mask over his mouth, rubber gloves over his hands. Charles entered and found himself at the top of a dark stairwell.

"I used my wallet as a stopper. I was hoping that enough of that neon light from out on the street would follow me down there . . . help me until I could find the real overheads. But it was obvious I'd be in total darkness very soon."

He was. And he used the stone walls as guideposts on the way down the stairs.

"But I misjudged them and stumbled down the last step. I hit a metal tray table on wheels and the crashing sound scared me deeply. I thought for certain I would get caught. That somebody would emerge from the darkness, a hand would grab my own. You know how they say a person's heart beats heavy when they're scared? Mine was beating so hard I thought it was my hand on my chest, but my hands were out in front of my face, trembling in the darkness. I felt along the wall for the lights. It took me quite a while, many minutes, and those minutes down there in the dark were very hard. Andi would be happy to know that, despite the horrors, I didn't once consider turning back. Love, Richard. Legendary love.

"Oh, I wish you could have seen it! When those lights came on I was privy to a side of Goblin that not many people see! I was *beneath* the city. Beneath even the graves, I'd say, as the graves are where the bodies rest. But at the morgue? Goodness, Richard, the morgue is a physical purgatory. Nobody *stays* at the morgue. Not for long. And so it struck me, looking to the many square metal doors in the walls, that whoever happened to be there that night also happened to have been unlucky enough to meet me in purgatory. Me, a creature with bad intentions.

"There were a number of steel tray tables scattered about. And on them were scalpels, needles, stitching. Clear canisters with chemicals. There were sinks against the far wall and many faucets of different colors. Green smocks hung from hooks on the walls. Face masks and safety goggles, too. They take great pains to keep a place like that sanitary. And here I was, breaking every rule."

Charles stepped to the square drawers, eyeing the clamps that held them closed.

"I got started right away."

Charles counted the drawers, saw there were eighteen total. Three rows high and six across.

"I decided I'd just start at the left and make my way across until I found a foot that I could pass off as my own. I pulled open the top left drawer. The handle was like ice in my hands. And the smell that erupted forth was terribly ugly, something like the opposite of love. And it soothed me, thinking that, of course, the only elements in play were love and its ghastly opposite. Do you see? Some would call that balance. But I felt more like I'd stepped through a thin wall, a wall of Goblin rain perhaps, and that everything and everybody I'd encounter thenceforth would be mean-ingful, enormous, important. And to think . . . *haha* . . . it all started with something so simple as a toe."

14

The drawer slid open easily upon audible ball bearings. Charles felt a tremendous rush. What would he see in the darkness of that drawer? How long had it been dead? He stood on his toes and looked inside, to the back of the long rectangular shadows. There was nothing but icy air and steel. And that smell. The memory of tenants past. A cold, graceful gust of air washed over Charles.

The drawer was empty. And so was the next one. And the next.

Charles looked down at his own shoes. The toes hidden within seemed so innocent, unaware of the fact that, if he were unable to find a body, he'd come for them in the end.

But the eighth drawer delivered him what he wanted.

The second drawer from the left on the middle row. It had a little more weight to it and Charles knew before seeing it that a body was indeed inside. He opened it slowly and stopped at the shin.

"There was really no reason to look the person in the face," he said. "After all, what I needed was far from it."

The body lay level with Charles's waist. The feet looked very old. Would Andi be able to tell the difference? Would she accept that a toe looks different once it's removed? Is a man's age visible in his baby toe?

What about the next time she comes to Goblin? Will it break her heart? Will she feel deceived when she asks to see your feet, Charles?

He brought the scissors to the body's foot. No use thinking about *that.*

He lined up the edges of the blades to the cold rubber flesh. He thought of Wayne Sherman fashioning the topiary that stood outside his own apartment. Sherman would give it one good whack.

Be an artist, he thought. *And art.*

The shins jutted out of the darkness like withered bundles of birch.

On three.

Charles looked at where the light became shadows, just below the knees.

One . . .

He imagined a face, living, deeper in the dark drawer.

Two . . .

A face waking, screaming, hands erupting from the shadows, grabbing hold of the scissors, of Charles . . .

Three.

Charles gave it his all.

He heard a flat squishy sound, as if he had dropped pudding on the morgue floor, and felt the blades cut through muscle, tissue . . . tendon . . .

"But it stopped at the bone. Stopped so suddenly that it was like the body itself was telling me, *No more.*"

His shoes squawked as he left the scissors stuck in the purple grooves and inched back from the open drawer. Would he be able to break through that bone? Was it brittle enough?

He wiped sweat from his brow and reset himself.

"I needed a minute. The emotions warring within me were as big as any I'd ever felt. And the way the scissors stuck to the body like that, it was just the kick I needed. For they made it all . . . cartoonish. A game. As if I'd been tasked with removing all ten toes in a finite period of time, and a whole crowd of fellow children were rooting me on, watching to see if I'd do it. So I got back to it. And this time I was prepared. I gripped the scissors much harder the second time."

But the bone wouldn't give. Charles yanked, side-to-side, exposing more of the bone as he did. He grunted and cried out, placed a sneaker against a drawer beneath, pulled with all the strength he had.

Snap, dammit! BREAK!

He pressed harder, pleading now into the cold dead steel of that drawer. And finally, as a cry for relief came from deep in his throat, Charles felt the give, the snap he was looking for.

He stumbled back hard and fell heavily to the linoleum floor.

Across the room, the drawer rolled all the way open from the force.

Charles sat on the ground, looking up to the drawer's handle, to the body that he still couldn't quite see.

In his hands, the scissors held the toe like a diamond in the grip of pliers.

Charles inched across the morgue floor on his butt, then planted a sneaker against the drawer and kicked it shut. It rolled back easily and slammed closed with a great steel echo.

He lay on his back, breathing hard, looking up to the ceiling.

"I fell asleep that way. I realize how foolish that sounds. But the relief was so great that it affected me. I imagine drugs do the same thing. And when I woke, I still held the scissors and the toe within them."

Before getting up, he waited. He listened. How long had he been asleep? Long enough for the morning shift to arrive?

Hearing nothing, Charles rose and, scooping up his wallet on the way out, let the strong steel door slam closed behind him.

"I thought of Andi. Over and over. As if she were only a name and that name was powerful enough to propel me. The love I felt in that moment was *pure,* Richard. I had done what she asked of me. What more can we do?"

Outside, the Goblin sky was still dark and Charles ran under it, hailing a cab with one hand, a severed toe clamped by twin blades in the other.

"*Andi,* I thought. *Andi, Andi, Andi, Andi . . . I did it. For you, Andi, I did it. For Andi, for you, big love, legendary love . . . Andi.*"

15

The people at the post office waved to him as he came in the next morning. "A present for your lady friend in Minnesota?"

"Sure is," Charles said.

"A happy girl is a happy boy."

Charles thought about that.

"Sure is."

After leaving the post office he drove south on Christmas to the Transistor Planet. He had to work. It wasn't going to be easy. Standing around selling electronics while thinking about whether Andi was going to like his gift. Would she have questions?

He helped people with the newest printers and tried not to think about the images he'd seen in the morgue. A body half in shadow. The bone that broke like old bark. The toe in a plastic bag in the mail.

16

Two days later Andi called. She was electrified.

She told Charles she loved him and that their love would go down as one of the all-time greats. She even hinted at marriage.

Charles's blood flowed masculine through his body. He was basking in the bright light of love.

But Andi wanted more.

"I couldn't believe it, Richard. She asked for a *finger*. She said that no man had ever sent his lover *two* parts and that we stood a chance at 'upstaging' Van Gogh and all the lovers who ever came before us. And those who'd follow, too. What could I do? If Andi wanted a finger . . . I'd send her a finger. Besides . . . it wouldn't be mine. What harm was there in saying yes?"

The second time Charles was prepared. He brought with him a small hacksaw and a plastic bag.

Once again he found the side entrance open, and again he used his wallet to hold open the heavy metal door. After turning on the lights he was accosted with the strange feeling of returning to a place he never thought he'd see again. He walked straight to the second drawer from the left in the middle row and slid it half-way open. It was the same body. There was no doubting that. And Charles had no more intention of seeing its face this time than he did the last.

And yet the body did look different. Being less afraid, Charles studied what showed for longer periods of time than he had before. Wrinkled, shriveled legs gave way to veiny bloated thighs and a rubbery flaccid penis. The hairs on the legs and around the purple testicles were wiry and white.

Maybe I ought to find one with more of a . . . likeness.

He looked down at the crude jagged space where the toe had been.

I've already started on this one.

The wrists jutted out from the shadows of the drawer's inner space. The harsh overhead lights rendered the details brighter than life.

Charles thought the fingers looked fat.

She's going to know . . .

But would she? If Charles really did send his own finger, might it not look different than she'd remember? And wouldn't the absence of flowing blood change it?

Of course it would. And the option was intolerable.

Charles retrieved a green mask from a hook on the wall. Wearing it, he carefully placed the middle, ring, and pinkie fingers under the palm of the body's left hand. The way he set it up, it was like the hand was pointing at something at its feet.

A missing toe perhaps.

Charles got to work. And this time it was easy.

17

Andi was bursting at the seams with happiness. Charles had done it. He'd sent *two* parts and for that she was convinced their love was legendary. Always would be. She was going to tell her mother that Charles was her soulmate. They would marry one day and they'd have children and live the loveliest, fullest, most enviable life.

Writers would study them. Charles was her beast slayer. Her blacksmith. Her king.

But as happy as Charles was, he was also beginning to have bad dreams. A body slowly rolling out of the shadows feet-first . . . its knees revealed . . . then a waist . . . a chest . . . neck . . . chin.

And a face.

Charles screamed every time it showed.

In his nightmare the body opened its pale lips and pointed at him with a missing finger.

She's gonna know, the body said. *A woman knows. And when she does, she's gonna take the train to Goblin, to you. She's gonna see you have all ten fingers and all ten toes and she's gonna know . . .*

And Charles would stumble back and trip over his sneakers and fall to the cold morgue floor.

Then the body would sit up and peer over the drawer at him. It'd swing a foot over the side of the steel, a foot with a missing toe.

I'm coming for you, it'd say. *I'm coming for your parts.*

Then it'd laugh and its laughter cackled in the stone room and rats erupted from the corners and took Charles in parts, in pieces, in slices.

So when Andi called him up and suggested he send her *just one more*, the phone shook in his hand, all five fingers gripping it, not wanting to let her go.

"Of course I can get you an ear," he told her.

And of course he could.

An ear because Van Gogh sent an ear, and when people debated the greats she didn't want people to argue Van Gogh was more romantic than Charles. Maybe an ear was worth more to some than a finger and a toe. Maybe it had something to do with being so close to the face.

After they'd hung up, Charles went to the bathroom and studied his ears in the mirror.

"I wanted to do it, Richard. I truly did. But here . . ."

He reached out and tugged gently on Richard's earlobe. The black sky thundered above.

"Can you imagine it?" he asked. "The pain? The loss?"

Then he removed his hand and looked ahead again, into the powerful Goblin rain.

"So I did the only intelligent thing I could. I went back."

18

One more trip to the morgue. One more walk to the basement.

One more opening of the drawer.

Charles entered the basement for the third time just an hour before calling Richard tonight. At the second drawer from the left in the middle row, he breathed deeply, braced himself for the face, and gave it one solid pull.

The drawer moved too quickly.

Inside it, he saw only shadows that, days before, hid so well the rest of the body.

Had the body been moved? Buried? Did they notice what he'd *done* to it?

Charles panicked.

He opened the next drawer over. It, too, was empty. So was the next. And the next. In a frenzy, Charles checked all eighteen steel drawers, and each held nothing but cold drafts and shadows.

He looked once around the stone room, as if expecting to find an errant body slumped in the corner. Then he ran out of the basement, breathing hard, images of Andi disappointed racing through his mind.

You'll have to tell her now, buddy.

Outside he hurried to his car, the same Oldsmobile he'd bought at age sixteen, and sped north on Christmas. Home again, he called Richard.

Richard would help.

Richard was his friend.

His only friend.

Now the rain beat on the roof of the car like it was the closed fists of the Goblin Police.

"Have I failed her, Richard?"

Richard squirmed in his seat like worms were crawling under his coat. One of the two of them had to get out of the car. He was going to go crazy if one of the two of them didn't—

"Have I failed her, Richard? Tell me. Please. I'll believe you."

Oh, Charles . . .

"Have I done something wrong? I feel like I have."

A car came up Lily behind them. In the headlights Richard could see that Charles's eyes were swelled with pending tears.

"It wasn't my toe," Charles said. "It wasn't *my* finger. But I'm not a liar. You know that. Right? I'm a good person. Right? Richard . . . please. Talk to me. You're my very best friend."

Richard couldn't believe it when his own lips moved.

"No, Charles. I don't think you've failed her. I think you tried your best."

Charles nodded.

"Thank you, Richard. Thank you for saying so. That's very good of you. I knew it was smart to call you. Who else would I call?"

Charles opened the passenger door.

"Where are you going?" Richard asked. He was sick with confusion. Couldn't even look Charles in the eye. The right thing to do hovered somewhere deep inside himself but he couldn't get ahold of it, couldn't determine what it was.

"I'm going to take a walk. I'll be okay. Honest I will. I'll take a cab."

But . . . it's raining like mad out there . . . you could get sick.

"Charles . . ."

"Thank you, Richard."

Charles stepped out of the car and Richard saw him swallowed up in it like he'd stepped through a submerged curtain shielding a sunken stage.

Richard sat that way, trembling, for the better part of an hour. And in that hour the right thing to do made itself known.

But Richard shook his head no. No, he couldn't be the one responsible for putting Charles in the hands of Mayor Blackwater or the Goblin Police. No.

It's not what a friend would do.

And yet . . . what option was there?

Go to him. Tell him to leave Goblin. Tell him that if he doesn't leave Goblin, if he doesn't leave you, you'll turn him in. Tell him, Richard. Tell him that those officers you saw patrolling the streets of downtown, way back when you two were eleven, those same officers will come for him tonight. If he doesn't leave Goblin.

If he doesn't leave you.

Tell him.

Richard pulled out from the corner of Lily and Neptune and drove.

19

And now, standing in that great Goblin rain outside Charles's apartment, face-to-face with that incredible Sherman topiary, Richard understood that all that tough talk was folly.

I'm not turning you in.

The thought played once, loudly, like the drum Charles once beat so many years back in the Goblin High band.

Drenched, depressed, defeated, Richard left the statue at last, and headed for his car.

I'm not turning you in.

Because it's not what a friend would do.

And the unseen hands shook once again within him.

20

Richard pulled into his garage and turned the Dart off. He sat still for a while, allowing his mind to go blank.

Charles was Charles and Richard was Richard.

Richard didn't have to feel guilt for being a friend.

Stepping out of the car, he couldn't believe how wet he was. Growing up in Goblin had taught him something about rain, but tonight's felt somehow more meaningful. Everything did.

Inside, he checked the mail then climbed the stairs and dried himself off in the bathroom. Looking in the mirror, he saw his face didn't look as troubled as he thought it might.

A priest isn't guilty of the crimes confessed to him. And neither is a friend.

Back downstairs, he sat down on the couch to watch television, but each show felt too violent, too full of anger.

He turned it off.

And heard movement upstairs.

Richard rose and started up the carpeted steps.

"Hello?" he called, one hand on the railing.

He stood long in the upstairs hall, but no second sound came.

In his bedroom he felt twice as tired as he did downstairs. He lay down on his bed and heard a voice from inside the closed closet.

"potts . . ."

Richard sat up.

"*potts . . .*"

Richard lifted the closest thing to him, a hardback book on his nightstand, and swung his legs over the side of the mattress.

He swung the closet open violently, raising the book above his head.

Behind him, the word again.

"Parts, Richard. I'm just short a few parts."

Charles stood on the other side of his bed.

"Charles . . . are you holding scissors?"

"It's your duty, see? I need you because I have nobody else."

Before Richard could respond, his friend was upon him. They tumbled onto the bed.

Charles struck and he swung until the sound of Richard's screams became one with the rain against the apartment . . . the windows . . . the street outside.

Blood splashed up onto the headboard and the wall behind it.

"You've always been there for me, Richard. She'll never tell your parts from mine."

Soon Charles sat hunched over his friend, greedily shoving his parts into small plastic bags . . . parts he would save . . . parts he would send . . . and parts he would thank Richard for forever.

And Richard . . . scattered about on the comforter . . . a body in pieces . . . a man in parts . . . a man in slices . . .

A friend.

KAMP

Walter Kamp sat up in bed, his enormous body trembling. A plump hand went straight to his chest. He was out of breath from the single sudden movement.

"What the hell was *that*?"

Since he'd long removed the interior walls in his apartment (now piles of drywall and dust on the wood floorboards) he had a view of his entire space. And from his bed to the kitchen, the strung-up holiday lights showed him nobody was there.

And yet . . . *something* woke him up.

It was raining outside, raining hard, but to a Gobliner the sound of rain was as commonplace as a train in a metropolis; certainly nothing to wake to. And aside from the heavy patter against the windows, his rooms were quiet.

"So what woke you?"

Kamp, sitting up on his transparent bed, the single blanket across his thick legs, his reddish-blond hair rumpled with sleep, often talked to himself in times like these. For usually the fear of giving yourself away trumped the horror of what might erupt from the silence.

He was absolutely sure the noise he'd just heard was *not* the rain. His mind commenced its customary roll . . . a ticker tape of possibilities . . .

The wind.

Something fell over.

Mrs. Doris fell over.

A rat on the fire escape.

A bird on the fire escape.

A person on the fire escape.

A person was in his apartment.

A ghost was in his apartment.

Kamp swung his big legs over the side of his bed and planted his feet on the wood floor. He reached for the closest lamp and pulled the string. The bulb was aimed at the bed itself and Kamp spread his legs, slowly, looking down to the floor beneath the bed.

And yet, if not beneath his bed . . . then where? What had woken him?

Kamp had a vague idea that things were getting out of control. The numerous traps set up around his apartment took up more room than they didn't. The shattered walls, the lack of mirrors, the Plexiglas bed. It was all in the name of removing the corners, all the places something might hide.

"Nothing's here," he said. But he wished he hadn't, for right after saying it he looked to a pile of drywall illuminated deep into the living room and imagined something rising from behind it.

Come on, old man. Keep it together.

Kamp wasn't that old. Forty-one by the time he'd fortified his rooms, ghost-proofing them as best as he knew how.

"*Nothing* is here," he repeated. But the wheel of disquietude had begun its roll.

He knew well that just considering a ghost would quickly eliminate the other possibilities. No matter what he saw or didn't see, within seconds he'd be convinced a ghost was down the hall, toying with him, going "bang bang" as he fooled himself into thinking he was protected.

The wind? You know better than that, Walter. The windows are sealed shut.

And you also checked the edges. Like you always do. The counter, the sink, the tub, the television. There's nothing to fall over.

And Mrs. Doris is fine. She's asleep, as always, in bed by seven, awake by five A.M.

And nobody got in here unless they took an ax to the door.

And so for Walter Kamp, there was no other option but a ghost.

"Shit!"

He jumped out of bed (his big body could move fast when it needed to, had always been limber) and he went to the small television set against the wall. Before it rested a Glasgow mixing console, the multicolored knobs making it very easy to REWIND, FAST FORWARD, PLAY, STOP, and RECORD.

Kamp pressed STOP and rewound the tape.

"Nothing's gonna sneak up on *me*," he said. Again he brought a hand to his chest.

His greatest fear, of course, was being scared to death.

He pressed the PLAY button and, placing his powder-blue rimmed glasses upon his nose and ears, watched with wide-eyed apprehension.

What woke him?

Five video cameras monitored his rooms, nowadays a single *room*, due to his removal of the walls (a task that had worried Mrs. Doris greatly, Kamp with a sledgehammer next door). Even the toilet could be spotted from where he stood. The cameras covered what used to be the bathroom, the kitchen, the front door and living room, his bedroom, and the hall connecting them all.

"Come on, show yourself."

The screen flickered, reflected in his big glasses. Standing in only his underwear and a Goblin High Marauders tank top, Kamp gripped his baby-blue blanket.

"How can there be nothing?" he said, shaking his head. "Nothing doesn't make noise! Nothing doesn't wake you up! You know what does that?" He looked down the length of his booby-trapped rooms. "Something!"

He rewound the tapes again, the Glasgow humming under the power of the falling Goblin rain.

"What's that?" he asked, bending at the waist, gripping his blanket tighter.

It looked like something, a shadow perhaps, may have shifted in the bathtub.

Kamp turned to face the tub. The holiday lights strung above it gave him a good enough view to see if someone was crouched in it. But what if they were lying down?

"Oh . . . *fuck.*"

Kamp felt pressure at his bladder. The sudden need to piss.

There was a ghost in his tub. He was sure of it. There was a ghost in his tub and it had knocked the shampoo over or struck the faucet or something, but whatever it *did do,* it woke him.

He was already sweating through his Goblin High tank top and now he felt a gripping in his throat. Was this what panic felt like? He never could remember. That was, after all, the wily nature of panic. Was he going to freak out? He lifted up on his tiptoes and looked over the drywall rubble to where the tub stood, as if this half inch of height might show him something lying flat in there.

He held his breath.

He stepped from the static of the television screen, then stepped over the drywall pile that was once the doorway to his bedroom. His big flat feet tested the floorboards beneath him.

Adjusting his glasses, gripping his blanket, Kamp approached the tub.

"No ghost," he said. Just like he used to, as a kid, sitting up in bed, shaking his head no. "No ghost, no ghost, no ghost." He wiped snot from his nose, licked his lips. "And you will *not* be scared to death, you will not!"

Halfway through the living room he was able to see some of the inside of the tub.

Were the lights strong enough to show him the bottom? Could he be certain what he saw and what he didn't?

"Look in the tub, Walter. Go on up to it and look inside."

Taking tiny steps, he advanced.

"No no no! Slow and feeble is how someone gets scared to death. Run to the tub, Walter! *Run!*"

His big feet thundered across the wood boards, and the piles of drywall shook with it. By the time he reached the porcelain edge he was moving too fast and when he tried to stop himself he slid, shins-first, against it.

"*Owwww!*"

But he was above the tub now. And he looked, wide-eyed, to the stained bottom before him.

"Nothing."

There was nothing.

"Nothing!"

Then, a memory, a replay of the sound that woke him.

His face lit by the hanging holiday lights, Kamp crossed his rooms again, floating, it seemed, to the secured window overlooking Neptune Street.

Below, on the closer side of Neptune, he saw a car idling in the rain. A Dodge Dart. From this height Kamp could see a man sitting behind the wheel, but no more.

"A car door," Kamp said, smiling. The anxiety broke, scattered, and looked so harmless now. "A passenger got out of the car!"

It was unlikely that anybody stepped out of the idling Dart, given the incredible rainfall they would have had to endure, but Kamp knew he was right.

The soft slam. The distant click.

It was a car door indeed that had woken him.

And yet, as relieved as he felt, he jumped at the sound of Mrs. Doris in the hall outside his front door.

"Waaaaaaalter?"

"Good God!" he cried.

"Waaaaaalter . . . are you okaaaaaaay in there?"

Kamp brought a sweaty hand to his chest.

Yes. Yes he was okay. No ghost in the tub. Just a Gobliner in the street.

"I'm fantastic, Mrs. Doris! And I apologize if I woke you! Now go back to sleep and don't worry about little ol' me!"

Silence from the door. Kamp recalled his own footsteps thundering toward the tub. The way he'd been hollering in here.

"Okay," Mrs. Doris finally said, unseen, beyond the door. "Good night, Waaaaaalter."

After she'd gone, Kamp gazed out the window a beat, then carried his blanket back to his Plexiglas bed, where nothing could hide beneath.

He sat upon it and looked once to the breadth of his illuminated rooms.

Then he fell upon his back, making one final loud thud before closing his eyes again.

Now he would sleep.

For now, the apartment was ghost-free.

And, thanks to his fastidious preparation, his industrious traps and triggers, and his keen sense of sound and sight, he'd avoided being scared to death once more, and could dream to face another day tomorrow.

2

Mrs. Doris, Kamp's eighty-eight-year-old landlady and next-door neighbor, watched with concern as Walter, a year after moving in, trucked up and down the five flights of stairs, carrying up tools and carrying out doors, sweating so hard he looked like he might pop. She wondered deeply at those doors he was removing, one of which she recognized as belonging to the bathroom. She wondered, too, at the blueprint he'd accidentally dropped in the hall, where it unrolled for her to see his vision of an apartment with no surprises.

She'd stopped him numerous times but gotten little information out of him. He'd simply smiled behind his big blue glasses and run a plump hand through his reddish-blond hair, before limping back up the stairs, carrying his saw or hatchet or ax.

She worried.

Though she had known Walter for a good long year, this behavior *was* certainly alarming. She believed he was good for the rent money, his numerous municipal jobs seemed to pay well enough, and yet . . . it was possible he'd overextended himself somehow. Or as her sister Maude once called it, it was likely Walter Kamp had *gone ape*.

And to see his ape-ish size trundling up and down the steps didn't help squash this blooming concern. But when Walter paid her for the next year in advance, a gesture Mrs. Doris had not been anticipating, she was pleased, despite fearing she'd been handed an envelope of, as Maude would say, *hush money*.

The truth was, until recently, Walter Kamp had been one of her best tenants. If only for his stature among the Goblin intelligentsia (a circle Mrs. Doris didn't run in but, by virtue of gossip and flyer, was aware of). Walter was bright. Funny. And nobody could argue his being the wisest Goblin historian the city boasted. The man could talk George Carroll like no other. And the Original 60 were like family to him. Yet wasn't it the best and the brightest that usually fell for what Maude would call *life's painful pitfalls*?

Lately Walter had been talking about fear. And being frightened. And how he was (as he put it one night, high on wine) afraid of being scared to death.

A strange concern, Mrs. Doris thought, but she'd heard stranger. And yet, watching Walter carry things in and out of the building, Mrs. Doris naturally opined that he'd be best served with exercise, if it was his heart he was so worried about. Walter, having just carried a stack of mirrors of many sizes outside, simply smiled and said something she'd long remember.

Did you know that some mothers scare their kids to death, Mrs. Doris? With a simple game of peekaboo?

And yet . . . unquestionably a brilliant man. A *historian*. A tenant who would sit up with her many nights, delivering detailed monologues of Goblin's dark past. Why, if it weren't for the renovations next door, Mrs. Doris might consider Walter Kamp the most interesting Gobliner she'd ever met. And perhaps if she'd only *heard* him working, hammering nails, drilling holes, maybe she could have let it go.

But Mrs. Doris wasn't above letting herself in when she knew Walter wasn't home.

And she'd seen what the rooms next door had become.

There were no doors in Kamp's apartment. No cupboard, no cabinet, no trash can lid, and no top to his toilet seat. Spotlights were supported by tall steel tripods, and Christmas lights hung in rows across the ceiling. The walls had been removed. Most of them anyway, as piles of drywall remained where each of them once stood.

The windows were sealed shut, including the one that led to the fire escape, and Mrs. Doris understood that she'd have to talk to Walter about *that*. And yet, where to begin? The bed frame was made of the same Plexiglas that had been used for the refrigerator door. Trip wires and alarms ran along every wall. The couch and bookshelves were nailed to those same walls as if Walter didn't want there to be any room, anywhere, for something to hide.

Mrs. Doris recalled Walter's concern with being startled, his worry about being "scared to death." In his rooms she found no corners, no crannies, no nooks.

Walter had successfully remodeled his rooms so that he could see everywhere at once, no matter where he stood.

Mrs. Doris stood in many places, shaking her head, wondering at the sort of decisions that would lead to such a state. *Was* Walter okay? Certainly he was allowed to move things around (and she had no doubt she'd had more troubling tenants in the past), but his rooms had all the hallmarks of a cry for help.

Was Walter Kamp crying for help?

There were no pictures on the walls. Certainly not. Framed photos behind glass would be a nightmare, Mrs. Doris realized, as they provided a glimpse of what might be *behind* Walter, a surefire path to a potential heart attack if he were to see a face reflected, a face not his own.

She wondered why she was thinking this way. Why she, too, was imagining supernatural experiences, sudden frights, jump scares. She'd never had a moment's unease in her building, and in the fifty-two years she'd been running it, not one tenant had complained about a ghost.

Not even Walter Kamp.

He was putting ideas in her head, she believed, and the sight of his rooms was enough to cause even the most staunch realist alarm. Yet as she was locking his door behind her, after the first time she let herself in, she had to wonder why a man so smart, a man so *kind,* could let himself be turned around like this.

Scared to death!

The way Walter was carrying on, he was liable to scare himself to death!

With his year of rent in hand, and the continuation of his monthly visits to her rooms, where they drank wine and he spoke adoringly of Goblin past and present, Mrs. Doris decided to let it slide.

For now.

After all, being a Gobliner herself, and having let rooms to so many others, she'd seen her share of odd. Walter could paint the walls black and hang goats' heads from the ceiling and he might not surpass some of the people she'd known. Neal Nash, the now brash, rich, and famous hunter, used to fire his guns into the walls. Jonathan Woodruff had commanded unseen employees about and acted as if Mrs. Doris's building was the hotel he would one day build and own.

Perhaps Walter Kamp was simply the logical extension of such personae. The next Gobliner in line. Maude used to say it was *in the water.* And it always made Mrs. Doris laugh because she knew her sister wasn't talking about the tap. She was referring, of course, to the endless rainfall outside, and the fact that nobody ought to be tasked with maintaining their sanity forever in a city that never stopped crying.

3

Every other member of Kamp's immediate family had seen a ghost. His mother, his father, his sister, Carol, and brother, David, too. Even a couple of cousins and an uncle had stories that took place in the periphery. Stories that chilled Walter through the years. Once, at a family reunion in Perish Park, a cousin's husband told Walter that he'd been on the toilet when a tongue sprouted from the water and lapped at his thighs. Telling the story, the husband laughed. He added that he smoked a lot of grass and would Walter like to try some? And yet even this story, with its obvious detractions, caused Walter to worry. What would *he* do if a tongue rose from the water between his legs? Would he survive long enough to laugh? Long enough to tell himself he'd been seeing things . . . and nothing more?

It seemed, to Kamp, that everybody laughed after they told their particular ghost story. Even those with the worst ones. They flaunted them like party favors, like business cards, like winks. They tapped one another on the shoulder and excitedly blurted them out, projectile-vomiting tales that, if taken seriously, ought to change the way one sees all of living and life. Walter couldn't understand it. Didn't *want* to understand it. How dare someone flippantly describe a shape upon the ceiling without expressing the deep concern that should come with such a sight?

Was it possible that all these people had seen an actual ghost and not *one* of them was tortured or scarred by the experience? Kamp believed his family when they told him what they'd seen (each in their turn, through the years) but he couldn't get over the idea that they were able to carry on, reenter life, as if a door hadn't been opened, a deep truth not revealed. Why weren't they affected in a bigger way? Why wasn't his sister, Carol, haunted by what she'd told him? What about his brother, David? At twelve years old David woke to find a little girl searching the walls of David's bedroom for a door. That's what he said. That's what he saw! And somehow, *somehow,* David slept the rest of that night in his very own bed!

Kamp couldn't understand it. He didn't *want* to.

The night David told their mother what he'd seen, Kamp couldn't sleep at all. He sat wrapped in a blanket on the grass outside, watching the house until sunrise. Mom saw him in the morning, a chance glance out the kitchen window, as she brewed coffee for the day.

Everybody in his family had seen a ghost. All of them.

To Walter, this meant his turn was sure to come.

And when it did . . . would he be able to laugh it off? Would he be able to carry on? Would he happily flap his lips, telling his fellow members of the Goblin Historical Society all about the apparition he'd seen in his rooms?

An old chess partner once told him that God knew he couldn't handle seeing a ghost and so had never sent one his way. For days Kamp wasn't sure how that idea made him feel. Avoiding a ghost was not the same as refusing to ask a woman to dance. It wasn't a matter of bravery or what you could or could not handle. To Kamp, saying you weren't afraid of ghosts was tantamount to saying you weren't afraid of death. And who wasn't afraid of death but those who didn't adore living?

With his parents he could say, *Of course Mom and Dad could handle it, they are and always will be bigger, wiser, and stronger than us.*

But with Carol and David, Kamp had no excuse. His siblings took their sightings in stride. Hardly put out, they'd related the events to their parents and were emotionally settled within hours. And yet each of them did have their buttons, strings to be pulled that could scare them.

Carol was terrified of spiders. Walter was not. And what did she see when she saw one? Was it as overwhelming, as all-powerful as the ghost Walter believed was coming? For David it was needles; how he used to scream when the doctor took his arm. And how big, how sharp, did the needle look to David? And what precautions would he take to avoid it?

Would he tear down some walls? Put up some lights? Set trip wires and cages throughout his rooms? How far would David go?

Walter had gone pretty far. He knew this. About as far as one could go. The ache in his back from sleeping on Plexiglas provided that reality.

And so what? Kamp often thought. *They have their fears, I have mine.*

Ghosts. And yet . . . not ghosts alone, but his potential *reaction* to seeing one.

Oh, how many people shared their ghost story . . . their eyes wide and watered but without real terror? How many of them were *excited* to bring it up? How many couldn't wait?

Look at me. I'm in the supernatural club.

Never mind that they had to be in the same room as the thing to see it. Never mind that if it came once it could come again. And never mind that, if it wanted to, a ghost might sneak up on someone, show itself when he was least expecting it.

On a downbeat perhaps. Or an up. Kamp worried about both indiscriminately.

And tonight, having fallen asleep after determining the sound outside was a car door closing, Walter Kamp woke again. This time it wasn't because of an unplanned noise of the night. Rather, it was when one of his many alarms went off, set for one fifteen A.M. The first in a series of nightly checks, tape reviews, times to make certain nothing was floating through his rooms, avoiding the trip wires on the floor, sailing the stale air with a mind to tap him.

Walter reached out and turned off the buzzer. Then he sat up and stared long down the length of his rooms, one room now, searching for changes, like that game with the two photos, spot the differences, spot something that doesn't belong, spot it before it spots you and scares you, scares you to death.

4

Thirsty, he got out of bed. He stepped over the drywall rubble and crossed his rooms to the kitchen sink. The Goblin tap water always tasted good. Especially on the nights it rained. As if the city somehow absorbed it. In the silence following a gulp, Kamp imagined he could hear the entire building at rest. Mrs. Doris next door, dreaming no doubt of rent envelopes and those Thompsons on the first floor who gave her nothing but trouble.

He thought, *But who would want to haunt you?*

He hadn't been thinking directly of ghosts but ghosts always hid in the one place with corners he could not remove. His mind.

Returning to his room, sitting now on the edge of his bed, his great weight testing the indomitable Plexiglas material, he thought this over.

"Who would want to scare you?"

Because most people's stories were of dead family members, a grandmother who had recently died, a father returned to calm a sad son.

Kamp gulped some more water and decided that he didn't have an answer to his question. Certainly no one he once knew would want to do this to him.

So, who's coming?

Because whether or not he had any proof to tell him so, Kamp was sure something was coming. He could feel it in the joints in his knees, in the muscles in his back and neck. Something was going to show itself soon. And when he tried to imagine himself reacting well, the vision cracked and shattered, as if he'd thrown a rock through the window of Mr. Bench's magic shop on Lily.

"Please," Kamp said. "I'm not ready."

He tried to believe he was. But those ghosts that swarmed between the thoughts and convictions of his thoughts refused to withdraw.

You know exactly how you'd react. You'd scream and bang on the wall and eighty-eight-year-old Mrs. Doris would come over. She'd knock and call for you until she couldn't call anymore. Then she'd call the Goblin Police. And those crazy, creepy cops would come and bust down the one door you've got left and they'd find you dead on the floor and point to you with their long gray fingers and say, "Walter Kamp has died. Bury him standing."

Maybe it'd go this way: He'd be sitting on the edge of the toilet, clipping his toenails. He'd get one foot done when a squishy sound and a little motion caused him to look up and see a half-rotted woman in the tub.

She'd say, *What? Aren't you glad you have a story to share at parties now?*

And that would be it. Walter's heart would go out. Snap. Like the dead woman had turned off the lights. And Mrs. Doris would find him that way, his ass still on the toilet, his huge naked body slumped forward, his head hanging over the edge of the tub.

Something's coming. Who?

Still sitting on the edge of his bed, Kamp was sweating now.

Something was coming, indeed. *Something* was going to show itself and *Something* wasn't going to be good. It'd been keeping tabs on Kamp's precautions, breathing in the blackness, the one place Kamp hadn't thought to prepare.

"Are you in here? Are you here already? Please let me know. Please don't leap. Don't come suddenly. Don't . . ." He held his head in his hands. "Don't scare me to death."

The silence following his own words affected him. What was he doing? *Trying* to make contact? In the silence he could almost hear the air around him *push* out a bit . . . bend . . . like words were about to be returned to him.

The rain pounded hard against the windows. Heavy fat hands. *Let me in.*

Kamp pulled his blanket up to his nose. The Goblin Marauders tank top felt like scant protection against whatever was coming.

Something was.

He looked out across his rooms, down the lit path to the kitchen. His heart beat heavy and he pressed the blanket to his chest.

He tried to think good thoughts. Good things. Goblin. Chess. History. Mom.

But Mom had died and so thoughts of Mom led to thoughts of ghosts once again.

"Don't show yourself!" he suddenly called out. And across his rooms, through the far kitchen wall, he believed he heard Mrs. Doris get out of bed. He thought he heard her in her own kitchen, adjacent to his, where the unmistakable sound of a glass against the wall could be heard.

As if listening to him. Listening to see if he was okay. Or, Kamp worried, listening to be able to say one day, excitedly, at a party, that she had a ghost story of her own, one that topped all the others, yes yes, the time she heard a man die through her kitchen wall, the time she heard a man scared to death.

5

Kamp, still awake, still sitting up on his transparent bed, was still thinking.

His mother and father made it forty-six years together before Harrison (sixty-eight) died of cancer. Judy (also dead at sixty-eight, but four years after her husband) went for no reason at all. Died in her sleep. Kamp, coming to take her to a movie, found her sitting up on the couch, eyes open, unmoving. He shook her once, then twice, then sat down beside her on the couch with his hand to his chin, wondering what might happen to her soul, how long she'd actually been dead, and if maybe she wasn't still in the room with him.

If I didn't see a ghost that day . . .

His relationship with his mother was a fantastic one, underscored somehow by the fact that he was the one to find her. Of the three Kamp kids, Walter was most like her in physique and spirit.

Judy Kamp was a big woman with a bright light inside.

Halfway through her pregnancy with Walter, she knew she was carrying a big boy. And through the grit and grind of labor, she knew he would be *her* boy.

And in a way, he was. Growing up, there could be no argument that Kamp was his mother's son. They shared the same mannerisms, the same gestures, the same predilection to eat the leftovers on the next plate over when their own plate was eaten clean.

They shared the same laugh, too. The hallmark bellowing of the heavier set.

To all, Judy Kamp was a riot. Friends and visitors felt safe in her sphere, knew they were in good hands; Judy could hold court at any table and made society simple and exciting. She had opinions, ideas, sayings, and phrases that stretched not only to all the laughing guests, but well beyond, all the way to the classroom Kamp would briefly teach in years down the road.

No one spending an afternoon with Judy Kamp would remark on how smart she was, but how *right* she was. And Walter's great intelligence never stepped over his mother's great reason. It was their sense of humor that served as their clubhouse. *The smarts barometer,* she used to say. *They ought to test IQ by how many funnies a kid can make.* Yes, their secret hideout. The place where their exclusive versions of reality came together in a sort of celebration of two. Kamp treasured these moments most. From peals of sincere laughter at the kitchen table, to something she might have said, just to him, in an aisle at the grocery store. But Judy gave him much more than her jokes; she also gave him her spirit, her insatiable thirst for knowledge, and the energy it took to seek it out. Judy Kamp was not religious. Not righteous. Never stubborn nor severe.

Her death left quite a hole in Walter's life.

Would she think to come to me now? he considered, the blanket held tight about his shoulders.

Oh, Mom. What if I don't recognize you?

How he loved that woman!

Kamp flopped onto his back, his reddish-brown hair wet with sweat. He pushed his glasses up his nose.

All these thoughts of Mom. Of death. Of ghosts.

Even while recalling his mother, his best friend, Kamp couldn't help but feel the horror that awaited him. Why wouldn't he *want* to see his mother again? He missed her terribly. Could she see the precautions he took? What if Judy, floating about in the abyss of bodiless souls, caught for a moment a glimpse of her son . . . still living . . . cleaning his curtainless tub and (excitedly) decided to make contact? And what if (in the rush of this encounter) Kamp didn't recognize her as his mother? Who could say for certain what face the dead wear? How different might she look? How thin? How awful! For Kamp to be frightened of the woman who taught him everything! Would her face have aged the ten years since dying? Aged without the beauty enhancements of such things as . . . *blood*? Would Kamp be able to sense in that leathery shape a kindred spirit . . . a like-minded soul . . . his mother . . . the same way she sensed it in him the day he poured forth, bloody, from her womb?

"I gotta think of someone else," he said. He got up again, still clutching his blue blanket. "Anybody else."

So, without him wanting them to, his thoughts turned to his father.

"Dad," Kamp said, eyeing the tub. The sleeping spotlights up by the ceiling. The rat traps meant for ghosts.

Harrison Kamp was, by all measures, obsessive. But he adored Judy and that was enough for a young Walter. He openly flirted with her till the end. For a man as conservative (monetarily, politically) as Harrison was, nothing stopped him from kissing Judy full on the face upon coming home or taking hold of her hand on the couch.

Dad, Walter thought. *What if it's Dad who's coming?*

He blinked and realized he'd reached the middle of his rooms. The shadows of the many raindrops danced upon his Goblin Marauders tank top, and Walter looked down to see he'd dropped his blanket at his feet.

"Dad?" he said. "Are you the ghost I'm fearing?"

He barely made contact when he was alive!

It would surprise Kamp to know that, somewhere on that other side, his father might be looking for him.

And would he recognize him if he came? Both Harrison and Judy were buried standing up in the Goblin Cemetery and had

been for a long time. It didn't take an artist's imagination to endure a vision of Dad in the kitchen, half rotten to the skull, bones
making sharp angles out of his brown death suit.

Maybe it'd be his father's one big chance to play father-
educator by returning from the grave to tell Walter not to waste
so much of his life on obsession.

Wanna end up like me, son? Carrying all your concerns into the ground?

Kamp paced between the refrigerator with the see-through
door and the secured windows against the wall. He nearly stepped
on the bear trap on the way.

"Dad," he said, "Mom. Please don't come to see me. Not yet!
I'm not ungrateful. I love you both. I'm just not ready. I can't
handle it. My heart . . . my—"

He looked down the length of his rooms and saw that his
blanket was balled up on his bed.

Kamp brought a hand to his chest.

He looked to the ground, to where he was sure he had left it
last. And yet he had been pacing. To and fro. From one end of the
apartment to the other. Was it possible he'd picked it up and set
it down on the way?

A long, gurgled moan rolled out of his throat and Walter felt
a sudden need to piss.

"There's something hiding under my blanket on my bed," he
said.

The words were too real, too immediate, and he had to cover
his eyes with both hands. When he pulled his big fingers away, he
saw that the blanket was still there, bundled upon his bed.

Go on . . . push it aside.

But the thought was a bad one. A mean one. Walter couldn't
walk across his rooms any more than he could find the nerve to
pull the blanket aside.

He stared at it for a long time. As the rain pounded against the glass. As his heart pounded against his ribs.

How long had he been thinking about his mother and father? How long had he been off his guard? Traveling through nostalgic woods, stepping under nostalgic archways . . .

Go on. Pull that blanket aside.

He was walking toward his bed at last, without the conscious knowledge of having decided to do it. When his big toes touched the Plexiglas base, he bent at the waist and reached for the line-switch that would ignite the bulb aimed at his bed.

On three. Turn it on and pull back the blanket. One . . .

Kamp felt the cool knowledge of inevitable death upon him.

Two . . .

And what might it look like?

Three . . .

He pulled the blanket back and flipped the switch.

He screamed.

There was something there. Mom's corpse flat on her back. Dad wearing a suit of centipedes.

"Get out!" Walter called, closing his eyes.

But when he opened them, he saw that the crinkles in the blankets had made funny shapes and that was all.

From out in the hall he heard footsteps.

"Mrs. Doris?"

Maybe. Maybe something else.

Kamp got back into bed and pulled the blanket tight to his nose. He stared out at his rooms for a long time, but not long enough for the sun to come up again. Not even close. By the time he fell asleep, the rain was the heaviest it'd been all night, and the Goblin sky was as black as an unaccounted-for corner where death might be found crouching, readying itself for the spring.

6

At two fifteen A.M. the alarm nearest his bed went off.

Kamp sat up with a gasp. He looked the length of his rooms before he understood that the sound was coming from the small box beside him.

With a plump pointer finger he turned it off.

Silence.

It was time to check the tapes again.

Stepping over the rubble of former walls, he sat at the television and rewound the tape an hour. At the beginning of the footage he saw himself pacing the apartment. He winced as the him on the screen pulled back the powder-blue blanket on the bed and screamed.

He watched the rest in fast-forward then, sleepily, got up.

But halfway to the kitchen he turned right and stepped to the front door.

Somebody was out there. Walter heard him.

His ear to the wood, he waited for a sound. It didn't take long as he could distinctly make out the steady breathing of someone in the hall.

"Mom?"

"Walter?"

Kamp jumped at the sound of his name. He inched back from the door with his hands raised before him.

"Not yet, Mom! I'm not ready! It'll kill me! It'll scare me to death!"

"It's me! Mrs. Doris!"

Kamp recognized her voice. He lowered his hands. "Mrs. Doris? What are you doing out in the hall so late at night?"

"I'm restless. Sounds like you are, too. Come have a drink,

teach me some history. On a night as rainy as this, I could use to reconnect with Goblin before it washes clean away."

Of course! *History!* This was a topic that could take Kamp's mind off the ghosts. Funny, no?

"I'll be right over," Kamp said. Then, to himself, *Incredible how bringing up the ghosts of Goblin make me forget my own.*

He'd majored in history at the university and later taught the subject at Goblin High, pulling off the very tricky task of making the subject fun. In those days students clamored to get into his classes. They could spot an enthusiast a hall away. Kamp spent so much time reading up on the city's history that the editor of *The Green Goblin,* the biggest newspaper in town, showed up at one of his classes to ask Professor Kamp if he might proofread an article about the Original 60.

"The Original Sixty," Kamp said. For the first time all night, he smiled. He unlocked the front door and entered the hall. Mrs. Doris was peering out her apartment.

"You wanna put some pants on?" she asked him.

Walter looked down. Saw he was still in his tank top and undershorts.

"Oh."

"Well, I don't care if you don't. I live half my life in a bathrobe."

Walter smiled again. He locked his door.

"The Original Sixty," he said.

Now Mrs. Doris smiled.

"One of my favorite subjects. Come on in for some wine, Walter. Let's see if we can put our ghosts to bed."

7

"It's my favorite stretch of Goblin history," Walter said, sitting at Mrs. Doris's small kitchen table.

"I like it, too."

"And what are you doing up so late?"

"So late? It's early is what it is. And what can I say? I heard you rummaging about."

"Was I?"

"Yes, Walter. It was you. I heard you, I came and knocked, and you answered."

Kamp seemed satisfied with this answer.

"Now," Mrs. Doris said. "The Original Sixty."

Kamp had a sip of wine. "They were the first to fall in love with all this shit," he said. He fanned a hand toward her open windows, where the heavy rain came in. "As if they were some variety of snowbird. Like . . . like . . ."

"Rainbirds."

Walter shrugged. "The word has long eluded me. But rainbirds will do."

They cheered their glasses.

"This land had long been watched over by a community of indigenous people who turned out to be not so much indomitable as they were justifiably unwilling to assent. They didn't think *anybody* should occupy this land. Not even themselves! They were a tribe run by a very strong, very smart man named Chief Blackwater, the very ancestor of our current mayor."

"I love him."

"So do I."

"But I worry."

"Worry about Mayor Blackwater?"

"Sure. A lot of unrest in Goblin. Not the people necessarily, not in that way, but the . . ."

"The land."

"Yes. The land."

"Yes, well, Chief Blackwater recognized that same 'unrest.' He called it 'dark land,' and was protective enough of all this"—he fanned a hand to the window again—"and wise enough to refuse all negotiations with the white man and made it a tribal law to scare off any who stayed too long."

"Or talked too much."

"That's right. It was obvious to Chief Blackwater, from the start, that the white man had one thing in mind."

"Theft."

"That's right. Blackwater's personality was the sort not to take chances. To him, Goblin, or the land that was to become Goblin, wasn't a place *anybody* should settle. The land was sacred and the rain suggested great power. I agree. I feel it, too. This land wasn't for dwelling, Mrs. Doris. It was for . . ."

"Spirits."

They stared at each other across the small table. Kamp looked over his shoulder, to the many corners and doors of his landlady's apartment.

"Yes. Spirits."

They sipped wine at the same time.

"They say Blackwater went nuts up in the North Woods. Rumors of a witch spread quick, and his tribesmen spoke of her quietly when he wasn't around. About how he met her in those woods and she stole the remains of his sanity. They saw a void in his gaze, upon exiting those woods, when he declared all of Goblin off limits to any human being. That included the indigenous people, too. It would be years before anyone would step foot here again."

Mrs. Doris smiled and her eyes became two youthful slits behind her own pink-rimmed glasses.

"Then the Original Sixty came," she said.

"The first sixty settlers," Kamp said, nodding. "The arrival of the white monsters Blackwater had anticipated. The kind that wanted to stay. At first he and his tribe watched from a distance. He instructed them to wait. And so they did, in the marshy banks of the West Fields. Let the *pale shades* settle in. His term, I've read. Let them get lazy first. Then?"

"Then?" Mrs. Doris asked, her eyes wide open again. But she had heard this story many times.

"Well, what happened next is a hotly contested point in Goblin history, Mrs. Doris. One book will tell you something a little different than the next."

"But what do *you* say happened next?"

"Me? What do I say?" Kamp leaned back in the kitchen chair. The wood groaned in retaliation. "I tend to believe the story about a woman, a wife and a mother, who set out to retrieve a horse that had broken a fence and run away. She tracked the animal out to the far southern entrance to the North Woods, where she came face-to-face with Blackwater himself."

Mrs. Doris wiggled her eyebrows.

"Bet she wasn't expecting *that*."

"Indeed. Before she could say 'neighbor' he'd scared her so thoroughly, she turned whiter yet. Blackwater did such a good job running the rest of the settlers off that, two months later, when two male explorers came through, they recorded in their notebooks that the land they'd discovered was being seen for the first time by human eyes. That's how completely the Original Sixty had fled."

Outside, the sound of police sirens caused both Kamp and Mrs. Doris to get up from the table and go to the window. Down on Lily, four cruisers passed fast, their lights spinning red and blue, turning each drop of rain into a prism.

"Looks like Christmas out there," Mrs. Doris said.

"No," Kamp said. "Only Lily."

"Tell me about Perish Park, Walter. Unless you're ready for bed."

Walter turned and looked into her eighty-eight-year-old eyes. For the first time all night he had the sneaking suspicion that Mrs. Doris had asked him over with the intention of calming him down. But the thought was fleeting and it vanished before he could consider it.

In his mind's eye he saw the historical marker at the gates of Perish Park. Mrs. Doris probably thought of it, too.

PERISH PARK.
WHERE COLONEL WES FARRALINE
CHEATED CHIEF BLACKWATER'S SON
WITH A CONTRACT MADE OF DUST.

"Pretty soon other settlers and soldiers south of Goblin got wind of the unflappable indigenous chief who wouldn't allow anybody to step foot in what is now our beloved Goblin," Kamp said, still eyeing the wet street below. "It had been twenty-five years since the Original Sixty. George Carroll, who, as you know, is one of the two Sherman topiaries that greet people upon entering our city today, mustered a couple hundred men, women, children, and dogs to follow him north to a 'unique land' he'd discovered where it 'rains all the time.' He wasn't afraid of the rumors. I think he might have been crazier than Blackwater."

"Come," Mrs. Doris said. "Let's sit again. I'm too old to stand up for a story."

Kamp followed her to the table.

"By then," Kamp said, "Chief Blackwater was sick. He was getting older and he was getting ill. But that didn't mean he'd forgotten how to protect this land. When he got word that a group of white people were trying to settle all over again, Blackwater instructed his tribe to let them. To wait. Just as he'd done a quarter century before. But as you know, Carroll was a bit of a . . ."

"Kamikaze?"

"Yeah. A kamikaze. My God, you can almost imagine him parachuting right into Blackwater's anger, can't you?"

"Yes, you can."

"Carroll's community had been living here three months when the indigenous people emerged from what one boy called *the rippling space.* I've always loved that. He was no doubt referring to the waves we're all so used to seeing, walls of rain, walls of water. But it sure gives the scene a science-fiction nod, doesn't it?"

"Indeed, it does."

"They were working on a schoolhouse then. A battle ensued."

"How bad was it?"

"Both sides lost lives. Carroll's more so than Blackwater's, but the natives were faced with the reality that this group of white people would be more difficult to get rid of than those sixty from years back. From his sick-cot, Blackwater demanded his tribe gather these white men from their beds before things escalated any further."

"Because of the spirits."

"What's that?"

"Blackwater didn't want these men or any men bothering the energy, the spirits that live here."

"Live . . . or lived?"

"Oh, *lived,* I suppose." Then, "Why didn't he just warn them? About the spirits?"

"From what I've read," Kamp said, "Blackwater didn't want to have to talk about what he'd seen in the North Woods."

Mrs. Doris shook her head. "Sounds like he saw something that shook him up."

"Indeed."

"And?"

"And what?"

"And so what happened? Carroll's men were sleeping . . ."

"Some died."

"Ah."

"Carroll sent word south."

"For help?"

"For help."

"And?"

"Here's where the history leads to modern day. A platoon of soldiers, headed by Colonel Wes Farraline, was sent north to bail George Carroll out. Farraline was shocked when, greeted by a half-bearded and fully disheveled Carroll, he learned the settlers had already lost fifty percent of their personnel. And not just the men."

"Tsk tsk. See where trying to steal gets you?"

"Absolutely. But when Blackwater heard of the cavalry arriving he was flattered. To him, seventy soldiers meant more numbers to overcome. He instructed his men to bring him seventy heads by sunup. Legend has it he wanted the tribe to use them as soup bowls at breakfast. But Blackwater's son knew better. He saw the weapons Farraline had and he wasn't going to have his chest blown apart to appease his dying, raving father. He decided he'd do what Dad never did: strike a deal with the white man."

Kamp sipped his wine. His big elbows dwarfed Mrs. Doris's little table.

"A deal in dust," Mrs. Doris said.

"But not yet. When Farraline got word the indigenous people wanted to make a deal, he silently patted himself on the back. He figured they wouldn't be any more difficult to dispense with than any others he'd encountered. He walked tall through the settlement with the news. But as goes 'good news' in history, Farraline got a little greedy and ignored the omens that came with it. He brought Carroll into his tent and suggested they try to trick Son of Blackwater. Get him to sign a contract that would allow Carroll's gang to live on the land. Then have a second contract drawn up, for Carroll to sign, that stated the natives still owned the land and would be awarded a tax from the settlers. Farraline's plan had Carroll signing his name in *sand*. A quill loaded with fine dust; Blackwater's son would see that Carroll put his name down, but when he put the contract in his satchel the name would slide off, vanishing into nothing but dirt. Then the only *legal* document would be the one saying Carroll had permission to settle. Carroll readily agreed. His likeness doesn't grace the Goblin gates for his morality, after all."

"Not many likenesses do."

"Do what?"

"Look like what they say they do."

"No. They certainly don't. Farraline and Carroll, in full regalia, met with Blackwater's son in what would become Perish Park." Kamp fanned a hand to the window, though Perish Park was a few miles east. "The natives agreed. The contracts were signed. Farraline was nervous when Son of Blackwater turned to leave without immediately putting the contract in his satchel. But two steps farther away, he did. And so it appeared their scam had worked."

"So it appeared."

"Later that night, drunk on his own cunning, Farraline foolishly answered a tapping on his tent. Unarmed, he was confused to see what looked like a lantern floating in the darkness. He thought it might be an angel, a congratulations from the God he adored. He had no way of knowing the natives had painted themselves night-black and planned on bringing their visionary chief those seventy heads after all. Blood erupted. The indigenous people were like a physical manifestation of Blackwater's mental landscape. Chaotic. Righteous. Unstoppable. Carroll, leading a group of women and children through the outskirts of that slaughter, saw three lights off in the distance. Hoping it was Farraline, he followed them. Turned out it was. Farraline's face was wrapped around a lantern set on a tree stump. Three lights shone. Two out the eyes and one big beam out the mouth."

"Clever. Good one."

"Carroll rounded up whoever was left for Goblin's first makeshift militia. He wasn't giving in. Not yet. But he wasn't sure exactly how to proceed. Nobody was. And then, in South Shilling Field, a farmhand named John Phillis hatched a plan that would salvage Carroll's gang, and secure what would become Goblin, for good. The remaining settlers *pretended* to evacuate. They staged a faux fleeing. They admitted defeat by packing up their belongings and heading north. And after they were sure the natives saw them leave, they hid out in the North Woods. The very woods that, legend says, drove Blackwater insane a quarter century before. Goblin's great expanse of brittle black trees, thousands of twisting trunks, nature in chaos, with no path or clearing to guide them."

"I've never stepped foot in the North Woods."

"Nobody will go more than a hundred feet deep. I've heard you can see beer cans near the entrance. Teenagers, I suppose. But even cocksure youth won't go any farther than that. There's a witch in there, didn't you know?" Kamp smiled.

Mrs. Doris shrugged. "It's the Great Owls' domain. Let them have it, I say."

"No doubt. And they don't need us ruining it for them."

"So did they make it out of the woods sane? They must not have, if they're our ancestors, after all."

"John Phillis, George Carroll, and the highest-ranking remaining officers mapped out their course of action. Restless members of the camp could go walking along the winding paths so long as they were secured by rope. Kind of like lowering someone into a cave, I suppose. Volunteers stood post at the head of the trails, and if you wanted to go deep you asked for a rope, one end of which would be fastened to your waist and the other tied to the hand of the volunteer. If someone tugged on the rope violently, men would be dispatched to check it out. These men would have to be tied to the volunteer as well."

"I hear the Great Owls can eat up an entire man. Is that true, Walter?"

"I don't know. But for some reason I'd like to believe they can."

Mrs. Doris smiled. "That's because you're a true Gobliner. Truer than any other. Most of us are passing through, but Goblin has gotten into your bones."

Walter smiled. Mrs. Doris had meant it as a compliment and he'd taken it as such.

"Blackwater's illness worsened. His grip over his tribe loosened. His progressive son, having proved his worth by driving the white men out, ignored his father's archaic laws and, eventually, allowed the tribe to live on the very land we live on now. They occupied the small village erected by the white settlers. They'd seen Carroll's exodus with their own eyes. The land was fair game."

"They relaxed."

"They sure did. And then Carroll called the shot. Six months to the day after their staged evacuation, the settlers returned to burn down their own village with the natives sleeping inside.

Mothers set fire to the very houses they tended to half a year back. The schoolteacher tossed the torch into the schoolhouse. Carroll located Blackwater, sick bed and all, and boasted about what he'd done. Blackwater told Carroll that Son of Blackwater would come back from the dead. That he'd 'deliver an evil' to all who were present upon his return. Then Carroll left Blackwater out by the West Fields, alone, where he slowly starved with no one near to nurse him."

Kamp remembered a related yarn. How a young girl convinced a volunteer she was old enough to walk the North Woods alone when the settlers were hiding out. How the volunteer fastened the rope around her waist and sent her on her way. After four hours passed, with no sign of the girl, the volunteer grew nervous. He signaled for the remaining soldiers and told them his concern. They fastened ropes to their waists and followed her trail. Twelve men wound their way through the impossible woods. Lit by lantern, the men were scared no doubt, replaying the witch myth on repeat. They followed over half a mile of rope before finding the end of it bloodstained and chewed. Kamp remembered how one of the twelve went a few feet farther and found, in that soft lantern light, the young girl with her chest sprayed purple. Like a wolf had eaten her from the back to the front or like her heart had exploded.

With that thought, he brought a hand to his chest.

"What do you know about Jonathan Trachtenbroit?" Mrs. Doris asked.

"Trachtenbroit? I know a great deal. But in my opinion, his history isn't as interesting. He wasn't a Gobliner, after all."

"That's sacrilege," Mrs. Doris said, smiling. "In these parts."

"That's just my humble opinion."

"And what do you know about the key to the city? I should think a man like you ought to have it."

Kamp shrugged. "I know it's a symbolic story. When people say the key to the city belongs in city hall, that Goblin's history runs amok when it's not, they're just trying to make excuses for why the present is so messed up. And as you know, the key has been lost for . . . how long now? Gosh, I don't even know. Years. Mayor Blackwater says he'd like to locate it, but I think he's just putting us on. Having fun. You do know that when someone gets the key to a city they're not receiving an actual key, of course. It's all symbolism. And to suggest that, whenever the key isn't where it's supposed to be, that all of history, that all the ghosts of Goblin . . ."

Kamp trailed off. He still had his hand on his chest.

"Walter," Mrs. Doris began. And for the second time tonight Walter wondered if she had asked him over with a mind to distract him. Exactly how much did Mrs. Doris know about Walter's personal life?

"Yes?"

"Why don't you head to bed. Lord knows one of those many alarms is about to go off. You could silence it now, before it begins, and get some good sleep."

Walter stared long into her eyes.

"Have you been inside my rooms, Mrs. Doris?"

The way he asked it, the accusation in his voice was naked.

"Walter Kamp, I would never enter your apartment without your permission in a hundred thousand years."

"Then how did you know I have numerous alarms?"

Mrs. Doris shrugged. Kamp couldn't read her reaction. The idea of someone gaining access to his rooms meant that anybody could.

And then maybe any*thing*.

"A woman knows," she said, getting up, leading Walter to the door. "And besides, your apartment sounds like a bloody battle-field through these thin walls."

8

"Waaaaaalter?"

Kamp sat up in bed, sweat dribbling down both sides of his face. He'd been dreaming of Mrs. Doris in his rooms. Only she was dead, like Mom and Dad, and her wrinkled flesh had fallen to her wrists, her shoulders, her ankles, exposing bones that looked just like the trunks of the twisted trees in the North Woods. It was as if she no longer had the strength to carry her own skin, and now it all sat rumpled like oversized leg warmers, puffy scarves, in piles.

"Waaaaaaaalter?"

It was Mrs. Doris's voice, no doubt, calling from the hall. But while Kamp knew this, he couldn't help but wonder if perhaps she was inside.

He scanned the length of his rooms, still seeing in his mind's eye the eighty-eight-year-old woman, slowly inching toward his bed. What had she been saying?

Of course I've been inside your rooms. I'm here all the time. And I've found a hiding place, Walter, a place to jump out from, a place from which to scare you to death . . .

BANG BANG!

She was knocking on the door.

"Mrs. Doris!" Kamp called. "Are you okay?"

"That's what I came to ask you, Walter. Are *you* okay?"

"Me?"

"I heard you scream. Were you having a nightmare?"

Kamp reached a hand to his throat, as if he'd find evidence of a scream.

Had he cried out? He'd certainly been having a bad dream.

He swung his legs over the side of his Plexiglas bed and

planted his huge feet on the cool wood floor. Awake again. And how long had it been since he was waxing history with Mrs. Doris next door? He looked to the clocks.

Three twenty-five A.M. meant that he'd somehow slept through an alarm.

Lord knows one of those many alarms is about to go off.

Mrs. Doris had said that. Not in his weird dream, but when he was leaving her apartment, only hours ago.

Had he screamed?

"No . . . no . . . I'm fine," he called. "I mean, yes . . . I had a nightmare. Thank you, Mrs. Doris. Thank you. Good night!"

He imagined her out in the hall, pocketing the key to his rooms.

Had she been in here? Was it so easy for someone, anyone, to get in?

Kamp rose and moved quickly to the door. Getting on all fours, he looked through the ankle-high peephole he'd installed himself two weeks ago to the day.

He saw a pair of dark naked feet slowly stepping out of view.

"Ah!"

Kamp recoiled and fell onto his ass, facing the bolted door.

Who was that? WHO WAS THAT!

"Waaaaalter?"

Mrs. Doris again. Out in the hall.

"Mrs. Doris! Go to your rooms! There's something out there in the hall with you!"

Quiet. As if she was checking. Or as if the thing with dark naked feet had silenced her.

Kamp, breathing very hard, waited for her to say something, anything. Then he got on all fours again and scurried to the peephole.

Only a pair of yellow slippers.

"There's nobody out here, Walter. Nobody but me."

The name Blackwater crossed Kamp's mind. Those dark naked feet had strength to them. The strength of a man who lived off the land, who didn't need shoes at all.

"You're losing your mind," Kamp said.

"What, Walter?"

"Nothing, Mrs. Doris! I had a bad dream! I'm sorry. Must've been the wine."

Mrs. Doris sighed beyond the door.

He saw it through the peephole when she turned and vanished deeper down the hall. He stayed that way, looking, waiting for any sign of naked feet.

Then he smiled and a laugh escaped him, a hearty bellowing laugh that sounded like a replication of Judy Kamp holding court.

Still chuckling, he turned and sat with his back to the door. Looking down the length of his rooms, he saw his great bed illuminated by the hanging holiday lights.

Did I scream? When I woke up?

He tried to remember. It mattered to him. Because if he hadn't, what had Mrs. Doris heard?

"Goblin history," Kamp said. "It got to us both."

But while this felt good to say, Kamp couldn't be sure it was true.

Kamp got to his feet quickly.

What exactly did she hear?

He was starting to sweat now. Imagining the screams of the Original 60 on the very land on which his rooms were built.

Goblin.

You're a true Gobliner. Truer than any other. Most of us are passing through, but Goblin has gotten into your bones.

Mrs. Doris had said that. And what exactly did she mean?

An alarm went off in his room. He gasped and stumbled back against the door, his hand to his chest.

He barreled down the hall to his bed.

The clock read three forty-five A.M.

Had he set it for that? He couldn't remember. But if he hadn't, who did?

"Mrs. Doris?" he asked.

The thought chilled him. His landlady, like she was in his dream, carrying the folded rungs of flesh, changing his alarms, erasing his tapes, adding corners and small doors to his rooms.

"Stop it," he said. "She would never."

But if not her, then who?

To Blackwater, he'd told Mrs. Doris over wine, *Goblin wasn't a place anybody should settle. The land was sacred and the rain suggested great spiritual power. This land wasn't for dwelling, Mrs. Doris. It was for . . .*

"Spirits."

Kamp looked to the kitchen. He surveyed his rooms.

Was something in there with him . . . right now?

He felt the first tingling rise of panic.

If something was there, if something had reset his alarms, now was the time it would show itself. He was as sure of this as he was the spelling of George Carroll's name. He could feel the air pressure in his rooms change, making space for another, something squeezing itself into Kamp's domain. Something with a need to show itself.

"I'm not ready!" he screamed. Then he clamped a hand over his mouth. The last thing he wanted was Mrs. Doris coming over again.

He was stuck that way, like a Sherman topiary of himself. Standing there like Eula the gorilla at the Goblin Zoo. But Eula was strong. And he felt helpless.

He thought of his heart. That unreliable muscle no bigger

than his fist, pulsing uncertainly, ultimately a false support. Oh heart! Tell me . . . can you withstand it? The day the ghost shows itself . . . how will you fare?

He stepped to the television and rewound the tape. Saw himself on all fours by the front door. Saw himself in bed.

Saw himself scream, too.

You sonofabitch.

He pumped his fist in victory and allowed himself another legitimate smile. And yet, relieved as he was, he understood that a smile born of relief was very different from one forged in joy.

But he *had* screamed. And Mrs. Doris had invited him over tonight because, as she said, a woman knows. Especially a woman who lives next door and hears everything through the thin apartment walls. Mrs. Doris had been a friend tonight. She gave him company, she gave him wine. She gave him a chance to talk at length about subjects he adored.

Goblin. History. The strength of Blackwater and the cruel cunning of George Carroll and Wes Farraline.

"There was no native chief in the hall," he said, rewinding the tape farther yet. "It's just . . . in your bones tonight."

He saw himself leaving then returning to his rooms, then leaving, then pacing, waking, sleeping, waking, sleeping.

He pressed PAUSE when he saw himself setting the alarms before going to bed. He froze the frame as his hand lifted from the alarm clock in question.

The numbers read 3:45 A.M.

He'd set it after all.

Kamp sighed.

Then he got up from the monitor, stepped over the drywall rubble, and fell flat, exhausted upon his bed.

9

But he did not sleep. Instead he reveled, for as long as it would last, in the cool rainy waves of amelioration, having made it so deep into the night, without dying, without giving up, without being scared to death.

10

For the first time in many days, Kamp felt like a grown man capable of telling children, *There's no such thing as ghosts.* DON'T YOU WORRY ABOUT WHAT'S UNDER THE OL' BED! DADDY'S HERE!

Trust Daddy.

Another alarm went off.

Kamp, lost in his new mood, simply rolled on his side, pulled the sheet, flashed the bulb, looked under his bed, turned the alarm off, and settled again on his back. Hardly any more effort than turning the air conditioner on or off.

His gaze drifted. From the small monitor hooked up to the video mixing board, to a small pile of clothes on the floor in the closet with no doors. Up to the ceiling and up and down the walls. He looked over to his nightstand. Four identical alarms bought at the Transistor Planet downtown. Kamp peered over his bed. On the stand's shelf stood the state championship debate trophy: a golden woman holding an old-timey microphone. Kamp coached Goblin High to the school's one and only state championship. Had his photo taken for *The Green Goblin.*

His own history had never been as fascinating to him as the

city he loved, the city that had *gotten into his bones,* but tonight it sparked, tonight it made a simple flame.

He'd gone from shelving books at the library to teaching high school history in what now felt like a matter of minutes. Then he'd quit. For no real reason he could point to. The kids loved him. He was making a difference, one he could see, and yet . . . quit. Just like he had the courthouse, the medical examiner, the library, the chamber of commerce. Mister Municipality. He'd even worked a stint at Carroll Hospital. He'd run into his former boss there, Principal Donner. Donner, with a Velcro cuff around his arm, asked Kamp if he'd like to return to Goblin High. Teach history. Coach the debate team again. He told Donner he'd think about it.

But you didn't, Kamp thought. *You didn't think about it at all.*

He got up out of bed and went to the window. The rain was positively forbidding.

He put his hand to the glass. Part of him wished it would open. He'd put his head outside and let the amorphous Goblin landmark drench him to his soul.

Or maybe he'd jump, and make it so nothing could ever scare him again.

Kamp remembered something his sister, Carol, had told him. She was getting ready for a night out when she saw her ghost. She'd closed her eyes and opened them to find a man sitting next to her before her vanity doing the same thing. Putting his own face on. She'd screamed and leapt from the seat. But when she looked to the bench again, he was gone. She told Kamp she was positive the experience actually happened because she and the man made *eye contact.*

It wasn't a peripheral encounter, she'd said. *We . . . connected.*

From that day forward Kamp couldn't walk past Carol's room

without thinking he'd see a man sitting at her vanity, applying eye shadow. This gave him nightmares and he'd wake Judy up. Judy always answered him that what Carol saw was her own reflection.

What do you expect from someone who throws up at the sight of a spider, Walter?

Mom had a way of calming him down that he hadn't found a replacement for yet.

Everyone in Kamp's immediate family had seen a ghost. Even his practical father had a story of his own. He said that, before Judy and he were married, he came home to his apartment and, stepping toward the television, saw a figure leap out from behind it, arms up, warning him of something. Judy told Walter that this story was bogus.

Your father drank more in those days.

But what about Judy herself? Kamp overheard her on the phone with a friend, her big hand cupped over the receiver, relaying how she woke up to the sound of shuffling under her bed. She looked over the edge of the mattress and saw a pair of sneakers slip underneath. She heard children giggling. That's what she said. She said that of course she assumed it was the kids, Walter himself, but when she rolled off the bed there was nothing but lint beneath.

Kamp stepped away from the window. He sat at the kitchen table and absently fingered a piece of charcoal he'd worked to a small chunk, making measurements on the walls, where to place the spotlights, where to chop down the walls.

Then he started drawing lines on his face. War paint. Thick black lines that began near the bridge of his nose and curved up and over his round cheeks. While doing so, he eyed a pineapple on the kitchen counter.

The head of it looked like feathers. Enough like them. In fact, the longer he stared at the pineapple, the more that whole fruit looked like Blackwater himself. A native who knew this land was bad news long before the pale shades found out for themselves.

"We didn't believe you," Kamp said, putting the finishing touches on his war paint. Protection, perhaps, against a ghost. "And most of us still don't believe you now. But I do."

Then he got up and, as the same admonishing rain that Blackwater himself must've faced without a roof, as he lay dying in the West Fields, pounded against the secure windows of Kamp's rooms, Kamp cut the top of the pineapple off and placed it gently upon his reddish-brown mop of hair.

"This land is for nobody," he said, facing the length of his rooms, looking through the haze of holiday lights to his transparent bed. "This land is . . ."

But he didn't want to say the word. Not even dressed as he was, prepared to face the entity that was coming to steal something from him.

He didn't want to say *haunted*.

Then, crying out like Blackwater might have, he threw the knife he'd used to chop the pineapple across his rooms, saw it land short of his bedroom and slide smoothly under his bed.

11

Carol's phone rang seven times before she answered. Carol, whose name, being so close to George and Hardy Carroll's own, delivered a young Walter Kamp a ceaseless and bitter envy.

"What is it?" she cried. "Is someone hurt?"

"Carol, it's Walter. No one's hurt."

"Walter? What's going on?"

"How did you handle it, Carol?"

He sat on the couch, the pineapple top balancing on his head.

"Handle what, Walter?"

"How did you handle it when you saw your ghost?"

"What ghost?"

Kamp nervously played with the phone cord.

"You know. The man. Sitting next to you. The vanity. That whole thing."

"What time is it?" He could hear her shuffling on the other end. "Are you fucking kidding me, Walter?"

"I need your help, Carol. Tell me how you handled it. How were you able to sleep in your room that night? Tell me. Why aren't you afraid of being scared to death?"

"Is this about Mom, Walter?"

"What? No."

"Then what the fuck? Did you see a ghost tonight?"

His heart thundered. Sounded like the footsteps of an angry tribe.

"Carol, don't *say* that! Please, just tell me how you did it. You went straight to sleep that night!"

"I never saw a ghost, Walter." An alarm went off in his bedroom. A bead of sweat ran down his cheek. "I was probably trying to scare you. That's what big sisters do."

"That's impossible," he said, trying to remain calm. "And look, I need your help on this."

"I've never seen a ghost, Walter. Trust me. I'm sure I'd remember it if I had. You're reading too much history again. Goblin has . . . gotten into your bones, man."

Another alarm went off.

"What did you say?"

"What the fuck is all that noise? Walter, call me tomorrow, huh?"

Kamp looked back toward his bed. The alarms sounded like a tribe shrieking, coming for the pale shades who didn't believe in ghosts, weren't wise enough to sense them.

"Carol," he said, trembling now, "I need to know the secret here. I need to know how you handled it. I—"

"I was *trying to scare you, Walter! That's what big sisters do!*"

"But that's crazy. You all saw ghosts."

"All who? Mom? Dad? David? Nobody saw any ghosts, Walter. We tell stories. Like every other normal human being. Are you okay?"

A third alarm started.

Walter stared at his bed. Had he set three so close together?

He lifted off the couch a bit, leaned forward. *Was* that something under the bed?

"Walter?"

Yes. There was. There absolutely was something under his bed. Something that shouldn't be there.

"Walter?"

He hung the phone up.

He stood up. The alarms played together, out of tune, loud.

NEEP-NEEP-NEEP!

He heard footsteps in the hall. He started for his bed.

He thought of Son of Blackwater. Thought of how angry he must've been when he pulled that contract out of his satchel and saw the white man's name was no longer there.

He leapt onto the transparent mattress. On his knees. He grabbed the line-switch.

"This land is no place for human beings!" he cried, fortifying himself for what he would see beneath his bed. "This land is . . ."

He flipped the switch, flooding the bed with light.

He pulled the blanket aside.

"Ah!" he cried.

He put the blanket back.

Turned the light off.

There was something. *Something.*

"I'm not only protecting my tribe," he howled, "I'm protecting you, Pale Shades, from the same nefarious spirits!"

Again, he flipped the switch and pulled the blanket aside.

Then he did it again.

And again.

And beneath him, through his Plexiglas bed, Kamp saw a face looking back.

He covered his bed, turned off the light. Then removed the blanket and turned the light back on.

Again.

Again.

Yes, a face, looking up at him.

Did it look like . . . *Mom?*

Oh my God.

FLASH!

It's got the same face as Mom . . .

(pull it aside, put it back, pull it aside, put it back)

FLASH!

"Waaaaaaaaaalter?"

A voice . . . behind him.

"Mom!" Walter cried, turning the light on and off, on and off.

But it wasn't Mom. No. Couldn't be. Because Mom never wore war paint. Mom never looked like a native chief dying out in the West Fields, nobody there to nurse him.

FLASH!

He sat up. His back erect. Still, on his knees, pulling the blanket aside, putting it back.

"Mom, it's not you! It's . . . it's . . ."

He was breathing too hard now, the veins coming to the surface in his forehead, the atonal cries of the alarms and that great Goblin rain thundering about him.

And his name, too. His name called out by a voice as old as Goblin.

"Waaaaaaalter?"

"IT'S BLACKWATER!" Kamp howled. "HIDING BENEATH MY BED!"

Kamp howled and the face of the chief howled back.

Then Kamp felt something tug below his throat. His eyes bulged.

He dropped the line-switch. He clutched his chest.

"Oh God! It's happening. I'm dying. I'm scared to death!"

He stumbled forward on the bed, still gripping the blanket.

I saw it, he thought—relieved, it seemed. *I saw it . . .*

He fell forward and rolled off the bed, pulling the blanket with him. His body shook his rooms as it fell to the wood floor.

The alarms rattled on the dresser. The television monitor shook.

And was it so bad? he asked himself. *Being scared to death?*

"Waaaaaaaaaalter?"

Whatever it was still beckoned him, calling his name in an old, historical voice.

He rolled onto his back. He started to drift.

Mom, he thought. *I can't wait to see you!*

The last thing he thought of before he died was the story of the girl who was found in the North Woods. The one with her chest exploded.

She saw a ghost, he thought. *She ran into a ghost big enough to scare us all.*

Goblin. And the word, the name of his city, still shone.

The last thing he *saw* was that debate team trophy reflected in the knife beneath his bed. The knife he didn't remember throwing there.

His grip on that blanket loosened.

The alarms sounded like the Goblin Police, driving by fast, chasing someone down on Lily.

And his name still came, called from somewhere deep inside the North Woods, the one corner of Goblin even Walter Kamp couldn't remove.

"Waaaaaalter?"

"Waaaaaaaalter?"

"Waaaaaaaaaaaalter?"

HAPPY BIRTHDAY, HUNTER!

1

YOU ARE INVITED TO
THE 60TH BIRTHDAY BASH OF
GOBLIN'S MOST DECORATED HUNTER:

Neal Nash

(Believe it!)

COME TO

6 Marbles Lane, Rolling Hills

ANYTIME AFTER

9PM

AND THROW YOUR CAR KEYS IN THE

Barracuda Tank

BECAUSE YOU AIN'T DRIVING HOME FROM THIS ONE.
(Bunk beds available in the lodge: Sleep with a stranger?)

EXPECT FIERCE ENTERTAINMENT, LIVE MUSIC,
ALL-YOU-CAN-EAT MEAT

DO NOT RSVP

IF YOU CAN'T ATTEND, YOU AIN'T WANTED

—Barbara and Neal Nash

2

To enter the Nash compound one took a chain of uneven dirt roads through the deep woods cloaking the beautiful northeastern residential section of Goblin called Rolling Hills. After so many unannounced twists and turns, incalculable shapes seen in the shadows, and myriad concerns with having somehow passed the address, great golden pillars peeked out from above the pines, declaring X marks the spot indeed. The gatekeeper, a robust and flaky-haired man named Duggan, sat in a luxurious oak stall with a golden flat roof, a gun at his hip, and a list of the names that had been okayed by Barbara Nash herself. A gorgeous cluster of evergreens reflected off the glass window he pulled aside to greet those who pulled up. The night of Neal's sixtieth birthday party, a woman sat in the booth with him; a stunning, half-clothed blonde with a rainbow party hat upon her head, a glass of amber liquid in her hand, and what appeared to be an indefatigable smile upon her lips.

Duggan's hair was uncharacteristically unkempt; even the top button of his shirt was undone. Some guests knew Neal and Barbara well enough to know that they'd ordered poor Duggan to dress the part. The part of *fun*. And how Duggan played along; he informed each new arrival he had a message from the house, then, as husbands and wives waited with clear curiosity in their eyes, he pulled a foghorn from beneath the window and blasted it in the face of the guests.

"No bullshit tonight," Duggan said, and it was clear to those that knew him that these words were rehearsed. "And, um . . . leave the, um . . . sucky stuff behind."

The blonde then asked how many people were in the car while

stumbling out of the booth. She handed each guest a bag of confetti and instructed them all to dump it over their heads.

Nobody refused.

Roger Fletcher, one of Neal Nash's oldest hunting buddies and one of the first arrivals for the big bash, laughed most of the confetti from his face and said to his fellow passengers, "Neal is trying to set records tonight."

After Duggan flipped a switch, the white gates drew apart, and the visitors drove up the short and winding drive to Neal and Barbara's astonishing home. On the way in, Marie Fletcher, wife to Roger, mother to none, remarked how wonderful the craftsmanship of the white geese of the gates was.

"I hate to say it, love," Roger said, smiling so big his eyes disappeared. "But those were once alive. Only now . . . dead. And painted."

And the other guests smiled with him.

Neal Nash was, as the invitation for his party proudly boasted, the most celebrated big-game hunter in the history of Goblin.

"Look," Andrew Belle said, pointing through the glass of the backseat window, confetti on the tip of his finger, "that's a hell of a team of Shermans."

Between the front gates and the Nash compound, set squarely on the front lawn, stood the second tallest pair of Sherman topiaries in all of Goblin. At thirteen feet and three inches, the pristine renderings of Barbara and Neal looked something like a president and his First Lady.

But the rain ruined the perfect view. Even the four people in Roger Fletcher's car, native Gobliners all, had to acknowledge its severity.

"Like the sea is somehow above us," Harper Belle said. "And leaking."

With the assistance of a man in a white slicker, Roger parked his BMW beside a dented Ford truck. The Nashes hadn't invited only the city's finest; as the Fletchers and Belles knew, this wasn't the sort of night for fellow magnates to sip brandy and exchange political concerns. Neal Nash was attempting to throw the biggest, most varied, most all-inclusive party Goblin had ever seen. It was as if he was hoping to add a bust of the party itself to his hangar of severed beast heads beyond the house.

The mail carrier of Rolling Hills had received the same invitation as the biggest investors in Nash & Crawford, Inc. The beat-up Cavalier belonging to Barbara's favorite waitress, Jenny Sparks, was parked beside Senator John Garret's Mercedes. The VW Bus belonging to Hank Houghton blocked the view of the marble fountain, now overflowing, in the yard.

By the time Roger parked, the Nash compound was most certainly already alive. Guests honked clown horns made to look like guns, pointing them at one another, *beep beep,* as the rain pounded the manicured green grass. Multicolored lanterns fashioned to look like Colonel Wes Farraline's distended face floated between the cars, carried by guests already two, three drinks deep into the night. Some wore headlamps. Some wore masks. The top of a hot-air balloon showed just beyond the home's east wing, and the brave wildlife, deer and rabbits, watched from the evergreens bordering the lawns.

Roger parked no more than a hundred feet from the toes of the great Sherman topiary of Neal himself.

It was nine oh nine P.M.

"This is how most parties look when they *end,*" Harper Belle said.

Welcome to wasteland, Roger thought. He wondered how many blond women were roaming the compound, women something like the one back in the booth with Duggan.

Then he grabbed hold of the umbrella for his wife, exited the car, and entered another man's dream.

3

For those who arrived first, it quickly became hard to say exactly when the party began. Some people had come by early in the afternoon to set up the stages, the speakers, the surprise. Around then, Barbara began overseeing the thirteen cooks who would ready the Festival of Meats. The smokers and bi-level grills were protected from the Goblin sky by large white tents erected beside the Nash's swimming pool. Carcasses hung from racks like the sort bellboys used to cart the Nashes' luggage in and out of hotels, and Paul Romeo, Goblin's best-known butcher, sliced and shaved.

The meats were as varied as the guests. A game ballet.

Suspended from the upper supports of the tents, as if suspended in flight, were the ducks, pheasants, quail, geese, grouse, partridge, and swans. The walls of each tent were made of caribou, elk, moose, antelope, boar, and bear. Tabletops of gator, mountain goat, jackrabbit, and hare created aisles for Barbara and the cooks to walk about and check the status of their dishes.

Barbara breathed in the cumulative scent of so much dead. She smiled, because she understood better than most the preparation that had gone into bringing the Festival of Meats to the party.

"Thinner," she said, pointing to where a cook had half sliced through a reindeer's flank.

She looked out from under the tent to the house, where she knew her husband was sitting cross-legged before a mirror, readying himself for the night.

She smiled. Whereas some men would be frightened of the aging, the number sixty meant a great deal to Neal. Goblin's Original 60 settlers came to mind (and oh, what Neal would give for even a phalange of one of them), but there was more significance than that.

"Every year he lives," she said to nobody but herself, "is another year in which he triumphed."

As if being a renowned hunter, he had managed, thus far, to elude the greatest hunter of all: Death.

"Mrs. Nash!"

She turned to see a cook holding a skinned rabbit by its ears.

"Stew," she said. And again she thought of the preparations her husband had made, the work he had done for this day.

A week prior, Neal had rounded up his inner circle, his oldest and wisest hunting buddies, and proposed they hunt the meat for the party themselves. Roger Fletcher was there. Harvey Buttonbuck and Saul Stein, too.

"How the hell are we going to pull that off?" Harvey had asked. Practicality was his way.

But Barbara knew Neal better than that. And his response was no surprise.

"The animals are already on their way," he said. "And they'll be running free on the estate when they get here."

Caged. Gated. And yet . . . a hunt.

Barbara watched as Neal handed out leather jackets to the fifteen hunters he'd invited.

"Notice the patches," he told them.

0-60 was stitched into the right shoulder of each. Some, like Saul, thought it referenced the speed at which Neal moved, zero to sixty every day of his sixty years. But most of the others knew what it stood for.

The hunt was simple. The game had nowhere to go. And despite the favorable odds, the men experienced a thrill they'd never known while hunting before. The immediacy of multiple kills. One after another. Rapidly. Repeatedly.

Relief.

All but Neal himself, who participated mightily at the onset but lost interest early on, as he paused to study a particularly twisted tree in his yard. One that resembled the impenetrable trunks of the North Woods.

He thought of the Great Owls. And once he started thinking about them, he couldn't bring himself to stop.

Endangered or not, protection be damned, Neal Nash would give anything to have one of Goblin's sacred untouchable beasts in his hangar for show.

Nobody had ever hunted a Great Owl. Nobody had ever had the nerve. If the North Woods legend of the witch didn't stop you, the Goblin Police most certainly would.

And yet, staring up at the winding branches, the uneven trunk that looked something like a question mark erupting from the grass, Neal imagined the beast, just one, under glass, here at home.

Even then, seven days before his sixtieth birthday party, as Barbara noted who was coming and the staff prepared the many feasts; as Harvey murdered movement and Saul shot snakes; as the voices of his inner circle rose to the Goblin sky in joyful unison, exclaiming the hysteria of the hunt; Neal thought of the one animal he was not allowed to have.

4

At ten seventeen P.M., the party well under way, a stoned man turned to a drunk woman and asked, "Does Nash turn sixty *today*? Or does he turn sixty tomorrow?"

The woman, leaning against the hall wall for support, squinting to see the man through the color wheel of lights, shouted over the music. "The party's tonight! We're at the party *right now.*"

"Yes but . . . does he turn sixty before or *after* midnight strikes?"

Then the woman laughed and accidentally knocked her nose on the wall.

Outside, nobody cared that it was raining. It was as if the Nashes had arranged that, too. Gobliners all, even a heavy rain was hardly something to run from. And the more the guests drank and smoked, the more pills they swallowed, the more righteous this particularly brutal rainfall became.

"A coronation," someone called before pointing their gun-horn at their own head and honking.

"The sky is partying, too," said another.

But there were some who worried.

"It's too much," one man said.

"Too debauched," said another.

"The sky knows," said a few more.

And these voices were lost in the throng of celebration. Bankers talked to busboys. Executives sang songs with cabdrivers. People dressed in owl costumes honked gun-horns for hoots. Lines of people talked at the meat tents. Guests played games and shot arrows at bundles of hay. People were encouraged to toss their plates and glasses against an enormous wood board situated above a trench. Men and women, men and men, women and women stole away into the evergreens to do what was done in the shadows. Danceable, rhythmic, drug-friendly music erupted from the stage, where Goblin's own Eulas played. The music sailed through the trees and traveled the course of the grounds, entering every open window of the house.

The house was even livelier.

One man found the line for the bathrooms too long and looked for a sink instead. Stumbling already, passing a hundred somewhat recognizable faces on the way, he found himself standing at the doors of the master bedroom, the very place where Neal and Barbara Nash's skunk-furred comforter enveloped their enormous bed. Taped to the door, a sign read:

NO FUCKING IN HERE!

And the man pissed where he stood.

5

By eleven P.M. no one had actually seen Neal anywhere at the party.

Soon rumors spread.

Neal Nash was dead. He'd died the day before his party and Barbara decided he wouldn't have wanted it called off.

This was now his funeral, not his birthday.

Some even said he requested his body be tied to a tree where every mourner could take a shot with a .22 until there was nothing left but pieces for the dogs to dine on.

A new kind of party, a dark trip, a wild meat-fest, a drunk and dangerous party thrown for the birth of a dead man!

The idea was too good. People almost wanted it to be true.

And the celebrating swelled.

People swam with live bass in the pool. Others took showers indoors still wearing their suits and dresses. People passed out and got back up.

There was a sizable dent in the fort of food the thirteen cooks presided over. There was a dip in the ocean of booze.

And there was so much rain that, after a while, it felt like there was none.

Neal appeared thirty minutes before midnight. On the shoulders of fifteen men wearing leather jackets with 0-60 patches sewn into their right shoulders.

"Make way!" they laughed. "Make way for the most decorated hunter in the history of Goblin!"

Neal was hooting like an owl when they tossed him into the pool.

6

Guests gathered by the pool and were led in song by a man whose eyes were half closed and who teetered on the edge of the water like a child about to fall down.

"*Happy birthday to you!*"

Those who were indoors followed the singing outside. Barbara slid into the water beside her husband.

"*Happy birthday to you!*"

Neal looked like he stood between two pools: the one that went up to his waist and the one that fell upon him from the sky.

That great Goblin rain.

"*Happy birthday dear Huuuuuuunter . . .*"

Hunter.

Neal's nickname. For being the best. The best hunter. A big-game hunter. A *trophy* hunter.

"*Happy birthday to you!*"

The guests erupted into cheers, and the sound of smashed glasses crashed through the falling rain.

Neal bowed.

Guns were shot into the sky. Half-naked, half-painted jockeys rode horses around the house. People threw food. Arrows were sent into the sky.

As Neal got out of the pool, helping Barbara out by the hand, a pickup truck pulled up onto the lawn. The bed was loaded with boxes: presents wrapped in every color. A blue tent protected them from the sky. Neal stepped up onto the opened truck-bed door and waved his hands for silence.

"This is fucking great," he said. "Where did we learn to have so much fun? Who taught us how to have so much goddamn *fun*?" More cheers. More laughter. "Tonight I'm sixty years old and thanks to you people I feel . . . *eighty*!"

"Where's Crawford?" someone yelled.

"Crawdaddy?" Neal answered, his face a half scowl. "Crawdaddy couldn't make it. Hell, someone has to work tonight, yeah?"

Laughter. Cheers. False boos for Dean Crawford.

Dean Crawford was the other half of Nash & Crawford, Inc. Neal knew exactly where his partner was. Waiting at his own home in Rolling Hills; waiting for the delivery of a crate.

"And where's Mayor Blackwater?" someone else said.

Neal chuckled. "Everyone Gobliner is welcome to break some laws in the Nash household, all except those who make them."

Laughter. Riotous. Applause that became a word:

"Caaaaaaake!"

Saul Stein led Neal through the guests, then the back deck's glass doors and into the house. Neal's shoes sloshed on the brown carpet as he walked through rows of people more drunk than himself. He believed he was happy.

Seated at the head of his oak dining room table, Saul told him to sit tight, then vanished into a wall of guests. The tablecloth had embroideries of deer and fox humping in various positions. The walls were lined with antlers, and in this room stood a zebra so well preserved it looked like it might be a guest.

It was cake time.

Everyone that could fit packed into the room. Some watched from the yard through the windows and many lay down on the grass, too drunk to stand up. Neal grabbed a fork and knife and pounded both on the table like an impatient child.

"Where's my cake, Mommy?" he yelled.

Honk! Honk! Gun-horns blared as Barbara entered, pushing a great steel cart before her.

Sixty candles, bright as police lights.

"Barbara!" Neal exclaimed, eyeing the cart she rolled.

It was a meat cake. A cake of meat. At one hundred and ten pounds, it weighed more than some of the guests.

It took two men to lift it onto the table.

"All right, friends," Barbara called sweetly. "You all know how it goes."

"Happy birthday to you!"

The song again. A birthday so big they had to sing it twice.

Neal looked at the hot dogs used as candleholders.

"Happy birthday to you!"

Slabs of venison and moose were packed so tight, blood oozed out the sides, staining the tablecloth beneath.

"Happy biiiirthday . . ."

Ground beef, duck, and goose made up the middle. So fresh it looked like a wound.

". . . dear Huuuunter . . ."

Bacon fat decorated the top like frosting. Neal recognized quail, woodcock, dove, squirrel. Chunks of pork were set at the corners; the decorative details that any baker would've employed.

Small bones were arranged to read:

HAPPY BIRTHDAY, HUNTER!

"Happy birthday to you!"

Tears rose in Neal's eyes.

"Blow out the candles!" someone yelled.

Sixty candles for sixty bludgeoned settlers, for sixty years alive.

Neal sucked in a deep breath of air and closed his eyes and thought:

I want an owl.

And the Gobliner's guilt following this wish rose and for one second Neal believed he had done something horrible already.

He blew out the candles.

The famed butcher bent in to cut the cake but Neal comically elbowed him out of the way and grabbed hold of the knives.

People cheered as he cut himself a wedge of bacon, duck, and cow tongue then rammed it into his mouth.

I want an owl, he thought again. This time with no guilt.

Somebody asked him, "What did you wish for, Neal?"

But Neal only waved a hand, waving the question away.

And thoughts of an empty space in his hangar rose like birthday balloons in his mind.

7

"I'm not going to make you all watch me open that mountain of presents," Neal told the room. "But I'm gonna make you watch me open *one*."

Barbara smiled and handed him her gift.

"Happy birthday, dear," she said. Then she kissed his cheek. Neal pulled her close with his arm around her waist.

It was a small thin present wrapped in gold paper. Neal opened it gently.

"Trachtenbroit," he said.

He held a Goblin city postcard with a photo of Jonathan Trachtenbroit. It cost Barbara $1.19. Green letters read:

GREETINGS FROM GOBLIN!
FIND YOUR TARGET HERE!

"Where'd you get it?" Neal asked.

"You know very well where I got it," she smiled. "The same place you get your crappy energy sodas."

The guests laughed.

Neal looked into the face of the man who had discovered Goblin's Great Owls so long ago.

"I know how much you love him," Barbara said. But they both knew this was an understatement; Neal Nash collected everything Trachtenbroit-related that he could. Letters to colleagues. Notes for assistants. Journals he'd kept while studying his prized birds. Photos. Paintings. Drawings in dirt. From the rarest item (Neal believed he owned the very wire that was used to strangle Trachtenbroit on Freedom Hill) to the most common (a keychain in the Scottish hunter's likeness). Neal knew better than anybody that Trachtenbroit was the actual hunter's watermark. The best. The best hunter Goblin had ever called son.

And every time Neal referred to himself as such, Trachtenbroit's visage hovered in his mind like a ghost.

Tsk, tsk, he seemed to say. *For I found the Great Owl.*

Neal could never rid himself of the possessive in hunting. He wanted to have and to own. To stuff and to show. But Jonathan Trachtenbroit bred and fed and then freed. For Gobliners, this made Trachtenbroit an easy guy to root for.

The hunter with feeling.

The exact hunter.

The gentleman hunter, to all.

Not even Goblin historians could be sure when the Scotsman first came to the city, though it was known he met George Carroll on the latter's way out. He kept to himself, a strange and solitary stranger, always dressed in a red velvet jacket, who quietly studied cats and rabbits, dogs and squirrels. What *was* known was that, after six months of studying the animals who called Goblin home, he stood before the blocked entrance to the fabled and feared North Woods. A sign blocking the entrance read:

A DANGEROUS WOOD

He wondered what might thrive in there.

Back in town proper he quietly, selectively asked about the "dangerous wood" and could anybody tell him any more? But nobody could satisfy his hunter's curiosity because no one had ever been inside.

It was illegal, they said.

But why?

He was told the legend of a witch who inhabited those woods. A witch who could enlarge your heart with a story, a whisper, until it exploded inside your chest. He was told of Chief Blackwater's madness and how it was forged among those twisted trees.

But Trachtenbroit was a scientist first. And though he enjoyed stories of this nature, he wasn't going to let them stop him from exploring. He asked whom he might speak with about breaking the rule of entering. He was directed to George Carroll. By then Carroll was eighty-something years old and when the fresh-faced Trachtenbroit introduced himself, Carroll laughed.

"I know why you're here," he said.

"Why?"

"You're the man obsessed with the animals."

"Yes."

"And you wonder what's living, what's breeding, what's dying in the North Woods."

"Yes."

"And you want to ask me if you may break Goblin law and enter."

"Yes."

"I daresay," Carroll famously told the young hunter, "dying is up to you."

Carroll knew firsthand how easy it was to get lost in those woods. There was no logic in there. No pattern to follow, no code to crack. In the North Woods, you might be walking what felt like level ground before you started panting and discovered you were walking uphill. Things were *different* in there . . . laws of nature weren't followed. No maps existed because no one was allowed inside.

"Can you tell me," Trachtenbroit asked, relieved by Carroll's permission, "how best I can go about not getting lost?"

Then Trachtenbroit removed his velvet jacket and listened to eighty-something-year-old Carroll explain the rope system they'd used so long ago, when they'd staged a phony evacuation to fool Son of Blackwater and more.

The tales of the witch and exploding hearts meant little to the Scotsman, but he felt a burning in his chest all the same.

It's what he called *target*.

Purpose, direction, intent.

Target.

A word Neal Nash would think of every time he took aim with a gun, every time he added false bricks to the base that supported his title of the best hunter in the history of Goblin.

Even on his birthday.

8

"Let's blow some shit up!"

Nash was in a groove. The whole place was. There was constant chatter, constant coming and going. Mob motion. Like the house and grounds (the stables and the hangar included) were a living thing trying to *lift off* from the grass to head sailing to where the rain originated. Nash was a key part of this. But his motivations were varied. The owls lurked, perched upon the gnarled branches of his deepest desires, their shadows cast upon the party. And as he stumbled through the crowd, he looked different to some guests, some who knew him, and those who knew the look of a predator with a sudden thirst for a particular prey. He tried to blend in. He entered and exited conversations, often gripping random unfinished drinks and tossing their remains down his throat.

And yet he couldn't blend in. And he couldn't get drunk, either. Not the way the star of the party ought to.

After making a full round of the house, with a drink in each hand, Neal slumped between two women on the couch in his office, breaking their conversation in two.

"Get out," he said.

The women laughed. Neal Nash didn't demand people leave, he demanded they come.

"*Get out,*" he repeated, an echo like a hoot, and the women, flustered, removed themselves from his office.

"*Get out!*" he shouted, long after they had gone.

Then he sat behind his desk and opened the top drawer. There he eyed a book he'd had for the better part of forty-five years, picked up for a penny when he was but fifteen.

Get to Know Jonathan Trachtenbroit

More of a pamphlet than a book, with only so many pages and pictures.

But Neal could think of nothing else. So as the people celebrated in his honor outside, Neal flipped through the pages, hardly reading the words at all, gazing dumbly at the pictures, and staring extra long (and longingly) at the midnight-black birds drawn by artists who could only estimate, as Trachtenbroit had destroyed all evidence of what his prized find looked like days before he died.

"He didn't find them here," Neal said aloud to nobody. Then he shook his head because it was incredible to him that something so integral to Goblin could have been imported. "He *brought* them."

9

Neal Nash wasn't an Anglophile but those British sure could hunt.

Trachtenbroit, after spending a week inside the North Woods, did not go insane. Nor did he see a witch or get lost. But he left Goblin for so long that when he returned, almost ten years later, he was nearly unrecognizable. No longer the ruddy-cheeked scientist of thirty, he rode into Goblin a driven (and informed) missionary. Those who had encountered him before knew him to be focused, but the focus one employs when determining *how* something will be done is very different from the focus one uses to do it.

Trachtenbroit discovered his Great Owls in the backyard of a colleague's home, at a party, when he'd stepped out for some fresh air. Walking through a lemon grove, wearing his signature red velvet jacket, the young scientist saw what looked like a black sweater left upon a tree branch. He went to take hold of it and was shocked when the top of the sweater rotated to reveal the two most remarkable eyes he'd ever seen. Ovals the size of cake plates, the eyes were entirely black save red irises that might have brought a groundskeeper to faint. It was an owl. An owl with feathers as black as an English coach and talons as long as certain snakes. Trachtenbroit was mesmerized.

"You," he said, "you."

Over and over again. *You.*

Then, with an excitement that was entirely unknown to him, he made to rush back to his colleague's home. Then he stopped.

Something self-preserving took over.

Something he recognized, even then, as greed.

This is my discovery, he thought. *Mine.*

Years later, Trachtenbroit would come to believe the owl knew it was one of only four in existence and that Trachtenbroit was delivered to save them. *That,* he reasoned, was why the owl had showed itself to him and not to his friend who had traversed the same lemon grove so often.

Trachtenbroit did return to the party that day and casually asked his friend about the local wildlife. But he took great care not to mention the owl. His friend replied that his property housed "the ordinary Scottish thing" with "nothing unique to report" and since Trachtenbroit detected no hint of insincerity, he believed he, himself, was the only man yet to see one.

Later, Trachtenbroit slipped outside and approached the owl once more.

"I will return," he told the bird. "And if you wait for me, I will find you a home more deserving of you than this paltry place of lemons."

Trachtenbroit searched long in Scotland, then England soon after. But it wasn't until overhearing two Irishmen discussing America that he decided to set his sights overseas.

America the less populated. America the unknown.

He'd maintained constant contact with his colleague who lived by the lemon grove, sending letters that asked about "any new discoveries" and "any big news." The lack of any thrilling response told the Scotsman all he needed to know. And yet anxiety came after all, as the colleague sent word that he would be moving soon, and would Jonathan like to see where to?

That very day, on a walk intended to calm him, in which he'd hoped to find some internal answers, Jonathan Trachtenbroit discovered the North Woods and the admonishing wooden sign that thrilled him.

The legends made it only better. Gobliners, it turned out, avoided the one place he was looking to store a secret.

After finding what he was undoubtedly looking for, Trachtenbroit returned to Scotland and set out to befriend the new inhabitant of his colleague's old house. By any means, he had to have access to that lemon grove. When he discovered that the new tenant was a former brigadier in the Scottish army, and that his tastes included beer, sport, women, and little else, Trachtenbroit understood he had nothing in common with the new tenant.

But he was determined to connect.

He came to call the man Red for his cropped, rose-red hair. And one evening he followed Red to his favorite pub. After eavesdropping booth-to-booth for four hours he surmised that approaching the former army man as a scientist would be useless.

The next morning Trachtenbroit hired a prostitute to act as his own sister. This part of the story always made Neal Nash smile. The lengths Trachtenbroit went to were the stuff of Goblin legend.

"For a few nights," Trachtenbroit said, in the darkness of the alley he met Lula in. "No physicality. Not for me."

He paid her with moneys he'd received from a science grant that assumed he was studying bees, and that night he brought her to the pub. Red sat hulking at the bar, swallowing whole beers and hollering obscenities at whoever stepped in view. As hoped for, he had his eye on Trachtenbroit's sister from the start. He asked the pair to join him at the bar, and the three drank until the pub closed for the night.

Trachtenbroit could *feel* the owl in his hands when the man, without reservation, turned to him and said, "What say you and your sister come back to my place and we continue the party, eh?"

The prostitute feigned excitement but Trachtenbroit felt it for real. They climbed into the scientist's black coach and rode out at last to the house whose lemon grove had consumed him for four long years. Once there, the prostitute wasted no time distracting Red with kisses and Trachtenbroit pretended to fall asleep drunk on the couch.

"Eh," Red said, eyeballing the scientist suspiciously as he was led down the dark hall to his bedroom. "He's not going to rob me now, is he?"

The prostitute giggled and tugged on Red's arm. "Rob you?" she said. "He couldn't rob himself, he's so sussed."

"Aye," Red said. "But if he *does* . . ."

The moment Trachtenbroit heard the bedroom door click shut, he got to his feet and carefully left through the front door. From his coach he grabbed a wire cage, then went back through the house, tiptoeing and holding his breath. At the back door he turned the knob and heard Red say something from down the hall.

Trachtenbroit set the cage on the ground and hurried onto

the couch, reaching a slumped, sleeping position just as the bedroom door opened.

"Eh?" Red said, peering through the dark room at the lump on his couch.

"Come back," the prostitute called. "He doesn't even know where he is."

"Eh . . ."

Trachtenbroit kept still as Red returned gruffly to his bedroom. Then he waited. And waited. And got up and went back to the back door overlooking the lemon grove at night.

Lifting the cage, he slipped outside.

The fog collected then split at the ankles of his boots as he traversed the small grove, having decided to start with the very tree in which he'd seen the magnificent bird. Once there, he thought he saw an article of clothing upon a low branch. But he knew better this time. And the bird that had flown for four years through his mind was perched exactly where he'd seen it last.

Its black eyes were difficult to discern in the darkness, but its red irises were unmistakable.

"Hello," Trachtenbroit said. "My dear, sweet friend."

The owl hooted.

"Oh," Trachtenbroit said, bringing a hand to his chest. He laughed. For such a magisterial creature, its voice was certainly crude. Its hoot sounded very much like a horn.

Trachtenbroit advanced, preparing himself to get the animal into the cage. But movement brought him to a stop. Something was rotating beside the black bird.

To Trachtenbroit's astonishment, he saw it was another owl. Then another. And another yet.

On his travels, searching for a place unlikely to be ruined by the human touch, the Scotsman had indeed considered the idea that there was more than one bird. But the way in which they

presented themselves, that night in the lemon grove, Trachtenbroit simply couldn't help but wonder if they felt a reciprocal kin-
ship with him.

Were there more?

He'd take a look.

But a loud sound from inside the house caused him to drop
the cage and hurry to the back door. There he saw no sign of Red.
He slipped back in and dove onto the couch as the bedroom door
clicked open once again.

"Eh . . ." Red grunted. He approached Trachtenbroit on the
couch and poked him with strong, fat fingers. "Drunk are ya?" he
said.

Trachtenbroit moaned.

"Sick, are ya?"

Trachtenbroit snored.

Then Red laughed.

"*Asleep,* you are!"

Then he kicked Trachtenbroit's slumped body and barreled
back down the hall to the hired sister.

Trachtenbroit leapt from the couch once more. His velvet
jacket was worse for the wear and his side smarted from the kick.

But there were four of the most beautiful birds he'd ever seen
outside, and he needed to get them into the coach.

And so deep fear consumed him when he arrived at the tree
and found it empty.

"Where are you?" he cried. His voice seemed to echo into the
fog, to reach every tree in the grove. "Come back!"

He made to step farther and felt something strong at the tips
of his boots. Looking down, he saw three of the enormous owls
huddled tightly inside the cage. The fourth perched upon it.

"You guys want to come with me," he said. He looked over his
shoulder to the house. The fog covered most of the back door. To

the owls he said, "If you are capable of knowing that I am here to assist you, what else might you be capable of?"

The fourth owl rose from the cage and settled upon Trachtenbroit's shoulder. The Scotsman had no way of knowing that the very posture he held, bird and velvet coat, would one day be cut into an enormous topiary statue, Wayne Sherman's second masterpiece, standing sentry at the gates of Goblin.

He lifted the cage and carried it back through the house and out to the coach. As he placed the birds inside he understood how close he was to delivering them to a sanctuary no man or woman would dare intrude upon.

A voice behind him rattled his repose.

"Are we leaving?" Lula stood half dressed in the dark.

"Yes."

Then he stepped aside and Lula saw the birds for the first time. "What are *those*?"

"Those," Trachtenbroit said, "are for the church. We call them . . . *living gargoyles.*"

"Well," she said, shaken but satisfied. "If I'd known I was being paid by the church tonight I might've been less discreet."

That night, alone in his lodgings, Trachtenbroit studied his owls for the first time. There he named them.

Neal Nash always envied this part of the story. The moment Trachtenbroit discovered how violent his precious creatures could be.

The Scotsman had been taking notes, observing them upon the piano, when all four leapt upon something in the corner of the room. Their beaks sounded like steak knives, clacking together, the swishing and swooshing of sharp steel. When the owls were finished they turned their big eyes back to him, and he could well see the small pile of fur and bones behind them.

"Oh my," Trachtenbroit said. "You just ate my cat."

The next morning, he carried the four onto a boat, two each in a pair of wire cages. He also brought aboard a pig; it was going to be a long voyage back to America and his carnivorous birds would no doubt grow hungry. On the ride across the Atlantic, Trachtenbroit felt as if his life's work had begun. He felt no sympathy when reports surfaced of people's pets going missing.

The Great Owls, as he'd come to call them, were above reproach. And they would add life to a wood no living thing dared enter.

10

Somebody handed Neal a drink. Things had been spinning since he left the office, images of owls swarming his warring mind. In the foyer a friend nearly spilled his drink on Neal, and the birthday boy angrily grabbed his wrist.

"Be careful!" he bellowed. "It's velvet!"

But the coat he wore was not.

Covered in white confetti, searching the party for specific guests, Nash allowed his birthday wish to rise to the surface, unfettered, at last.

"I want an owl," he said. But nobody heard him over the band.

Yes, he could admit it to himself now. What a tease it had forever been! For Neal and every other hunter who called Goblin home . . . to have such splendor so near, the incredible expanse of unchartered territory, the North Woods, the Great Owls, only miles from the bed in which he dreamed.

"Where would you set up a blind in a place like that? How would you get a clean shot off in that cluster?"

Already, images of himself armed in the woods.

But the Great Owl was sacred in Goblin. Bagging one would

be tantamount to taking a chisel to Mount Rushmore. The owls were something to boast about. Something to think about when the rain was too heavy to do anything else. The Hedges, the North Woods, and the Great Owls made Goblin *different*. A species that couldn't be seen anywhere else in the world did something for the city that no department store could do. It made it special. Put it on the map. The individuality afforded Goblin by Trachtenbroit's big find wasn't meant to make the city money. Trachtenbroit, for all his contributions to the city, wasn't thinking of Goblin at all. And somehow through the years the purity had been distilled.

"One owl," Neal said, "won't change a thing."

Deep in the recess of every Gobliner's mind sat an owl on the branch of an impossible tree.

Goblin pride could always be traced back to the magnificent coach-black birds Trachtenbroit delivered. The people didn't need the ordinance or the fear of the Goblin Police; the Great Owls were not to be touched.

And yet ... Neal Nash often felt bigger than the city he lived in. And this dirty thought had peered around the corner of his inflated mind many times before. But tonight it was in full view. And thinking it over, now, walking through a haze of smoke and bodies, Neal understood that it wasn't so bad a thing after all.

Christ, Trachtenbroit had *stolen* the things in the first place!

Neal stepped out through the back door, downed the drink in his hand, and tossed the glass on the grass.

He didn't see the thousand people dancing in the rain in his yard. He didn't hear the thunderous music of the band.

In his mind, he was already crouched among twisted trees, smoke still rising from his gun, bagging an untouchable bird.

"Nobody ever died of guilt," he said. Then he crossed the lawn toward his hangar.

Friends called to him as he passed. A woman placed a hand on his shoulder and he brushed it aside with a sneer.

At the door to the hangar, he looked once over his shoulder at the party in his honor. It registered as fog. And he entered the building at last.

"Hello," he said, turning the overheads on. "Daddy's thinking of bringing you a sister."

He walked the rows of big game, a rhinoceros and a puma the first to greet him. Beyond them stood two zebras, a lioness, and a lynx. Each row was ten animals deep, so that Neal felt a surge of power so great it was as if he were passing them in the afterlife, *their* afterlife, where he reigned king, all of them belonging to him.

He came to an open space among the birds of prey. An empty case upon a column painted white. Between a condor and a bald eagle, Neal saw his own face reflected in the glass. He saw a black bird within, one that was not yet there.

"You delivered us these birds, Jonathan Trachtenbroit. You hunted them once and brought them to me to do the same. We'll be in the books together. The only two men to ever call them our own."

He looked over his shoulder. Took in the game.

The overhead lights made the animals look alive.

For a moment, he couldn't help but feel the ground beneath him had gone slippery. As if a hole were opening up, a grave in the Goblin Cemetery, a space just big enough for Neal to fall straight into, to be buried standing up forever.

Perhaps he was falling from grace. But he was okay with that. So long as he caught an owl on the way.

11

By the time Neal found Roger (in the garage, in a cloud of smoke as thick as exhaust, smoking a joint with a cook from Barbara's favorite restaurant and a lawyer who once helped Neal out of a pickle) the party was so out of control it was like a *spill*. There was no more separation for Neal. It was one sweaty, heaving mass, bending and writhing, singing its song. Barbara and he hadn't invited one thousand people but an unruly creature called *the Party* instead. If it wasn't Roger Fletcher's face (and it seemed like it wasn't for a hell of a long time) then it was just more of the monster. But the difficulty he'd had finding his oldest hunting buddy comforted him, too. The cloud of bodies might provide cover for their exit.

"Roger," he hollered over the psychedelic noise. "Find Harvey and Saul and meet behind the showroom."

Roger, stoned silly, smiled. "What's up, Neal?"

"Never mind what's up. The four of us are going to have a little fun."

He'd already had his cake. Opened Barbara's present. Made himself known. The last thing people would be thinking was *Where's Neal Nash?*

And Barbara . . . Barbara understood impulse better than most.

Less than ten minutes later Neal was behind the wheel of his Jaguar, parked behind the hangar, tapping his fingers to an inaudible beat on the steering wheel, waiting for his friends.

"A hunting party," he said. "That's what it's called on a night like this. That's what you call it when a party goes hunting."

12

"Y ou can't leave your own party," Harvey said, drenched
and happy.

The four men sat in the idling Jaguar. Roger blew
smoke out a slit in the window.

Neal cleared his throat.

"You know what I *really* wanna do for my birthday?"

"You wanna go hunting," Saul said.

"I wanna go hunting."

Cautious excitement brewed in the car; the honor of being
inside Neal Nash's inner circle always came with a holding of
breath.

"Sure, Neal," Harvey said. "Where do you want to go?"

"The West Fields," he said. "Let's shoot us a deer. A pheasant.
Something I can take home and stuff. A birthday bird. We could
be back in an hour. This party will still be going. Hell . . . it ought
to still be going tomorrow."

"Right on," Roger said. "I'm game."

"Don't say that," Neal said, "or I'm liable to shoot you."

Then he started the car.

Roger, Harvey, and Saul had been to Africa with Neal. They'd
tracked elephants and leopards. They'd stood up in one another's
weddings. They knew him as well as anyone would. And yet none
mentioned the strange route he took to the West Fields.

Perhaps he was avoiding the Goblin Police.

As they barreled down dirt roads, Harvey, drunk, imagined
they might surprise a kid getting his first hand job: Here come
four sixty-year-olds, falling out of a Jaguar, looking to shoot the
first thing they see.

The grass framing the roads, so Goblin green during the day, looked transparent in the Jaguar lights. As if every blade of grass were a tiny mirror, reflecting the gushing Goblin sky.

"Where are we going again?" Saul asked at last. The first to question where the night was leading.

But Neal didn't answer. As the roar of the engine rose to meet the roar of the sky, the Jaguar howled like a living animal, as if, finally, the hunters had been swallowed by the beast.

13

The Jaguar didn't handle well in the rain and, with Nash visibly drunk, Saul started to worry. The car was hydroplaning and Neal took some of the turns far too tight. Roger was nearly passed out in the passenger seat and Harvey stared dumbly out the window.

But Saul wanted to know what was making him so nervous.

Mayor Blackwater was as serious about the North Woods as any mayor before him. And the Goblin Police were severe. Of this there was no doubt. And yet he wasn't afraid of Neal getting pulled over. Surely Nash could handle it if they were.

So what was it?

An accident? Was Saul holding the door handle tight because he was afraid Neal was going to drive them into a ditch? The roads were slick, yes, but whatever was bothering Saul, that wasn't it. There was something heavy, it seemed, inside the car; something bigger than Saul thought he'd agreed to.

"I thought we were hitting the West Fields, Neal," Harvey suddenly said. Neal had made a right on a dirt road called Blatty. They were headed north now, not west.

Nash looked in the rearview mirror.

"I ever steer you wrong, Harvey?" He was smiling. "Just because we left the party doesn't mean the party's over. We're going to remember this night for a long time."

He was right, Saul thought. In all their years, all their adventures, Nash had never steered them wrong. He'd shown them three lifetimes of the time of their lives. As unpredictable as he was, Neal Hunter Nash knew right from wrong.

That's why, when Neal stopped the Jaguar and killed the lights fifteen yards from the south entrance to the North Woods, Saul breathed deeply and thought,

Not anymore.

14

"You're drunk," Harvey said. "And out of your mind."

Neal turned around in his seat. The Jaguar still idled.

"Scared of getting a little lost, Harvey? I've taken care of that."

Neal got out of the car. Harvey and Saul watched as he passed the back window. They heard him open the trunk.

"I'm not going in there," Saul said.

In his whole life he'd never—not once—considered going inside the North Woods. Like most Gobliners, the admonishment had been branded into his brain:

Chew your food before you swallow it, Saul.

Look both ways before you cross the street, Saul.

And if I ever catch you near those fucking North Woods . . .

Harvey simply didn't believe it. It didn't catch in his mind. It was late as hell. It was raining like crazy. They'd all drunk enough to drown. *Now* Neal Nash says hey, let's go into the North Woods? Harvey wasn't scared. He didn't have time to feel fear. Maybe in a few seconds he would. But just then he didn't believe it. Couldn't.

A midnight hunt sounded like an adventure. Entering the North Woods sounded insane. If he was ever going to have done this, it would have been forty years ago with a blonde named Rhonda.

But this? Here? Now?

He had an image of himself lifting the last rock on Earth. Opening the last freaky door.

Neal returned to the front door and tossed rope on the seat.

"See now?" he said. "We won't get lost."

Then he threw two green ponchos onto the rope. He put a third one on.

"What about Roger?" Saul asked.

Thunder erupted high in the Goblin sky.

"Forget him," Neal said. "He can wait in the car."

Then Neal went back to the trunk.

Harvey put on his poncho quickly.

"This isn't a good idea," Saul said.

Harvey seemed unnerved by it. Like Saul was voicing something he didn't want voiced just then.

"And why not, Saul?" Harvey said, stiffly. "'Cause of a witch?"

It sounded silly, of course, but when their eyes met, both looked away quickly.

Saul got out of the car and Harvey soon followed. Roger remained sleeping with his head against the passenger glass. Neal was carrying a big box.

And the three men started walking intentionally toward the dark entrance of the North Woods for the first time in their lives.

Neal had a bow strapped to his back. A quiver of arrows, too.

"What do you got in the box, Neal? Breadcrumbs?"

Neal turned to Harvey as the rain came heavier upon them.

"Yes, Harvey." He slapped a hand on the box's side. "Breadcrumbs."

Saul remembered a time when he was eleven years old, on the

playground behind Goblin Elementary, when Carl Clay told him he'd been in the North Woods. Without bravado. Without bragging. Just a kid that had to tell someone that he'd stumbled over a dead deer out there with its chest cavity torn open like the lid of a cardboard box. Carl told Saul never to go out there. Shook when he said it. Cried, too.

"Really, Neal," Harvey said.

Neal paused just a few feet from the entrance to the woods. Nothing more than a space between two tangled trees.

Neal opened the box.

"It's empty," Harvey said.

Then Neal slammed it shut. And Saul understood, clearly, that Neal hadn't had a sudden impulse to go to the North Woods at all. He had a plan.

A plan to take something out.

"No flashlights, Neal?" Saul asked.

But Neal only laughed.

"You want them to see us coming, Saul?"

Then he tossed Saul a penlight.

"Only use it if you have to."

"Thanks, Neal," Saul said. But he wanted to say . . . *Who's "them"?*

15

Nothing terrible happened when they crossed the threshold. While Saul imagined they'd be sliced to pieces upon entering, nothing came at them at all. No wolf howled hello. In fact, he experienced a rare sense of freedom, as if, by breaking his hometown's ultimate rule, he had returned, momentarily, to childhood.

He hadn't noticed any particular sounds on the walk from Neal's Jaguar to the south entrance, but he certainly caught it when they were cut off. As if the trees acted like foam padding, eliminating all but the noises of the North Woods. Even the rain was muted; the trees like one of the meat tents back at the party.

Oh, the trees.

Saul couldn't believe them. In person they were more confusing than any fabled version he'd imagined as a kid. Any Gobliner could see their tangled, gnarled trunks and branches from the outside, but being within them changed everything. Like the difference between knowing a man is crazy, and then stepping into his mind.

Things got much darker. For a moment Neal and Harvey disappeared ahead, taken by the trunks. But by the crooked moonlight coming through the treetops, Saul saw that the trail took a hard left. There he found that his friends had stopped and were whispering.

I've been inside the North Woods for thirty seconds and I almost lost them, Saul thought.

He was scared in many different ways. Scared like a good kid who was suddenly involved in a bad prank. Scared like a sixty-year-old man, a hand to his chest, wondering how much of this particular brand of excitement he could take.

Scared in a deeper, more absurd way, too.

Scared of a witch.

Nash held up the rope.

"Like they did in Carroll's day," he said. "We'll tie our two around you, Saul. You'll be our post. You stay here."

"Stay here? Why not tie it around a tree?"

Nash shook his head no. "Animals might chew it off. Can't chance it. Need one of us to make sure we get back to this very spot."

Before Saul had a chance to retort, Nash was securing the rope around his waist.

"Now," Nash said, tightening the knots and whispering far under the sound of the muted rain. "If you feel us tugging hard, like we're in trouble, that means we are. If that happens, tie it to a tree and come after us. Here." He handed Saul a pistol.

"Trouble, Neal? What kind of trouble could there be out here?"

But he wished he hadn't asked it because, when Neal looked him in the eye, Saul saw his old friend was wearing a face he'd never seen him wear before. In that moment Neal Nash, the bravest man in Goblin, acknowledged the myths of the North Woods.

Then Neal tied the rope around Harvey's green poncho and brown suit coat. He tied a second rope to the first and secured it to his own waist.

"We've hunted rhino," Harvey said. "But we've never needed rope before."

"Nope," Neal said, the rain a never-ending thud above him. "A new first."

A lot of "firsts" tonight, Saul thought.

A whisper of wind came from farther up the trail, and the three looked into the darkness ahead. A tunnel through their imaginations; fears and desires twisting, tangled with thrill and shame.

"Cheers," Neal said, "to whatever calls these woods home."

Then Neal and Harvey advanced, and Saul was left in the darkness alone.

16

Harvey was well shocked. The skinny trails were as tricky as all the terrible stories said they were. Neal used a penlight of his own and, as meager as the beam was, Harvey didn't know what they would do without it.

He and Neal turned right and came across their own ropes from an earlier turn. Harvey had been sure they were headed in a zigzag route *away* from where they started. Clearly, they were already mixed up. But Nash, always optimistic on the hunt, didn't acknowledge it other than to turn around.

There was space enough for a man to walk alone. The trails gave them that much room. Harvey kept expecting things to be grown over, for a meeting of trees to block the way, to cause them to start over. But that never quite happened. And rather than finding comfort in this, he couldn't shake the feeling that the woods wanted them to descend.

Descend? Harvey thought. It seemed like a peculiar word to use considering they were walking forward, not down. And yet no other word felt as fitting.

The pair didn't speak. Nash stopped often and studied the trees. For this, Harvey understood his old friend was looking to bag a bird on his birthday.

"Pheasant?" Harvey asked.

But Neal didn't respond.

And they continued to . . . descend.

Another dead end. Another turnaround. Harvey started to see their rope as something as tangled as the branches he ducked and dodged.

Neal's penlight seemed to grow dimmer as the darkness of the woods increased. The logic-less terrain was wearing on Harvey.

He thought of the dancing women back at the party. The drinks he was missing out on. Neal's light settled on a cluster of trees and then another, then another, and they all looked the same. Harvey suddenly wanted music. Smoke. A woman's body to hold. The deeper they walked, the greater the distance behind them became, and Harvey felt like he was standing still as the forest grew wide around them. But Nash was all business.

"Look for red dots," he said. First thing he said in a long time.

Harvey had no idea what this was supposed to mean but he imagined a red-eyed witch crouched on the trail ahead.

"Let's bag the first thing we see," Harvey said. "Then let's go get trash-canned."

Nash didn't respond, and it bothered Harvey. Neal always had a way of making you feel *included*. Like you were in on the hunt no matter how little you knew or how big the game. But tonight Harvey felt like he was playing a small role in a story only Neal Nash had read.

Harvey thought of Saul, drunk, wobbling in his white linen suit and green poncho, waiting for his friends to return.

Alone at the entrance. Alone in the North Woods.

And Saul thought of Harvey at the same time. As if the angular branches deflected thoughts, sent them spiraling through the spaces, a living web that delivered one man's idea to another.

Saul shifted his weight from one foot to the other. The rope was heavy against his waist.

He'd heard whispering a minute ago. A scratchy voice, a group of voices, sounds Neal would no doubt ascribe to the wind.

But the witch was said to whisper.

"She tells you a story," Saul said, shining his penlight into the thicket surrounding him. "Until your heart explodes with it."

He didn't like the sound of his own voice. Didn't like the noise it made.

He looked deeper into the woods. Down the trail he saw his friends go.

I could tie the rope to the tree, go join Roger in the car.

He chewed his lower lip, considering.

A chorus of whispers rose to his right.

Once upon a time, he thought, *your heart exploded . . .*

BOOM!

Something loud deeper in the woods. A gunshot? Saul didn't know. Didn't look ahead with the light, either. Instead he fell to his knees and held his head in his hands.

"No, no," he said. "Everything's fine. *Everything's* fine."

But when he looked up he saw a pale face pull back behind one of the gnarled trunks of the trees.

Saul couldn't find a scream within himself. Not even a gasp. So he remained still. Very still. Staring where he believed he'd seen a pale face. Then his mind overlapped ideas, as if the bent branches had something to do with the way he thought, and Saul imagined he'd seen not only a pale face, but a *white man,* hiding out here, hiding from a tribe of indigenous people that would remove his face and tie it around a lantern if they caught him.

"Everything's fine," Saul said.

But it wasn't fine. Not when the whispering picked up again. Not when Saul heard it so clearly that, even if Neal had insisted it was the wind, Saul would've known the truth.

17

Neal and Harvey were lost. At least Harvey believed they were. And how could they not be? The longest straightaways went ten feet before another severe turn rubber-banded back in the other direction. A map, Harvey realized, would be useless.

What was Neal thinking? He certainly wasn't acting like a birthday boy out for a joyride. No. He had the same determined gait that Harvey had seen a hundred times on five continents.

"He mistook their backs for a sweater, for night sky," Neal suddenly said. "But everything looks like night sky in here."

"What was that, Neal?"

Finally Neal turned to face him. "You're not holding out on me, are you, Harvey?"

"Holding out? What do you mean?"

Nash studied his face suspiciously, then forged ahead again.

He took the turns tighter. Uphill and down. Forward and back. He made decisions faster, now, like he was getting to know the woods.

Harvey had difficulty keeping up.

"Easy, Neal. I'm drunk."

Another quick turn and *duck!*

Uphill, downhill, step over a low-reaching branch.

Breathe, Harvey thought.

Winding one way, then the other, then the first again.

Lift the arms, raise the knees, *duck!*

Turn right, turn left, get on the ground to crawl under a cluster, back up again, turn right, turn left.

Mind the ropes. Mind the ropes.

"How deep are we?" Harvey asked. But he wanted to ask, *How deep are we going to go?*

Then Harvey got dizzy. Neal's light gave him just enough of a view to keep going, to take another step, but never enough to explain to him where they were. All this darkness . . . all this night. The woods felt huge now. Overwhelmingly so. He imagined Saul standing where they left him, the one brick of reality he could count on. Harvey had to get back there. Sooner than later. The deeper they walked, the more anxious he became. And the whispers, too. The rising tide of wind through the branches, the sound of many thoughts, as if the trees were (yes) capable of orchestrating such things. Neal made a hundred quick decisions and they all blended into one bad one to Harvey.

The terrible decision they'd made to enter the North Woods.

"Here," Nash whispered. And the one syllable was strong.

Nash came to a stop. He laid the excess rope on the ground and illuminated the space ahead with the penlight.

Neal started to take off his poncho.

"What are you up to, Neal? I know you're not firing at random out here."

Neal nodded. "It's my birthday, Harvey. I thought I might dress up for the occasion." He pulled the poncho up and over his head. Then he removed his suit coat, too. And beneath it, Harvey saw a red velvet jacket.

"Where'd you get that?" Harvey asked. But what he wanted to say was, *What are you hunting for out here, Hunter?*

"It'd be nice to think that the owls were attracted to Trachtenbroit himself, wouldn't it, Harvey?" Nash let the poncho fall to his feet. "That they saw some sort of . . . protector in him?"

"What are you talking about, Neal?"

Neal smiled. He actually shone the light on his lips so Harvey could see him smile.

"The birds weren't attracted to *him,* buddy. Any great hunter knows that. They liked his *coat.*"

Then Neal extended his arms outward, palms up. He looked high to the treetops.

Above him, in plain sight of his old friend, a small piece of night, seemingly resting upon the branch of an impossible tree, began to rotate, a head turning, a mythic face coming into view.

"Neal . . . is that a—"

"Come to he who owns you!" Nash demanded.

The red dots that marked the Great Owl's eyes looked down at the two Gobliners.

"Neal."

But Nash was already reaching over his shoulder, into his quiver of arrows.

18

Saul had long lost his nerve; now he was losing his mind. The darkness of the North Woods wouldn't stop staring back at him. He was scared. Scared *good*. Every noise was a witch. Every drop of rain the beginning of a story.

He wanted to wake Roger up. Wanted badly to untie the rope, go to the car, wake Roger up and tell him, *Look man . . . I just can't be alone in there anymore!*

He untied the rope from his waist.

How far in could they be? Surely they're snagged on a tree or two out there. Why, it won't matter at all if I leave them. I could just drop the rope and go.

This sounded real good. Sounded better than wrapping his arms around a tree, discovering that something with a pale face was standing on the other side.

Come on, Saul. Tie the fuckin' rope to a tree.

So he did.

And once the rope was secure, he started to walk back to the south entrance. Back to the Jaguar. Back to the party.

But the darkness that ogled him a minute before seemed

to move now. It looked like the trees were wet with sweat, not rain, that they could flex, curve in on him, hug him, crush him whole.

He stopped and turned around. Walking back to the rope he thought, *This is the dumbest decision you've ever made.*

But it was too late. He'd made it.

Picking up the rope, he started to follow it, hand over hand, tracing the route of his old friends.

"Neal!" he called. "Are you guys okay?"

Because he wasn't sure. Because they'd been gone so long. And because he wanted to be there, on this night, when Neal Nash got what he was looking for.

Saul thought he knew what it was. Hell, Saul *definitely* knew what it was.

"You see a Great Owl in here?" he called.

Emotions warred within him. Guilt. Shame. Thrill.

The hunter in him was curious. The subservient friend in him couldn't turn himself around.

If Neal Nash was going to bag a Great Owl tonight, it'd go down as one of the most legendary moments in the history of Goblin. Not good, necessarily. Not flattering. And yet . . .

"Neal? What do they look like? You seen one yet?"

He shoved the image of a pale witch out of his mind. It was easier to do while walking, while leaning on the strength and bravado of his good friend Neal, while imagining what it might be like to see one of the black birds in person.

Who else could say as much?

So scared as he was, hand over hand, Saul continued. And the adjustment to the dark that he expected never came.

"Neal! You see one yet?"

And his own voice sounded like a whisper. Like he was the one beginning to tell a story.

Once upon a time, a fabled hunter tracked the one thing he was not allowed to have . . .

"Neal!" he called, louder. "I'm coming! If you're going to fall from grace, I'm going to fall with you."

19

Harvey wanted to say, *Neal, you can't.*

But it looked like he could.

The bird was incredible. The hunter in Harvey felt clean, warm water wash over his soul. For starters, the eyes, dark as they were, seemed to glow. The branch it was perched upon was illuminated, just enough, to show its astonishing feet.

Harvey turned to face Nash and saw that his old friend, his *best* friend and idol, was moments away from breaking the biggest rule, about to let fly an arrow through the chest of their hometown secret, the untouchable bird, Trachtenbroit's Great Owl.

He had to say *something.*

And yet . . . he *wanted* to see it happen.

Nash lifted his bow and took aim.

The owl acknowledged the movement below but didn't make to fly. Nash kept statue-still, his arms raised at a direct angle to the black bird. The bowstring looked like it was going to snap. But it didn't. Not yet.

"You," Nash said. "*You, you, you . . .*"

In his red Trachtenbroit jacket, Nash looked like something from the past. Harvey couldn't help but think of the settlers who hid in these woods.

Neal was a finger's release from being tied to his hero forever. Like winding rope through an impossible wood.

"Is this . . ." Harvey started. "Is this beneath you, Neal?"

He wished he hadn't asked it.

"Is Goblin *beneath* me?" Neal asked. "Is *history* beneath me, too? This is the finish line, Harvey. We've circled the globe together. Tracked giants and brought 'em back. But after all that effort . . . the *trophy* has always been right here, here at home."

"Neal . . ."

"I want an owl, Harvey. And I want it now."

Harvey looked up to the big black bird.

Why doesn't it just fly away?

Neal bent the bowstring farther.

"Harvey," he said. "In my right pocket is a camera. I want you to take a photo of this."

"A photo, Neal?"

It sounded more mad than the murder. Nash was asking for evidence of his crime.

"I'll need something to send Wayne Sherman, when he's commissioned to carve a topiary of this moment, the biggest statue he's ever done, the biggest moment in the history of our Goblin."

The rain fell through the treetops, between the mythic bird and the hunter, Neal Nash, who wanted him.

20

Saul was now terrified. Not only had he not found his friends, but he hadn't seen a thing but trees, distorted unending trees, since starting out. He was taking it slow because he had to. Because he couldn't see any other way to take it. And he was so scared of encountering something, something he couldn't hear over the noise of his own feet, that he stopped every couple of steps to check his ears. It was horrible, in its way, and he felt something close to embarrassment for the loyalty he gave Neal.

Once upon a time, a hunter fell from grace . . .

Oh, there was no question Neal was going for one of the Great Owls. No doubt about that.

Snap!

"Just a twig!" Saul cried out. "Just a twig . . ."

You're sixty years old. Your name is Saul. Your mother's name was Virginia. You used to sell fancy cars but now you don't need to. You're sixty years old. Your name is Saul. Your mother's name was Virginia. You used to sell fancy cars but now—

Hand over hand he followed the rope. And with every creak in the trees, he stopped and squinted, frozen cold with the idea of a rising whisper, a wrinkled face, a sudden bloated feeling in his chest . . .

21

Harvey took aim with the camera.

"Ready, Neal."

He imagined the red dots in the bird's eyes would haunt him for a long time to come.

"The first Gobliner to bag a Great Owl," Neal said.

"That's right, Neal."

But it didn't feel right. Felt like Neal had shown him a back door to his office, a room Harvey hadn't ever seen before, where a young woman was kept in chains.

"On three now, Harvey. I'm going to let it fly on three. You'll hear the snap. You take that photo a *quarter second* after you hear the release. I want that arrow *inside* the bird when you snap it. You got it?"

"I got it."

"Three and release then snap."

"Got it."

"Got it?"

"Yes."

Nash started counting.

"One . . ."

Jesus, Neal.

"Two . . ."

This isn't good.

"Three!"

Harvey thought, *Miss it.*

The bowstring snapped, Harvey took the photo.

FLASH!

The light from the small bulb was blinding. For a moment Harvey could see what felt like the entire forest: an infinite maze of broken branches . . . trees weaving in and out of one another's trunks . . . twisting up and wrapping over but never quite touching in the end.

And Nash.

Nash's back, the pull hand open and empty, the other still steady on the bow. High up in that incredible image (an image burned into Harvey's mind as he closed his eyes) the owl looked frozen in surprise and preflight . . . its eyes even bigger than they'd looked in the dark . . . everything about it bigger . . . an enormous feathered beast with long sharp talons and a beak as sharp as an arrowhead . . . its chest purple upon the black . . . Nash's arrow wedged well into its heart.

The image was almost more lucid than what he saw when his eyes were open. But as he put a free hand up to his closed lids and saw *Still Life of Owl Death* in great detail, *sound* continued . . . and Harvey heard the thud of the arrow piercing meat, the crackle of the black body breaking many branches, and the bass *whump* as it hit the ground.

Nash had done it. With something as simple as a red velvet jacket, Nash had attracted Goblin's off-limits bird.

Harvey opened his eyes.

"Uh-oh, Neal," he said. He was looking up to where the owl had perched, seeing there many more patches of black rotating to face the two Gobliners below.

Harvey counted thirty, maybe more. And the noise of their necks creaking sounded to Harvey like a casket lid opening, releasing something far more dangerous than the Goblin Police.

Sixty Hell-red dots in the darkness. A canopy of the black feathers that had given Goblin such pride.

"We gotta go," Harvey said. "We gotta go *right now.*"

Neal held his eyes on the black lump at the foot of the tree.

"Neal . . ."

"I'm not leaving empty-handed. Not tonight."

"Let's be happy we have our hands at all. Trachtenbroit fed his birds cats, Neal. These aren't robins looking down at us."

"Harvey," Neal said, removing his jacket, careful not to turn his back on the birds, "put this on."

"What?"

"Put the jacket on. The owls, they're fixated on it. Put it on, so I can get in there and get what's mine."

Harvey stood stiff. Whatever drinks and drugs he'd enjoyed at the party had long worn off.

"You know you got her, Neal. Isn't that enough?"

But the way Nash looked at him, Harvey wasn't sure who was more of a threat: the birds . . . or Neal?

Nash extended his arm, the jacket in hand.

Run, Harvey thought. *Follow the rope. Run home. Leave Neal here. He's lost his mind. He's crossed the line. RUN.*

He took the coat and put it on.

Always Harvey, always loyal.

Nash crouched slowly to his knees. He crawled toward the black body at the foot of the gnarled tree.

The Great Owls shifted above on the branches. One fluttered its dark wings.

Nash crawled closer.

Closer.

More movement above.

Nash grabbed the dead bird by its ankles and pulled it to his chest. He held it with both arms, protecting it, it seemed, even from Harvey.

One of the owls flew down and landed on Harvey's shoulder.

SWOOOOOOOP!

"Neal!"

But Neal just stared at Harvey and the bird.

"Easy, Harvey. It's the jacket. Like I said. Don't let it know you're scared."

Neal stepped closer to his old friend and took the camera from him.

"It's on me, Neal! What do I do?"

Nash looked his old friend in the eye.

"I'm sorry," he whispered.

Then he ran.

Back into the dark tunnel from which they came. His trophy in one hand and proof of it in the other. He ran like it was his *twentieth* birthday. Behind him, in the black, above the sound of his own boots cracking sticks, Neal heard a chorus of owls lifting off, taking violent flight.

SWOOOOOOOOOOOP!

Then Harvey screamed. But his scream did not last long before it became a gargled distant moan.

Neal did not turn back. He did not call out to his friend. Nash ran.

22

Saul raced through the trails, gripping the rope, terrorized by silly thoughts of a witch.

How old are you? he asked himself. Many times. But it didn't help. Didn't squash the rising chorus of nerves within him. Like most Gobliners, Saul had never run through these woods as a child. He was sixty years old and he was afraid of this dark. He didn't want to die like this . . . drunk and alone in a forest he should have known better than to enter.

He was worried about Nash and Harvey, too. Worried Nash's reputation would be ruined:

BIG-GAME HUNTER CAUGHT DRUNK IN
NORTH WOODS, GREAT OWL IN HAND

So many worries. So much to be afraid of. He was out of breath, he was nervous, he was coming down, too, from about ten whiskey drinks and a snort of white powder. His hands hurt from grabbing the rope, and all the uphills and downhills were starting to feel like needles in his feet and legs.

You shouldn't be in here!

For all Saul knew, Neal and Harvey could already be cuffed and in the back of a Goblin Police cruiser.

Saul shivered at the thought of an officer's pale soft hand falling upon his own shoulder.

You're coming with us, now. And we'll show you what happens to men who hunt things they're not supposed to.

Saul couldn't tell anymore if his shirt, beneath the poncho, was wet from the rain or from his own fear spilling out of him in sweat. He was like an animal himself now, hunted by unknowns, his mind reduced to a few directives.

Find

Nash

Find

Harvey.

Get out.

Saul heard something moving fast ahead.

"Oh God, what is it?"

It was coming his way. He was sure of this. The noise was getting louder, closer, louder, closer. Swift as a big cat.

Whatever it is, it's coming to kill me.

It sounded so close now that Saul thought it must be upon him, that there wasn't any more room for it to get any louder.

But it did. Louder and closer still.

"Please head in another direction," Saul mumbled, rooted to the ground. His hands shook on the rope.

He cried out as a shape came into view ten feet ahead and blew by him as quickly as it came.

Saul stood stiff, feeling the wind of its passing still upon him.

"It didn't see me," he said. Then he yelled it. "*It missed me!*"

He wanted to kneel in this impossible maze and weep.

Instead he forged ahead, faster than before. He pushed himself until the rope he'd been clinging to, the rope that was his only source of security, his one link to the world he shouldn't have left, went slack.

Saul stopped, fingering the rope to make certain there was no longer any pull from the other end.

He felt no resistance at all.

He pulled the slack rope until he came to its end.

He studied it under the penlight.

"Chewed," he said, matter-of-factly, before realizing what that conclusion meant.

He could hear his own breath like it was an icy wind now . . . the sound of that muted rain was somewhere miles above him.

He stepped forward without the guide of the rope now.

Images of a witch just ahead accosted him. Visions of the Goblin Police on their knees, chewing the rope.

Saul felt a lump like a soggy log at his feet.

The word *laundry* crossed his mind.

Saul squatted. He turned on the penlight.

But after seeing what he saw, he closed his eyes.

Weeping now, after all, Saul reached out and felt a leg, a thigh, the side of a man's fallen body. Saul's fingers sank into where the belly and chest ought to be. He cried out and pulled his hand away.

He reached up to the person's head and blindly felt the features of his face.

Then he turned on the penlight and opened his eyes.

It was Harvey. It had to be. But what Saul saw was an approximation of his old friend.

Harvey's eyes were pulled out, leaving two purple swollen circles where they once rested. But his eyes were not missing; they hung by their stalks on his bruised cheeks. One was looking right at Saul, as if Harvey was saying, *I see you, buddy, but I'm not doing too well.* His mouth was open and where the lips met, at both ends of a grimace, the cheeks had been chewed out, exposing dark gums. Holes ran down his neck and shoulders. He wore a red jacket that was torn to shreds. His stomach and chest were indeed scooped out; half-eaten lungs hung over the corrugated edge of his abdomen. Saul thought of a torn car seat in his mother's old Buick.

He jumped back from his old friend.

"The witch," he said. "The witch did this!"

He replayed the moment when the body rushed past him in the woods.

He now knew it was Nash. Running from the witch.

Then, after staring for a moment more at the remains of Harvey, Saul ran, too. He followed the rope, hand over hand, shaking his head no, no he didn't want to hear a story, no, please, no *Once upon a time,* no pressure in his chest, no terrible myth made real.

And when he made it all the way back to the south entrance of the North Woods, he did not feel good about it. He did not feel the relief he so desired. Looking back at the twisted puzzle of branches and trunks, he thought,

Harvey's still in there.

And it looked like a tomb to him then. A complex carving of the lid of a coffin.

Looking ahead, he saw Nash's car was gone.

So, as the brutal Goblin rain fell upon him, Saul began the long trek homeward on foot.

"Nash," he said, a hundred times, his voice muted by the poncho's green hood. "You saw the witch, didn't you. Didn't you? That's why you left Harvey. Right? It was the witch, after all. It wasn't because of . . . because of . . ."

But he didn't want to say it. Didn't want to ask,

Neal, did you run off with a bird?

23

Neal stood in the doorway of his big-game hangar, dripping rainwater on the floor. He ran a hand through the silver hair framing his sixty-year-old head. Carrying the thing was more work than he'd planned on but that no longer mattered. He was home. And he wasn't empty-handed.

He flipped on the bright overhead lights and brought to life a room that was remarkable to anyone privileged enough to have seen it. Tonight, after he'd placed the Great Owl in its empty glass case, Neal Nash would find it remarkable, too.

The sounds of the party continued outside. He didn't think anyone had seen him drive up and he didn't really care if they had. It was his birthday. He could drive through the house if he wanted to.

He didn't think of Harvey and he didn't think of Saul. Roger still snored in the passenger seat of the Jaguar outside but Neal hadn't acknowledged his friend as he drove home. Hardly knew he was there.

"Jonathan Trachtenbroit," he said as he stepped past the stuffed buffalo, the stuffed lioness, too. "Only us."

He knew he needed to stuff the bird before displaying it, but right now he just wanted to see it.

He had to.

He held the owl chest-high, both arms beneath it, as if carrying a dead lover to her grave. He passed the enormous rhinoceros he'd bagged in Namibia. The Russian lynx. The Icelandic reindeer that had taken ten days to track.

But his eyes remained fixed on a point ahead: a glass case with nothing to show.

"The first," Neal said, swatting away the pinpricks of guilt that arose. Then those feelings of guilt froze over and died within him.

He'd made his decision. He'd chosen history.

"Oh, Jonathan Trachtenbroit . . . we are colleagues now. We are unique. Only us."

Nash's friends had seen his face this way before; snowy nights where the liquor worked against him. Harvey would've said Neal was "getting edged." Saul would've braced himself for a night of Nash bragging.

Neal stepped past an ape, its face so well preserved it seemed to watch him.

"You did wonderful work, Trachtenbroit," Neal said. "I admit I couldn't have done it without you."

He laughed, each syllable rising to the hangar roof.

His Alaskan grizzly stood at full height above him. His Spanish ibex glowed.

"I killed 'em all, Jonathan, with my skill alone. With my dedication to the sport."

He'd come to the empty case. The bird weighed nothing to him now.

"Trachtenbroit and Nash. Jonathan and Neal."

He gently set the owl on a square of carpet at his feet and rubbed his hands together.

"The pride of Goblin," he said. "Right here at home."

Rain pelted hard against the hangar's roof as Neal lifted the glass case and set the limp bird beneath it. He knew he had much work to do—hell, the arrow was still sticking out of her heart—but he'd never seen a sweeter sight in his life.

"Happy birthday, Hunter," he said.

The bird lay unnaturally bent on the display podium.

"Mr. Trachtenbroit, say hello to me," Neal said. "I am forever inscribed . . . beside you . . ."

The hangar door slammed open behind him.

Neal turned quick, angry.

"Who's there?" he called. He raised a hand to cover the Great Owl.

Then he heard the sound of heels clicking against the floor and knew who it was before she said his name.

"Neal, really," Barbara said, her voice falling like leaves between the stuffed beasts. "Disappearing from your own party. It isn't like you to avoid the spotlight."

When she came into view, Neal stepped toward her. They met a few feet from the bird, surrounded by so much game.

"Barbara," he said, taking her hand, "I have something to show you."

Barbara lifted a finger to shush him. "But first, I have a gift for you."

Neal now noticed she was carrying a box. "I've already opened your present, dear. You wouldn't want to spoil me, now, would you?"

"You opened the present I wanted the others to see," Barbara said. "But this"—she held the box out to him—"this is my real gift to you. Happy birthday, Neal."

Neal took the box and held it against his poncho, still wet from the hunt.

"Thank you, Barbara. Love of my life."

He opened the box.

Barbara smiled as his eyes widened. A deep low moan rose in his throat.

Neal stuck his hand in the box and pulled the bird out by its feet. Its black feathers looked no different under the hangar overheads than the feathers beneath the glass behind him.

"Barbara . . ."

"I know," Barbara said. "I almost feel *guilty* about it."

A Great Owl. No doubt the first.

"B-Barbara . . ."

Neal stumbled back. Shaking his head no.

"Barbara. I was supposed to be the first . . . I—"

"Oh, don't fuss over what's right and what's wrong, Neal. You wanted an owl and I got you an owl. I did it last week."

A cloud as misty as the Goblin sky passed over Neal's eyes.

"What have you done?"

His voice echoed harsh through the hangar.

Barbara was taken aback. "Why, isn't that obvious, dear? I bagged you a Great Owl. The first in the history of Goblin, I daresay."

Neal fell to his knees.

"Neal . . . what *are* you doing?"

The bird fell in a feathered pile beside him. He could feel himself slipping . . . falling . . .

"Neal, dear. You *must* get ahold of yourself."

But Nash no longer heard the pleading of his wife . . . the voice of the first Gobliner to bag a Great Owl.

He felt himself slipping. Falling.

From where?

"From grace," he said. "From the books . . ."

"Neal . . ."

Neal Nash screamed; a deep bellow of rage that rattled the rafters of his trophy room . . . the nerves of his wife . . . and the glass that shielded his meaningless catch.

"Stand up, Neal," Barbara said, impatiently. "For Christ's sake. You're making it sound like I did the most terrible thing in the world. It's not like I'm not worried as it is. I broke a *rule,* Neal. A big one. For you." She shook her head. Neal wept. "You might've thought you'd been hiding your desire for that bird all along, dear, but a wife knows. *A wife knows.* And no silly ordinance has ever stopped us before. It's a wonderful gift, Neal, and when you finally come to see that the North Woods aren't going to miss *one* owl, you'll thank me for giving you the greatest gift of your life. Happy birthday," she said, flummoxed still. "Happy birthday, Hunter."

Then she turned and walked out of the hangar, back out under the crazed Goblin sky. The party was still going; Barbara would even say it was growing. And as she reentered the throng, she recalled the sound of her husband whimpering, the snotty sobs she'd heard as the hangar door closed behind her. She heard his cries in the music played by the band, in the laughter and shouts of the guests.

She even heard it in the falling rain, each drop a reflection of the sound Neal was making as he knelt among his trophies, crying rain among his game.

PRESTO

Dick Mable sat in the eighth row of a small crowded theater and might not have known his wife sat next to him if she weren't gripping his arm in terror. It was dark in there (*cave black,* he'd called it, finding the description to be clever) and, except for what was happening on the makeshift stage, you couldn't see a thing. Dick couldn't get over it. The show.

This guy Emperor was honestly unreal.

What he and his wife and about fifty others had witnessed so far was easily the best magic show they'd ever seen and *well* worth the eight-dollar tickets. It was crazy. Truly. *Crazy.* It was nothing like watching TV and nothing like those out-of-control Las Vegas shows where the men in glittering capes rode polar bears. This show was gritty. Almost to where Dick could feel the gravel beneath his dress shoes. The magician, Roman Emperor, was *right there,* fifteen feet in front of him at the most, using foldout tables as a stage and doing tricks Dick wouldn't have been able to figure out if you gave him a pencil, a pad, and a month. The Stake, the black-box theater on Main, was the kind of intimate place where, when a play came through, you could see the anxiety on an actor's face. The place was small. Tight. There was simply nowhere to hide the tricks! Mirrors and trapdoors, strings and pulleys . . . Dick couldn't spot any of it. And he'd certainly been trying.

"I'm scared," Theresa had whispered a few minutes ago, and Dick didn't blame her.

With TV, you always carried the indomitable suspicion that the reality of the illusion was somehow edited out. And the big Vegas shows may as well have been TV, you were so far from the stage anyway. But Dick Mable was forty-four years old. He'd seen a lot of shows. His nephew was in a loud grunge band and his niece sang opera in Kansas. He'd seen big productions and small, great shows and ones that weren't so much.

But this one? Christ, Dick could *smell* the show. And the smell was part grease, part sweat, and the unmistakable odor of honesty.

And yet . . . it was a magic show. Built on dishonesty.

"I can't look," Theresa said.

I can't stop, Dick thought.

He'd seen the show in the local listings in the back of *The Other,* the weekly alternative magazine that had proven much more interesting than the *Times.* Roman Emperor. The name was either cheeky or awesome, depending on how you looked at it, and Dick was sold.

Now, seated before the man and his assistant, Dick couldn't wrap his mind around what he was seeing. Of course every magician has secrets, but this maniac Emperor was *good.*

"Oh God," Theresa whispered, leaning into Dick. "What are they doing *now?*"

Dick had to admit, the trick looked dangerous. Emperor stood on one side of the stage. His master of ceremonies, a blonde whom Dick couldn't get a handle on (*Is she pretty? Is she sick? Is she perfect?*) stood across the shaky stage, an ax raised high in her hands.

"I will stop this tool with my mind," the blonde said. And everybody knew what that meant. She was going to throw it at Emperor and . . . stop it with her mind.

Dick looked for the strings.

A wood log stood at Emperor's feet. The blonde did the whole ring-around-the-weapon thing to show the audience there were no strings attached and even went as far as to hand the weapon out for the audience to inspect themselves. Dick wanted to hold it, but Theresa pulled the arm of his suit coat back as he reached out. Like she was scared he might catch something. Dick didn't entirely disagree with her.

Emperor paced as the audience inspected the weapon. In fact, he'd been pacing most of the show, as the (*sick? gorgeous?*) blonde did all the talking.

"It's so *dark*," Theresa whispered. Dick wasn't sure if she meant the lighting or the show itself.

Emperor finally stood motionless, but the animal energy within him still seemed to pulse. He had his back to the audience now, his head cocked toward the blonde. Dick guessed the magician was under forty, but it was very hard to tell. He was a throwback, to be sure, a character you'd see in a dramatization of the Old World. He wore tight slacks, black boots, a vest, and a white, ruffled button-down shirt, what Dick knew some people called a poet's shirt. Some gray showed in his mustache and sweaty black hair, but not much. So little, in fact, that it might have been applied for effect. Dick thought he looked like a poet bullfighter. A philosophical hunter. Despite his masculinity, there was something deeply neurotic about him. The way he paced. The way he stood. The unglued look in his eyes coupled with an unseen, but felt, confidence in his craft.

Beyond the prepared look of a showman, Dick detected fear.

And the blonde ... what was her name? Had she given it? When she first came out from backstage, Dick thought Theresa was going to kill him.

Oh, sure, Dick. Nice night out.

And yet as stunning as she was, there was something unnerving, too, a sense of fakery that outweighed her features.

She wore a cut-up version of a green-and-yellow Victorian dress, her chest testing the seams, her ivory skin smooth under the lights. The dress had been chopped into a skirt and her boots gave her tall frame a few extra inches. Shoulder-length blond hair half hid a face that came in and out of focus under the overheads.

She was feminine, Dick thought, absolutely. And yet ... animal, too.

Theresa didn't say a word about her. And Dick understood. The show was so good, so *fast,* that they didn't have time to look at her legs. And besides, in his way, Emperor was just as striking. If not more so.

"Oh God," Theresa said as the blonde received the ax back. "Here we go."

The blonde had dipped her hands into the darkness of the audience, and the weapon she brought back under the lights looked every bit as real as the tools Dick had seen about Theresa's father's toolshed. The blonde took the opposite side of the stage from Emperor and raised her eyebrows, silently asking if he was ready.

Emperor nodded once. Dick saw a bead of sweat drip from the tip of his nose.

The woman hurled the ax at his head so fast that the audience screamed as one.

SWOOSH

Dick closed his eyes. He had to. And when he opened them, he saw the ax blade suspended less than an inch from the magician's face.

The sound of the ax cutting the space between them remained strong in Dick's mind; the blonde's boot stomp upon the stage, too; the communal gasp of the audience when it seemed too late.

"Jesus *Christ*," Theresa said. "I can't take any more of this."

The blonde held her arm out as if an invisible beam tied her to the suspended ax. Dick looked for the strings.

Or was it Emperor that employed the trick? With his eyes on the blade, the magician's mouth formed a small circle, and he lifted his left hand. He made a subtle motion, as though wiping dust from the shoulder of his vest, a flick of the wrist, and the ax rose a few inches higher into the air.

Silence now. The blonde with her arm out, the magician staring down the high blade.

Then Emperor moved again and the ax began to spin. The audience gasped again as the ax dropped, fast, to the wood at the magician's black boots.

CHOP

It split the log in two.

The stage rattled. The crowd held their breath before releasing it in nervous laughter and applause.

The lack of music, the lack of explanation, added to the grittiness and Dick slid his dress shoes subconsciously against the theater's stone floor.

The blonde nodded and Emperor took a bow.

"How is it that the whole world doesn't know about this guy?" Dick asked his wife. But Theresa just gripped his arm harder. Her heart, she said, could barely take it. She was sure that ax was going to split the man's face and she'd have to relive that image forever. She knew all about how magicians had their secrets, secrets they don't share, but there was something different about this show. Something terrible. Something scary.

The blonde came to the center of the stage and asked for a

volunteer. Emperor paced behind her. Dick wanted to do it, but Theresa took hold of his wrists and made her point known. A man to the right of the stage beat him to it anyway. Emperor clasped his hands together and the woman explained the next trick.

"This time, *you* throw the ax at him. And he"—she fanned a smooth palm toward Emperor—"will be blind."

The crowd moaned. This was too much. The room for error, human error . . .

"It's too much!" Theresa said, louder than a whisper.

The volunteer was clearly nervous, but before he could back out the blonde had the ax in his hand and was showing him the most effective way to throw it.

"Use force," she said. "Do not be shy."

A slight hint of an accent. Dick couldn't place it. Finnish?

"Thank you, Maggie," Roman said.

The audience laughed.

Maggie, Dick thought. Then Maggie turned Roman around so that he was facing the audience.

The crowd was very still. Theresa was about set to break Dick's arm off. Someone sneaked out. Couldn't take it.

"Are you ready?" Maggie asked.

Roman, his back to her, nodded.

Maggie looked to the volunteer.

"We're ready," she said.

The volunteer threw the ax.

The theater lights went out.

Something fell hard to the stage.

The audience was up, yelling, asking what happened, asking if Emperor was okay.

Dick had a terrible vision of the lights coming back on to reveal the magician on the floor, the ax splitting the back of his skull, Maggie kneeling above him . . .

It's a small show, Dick thought. He tried to resist the thinking but it wasn't easy. *They're not as practiced as those people on TV, those fruitcakes in Vegas.*

Then, *Jesus Christ, was there an accident? IS HE DEAD?*

"What have I done!" the volunteer wailed.

The lights came on.

Maggie was smiling. The ax was frozen an inch from Emperor's skull. The volunteer fell to his knees and looked like he might cry. Then he started laughing.

"Fuck!" he cried, and the audience felt his relief.

Then the crowd was on their feet and cheering. Dick knew that, if he were ever to see any of these people on the street, he could say, *Yes. I was there, too.*

The ax spun slowly behind Emperor's head and came to a stop. The audience, still on their feet, hushed.

The blade cried out as it bent behind him, the weapon warped, folding in on itself. The handle snapped in two. Maggie put her hands on her hips and shook her head theatrically.

"Showing off," she said.

Finnish? Dick wondered. *Czech?*

The ax vanished. Smoke hung in the air behind the magician.

And that was it. The end of the show.

No music. No set design. No pyrotechnics. And yet . . . the greatest show Dick Mable had ever seen.

"Magic," Roman said, obviously awkward, clearly anxious, "is real."

Then he and Maggie bowed and together they slipped behind the black curtain, backstage.

People were slow to leave.

"Wow," Theresa said, a hand to her chest. "That was . . . brutal."

"It was *great*," Dick said.

"Where to now?" Theresa asked. "Know any good shrinks?"

But Dick didn't want to leave just yet. He *had* to meet this Roman Emperor.

"I was thinking we should step backstage. Let them know how wonderful that was. It's gotta be good to hear."

Theresa looked to the curtain as if a childhood ghost might be behind it. The thing from under the bed. The bogeyman in the closet at night.

Dick took her by the hand and led her to a back hallway. It was one of the perks of attending shows you read about in *The Other*: no security, no bodyguards, no fame. There was no fanfare back behind the curtain. No hangers-on. The hall was dark, but Dick saw light from a partially open door. Still dragging Theresa along, he quietly peeked inside.

Maggie was standing at the far end of the room, looking toward Roman slumped in a chair. The magician looked exhausted. He held a hand to the side of his head, as if his mind was tired.

Maggie saw Dick. He shivered when their eyes met.

"Welcome," she said, and Dick had a strange idea that a fog was rising around her, that specks of dirt showed on her shoulder and neck.

"I just had to tell you guys," Dick stammered, "that was amazing. The best show we've seen in years. Wouldn't you say so, T?"

He gripped his wife close. As if, without doing so, Theresa might be swallowed by the dark of the hall, and he'd be left alone with these two.

"Yes," Theresa said, peeking into the dressing room. "That was . . . horrifying."

"Thank you." Maggie smiled. "It all starts with an audience willing to believe."

Dick and Theresa smiled. These performer types were so . . . right on!

"I get it," Dick said. "But I gotta tell you . . . I looked for the strings . . . and couldn't see anything. Like . . . *at all.*"

For the first time, Roman cocked an ear in Dick and Theresa's direction. Then he looked over his shoulder at the couple.

"Thank God for that," he said.

And his voice was sharp, foreign perhaps, so direct that Dick felt strangely childish in its presence.

"How is it that the whole world doesn't know about you guys?" Dick asked.

"Dick!" Theresa said.

"You get what you're after," Maggie said. Roman simply stared. "What are you two after?"

"Us?" Dick asked, genuinely surprised. He looked at Theresa. "I guess a good night out."

"And are you having one?"

"Yes, we are. A great one."

Maggie held up empty palms and shrugged, as if to say, *See?*

Dick thought about it. Maybe she was just saying things to say, or maybe Roman didn't care about fame after all.

"Where are you guys tomorrow?" he asked.

"Goblin," Roman said.

"Ah," Dick said. "Strange town. You two will fit right in."

"Dick!" Theresa gripped his arm.

Then the four were silent for some time.

"Well, okay," Dick said. "Just wanted to tell you both how good we thought it was. The best show we've seen in years."

"Goodbye," Theresa said kindly. Then she led Dick away from the dressing room door. But Dick sneaked his head back once more.

"Do you need directions to Goblin? I know the way."

"We do, too," Maggie said.

"Well then, uh . . . how about sharing a secret or two?"

Roman raised a hand and the door started to shut on its own.

"I understand, I understand," Dick said. He pulled his head out of the way just before it closed.

In the darkness of the hall, he whispered to Theresa, "Goblin is gonna love them."

But Theresa was just happy to be exiting the theater. Yes, it was a great show, but sometimes great left you feeling afraid.

2

When Pete found out that Mike got tickets to see Roman Emperor he was very, very jealous. *Pete* was the one who was into magic. Always had been. Everybody in Goblin Middle knew that. Without Pete, Mike wouldn't know a white rabbit from a levitation. And now every kid in Goblin Middle was getting tickets and Pete . . . well, Pete might not be able to afford one.

He needed eight dollars. And for as small as the number sounded to some, it was a big one to Pete. His parents might or might not take him to a midnight magic show, one that was announced last-minute, and one that featured the indisputable king of dirty magic. If Dad took one look at any issue of *Presto* he probably wouldn't let Pete go. Hell, he might even ground him for asking.

Pete couldn't chance that.

Wasn't even going to ask. He'd ride his bike downtown and get one for himself. He *had* to see Emperor. For Pete, Roman Emperor was what Captain America was for the other kids. He'd read everything *Presto* published. The monthly magazine was a wonder ground for his imagination. He'd read about *all* the traveling magicians. The Spell Circuit, as *Presto* called it. They were like modern outlaws! Sleight of human hands; nothing like the boring animal trainers in Las Vegas and New York City. No way. The magicians on the Spell Circuit were usually old-school men of magic who performed for peanuts. A whole medium of odd men with odder assistants (none more so than Emperor's Maggie) playing empty theaters, high schools, libraries, dive bars, comedy clubs, underground speakeasies, and abandoned churches. The more Pete learned about them the more he loved them. He loved that his friends didn't care. The circuit's obscurity made him feel like he *owned* it. Roman Emperor, whom Mike and the others just *had* to see now, wasn't even in the top five in *Presto*'s popularity poll! And though none of the magicians were famous, Roman Emperor was about as infamous as it got. Pete had been introduced to the rogue magician by Mr. Bench, owner of Goblin's Magic, the one magic store in the city, and Mr. Bench said that Emperor might be the *best*.

He had to get a ticket. For the love of justice, he had to.

At home, in a desk drawer, Pete had a black-and-white photo of a very young Emperor chained to a giant wheel. Maggie stood beside him, holding a set of keys. The caption read,

EMPEROR REFUSES TO ESCAPE BEHIND CURTAINS

"If there's a trick to be seen," Emperor was quoted, *"let them see it."*

Pete *loved* that. Anything Emperor did was done in the open. Unlike the most celebrated men of the circuit, he never hid backstage or behind a curtain; Roman Emperor never stepped foot inside a trick cabinet. That very article suggested Emperor was making the other magicians nervous with his bravado; they were concerned he'd slip up one evening and give trade secrets away. But Pete was awed by this. A magician so edgy that the others cried stop.

And yet . . . weren't they all just trying to deceive? As Mr. Bench would say, *Fakers crying foul is a bit like bullies crying tears.*

Other articles, later articles, talked a lot about the infamous Kerry Theatre show in Morgantown, West Virginia. Planned as a unified promotion of the circuit, it was attended by almost every magician. But it was here that Roman was confronted backstage by others in an attempt to *swap secrets.* Emperor refused outright, supported (always) by Maggie, citing secrecy as the magician's only true freedom. Pete read that Don Deanie said it was *bullshit* (he used that word!) and tried to strong-arm it out of the young Emperor. But (this was Pete's favorite part) when Deanie went to charge Emperor, he found he couldn't move. The other magicians searched Deanie for strings.

Emperor took Maggie by the hand and left before his turn was up. The article quoted Emperor as having said, *"There's nothing great about the great Don Deanie!"*

Mr. Bench laughed at this story and told Pete that it was exactly what the magicians were looking for: promotion.

Don't believe too much of that, Mr. Bench said. *Emperor isn't so dirty, and the others aren't so clean.*

But Pete was simply smitten. Like himself, Emperor was an outcast. Walking the halls of Goblin Middle, his black hair hanging in his eyes, Pete could relate. The other kids looked at him the way he imagined the other magicians eyed Emperor. And here, not only had Emperor snubbed the entire circuit by not performing for them, but he'd officially insulted one of its elder statesmen. It was the day the Spell Circuit blacklisted Emperor, no longer including his shows in their promotions. They claimed he dabbled in *dirty magic,* and Deanie said that hosting Emperor on a bill would be tantamount to inviting a dangerous criminal into a school playground.

Emperor was out.

"He's one of the villains," Pete's mom told him.

And she was sort of right. Just like comic books needed the evil genius, so did the world of magic. And yet Pete couldn't care less if Emperor was considered good or bad. Between the way he dressed, the things he said, and Maggie, Emperor was electrifying. And what Pete cared about most was his *tricks*.

He asked Mr. Bench how they might be done.

"This one here," Pete said, pointing to a photo of Maggie's head turned completely around. "She'd have to have been wearing her clothes backward the entire show, or ... oh ... I don't know how they did this."

"The secret is the fun part, Pete," Mr. Bench always said. And Pete understood that, as the proprietor of the city's one magic shop, he had to say that.

"But let me ask you," Mr. Bench added, his mustache curled up into a smile. "What makes you so sure there's a trick? Why can't it just be *magic*?"

Despite not telling (or perhaps not knowing) the answer to Pete's questions about Emperor, Mr. Bench spotted a legitimate enthusiast in Pete and performed simpler tricks for him all the time. Pete had no ordinary boy's interest in magic. He studied the magazines like other kids from Goblin Middle studied girls. So, encouraged by this audience of one, Mr. Bench brought out his tricks in a series of Sunday meetings with the boy. Pete, without knowing it, had forced Mr. Bench to brush up on a lot of things. The aged proprietor was suddenly rereading old issues of *Presto* and *Magic Magazine,* the very rags he'd been selling for years. Behind the red curtains that led to his office in the back of the store, he relearned many old gags and practiced the more difficult card maneuvers. He'd dusted off the glass of his longtime mirror and found in his reflection a fountain of youth, inspiration to be *magicking* again.

Pete had brought it all back to life again for him. A trick all its own.

And Mr. Bench, in return, encouraged Pete's interests and supplied him with everything he needed to know about the circuit. He was, of course, the means by which Pete learned that his hero was coming to Goblin.

A week before the show, Pete came in alone, as he often did, and Mr. Bench motioned for him to come to the counter.

"I *just* got some tour dates you may be interested in, Pete," he said, feigning a casual tone. He handed Pete a piece of paper.

The list of cities and dates conjured complex images in Pete's young mind. Places he'd never seen, but ones he'd heard of. And he certainly knew the magicians well.

Gail Gordon in Boise, Idaho.

Invisible Williams III in Des Moines.

"Card Shark Attack" Wills in Montgomery, Alabama.

Finn the Fantastic in New York City.

Pete recalled black-and-white photos of Finn the F pulling rabbits from the hats of people in the crowd.

"Read farther down," Mr. Bench said.

Pete did.

Sugar Jay and the Outlaws in Chicago.

Michael the Gifted in Detroit.

Roman . . .

Pete dropped the paper. Had to pick it up again, read the listing once more.

"I don't understand," he said.

Mr. Bench laughed. "Yes you do."

"But . . . but . . ." Pete's hands trembled, the paper waving like it was alive. "It says Goblin, Mr. Bench."

"So it does."

"But Goblin is . . . that's . . . that's right here."

Mr. Bench laughed again.

"And so it is." He looked through the front glass, through the big blue, reversed letters painted there. GOBLIN'S MAGIC. Out to the bustling city beyond.

Pete, still staring at the paper, suddenly squealed.

"Roman Emperor is coming *here*?" he yelled, as if only Mr. Bench could make it official. "This isn't . . . an old list? A *mistake*?"

"Hmmm . . ." Mr. Bench said, taking the paper back and pretending to study it. "Nope. No mistake here. This is a genuine listing."

Pete turned red. Then he turned his head to the ceiling and howled.

"Holy cow! Mr. Bench! What do I do? What am I supposed to do? Roman Emperor is coming to *Goblin*! *What am I supposed to do?*"

Mr. Bench laughed. "Hey, hey, okay. Calm down."

"Calm down?"

"On second thought, no. That's the worst advice I can give you. Never calm down. But what should you do? Well . . . you should get yourself a ticket is what you should do."

Pete took the list and read it again.

ROMAN EMPEROR — GOBLIN — DOMINO THEATER
(Peak Show) — $8

He wrinkled his brow.

"What does that mean, Mr. Bench? *Peak show*?"

"The peak of night, Pete," Mr. Bench winked. "Midnight."

Pete's joyous expression fell from his face. In its stead was concern.

Midnight.

Would his parents let him go? Could he even risk *not* going by asking them?

"What is it, Pete?"

"Nothing, Mr. Bench. Honestly. Just . . . *wow.*"

He'd figure it out on his own. He'd have to. Nothing was going to stop him from seeing this show. One of the *Presto* magicians, the most feared magician on the Spell Circuit, was coming to . . . *Goblin?*

Pete felt like his legs were on fire. He couldn't stand still. Roman Emperor was coming to *Pete's* Goblin. Man! This wasn't "cool." This was *huge.* Oh . . . he was going to go. There was no worrying about *that.*

"You probably don't have to worry about it selling out," Mr. Bench said. "Our industry is . . . obscure, as you know. But I'd get a ticket as soon as possible if I were you. Just to be sure."

Suddenly Pete felt like he didn't know enough about Emperor. As if he'd failed to study all the material required for this unbelievable pop exam. When Pete first started reading *Presto,* he'd gravitated to the more forthcoming magicians. The guys who put their tricks on display or published them in magazines so readers could try to figure them out. Emperor, secretive as he was, had always been a vague impression to Pete. A dark, mythic figure who graced the pages of the magic mags with the sort of mystery ghost stories were made of. Unlike a lot of the readers who sent letters to the editors, Pete was fascinated with his reluctance to expose his moves. But for this, and because the other magicians had more or less ostracized Emperor years ago, material was slim. There just wasn't *that much* written about him. Most readers wanted a trick, a code to crack.

Roman Emperor seemed to have no code.

"I hear his live shows are thrillers," Mr. Bench said.

Pete nodded enthusiastically. "Me, too. People have *passed out.*"

"Is that right?"

Pete nodded. Then he checked his watch. How much time did he have to reread everything he'd ever read about Emperor? A week?

"I gotta go," he suddenly said. "*Thank you,* Mr. Bench."

Then he was out the front door of Goblin's Magic and up on his bike, pedaling home.

He had a lot of homework to do.

Roman Emperor was coming to Goblin.

Pete cocked his head back and howled delight into the early-evening Goblin sky.

3

Pete was a good kid, but he also *did* know where his mom kept her money. And it could hardly be considered stealing in this case. He simply had to see this show. He was one of only nine hundred people in the *country* with a subscription to *Presto.* To have one of the magazine's "Top 40 Active Magicians" coming to his hometown was the biggest news of his life (Emperor came in at number thirty-eight, but the blurb about him said he could be in the top fifteen if he ever learned to play nice with the others.) So . . .

So Mom left Pete alone on Wednesday afternoons. Though it was difficult to swallow, he'd have to wait a few days. He couldn't do it when she was home. Just could not risk putting himself in a position to explain what he needed the money for. He hadn't worked out yet how he was going to tell her or even if he was going to at all. But come Wednesday, he'd sneak into her dresser, take the eight dollars, ride his bike downtown, and get back before she got home. The articles in the magazine, Emperor's meager recorded history, would have to suffice for now.

But reading about Roman drove Pete only crazier.

With his bedroom door locked, he studied. And with every article he read he was aware of a new sensation: the personal touch of reading up on a man who was coming to Goblin.

One *Presto* review of a live Emperor show was three years old. There was no photo, but the write-up was fascinating:

SPRAGUEVILLE, RHODE ISLAND—

WADE "MAGIC FINGERS" McGOWAN WASN'T ON THE STAGE BUT HE TURNED SOME HEADS ALL THE SAME WHEN HE ENTERED THE HARDY HAR HAR CLUB IN DOWNTOWN SPRAGUEVILLE. SEEMS McGOWAN WAS AS INTERESTED IN THE LOCAL DEBUT OF ROMAN EMPEROR AS THE TEN OTHER MEN AND WOMEN IN THE AREA WHO WERE IN ATTENDANCE. EMPEROR, A UNIQUE AND EXCITING FACE ON THE SPELL CIRCUIT, WOWED THE SMALL CROWD WITH DANGEROUS TRICKS THAT INCLUDED TOSSED SABERS AND AN ESCAPE FROM A BEAR TRAP. AFTER WARMING UP THE AUDIENCE WITH THE HELP OF AN ALLURING BLOND ASSISTANT (WHO, IN SOME RESPECTS, STOLE THE SHOW), EMPEROR WASTED NO TIME GETTING TO THE THEATRICS. THOUGH NOT ONE MUCH FOR GAB, EMPEROR IS A VERY EXCITING MAGICIAN WITH A HEADY RESPECT FOR THE CRAFT. McGOWAN HAD THIS TO SAY AFTER,

"ANYTIME I'M IN TOWN LONG ENOUGH TO CATCH ANOTHER GUY'S ACT, IT'S A GOOD THING. IT WAS A GOOD SHOW."

Hmm, Pete thought. *A good show.*

A lukewarm magician-to-magician review to be sure. Pete suspected jealousy. He picked up another magazine.

Magic Monthly printed photos of twelve touring magicians and listed their statistics beneath them. Pete loved this kind of thing. Finn the Fantastic was one of the twelve featured. So was Emperor. Pete compared the two.

AGE:

Finn the Fantastic: *49*

Roman Emperor: *35*

FAVORITE CITY TO PERFORM IN:

Finn the Fantastic: *Cleveland, Ohio. I love the nightlife. And the burgers!*

Roman Emperor: BLANK

ORIGIN:

Finn the Fantastic: *Minneapolis. The big city. Go Gophers!*

Roman Emperor: BLANK

ACHIEVEMENTS:

Finn the Fantastic: *MAA Newcomer of the Year. 5 time MAA Magician of the Year. Runner-up twice. First place in the annual Midwest Magician Convention 11 years running. Performed live on Channel 8* St. Paul in the Afternoon *and once on* Good Morning Alabama. *8 times on the cover of* Magic Monthly. *Thanks guys!*

Roman Emperor: *None.*

INFLUENCES:

Finn the Fantastic: *The Great Don Deanie. Art Andrews.*

Roman Emperor: *Every magician that has come before me.*

HOBBIES:

Finn the Fantastic: *Drawing. Driving. Shuffleboard. Starting my own line of tricks—Finntastic. Look for it soon!*

Roman Emperor: BLANK

FAVORITE TRICK OF YOUR OWN/SPECIALTY:

Finn the Fantastic: *Moving things with my mind.*

Roman Emperor: *Moving things with my mind.*

Pete knew Finn was being modest. He could have named fifty more awards he'd received. The entire Finntastic catalog rested in a chest in Pete's bedroom. But Emperor . . .

Pete experienced that personal touch again. Emperor had given answers Pete no doubt brushed past the first time he'd read the article. But now there seemed to be more meaning in them. As if even with the blanks, Emperor had spoken.

Pete imagined him onstage at the Domino in Goblin. In his mind's eye an amalgamation of every black-and-white photo of Emperor and Maggie became one, until the stage in the Domino was big enough to hold them all.

He read on.

Next up: *Presto*'s "Year in Review" from two years ago. The cover showed a top hat with white stars spilling out. The text read:

WHAT A YEAR FOR MAGIC!
PRESTO TELLS YOU WHAT HAPPENED WHERE
AND WHO MADE WAVES

It was a "best of" listing. And since there were only so many magicians on the circuit, the same names came up often. The Newcomer of the Year, Ron Dander, was a guy Pete remembered reading about. But Dander had dropped out of the business about the time the magazine came out. Top Magician went to Finn the Fantastic.

Emperor's name wasn't listed anywhere. Not once.

Whether it was because the issue came out so soon after the Kerry Theatre fiasco, Pete didn't know.

Not a single ranking out of the two hundred or so possibilities was awarded to Roman Emperor, a magician who, Pete knew, had more presence in the scene than a good half of the names. Reading this particular issue, one wouldn't think Emperor existed at all.

Pete found this odd.

Emperor must have had the recent respect of his peers to have been invited to the Kerry Theatre in the first place. So why, Pete wondered, the freeze-out *before* the incident? Chilled by the thought, Pete suspected Emperor was invited to the Kerry Theatre just so the others could ask him his secrets. Maybe Mr. Bench was right when he'd said Emperor could end up being the best of all of them. And maybe the other magicians, a union headed by Don Deanie, feared this.

Pete was liking Emperor more and more with everything he read.

He read on. *Presto* from the same time period.

FOR SOME, TOURING IS NOT A SEASONAL THING.
IT APPEARS THAT ROMAN EMPEROR IS SET TO

PERFORM IN EVERY CITY THE COUNTRY HAS TO
OFFER. HE CLAIMS NO PLACE OF RESIDENCE AND
YOU CAN PROBABLY SEE HIS BLACK MERCEDES
PULL INTO YOUR TOWN IF YOU LOOK LONG
ENOUGH. HERE'S TO HOPING ALL THAT WORK PAYS
OFF.

Pete figured it had. Somewhat, anyway. Emperor was as familiar a name now as Wade McGowan or Albert Rich. That seemed
a long way to come.

And the more he read, the more impatient he got for that
ticket.

4

Mike wasn't the only kid with his ticket that Tuesday in
school. Four other kids had theirs, and rumor was that
everybody was going to the midnight magic show at the
Domino Theater. It was the biggest topic at school. It was all anyone could talk about. Pete wasn't even sure how everybody knew!
One kid's dad said he'd take him himself. Another kid said his
parents bought three tickets. Girls, boys, *everybody* was going. In
one of Pete's classes the teacher mentioned Harry Houdini. Referred to him as the "best there ever was." Pete turned red in his
seat. He wanted so badly to get up and tell everybody about Finn
the Fantastic and Roman Emperor and the Kerry Theatre and all
the touring and every little thing he'd read. But he didn't want to
share this with everyone else. None of this! Magic was *his*. The only
thing he had to himself.

And here that prized possession seemed to be slipping from
his fingers.

By Wednesday morning another fifteen kids had tickets. Pete considered stealing the eight dollars from a fellow student. In class he eyeballed pockets, looking for loose bills, like he was starving and there might be bread in there. The wait was torturing him. The school hours sluggishly bumped into one another like bumper cars driven by children. By lunchtime the coming midnight magic show was the only topic of conversation and Pete was losing his mind.

Ryan Dickson called him Roman *Empire*!

Oh, how the misinformation was driving Pete mad.

"He can make any animal out of a balloon. Even a kangaroo."

"He dresses in a long black cape and pulls bunnies from a hat."

"He can read your mind and write down your thoughts before you tell them to him."

Animal balloons? Bunnies? These kids were in for a surprise. Wait until Maggie hurled an ax at Emperor's face!

Pete smiled. At some point in the impossibly long day, he'd come to understand that all these frilly rumors were proof that nobody in Goblin was closer to Roman Emperor than Pete himself.

Pete *knew* Emperor.

He was the only one in Goblin Middle who knew Emperor wore a brown vest. A white shirt. Black boots. That he had wild black hair. That he drove an awesome black Mercedes. That Maggie was more than the usual assistant and actually emceed the shows. That Emperor refused to hide his tricks from the audience while refusing to *show* them to his peers. That a long time ago he made some enemies in the business because of this. That he once left HOBBIES blank on a personal profile in *Magic Monthly*.

That some peers said Emperor used dirty magic.

Pete watched the clock.

The hour was approaching, his exile at last. When he got home he was going immediately to Mom's dresser, pocketing the eight bucks, and *finally getting that ticket*. And the closer that time came, the closer Pete felt to the curious magician. It was a bond he'd never felt before. Forget who didn't know what about Roman Emperor. Forget who said what. And when the bell did ring, things became a speedy blur for Pete, and he wouldn't even remember the bus ride home. It was as if he were traveling through black smoke, a mist the color of Emperor's car, as the frightening magician drove toward Goblin, the alluring Maggie at his side.

Entering his own house, Pete thought of Emperor's hands on the wheel of the Mercedes. Saw magic rings upon each finger. And within each ring was a swirling mist of black. The hurried blur of a true fan finally getting the money together to come see him.

And beyond those fingers . . . pale Maggie. She was smiling in Pete's mind's eye. Like she knew Pete was coming to see the show. Like she wanted him to come as badly as Pete wanted to himself.

As fields of dark-green grass passed by the car window behind her, Pete imagined her speaking directly to him.

Hurry up, Pete, she seemed to say. *Get a ticket. And come see our show.*

Pete floated up the stairs, as if governed by an adult desire, a deep propulsion he'd never quite felt before.

By the time he got to Mom's dresser, he was ticklish with eagerness, with swirling black joy, and he wanted to feel that way forever.

5

I *didn't even check if Mom was home.*

But it was too late for that. His hand was already in there, pushing her underwear aside. He was more worried about there being enough money. *That* would be a problem he didn't quite have an answer for.

But in the back corner of the drawer was a bundle of bills amounting to a hundred and ten dollars. He slipped out eight singles (and then one more just in case) and set everything back where it was.

I'll pay her back.

He held the money up and saw it as a makeshift stage with little figurines of Roman and Maggie upon it. In his mind's eye Roman held out a steady open palm and Maggie rose, arms at her side, toward the darkness of a theater ceiling.

He shut the drawer and raced downstairs. His shoes squeaked on the laundry room floor as he made it to the door leading to the garage.

His bike sat inert beneath the bright hanging bulb. As if spotlighted, on a stage of its own, ready to play a star role in Pete's journey for the ticket.

The green paint looked like the landscapes he imagined Roman and Maggie driving through, on their way to Goblin.

He pressed the garage door opener on the wall then rushed up onto the bike seat. To Pete, it felt like curtains were rising, a magic show about to begin. He half expected Maggie to be standing in the drive, raising a palm of her own, as . . .

As an ax comes barreling toward your skull!

Pete blinked the sudden vision away and tore off down the empty drive.

To downtown Goblin! His watch told him it was three twenty-nine P.M. He'd have to time the trip down so he'd know exactly when to head back. He had to beat Mom.

He made a left on Northsouth, Goblin's second main road. Christmas ran parallel to Northsouth on opposite ends of town and Pete thanked God he didn't have to burn rubber down that sloppy gravel.

The wind in his eyes, the cars whizzing by, and the faces of the

Gobliners who drove them all felt like part of the incredible mission he was on. Perhaps there were secret agents sent from Don Deanie's camp, watching Pete pedal, weighing when to leap out, when to stop Emperor from receiving another ticket sale?

Pete cackled a high-pitched laughter. Remote facts about all the magicians on the Spell Circuit rolled like bike wheels through his mind, spinning violently around a very powerful hub that could have been Roman Emperor with his ringed hands to the sky.

When downtown came into view, Pete's watch said three thirty-six. This was going to work out. He had plenty of time to make it to the box office at the Woodruff, Goblin's nicest hotel, then pedal home. He might even have time to stop by Mr. Bench's and show the ticket off.

The Goblin Zoo was built on the very northern edge of downtown, and when Pete passed it he thought of Eula the prized gorilla, as if she were part of the magic show. As if Emperor might pull her from a hat.

"From a hat!" Pete cried out, smiling, pedaling rapid-fire, his nerves electric with the prospect of holding a ticket for a legitimate circuit magician.

Making a hard right on Angel, Pete saw the municipal buildings ahead. He knew which was which because Dad forced him to pay attention to such things.

Quit reading that magazine, Dad always told him. *You're never gonna get the layout of downtown if you're not looking.*

And yet, Pete was actually biking the fastest route to the Woodruff. When he hit Concord people hollered at him to *watch it,* but he slowed down only when he saw two Goblin Police officers slowly trucking uphill on the sidewalk. Their long, rubbery arms swung at their sides, and the dark aviators hid their eyes. Pete didn't want to mess with the Goblin Police. Dad and Mom talked about them the way some people talked about spiders, or heights, or the dark.

By three fifty-two he was in the nicer part of downtown, closer to those municipal buildings. The courthouse. The waterworks. The morgue. He passed great glass storefronts with huge photos of beautiful women and ebony podiums displaying cologne. More than one store boasted Goblin souvenirs, and each of these had miniature replicas of The Hedges, the maddening tourist attraction at the far eastern border of town.

"The Woodruff!" Pete called out, spotting its roof between closer buildings. He felt the lump of bills in his pocket, Mom's money, to make sure it was still there.

Another police officer rounded the sidewalk ahead and Pete removed his hand from his pocket. The man turned his head slowly, tracking Pete it seemed, and Pete saw himself in jail, pacing, missing Emperor's show.

Then he imagined Emperor bending the prison bars with his mind.

Come out, Emperor might say. *Don't miss this.*

Pete wasn't going to miss this. No way.

He reached the lobby of the Woodruff at four oh six. It had taken him thirty-seven minutes to get there. He'd have to head back by four forty-five to be safe and home before five thirty. If it took ten minutes to get the ticket, he'd have twenty-nine minutes to spare downtown. Would he have time to stop by Goblin's Magic to show it off?

Yes, Pete thought, smiling. He would.

6

Pete left his bike outside. He waited impatiently while a man bought tickets for a singer Pete's dad liked. When his turn came up and he asked for a ticket, the balding but young man behind the window shook his head. Pete felt all the air escape his body at once. But the man wasn't saying no.

"I just can't believe how well this show is selling," he said.

Pete smiled, and suddenly he no longer saw the other kids at Goblin Middle as encroaching on his territory; rather he saw them as making up a big crowd. A crowd Emperor deserved.

Pete slid the eight dollars across the counter and the broker handed him a purple ticket. Pete held it like it was a baby bird.

GENERAL ADMISSION
ROMAN EMPEROR – DOMINO THEATER – $8
DOORS 11:30 – SHOW 12:00

"Hey, kid," the man in the booth said. "Wanna step out of the way?"

Pete looked up to see a woman, frowning, next in line. He'd been staring at the words on the ticket, lost in the incredible realness of it.

"Sorry!"

Then he bolted from the Woodruff lobby.

He knew Mr. Bench's shop was around the corner from Transistor Planet, and he could see that from where he stood outside the hotel. He walked his bike, experiencing a sense of floating, as if even the Goblin Police couldn't reach him, he was so high.

"Mr. Bench!" Pete yelled, leaving his bike out front and running up to the counter. "Look!"

The purple ticket looked even better in Goblin's Magic.

"Well, what have we here?" Mr. Bench said, adjusting his glasses. "You don't say, Pete. It looks like you're going to see Roman Emperor in person, after all."

"Yes!" Pete said, trying to keep his cool but failing. "Isn't it . . . isn't it *great?*"

"It's the best news I've heard all week."

"Thank you, Mr. Bench, for telling me he was coming."

Mr. Bench smiled. "Well, Emperor may keep secrets, but I do not. And that's not all you're going to thank me for. I looked around a little. Found some things you might be interested in. C'mere."

Mr. Bench knelt behind the counter and returned with a stack of magazines and newspapers and loose pieces of paper.

"Seems there's more to learn about Roman Emperor than we thought."

Pete thought he was going to wet his pants. "Holy cow, Mr. Bench."

The pile on the glass counter was tall. Pete reached out to touch the pages, wanted to absorb it all at once.

"For you," Mr. Bench said.

"But I don't have any—"

Mr. Bench shooed this away with a quick hand gesture. "Money is funny, Pete, but it doesn't make you smile like magic does. Go on. You'd better get. You've got a lot of reading to do."

Between the ticket and the magazines, Pete couldn't wrap his head around it.

He took the stack greedily.

"Thank you, Mr. Bench. Thank you! You're the best man . . . ever!"

Mr. Bench laughed. "Oh yeah? Well you're not such a bad kid, yourself. Make sure to stop in next week, after you've seen the show. I expect you to tell me how he does what he does. Deal?"

"Yes. Deal."

Pete made for the door.

"Pete," Mr. Bench said, "pay attention to him. He really might be the best."

Pete blushed like the compliment was given to himself.

He made it back home with minutes to spare. Time enough to start reading. Mom didn't get home until five forty-five. Pete didn't worry about whether she'd notice he'd been in her dresser. He hardly heard her call hello from downstairs.

The material Mr. Bench had just given him was unfathomably right on.

And there was one thing all the write-ups and reviews seemed to agree with, one idea that made itself known in every piece or blurb printed about the mysterious magician: Emperor was so good that it appeared, even to the experts, that his magic was real.

Pete stared at the ticket, imagining Roman Emperor walking into his bedroom, crouching beside his bed, telling him that it was true. That his magic was real. Then the man proved it, and Pete watched as his bedroom became a chamber of spells, the box from which all the impossible things were pulled.

Pete read on, ignoring the chill he'd felt at his vision. The horrible reality of how frightening it would be if it were true; if Roman Emperor had dabbled in dirty magic, and was able to do . . . anything he wanted to.

"How awful," Pete said, without realizing he had spoken.

How different, how awful, the man might seem, if Pete were to discover, somehow, that his magic was real.

He pulled his blanket over his shoulders and read on, subconsciously shaking these thoughts away, until the idea was in pieces, floating to the corners of his room, no strings involved, an unseen magic trick of his own.

7

Emperor's magic *was* real.

8

As a child, walking the sandy streets of the marketplace with his father, Roman Emperor was frightened by a man in rags who leapt out of the shadows with a cold grin.

Don't worry, Father said. *A street performer.*

But as Roman's father made to step around him, the man in rags leapt in front of the child once again.

Excuse us, Father said, gripping young Roman by the wrist.

But the stranger pulled out a playing card and flashed its face for the father and son to see. It was the ten of hearts.

You see it? You see it? the man in rags asked.

Yes, Roman said. *I see it.*

The man in rags let out a small cry of happiness. The child was interested. From his tattered shirt he produced a whole stack of cards, many more than a single deck, Roman thought. The man slid the ten of hearts into the middle of the stack. To Roman it looked like a knife slicing skin.

The man in rags shuffled the cards. To Roman, this shuffling was as graceful as a dance; it looked to him like the man was pouring cream from palm to palm. Satisfied, he fanned the cards out just inches from young Roman's face. The boy's dark countenance intensified. He was confused.

Go on, Roman, Father said. *Take one.*

Roman thought hard. He could only pick one? He wanted it to represent him somehow.

Go ahead, Roman.

Roman took the one at the far right side of the fan. The man in rags smiled. Emperor's father bent down and flipped the card over for his son.

Ten of hearts.

Bravo, Father said, only partially impressed. Then he took Roman's wrist again.

But Roman was rooted to the sandy street.

How did he know which card I'd take, Father?

Come on, Roman.

Father?

The man in rags put a finger to his lips, letting the child know he wasn't going to be the one to tell him.

It's called a trick, Father said, impatient. *Low art.*

But Roman stared at the man's sandy hands. He could have easily picked the next card over. He almost had.

Possibilities, things he'd never considered before, traveled fast through his mind.

All the cards in the stack were the same.

The man somehow made the card more attractive in the spread.

The man could predict the future.

The man could read minds or at least force someone to do something.

Whatever it was, in the end, it didn't matter. What got Roman's blood rushing was the *suggestion* the trick made. The hint that mysterious powers could exist.

His father dismissed it, but the man in rags had exposed Roman to the core of magic. Years later he'd call it his *first glimpse behind the curtain . . . down the comforting hall of the beyond.*

Roman started studying magic at a rapid pace.

At the library. At the bookstores. At school. In the early days, he didn't even want to be able to explain the tricks to himself. With each new trick he learned, he was struck by two very different emotions: the *satisfaction* for figuring it out and the *disappointment* for knowing how it worked. Roman learned fast that a magician had to remind himself how glorious magic was by eliciting that wonder on the faces of his marks.

He would struggle with this paradox for a long time.

He told his father about it but Father only dismissed it. Told him his mother wouldn't have approved. Roman didn't believe that. In fact, sometimes he imagined he performed for her ghost. He imagined her sitting up in her casket, the last way he'd seen her, her skin dry as parchment, flaking as she smiled, as she said,

How'd you do it, Roman? Tell me.

Other times he pretended his dead mother was his assistant, bringing him the table upon which he would work, adjusting the strings and small pulleys, even speaking to the audience on his behalf.

If Father had known how much Roman was practicing, he'd have sent him to the academy. And by hiding it, Roman had to work twice as hard; deception upon deception. And yet, he did not avoid Father altogether. Doing so would be admitting he was hiding something. Instead Roman overcompensated, trailing Father through the house, bothering him endlessly, and playing him twice daily at chess.

Father always won. Father loved chess like Roman loved magic.

This marked the period in Roman's magic education when he learned the beauty of being the only person in the room who knew the trick was on display. It was a sensation he came to adore. At a friend's house he pretended to lift silverware with his mind when only the friend's grandfather was watching. At school he talked to a fellow student, deftly slipping their things into their desk, giving them a little jolt when they turned to find the table-top empty. He pulled jewels from his aunt's pocket, feigning sur-prise as real as her own.

Roman was well past the point of it all being just a phase. He came to loathe the word *hobby*.

The thought he put into it, the emotional upheaval it sparked in him, and the grace with which he handled it were the markings of a man who'd heard his calling, and not the fancy of a child play-ing imaginary games. It was healthy for him (he would be tor-tured without it) but it was grave, too. He respected it more and more with each passing session ... each practice ... each new trick learned. And soon this respect swelled into reverence. Magic was a living thing he could identify with more than he could his own father. A beast. And when he rode this beast, the reins com-fortable in his hands, his name blazed in his mind as if on fire above infinite clubs across the globe.

ROMAN EMPEROR!

A real man of magic. But not yet a man of *real* magic.

9

The day Roman told his father there was no need for him to enroll in college was the day his father's most paranoid fantasies became real. Roman said he was going to be a magician, and that there was no schooling better than his own.

His father cursed the man in rags from so many years ago. Then he burned a ten of hearts in the kitchen sink.

Roman challenged him to a game of chess.

If you beat me, I'll enroll. But if I beat you, you must give me your blessings for this journey.

His father agreed. And Roman knew that to beat his father, he'd have to employ a little magic.

The two sat down at the kitchen table, facing each other in the light from the fireplace.

Roman had to be patient. He couldn't start performing his tricks until the pieces on the board were spread out enough to cause diversions. *Cover.* If he could remain in the game long enough for that to happen, he had a chance.

He was able to play it safe long enough to watch the two sides advance toward each other slowly. And then, heart racing, in front of his father's open eyes, he deftly switched two pieces from where they stood. Then he stole an extra pawn when he was supposed to take just one. His sleight of hand was so deft that his father made no sign of noticing the changes. The disappearance and reappearance of the pieces under the nose of an expert was, for Roman, the greatest performance of his life to date.

Did Father even know he was losing? It might not have concerned him if he had. His seventeen-year-old son had never shown the talent for chess that he hoped he would and every game ended the same. So when Roman calmly reached across the board and moved his rook (sliding Father's king one space over in the process), he said something he'd never said before:

Checkmate, Father.

Father eyed the board for a long time. He eyed the pieces Roman had taken. Then he looked to Roman's hands and Roman knew.

Father understood what happened.

Excellent, Father said at last. *Truly.*

Then Father cried and rose to hug his son.

Promise me, Roman, that you will never be a man in rags. That you will always present yourself with delicacy. That you will not magic for money.

The last part of the promise Roman made would eventually be stitched inside the very vest he wore onstage.

NEVER MAGIC FOR MONEY

Within a month of the compromised game of chess, Roman Emperor was living in the back of the Caper Clothing warehouse, performing magic for mannequins.

His first crowd. Living or not, he gave them his all. Just as he had performed for Mother's ghost so long ago.

Magic for the unliving. Magic for the departed.

Magic for the dead.

10

It wasn't difficult for Roman to go unnoticed as he trained in the warehouse without permission. He slept during working hours, high up in a forgotten storage loft, as the Caper employees boxed coats and hats far below. At night, the place to himself, he rehearsed.

An oblong cedar chest was his bed. Forgotten fur coats, his blankets. And the mannequins below, his people.

He performed for three dozen mannequins nightly, choosing volunteers as eagerly as Finn the Fantastic did with flesh and blood, breathing members of his own adoring audiences in clubs across America. With the bald, peach, lifeless forms amassed before him, Roman practiced every trick he knew and began to discover others. He tried to levitate a mannequin, using thin fabric he hung from high shelves. He sawed another in half using mirrors gathered throughout the space. It was here that he decided not to hide his tricks, as the mannequins gave him no reason to be shy. Often he held the props inches from their lifeless eyes, a habit he would never break.

His new boots (found in the very box he slept in) clacked on the cement floor, and the sleeves of his white button-up shirts flapped in the cold, dark warehouse.

Mother, he'd call out, his voice sharp off the stone ceiling. *Please inform the audience of the next illusion.*

Even while speaking to the unliving, his voice did not have the weight he wanted it to and he longed for an assistant like the ones he read about in the magic magazines, the pages he never had money to buy.

A slightly crazed look was added to his already dark demeanor. The look of a man halfway up the mountain of his own ambition. If someone were to sneak in and witness his performances, they might not be able to guess his age; Roman was in the timeless grip of frenetic passion.

In his more lucid moments, able to see the scene he'd created from above, himself dressed in clothes from the warehouse boxes, the mannequins angled toward his pacing silhouette, he was able to name it in a word:

Ghastly.

But very soon all manner of lucidity fled him, leaving him completely immersed, behind.

These six months became another at an abandoned sugar plant forty miles from the warehouse. Here Emperor performed for the machinery. The black boots he stole from the warehouse once again rang out against the stone floor but here the echoes were returned by a hard, steel audience that was ever less forgiving.

And yet, by then he was performing for faces. Eyes and noses, ears and tongues, expressions he conjured in his imagination and held fast to as one might reality. The machines became old people and kids, newcomers and regulars, too. In the right mood, he fielded questions.

Mr. Emperor, how is it done?

Look closely. I hide nothing.

Before ever having opened a book on magic, Roman knew not to reveal his secrets. Soon the ferocious hold he held over this principle would come back to hurt the very career he cared so much about cultivating. But the Roman Emperor-to-be was very different from the one performing for steel vats and rusted gearings. And to get from one man to the other, Emperor understood that it was time to play out.

To play out for *people*.

11

He got on an open-call bill at the Comedy Canteen, one hundred and twenty miles from the sugar plant, a venue he never dreamed he'd enter. He called from a phone booth, trembling, and they said yes, yes with a name like his they'd be happy to add it to the list. But you better be good! they said. *Yes, but you better . . . be . . . good.*

He was slated to play at nine thirty. Emperor was so excited he showed up three hours early. He didn't know how shows and times and timing worked, and he hardly understood it when a lady there told him to come back half an hour before he was scheduled to perform. Or, she said, if he wanted to come back at seven thirty, the first of the four magicians slated before him would be starting and if he wanted to see the others—

Of course I want to see them, Roman said, astonished that anybody could think otherwise. When he came back at seven thirty the same lady smiled, told him things were running behind, and let him inside. The room was on its way to being crowded. Roman felt a lump in his throat that shamed him.

Most of the booths were occupied, leathery men and women in leathery coats. He found a small table near the restrooms and sat down alone. He set a suitcase full of props on the floor by his stolen boots.

The first act came on at eight ten.

Roman was stunned. The tricks themselves were no better than those he knew well, but the performer was incredibly talkative and engaging and, Roman had to admit, even funny. The magician, Paul the Pretty Good, was obviously going for a certain thing, but between his well-timed jokes and the smile of his gorgeous assistant, he was achieving it. Roman wanted to dislike it, wanted to hate what he was seeing. But oh, how it worked.

The crowd applauded, laughed, oohed and ahhhed at all the places Paul wanted them to. A volunteer got onstage and didn't mind it at all when Paul broke an egg over her head.

The second act was just as successful. As was the third. The fourth . . .

Roman felt sick. It was suddenly very clear to him that not only did he have no help onstage, but he had almost no personality to boot.

Dark thoughts rose mistlike in his mind, coloring the entire club, and forcing him to consider leaving.

The fella who went on before him called himself the Titan of Terror and had the crowd roaring as he pretended to fail at feats of strength, then succeeded at ones that were much harder. *Can't lift a toaster? How about the whole stove?* He introduced his tricks with just enough flair to make them sound more difficult than they were. Roman had fallen into a psychological tailspin. The laughing crowd seemed to be laughing at him, seemed to be saying,

You better be good, buddy. You better . . . be . . . good . . .

He hardly relished the moment he'd been waiting for, as, for the first time in his life, his name was announced over the club's crackling PA.

Roman Emperor, folks! And with a name like that, this shoulda been a toga party. Make sure your money is secure, lest he make it disappear . . .

Roman took the stage.

The spotlight was filtered red and, looking down at the sleeves of his white shirt, it looked as though he'd been shot, many times, in the shoulders, elbows, and wrists.

The crowd looking back at him suddenly appeared so knowledgeable to him. As if each and every person in the club had read all the same magazines he had, had practiced the same tricks in empty buildings, had even defeated their fathers at chess to earn the right to call themselves magicians.

Roman understood clearly that he was not special. That he had no gag, no bit, no act. And all the eyes upon him would know that very soon.

Striking his best showman's stance, Roman began without speaking, opening his box and removing objects far too big for it. Nor did he talk while presenting the objects at the foot of the stage. And the silence of the warehouse and the sugar plant, the inaudible intensity and proof of his undeniable command, felt like rejection on the stage of the Canteen.

A radio began playing as he began a new series of tricks. Roman looked to the speakers, assuming it was a malfunction, expecting it to cut off again. But the club's manager gestured for him to carry on and Roman understood that the club felt some accompaniment was necessary.

Roman was bombing.

And when he looked into the faces in the booths, he saw he didn't have them at all. They observed him with humor, sympathy at best.

The faces of his first crowd.

Roman, unable to stop the rising tide of shame within, turned red under the red light, bringing a devil's countenance to his already angular visage. He ended his show without a word and left the stage as silently as he'd taken it.

Young man, the promoter said, whispering to Roman by the bar. *You got another twenty minutes to fill.*

Roman latched his box shut and exited the Comedy Canteen, his blood burning scorched earth in his veins. He knew what he'd overlooked in those vacant buildings, those two thousand rehearsals alone: The crowd didn't want magic tricks, they wanted a magic *show.*

He needed an angle. A lady. A better costume. A joke. A bit. This was all as clear as candy to him as he drove home from his first performance. And yet he was never able to make those things happen. Never able to think of the right changes in the first place. No matter how many nights he told himself what he needed to do, the next day he'd only practice, learn new moves, stare into the mirror at a face that didn't have any more answers than he did.

And the face in the mirror aged.

Roman floundered in this way for the next twelve years. He played a handful of clubs, brief shameful moments in which he believed he'd gotten good enough at his craft not to need the silly gimmicks so beloved in the magazines. And so he needed someone else to imagine him in a new way, someone else to tap him on the shoulder and say,

If you do this, you will succeed.

Those kinds of meetings, Roman knew, were as rare as brilliance. In which the artist meets his propeller, the engine who sends him motoring across the sea of his most coveted waters.

Then, twelve years after his bombing at the Canteen, Roman

met his propeller. And the sharp, strong blades chopped him into so many pieces that he no longer recognized himself for all the blood.

12

Sleeping in an apartment above a Laundromat, a dozen years after his initial flop, Roman woke to the sound of someone knocking at his door. He had no friends, no family, and he was up to date on his rent. Perhaps there was a fire, he worried. A criminal in the lobby. Could it be the police calling to ask questions about his neighbors? Maybe it was a neighbor at the door. He got out of bed and cautiously peeked through the eyehole and saw nobody there. He looked again, thinking a neighbor had a guest who'd knocked on the wrong door before realizing their error.

Then Roman heard a voice from behind him. Inside his apartment.

Roman spun fast, eyeing his one room.

Who's there? he asked, his hands up, prepared to defend himself. The dark of his efficiency gave him no answer.

Roman. The voice spoke again. *Roman Emperor.*

The way it was said, the lilt, reminded Roman of the thousand times he'd heard his name through speakers that didn't crackle, spoken by a knowledgeable lover of magic. It was the voice in his fantasies of the way his career should have gone.

Who's there!

He made to step from the door, to grab hold of an ax he kept by the closet in case of intruders.

But something in the darkness moved and Roman stood rooted to the stained carpet. He hadn't felt this stuck in place since encountering the man in rags with the tall stack of cards in the sandy streets of his youth.

A short woman stepped from the shadows where his bed met the wall. Roman instinctively wiped his hands across his abdomen and thighs, as if this woman had soiled him in some way as he'd slept.

Get out! Roman called, but, to his surprise, the words were not commanding.

The woman wore a buttoned-up shirt, a long plaid skirt, and smelled of pipe smoke. Her eyes were made eggs by large glasses and Roman saw the wrinkles of her face magnified through the glass. He looked to her hands and arms, her neck, and saw wrinkles piled like pants around the ankles of someone disrobing for bed.

Who . . .

Roman Emperor . . . the world's greatest magician . . . loved *for his silence . . .* adored *for his lack of gimmick.* The woman smiled and smoke escaped her lips, but Roman saw no cigarette, no pipe. *Sounds good, doesn't it? Making it to the big time without selling your soul to get there?*

As she stepped into the blue light cast by the CLOSED Laundromat sign below Roman's one window, he saw that her hair was purple and tied up in a bun. When she spoke again, her voice was marked by a hundred thousand smokes, and the wrinkles in her neck gobbled.

Wanna be in the pages of Presto, *big time? Wanna be as famous as Finn?*

Roman's entire body cringed. He flattened himself against the wood door.

Get out, he repeated, this time with even less force.

The woman wagged a finger his way. The way she did it, and the way she advanced, Roman thought one word: *promoter.*

This woman, this impossible intruder, was something like Roman's fantasies of a promoter had always been. The cigarette voice, the glasses, the business-casual clothing. And the way she wagged her finger when she wanted Roman to know that she knew better than he did.

The woman promoter burped and Roman saw flies escape her fishy lips.

Your act is shit, she said, stepping toward him. Roman pressed his back harder against the closed door. *And you know it is. Or you would've opened that door and run by now.*

With that, Roman reached behind himself and felt for the handle. The woman's magnified eyes watched, smiling, as his fingers found the knob then slipped from it. Yes, horrified as he was, Roman wanted to hear what she had to say.

Thatta boy, the woman said. Then she coughed and more flies poured forth. She swatted them away with a wrinkled hand, and for a moment Roman saw the hand had impossibly long nails that curled in upon themselves. Then those nails were gone and in their stead were shadows of Roman's one plant upon the wall.

"Help me!" he screamed.

But he didn't want help. Not from anyone outside this room.

That's what I'm here for, kid, the woman said, stepping closer yet. Her eyes were no longer smiling. Roman saw fingers in her hair, keeping it in a bun. *You need help. Boy do you need help.*

What do I need to do? Roman asked. The words sounded disgusting; syllables of a defeated artist.

The woman nodded and crushed a flyer for one of Roman's shows with the heel of her right shoe.

You need a gimmick. An act. A bit. You got no ruse, kid. No artifice. And in your line of work, artifice goes a long way. And yet . . .

What? WHAT?

She held up an open palm and Roman spotted hair there.

How about no trick at all? How about . . . She was suddenly standing so close that Roman could smell her perfume. Dead wolf. *How about* real *magic?*

When the promoter embraced him, all the terror ceased. Roman's frantic (but wide open; as if he were holding the doors) mind was flooded with pictures of himself performing, doing things he would never have imagined possible. Not for himself.

He saw a crowd as large as the ones Don Deanie performed for. He saw legitimate awe in the eyes of the crowd.

He heard applause.

You see it? she asked him, looking up into his eyes. Roman saw bones dancing in hers. *Ah yes, you see it. Keep seeing it, kid.*

Then she buried her face in his chest and the fingers in her bun touched Roman's chin.

And he kept seeing.

The audience applause died to a palpable tension, the kind of silence that meant the people wanted to see more. Roman marveled at his own tricks; he was playing with time and space until natural law was rent, until he could smell the unmistakable odor of the supernatural. A vehicle could be crushed with a gesture, the audience could be lifted with a glance. Roman moaned. Buried under all these incredible accomplishments was a young thin man challenging his father to a game of chess. With these powers he could—

He looked down again to the terrible thing holding him.

She pulled back from him and Roman saw she had a man's face now, harder features behind the big glasses, under a bun wig, testing the seams of the blouse.

Keep seeing, she said. *Because we're just getting to my fee.*

Fee. Yes. A top promoter would need a fee, of course.

A cut.

New, odd visions replaced those that were like ecstasy to Emperor. No longer onstage, now he was digging. His back ached as he tossed shovelfuls of dirt over his shoulders, sending it into the blackness of night. He dug and he dug until he reached a body.

Then he shoveled the body out of the hole piecemeal, too. And beneath this body, another. And another, until the piles of dirt behind him were rivaled by the piles of rice paper skin and bone. Roman looked up and saw hundreds, no, thousands of bodies lifted from their graves, a chorus of corpses sitting up.

The dead, he saw removed . . . taken from their places of rest. And Roman himself was doing the removing.

A *graveyard custodian,* he thought, but he did not know what it meant yet. What she wanted. Her cut.

I need help, too, kid, she said. And Roman saw she was now sitting on the ground at his feet. *I need . . . turnover.*

Turnover?

She coughed and this time images escaped her, rising in the space between them. Roman raising his arms to the sky, sending the corpses nightward. Then Roman carrying new bodies to the empty graves.

Turnover.

He understood.

Kill for her. Bring her bodies. Her cut.

That's it, kid. Kill for me.

Because even Death needed to clean house. Even Death found the stench unbearable.

Suddenly he felt shame. Not for considering this swap, saying yes to the thing in his apartment, but because he had ever doubted such a day would come.

Roman had no doubt that he deserved this. That he put in the time, the work, the care.

Yes, he said. And the woman melted into black shadows in the carpet.

Brace yourself, kid, she said, leaving him. *You're going to be big.*

Her voice trailed off, the tail of an animal in the dark.

There was another knock at the door.

Roman leapt from the wood and turned to face it.

The promoter again? Why? Did she knock on the way out as she had on the way in?

Or was it perhaps the neighbors, coming to ask if he was okay. Or maybe the landlord after all.

Did you just sell your soul, Romie? Are you FUCKING NUTS?

Roman looked through the peephole, expecting to find an empty hall again.

But the hall was not empty.

A blond woman, pale and strange, stood facing him. From what Roman could see, she was naked.

He opened the door slowly.

She was indeed naked, her white pockmarked body like a bumpy dirt road under the hall's half-dead light.

What . . . Roman started. *Who . . .*

I'm Maggie, she said. *I'm your act.*

Roman reached out and took hold of her wrist.

Then he brought his fingers back and looked at them.

Frostbite! he thought.

Come in, he said. *Before someone sees you . . . undressed . . . in the hall.*

Maggie entered the small apartment. Roman saw that, the way she moved, she was as powerful as the visions that nearly split his skull a moment ago. Pretty, yes, but that seemed unimportant. The naked woman was a draw.

I think we should get some sleep, Maggie said. *We've gotta get to work right away.*

All right, Roman said, already feeling the balm of realized dreams approaching. *Yes.*

He got into his bed first and Maggie followed. She lay still on her side, her back to him. Roman was careful not to touch her again.

Try it, she suddenly said. Her voice was tender, pleasing.

Roman understood. He sat up as though in a dream and looked about his apartment.

The stovetop, Maggie said, her back to him. Had she seen the pot on the stove? Was she able to see it, somehow, now? Without looking?

Roman stared at the pan until it rose from the stove. It came to him, gracefully, wobbling, slow.

When it was above the bed, he crushed it with his mind. The metal cried out and for a moment it sounded to Roman like it was telling him to turn back, that he was in danger of losing something more important than his dreams.

Then the pan fell to the bed between his legs.

He turned to Maggie smiling.

But she remained with her back to him. It didn't matter.

The peace he felt was extraordinary.

He finally had his separation from the other magicians. His spark of originality.

His act.

Thank you, he said, and his breath turned to frost above his new assistant, lying still and forever awake beside him.

Two words followed him into the hole of sleep. Two words that he didn't mind just then, that felt like a means to an end, bread and cheese for the starving.

Dirty magic.

And the dirt from the magic reminded him of a man in rags and so he dreamed of him; the man slipping a card into a stack so high Roman had to look up, where he saw corpses rising like robins to the sky.

13

Dirty magic.

Roman could do one of two things. He could spend his years feeling guilty for making the decision he had, or he could twist the memory of that night just enough to make it fit into the arc he always imagined himself making. Almost immediately, he opted for the latter. And anytime he questioned the moral fiber of what he was doing, he let his mind drift back to the days before his ship came in. Often he imagined the wrinkled promoter steering it. He'd remember those long dark nights when he thought all might be for naught. And then, lifting a book from across the room in his better apartment or making a flower on the street vanish for good, he could smile and remind himself that hard work paid off.

Within a year of the night Maggie came to his door, Roman Emperor was a fixture on the Spell Circuit and all his peers considered him a threat. People whispered phrases like *he could be* and *the best ever.*

His show was electrifying. It was dangerous. He did things with weapons so frightening audience members would leave an Emperor show with a sense of having survived it. His show was sexy, too, in its way. Maggie changed the show from one of introspective meandering to arresting spectacle. Roman was free to concentrate entirely on the magic at last, as Maggie took care of all the things the audience pined for. And for this, for *her,* Roman's seriousness came off as refreshing in relief.

At last, people were *getting* him.

And yet, how long could he expect to carry out real magic before his peers started to ask real questions?

The Spell Circuit grew suspicious. Magicians whispered. Even writers from magazines such as *Presto* had incredulity in their eyes.

Unrelated articles about cheating appeared more regularly. The history of dirty magic was brought up.

Anything fishy about Roman Emperor to you?

His peers could tell. Of course none of them had the imaginative capacity to piece together the night Roman met his promoter, but in the same way baseball managers can spot the pine tar, the Spell Circuit smelled a rat.

Roman had always been good but it was strictly on a skills level. If one had asked the top names what they thought about him, most would've called him competent at best. And while they might have respected his love for the craft, they could look one another in the eye comfortably, knowing that the overcast man with the tight lip wasn't going anywhere.

Now though . . .

Now the guys were shifting in their seats and shaking their heads no. Something was up.

Almost all of Roman's tricks looked impossible. And most of them were brand new; tricks nobody had seen him work out live. And who was the blonde? And where had he found her? It used to be a running joke that, if you needed a quiet place to go, you could get a ticket to the Emperor show.

So . . . what was going on?

Maybe if the girl was the only thing different about the show . . . but she wasn't. Roman was strutting into the club like a soldier, hellfire in his eyes, and he hardly spoke to the other magicians on the bill. This wasn't protocol. This wasn't politics. This wasn't right. Emperor was acting like he owned the circuit and guys were worried he might eventually do just that. Their opinions of him were contorted by envy. And that envy easily led to the two least desirable words in the scene:

Dirty magic.

One evening in Tahlequah, Oklahoma, Finn the Fantastic's tour route crossed paths with the blossoming controversial Emperor and he decided to take in the show. Finn, an amiable and shameless self-promoter, sat at the bar with his collar unbuttoned and a rum and Coke in both hands. His blond hair was as perfect as if he were on his way to shoot a publicity photo, which, of course, already hung on the wall of the Stardust Matinee.

He watched Emperor closely.

Finn, a student like Roman, detected not one reference in Emperor's act. As if Roman had done the impossible: invent a wholly new show.

The performance ended with Roman tied up in a chair. The audience held their breath as the ropes started to move and untie themselves. Finn knew Roman was using invisible thread, but he couldn't spot the angles, the places that thread should be connected to. The rope moved snakelike, as though living, and Finn downed a drink, marveling at the fact that, if you knew your magic, even the best illusions looked artificial.

Not this one.

At the conclusion of the trick, Roman tossed the ropes to the foot of the stage and he and Maggie made a somewhat understated exit to the sound of rapt applause.

Finn eyed the rope. He couldn't resist.

Walking casually to the stage, as though studying the curtains for a show of his own, Finn quickly inspected the rope. No thread. No *anything*. Finn knew what to look for and there was none of it there to find. All the circuit talk of dirty magic echoed in his ears. When he looked up to the curtain he saw the eyes of Maggie watching him from a pale, placid face.

Finn dropped the rope. He smiled at her but she did not smile back, and he couldn't help but feel like the rope was left there on purpose. That he had somehow ended up an animal in a trap that night.

He left his second unfinished drink on the foot of the stage and departed.

A week later, Finn ran into Don Deanie in Texas. Finn, political as he was professional, wasn't one to gossip or smear but after getting very drunk, he told his old colleague what'd happened in Oklahoma and how he felt about it.

Deanie was upset.

Emperor, he said, was going to ruin them. In an effort to circumvent this, he arranged the show at the Kerry Theatre, under false pretenses of uniting the circuit as one. He would lure the quiet Emperor by billing it as a sort of magicians' conference. Any man desperate enough to shake hands with the Devil wasn't going to miss an opportunity like this. There was too much potential notoriety to be had. And besides, Emperor was clearly enjoying the power he was accumulating over his peers.

Deanie believed they'd all get to see Emperor up close and then could ask him, in person and together, where he had learned how to bend metal. Make things explode. Stop axes from striking his skull.

Emperor agreed to attend. But Deanie blew up his own plan when he got drunk and confronted the mysterious magician before Roman had a chance to perform.

In front of the entire attending circuit, Deanie asked Roman to reveal his secrets. Emperor refused.

Deanie called him a cheater. Emperor denied it.

Deanie demanded Roman prove his tricks were clean. Emperor kept quiet.

Deanie punched Roman in the nose.

Emperor simply waved a hand across his face and the blood disappeared.

The room went silent.

Maggie, who had been standing in the shadows of the curtain, took Roman by the arm and quietly led him out of the building. Outside, she whispered, "The pettiness of mediocrity. Do you miss it?"

"No," Roman answered.

But he did.

14

Roman spent as much time sending corpses to the sky as he did practicing magic with Maggie.

He was the best now and he knew it. But *recognition* of that would have to come from the audience and not his peers. There was no proof of Roman having dabbled in "that other magic" and so the industry magazines kept mostly quiet. But the magicians talked. And anytime Emperor's name came up, a morbid mood spread through the clubs and bars. No matter what Roman did from that point forward, he would always have an asterisk next to his name.

*Probably cheated.

And yet the circuit was so small that the disdain of his peers was somewhat irrelevant. None of the magicians would ever fill a thousand-seat theater. There simply wasn't a fan base that big to tap. Most tickets sold were to people looking for something different to do. People who had never heard of Finn the Fantastic or *Magic Monthly Magazine*. There was hardly any publicity other than the trades and even these only reached a handful of people nationwide. It was a slim industry. And the crowds Emperor enjoyed following the Kerry Theatre fiasco were no different from those he had before it.

And it wasn't perception that was getting to Roman anyway.

He'd been spending all his evenings in the cemeteries of the cities he played. Ducking the local police. Checking the grounds-keepers' houses. Watching for grieving visitors. Drunk teens. Sick men. He was used to working through the night, but this was a different kind of show. Often he cringed at what he did: removing the dead from their boxes, sending them into the sky, only to fill those boxes again.

With locals.

And yet, terrible as it sounded, often he felt comfortable out there, in the night, in the cold, with Maggie by his side. As if this particular trick was the one he'd been working toward since meeting that man in rags in the sand.

The bodies! Roman couldn't begin to count the number of lifeless mounds he'd removed to make room for fresh meat. And Maggie encouraged it. She was never as relaxed as she was in the graveyards. To Roman, it was there that she made the most sense. No longer seemingly odd or mysterious, Maggie looked as commonplace as the tombstones. As comfortable as the moss that grew upon them.

To watch Maggie . . . her eyes rolling back in her skull . . . as soft moans of ecstasy escaped her blue lips . . . as her hands met at her waist, then vanished into the folds of her dress . . . as her back arched . . . Roman felt the true darkness of what he did. Many times Roman heard her breathing hard, gripping the iron gates, twisting her body into impossible shapes behind him.

Often the thought of where Maggie came from haunted him. Sitting with her in a restaurant. Standing beside her at the check-in desk of a hotel. Driving with her, always, by his side. He had no respite, no *break* from the presence of what she stood for.

Maggie squealed with pleasure as they passed cemeteries they weren't prepared to empty.

The night before their midnight show in Goblin, Roman and Maggie sat quietly in their dressing room following a show. The pair had just thanked an apparent fan and his wife for their kind words and Roman, in a playful display of magic, shut the door on them with his mind. After doing so he turned to Maggie and told her,

"Tomorrow, Maggie. Time to clean up again."

But Maggie never lost track of the days they were supposed to refresh Death, send new bodies to Roman's always eager promoter.

By the time they pulled into Goblin the next morning, Roman behind the wheel of his signature used black Mercedes, Roman Emperor considered himself to be the greatest magician in the world.

As he passed between the giant Sherman topiaries of George Carroll and Jonathan Trachtenbroit, he smiled.

"There have been eighty tickets sold for this one already," he told Maggie. "I'm sure she'll be happy with her cut."

15

Pete was at Mr. Bench's shop when he saw the black Mercedes drive by. He couldn't see the driver, but he was positive the blond woman in the passenger seat, looking up through the glass at Goblin, was Maggie.

He'd read every single magazine and paper Mr. Bench gave him. He knew as much as someone could about Roman Emperor. So when the Mercedes passed, Pete's only thought was to follow it.

"What is it, Pete?" Mr. Bench asked, sensing Pete was distracted.

"Um, I'm gonna run to the Transistor Planet for a second."

His mind raced. "There's a new game out about witch hunts. Brian at school told me about it. Said they might have it already."

"Witch hunts, huh? My, how games have changed."

"I'll see you, Mr. Bench!"

Then he was out the door.

He searched the streets, looking for the car and peering in every storefront he passed. He moved fast, covering three blocks in a hurry, and headed east. He stopped at a light, Lily and Neptune, and saw Emperor's Mercedes parked a block away.

Pete's body stiffened.

The light changed and he had to tell himself to cross the street. Legs like rubber, he passed the black car, hardly able to believe it was here, in Goblin, in person, and he was so electrified that he looked for them everywhere, it seemed, at once, until all of downtown was a shimmering steel blur.

He found them sitting in a booth in Davey P's Diner.

Pete was stupefied. Rooted to the sidewalk outside. This was a *Presto* magician. And yet the man looked so lifelike, so alive. Unlike the photos Pete had seen, Roman Emperor's face moved when he blinked, his hands moved when he brought the fork to his lips, and when a cloud passed in front of the sun, it turned his hair from dark to black.

A raindrop fell from the sky and Pete recalled, vaguely, that it was going to be a *boomer of a rainfall* tonight. That's what Mom called it. Said people in town were preparing themselves for a flood. But the only flood Pete was worried about right now was the possibility of wetting his pants as he stared at the two legends beyond the glass.

Pete entered Davey's in a dream. He could hardly walk normal, one sneaker in front of the other. As he stepped to the host stand, Maggie looked up, and Pete felt a chill. Eye contact. She could tell, he believed, that he'd studied them.

She knows.

Pete sat at the corner of the counter on a stool. Only ten feet now from Emperor's back. Out of the corner of his eye, he saw the magician's black hair, his brown vest, and the white long-sleeved shirt beneath it. Emperor looked so strong . . . so real . . . so—

"Kid," a voice said.

"What?" He swiveled on his seat. The waiter tapped his fingers on the counter.

"You want a menu? You know what you want? The Davey P special perhaps?"

"A . . . a coffee," he answered.

"Coffee? How old are you?"

Pete turned red. "Is there an age limit?"

The waiter frowned. "Okay, smart-ass. One coffee coming right up. But don't blame me if it stunts your growth."

Rain started to fall harder outside the diner.

He looked back toward the pair nervously. Maggie was blocked by the back of Roman's head.

Okay, Pete thought. *This is it. It simply has to be.*

His legs trembled.

"Here's your coffee, kid."

Okay. Your name is Pete. Three . . .

"Don't blame me if you go berserk from the caffeine."

Two . . .

"Don't blame me if you can't sit still."

One.

"Don't blame me if—"

Pete stood up. He walked to their table. Maggie saw him coming and held his gaze. Once he was beside them he stopped and opened his mouth.

But nothing came out.

When Roman turned to face him, Pete felt like he might melt into the diner tiles.

"Hello," Maggie said.

Up close, Roman did look different in person. To Pete he looked . . . sad.

"I'm sorry," Pete said. The words tumbled up his throat, out his mouth. "I'm your biggest fan in Goblin and maybe the whole world, too. I know everything there is to know about you." He reddened. "I mean . . . everything you've told anyone."

Roman blinked. His expression did not change. "That's wonderful," he said. And Pete thought he saw something *young* happen to Roman. As if suddenly the *Presto* legend was a kid himself again.

"Do you practice magic?" Roman asked.

This was too much. A *Presto* magician . . . ROMAN EMPEROR . . . was asking *Pete* if he practiced magic.

"Yes. I mean, no. Not like you do. But yes. I mean—" Then, without meaning to say it, Pete suddenly said, "Mr. Emperor, I know you're not into dirty magic. Because . . . because there's no such thing. Any magic is . . . is . . . clean."

Pete saw the distant rise of water in Emperor's eyes.

"Thank you very much," the magician said quietly.

Maggie leaned forward. "Are you coming to the show tonight?"

"Of course. Half of Goblin Middle is."

Roman and Maggie exchanged a glance. Suddenly Roman reached out and took Pete's wrist.

"Close your hand," he said.

"What?"

"In a fist. Close your hand."

Pete did as Roman said.

"I'm going to give you something," Roman said. "And if you promise to always treat magic with respect, I'll let you keep it."

Pete nodded.

"Sure. Of course."

Pete didn't feel it happen. But Roman released his wrist and when Pete opened his hand he saw four quarters on his palm.

"That's for your coffee," Roman said.

Pete looked into the magician's eyes.

"We will see you tonight then," Maggie said.

"Yes," Pete said, trembling.

Then he stumbled backward to the counter and left three of the four quarters for his coffee. He wouldn't let the last one go. It was a gift from Roman Emperor. He'd never spend it. He'd carry it with him into adulthood and frame it and tell his kids about the time he met the world's greatest magician and how the man bought him coffee with magic.

16

By seven o'clock Pete was praying his mom would be asleep by ten. Dad was working and Pete hadn't told Mom about the show. He couldn't risk it. Not a chance. But if she was out by ten, that would give him plenty of time. The Domino Theater was at the north end of the city. It wouldn't take long to get there, but there couldn't be any room for error. He watched the clock like it was the last minutes he had to live.

By seven o'clock Roman was asleep in his hotel room. Maggie sat silently watching him from a chair.

17

By eight thirty Pete was trying to get it out of his mom what time she was planning on going to bed without saying it outright.

"Pete," she said, annoyed. "Stop badgering me."

"It's just that I'm so tired, Mom. Aren't you?"

The rain outside had gotten pretty bad.

By eight thirty Roman was still asleep and Maggie sat patiently in her chair.

18

By nine o'clock Pete was in his room, pretending to be sleeping. He thought maybe he could spread a sleepy mood through the house.

He watched the clock obsessively. He cursed every minute his mother stayed awake.

By nine o'clock Roman still slept and would for another fifteen minutes until Maggie touched him lightly on the arm and said,

"Roman. It's time."

19

By nine thirty Pete was resigned to the fact that his mom never went to sleep before ten. The light was back on in his room and he flipped through a magazine Mr. Bench had given him. There was a photo of Roman standing in what looked like a backstage hall. The caption read:

EMPEROR READIES HIMSELF FOR A SHOW

By nine thirty Roman was in the shower, humming. Maggie sat in her chair. Patiently waiting in the dark room.

20

By ten o'clock Pete was insane. Mom was in bed but she wasn't asleep yet. Couldn't be. And it seemed like everything was happening too quickly. Exactly when should he leave? He couldn't make up his mind. He was going to have to walk his bike back through the house because he couldn't risk opening the garage. It was raining like mad outside and he'd have to bring a cover. He was nervous. Should he risk it and leave right now?

By ten o'clock Roman was behind the wheel of his black Mercedes. He wore a gray coat and he was smoking. The window was open, letting in some of the cold Goblin air and rain.

"Did you know that they're buried standing up here?" Maggie asked.

"Yes," Roman answered. "You told me so."

21

By ten thirty Pete could stand it no more. He sneaked downstairs quietly. As he took his raincoat out of the closet the door creaked and his body stiffened. He waited. Then he walked through the laundry room to the garage. He opened the door very slowly and went and got his bike, then carried the bike back into the house. He thanked the rain for beating against the house, smothering any noises he made. Goblin was a friend in that way. He worried about Mom. What if she were to wake up and check on him while he was out?

She'd be scared. He'd leave a note.

He crept back upstairs and left this on his pillow:

Mom,
Don't worry. I'm at a magic show at the old Domino Theater.
I wasn't sure if you'd let me go.
                                                    —Pete

He lifted his bike by the bar and opened the front door. The rain made a wall before him.

He stepped into that wall and closed the door softly behind him.

Mom would understand. She'd have to.

By ten thirty Roman and Maggie were walking through the gates of the Goblin Cemetery. Maggie held an umbrella over both their heads. They walked slowly and neither spoke. Maggie, Roman could tell, was yearning for it. Her quiet giggles gave her away.

They stepped around the tombstones, respecting the old idea that one shouldn't step on another's grave. Despite the fact that Roman was about to empty them.

The sky was black with rain. Roman liked that. Coupled with the trees surrounding the cemetery, he should have sufficient cover to do what he had to do.

22

By eleven o'clock Pete was whipping down Northsouth. The rain pressed hard against him, but it made the trip only more magically unreal. The wind, the rain, the time of day. Pete checked his pocket to make sure he had the ticket. The quarter, too. Both were there. Pete rode on.

By eleven o'clock Roman had his palms extended toward the sky. He stood at the head of the Goblin graves and made a violent motion with his arms. The sound of so many lids cracking open at once hid the noises Maggie was making. She watched from under a tree. She gripped the umbrella handle. This was her favorite part.

23

Because of the wind, the rain hit Roman at an angle that he found almost refreshing. It seemed that even the elements were aware of the importance of this moment. He never felt as powerful as he did just before removing the bodies. And this place proved to be spectacular.

Sometimes Roman laughed at how the deal he'd struck favored him twice over. This part, keeping up his end, was just a different show. And not just for Maggie, either. For himself. There were nights Roman wished to be nowhere else. As he stood with the lids unlatched, lids he himself had forced open, by magic, he felt like the child stupefied by the street performer. Like the young man stealing chess pieces from his father.

Maggie, under the tree, whimpered impatiently.

Roman's brilliant dark eyes fastened on the group of open holes spread throughout the wet grass. He inhaled slowly. He was prepared; a lifetime of work resting on the simple gesture of his hand. A flick of the wrist.

The dead, he thought. *The dead!*

He lifted his palms toward the black Goblin sky and made fists toward the falling rain.

Maggie moaned.

The bodies shot up from their graves, still standing, suspended now twenty feet into the sky. The moon cast shadows upon the holes in the grass beneath them.

Roman stepped under the fifty bodies, the dangling pale feet forming an awning, a rotted shoe falling to the ground beside him. Some were more decayed than others. Women with hair so long it almost reached their feet. Old suits, old clothes, fashionable, perhaps, the last time they touched air. Some bodies were rotted to the bone, others with holes just beginning to show. Fingernails reached the knees. Jeweled bracelets barely hung from wrists too thin now to support them. Yellow teeth. Rotting teeth. No teeth at all. Eyes turned to putty, no longer filling their sockets. One woman wore a grocery store apron, and the worms had taken her face completely.

Roman studied them. Maggie fell to her knees.

The pack of corpses hung perfectly still, the gorgeous Goblin rain crashing against them, washing some of their rot to the ground. Roman studied them from beneath like a child looking for the invisible string, looking for the trapdoor, trying to unmask the trick.

"Be gone!" Roman yelled through the wind and rain. *"BE CLEAN!"*

The bodies were lifted higher. Maggie began moaning so loudly Roman heard it twice over, echoing off the steel lids of the strange Goblin caskets. The corpses went higher . . . higher yet . . . and Roman could feel her, the promoter, watching from behind a tree. Which tree? Roman didn't look. He opened his hands, extending his fingers, sending the bodies higher still until they were indecipherable from the many drops of rain falling fast from the sky.

Maggie screamed in ecstasy.

And then . . . the bodies were gone.

Roman let his chin fall to his chest. Maggie came up beside him and covered him with the black umbrella.

"Presto," Roman said.

"That was your best work yet."

Roman looked to her.

"And now . . . the encore."

24

By midnight Pete was gripping the quarter so hard it left an imprint on his hand. Everyone was there. Mike, Victor, Randy, Susan, Christopher, *everyone.* A lot of their parents, too.

Pete thought of Dad working. Of Mom asleep.

The Domino Theater was smaller than Pete imagined. He'd read a hundred times how the Spell Circuit magicians performed for sixty people or less, but to see that part of it up close was staggering. It was really no more than a box of a room, four wood walls nailed together, hardly capable of containing a genius like Emperor. But Pete would take it. The stage was so close. And because Roman didn't hide his moves, Pete would be able to *see it all.*

The lights went out and his classmates' chatter ceased with it. The unbearable silence that followed was broken by boots on the stage.

The lights came on.

Maggie.

The crowd was shocked by her. Pete knew they must be. But *he* wasn't. He already knew all about Maggie and Roman. Everything there was to know. When Maggie started talking, Pete felt a power in her voice that no magazine had ever mentioned.

She introduced Emperor.

And from the cave-black shadows backstage, he emerged.

He walked out with such confidence and control that the tired face Pete had seen in person seemed like a false memory. He wore the brown pants. Black boots. White shirt and a vest. His hair was wet and Pete was proud that it was because of the Goblin rain.

Goblin.

Roman Emperor was in Goblin.

Without hesitation the pair went headlong into their show. Pete couldn't imagine how it looked to Mike, someone who had no idea what Emperor was about. And the parents, resigned to take their kids to a midnight magic show, were obviously taken aback. Pete knew they'd been expecting some square in a top hat, but not this brilliant, dark artist who could bend metal with his mind.

People gasped. People called for more.

Pete was fixated on Roman's hands and body. Every move Roman made lived up to what the magazines said it could be.

And yet, *Presto*'s description of him was a crime compared with what Pete saw for himself. Roman moved so fast it was hard to keep up.

He escaped from chairs without moving his body.

Rope moved snakelike, alive.

Maggie threw an ax at his head that stopped an inch from his nose.

Objects appeared and disappeared, bent and broke.

Pete was speechless.

When Maggie announced they'd be doing their final act and that they needed volunteers, Pete felt a sinking in his stomach. He didn't want it to end. He didn't want it to ever end.

But he raised his hand all the same.

Roman was bent over near the back of the stage, drying sweat from his hair as Maggie surveyed the crowd. A small sea of hands waved frantically before her. She stepped to the side of the stage. Making room.

Roman rose and returned to face the crowd. He was loose now. His work almost done.

You wanna be a star, big time? You gotta give me my cut, too.

How?

Roman's dark eyes traced the hands before him, wagging, begging.

Fresh death, kiddo. Just can't stand the smell of the old stuff after a time.

Roman stepped to the edge of the stage and spoke the first words he'd spoken all night. With his palms extended toward the ceiling he said,

"All right, children . . . who wants to disappear?"

The Domino went nuts. Kids jumped out of their seats. Pete climbed up on his foldout chair and reached his hand higher than any other.

My cut, the promoter had said, *has nothing to do with how well you*

empty their graves. She smelled of dead wolf. Of bear. *It's how you fill them back up again that counts.*

Pete was screaming himself hoarse. But some kids were scared. And their parents, smitten by the show, weren't having it.

Roman watched it all as a boy himself, rooted to the sandy streets of his youth.

"Get on up there, Sarah," Mr. Anderson said. "Don't you want to disappear?"

"Come on, John! Don't be so shy!"

Maggie tilted her head. Licked her lips.

"Get on up there!" Mrs. Jones said.

"Go on!"

Roman raised a hand, ready to choose the volunteers, those who had decided to say yes to real magic. Those who were willing to dabble.

"Don't you want to disappear?" Mr. Parks asked his son. *"Don't you want to disappear?"*

A MIX-UP AT THE ZOO

1

Dirk Rogers woke every day an optimist and fell asleep despaired.

Truth was, he was getting tired of the tours.

You got fifteen 8-year-olds wetting their pants to see Eula, Dirk. Break's over.

It might not have been so bad (he might not have woken from nightmares of himself leading packs of children down long hallways built of a stone older than the pyramids, coated in a webbing made by no insect he knew of) if he had to work only *one* tour. One *type* of tour. Because the zoo had him running all week (from nine to five every day) and the slaughterhouse had him on the weekends. At night, home again, Dirk was beat. Bushed. It didn't matter what day it was or, really, how the day even went. Chasing the kids around, constantly counting heads, locking/unlocking doors, locking/unlocking cages, feeding the animals, cleaning the sludge from the gutters, giving directions, taking orders, answering questions, doing what he could to pick up his co-workers' slack and worrying a lot about his own. He had strong fantasies of an elusive nightlife. He *wanted* to get off work, shower, and hit the town. He wanted a drink. He wanted two. He wanted company. He certainly wanted to pick up a woman. But no matter how realistic this prospect sounded during the day, once home, it was a *different* Dirk that entered his apartment and opted to sit down/lie down instead. It was a different Dirk that brushed his teeth at night than the one who did the same in the morning.

Often, *before* work, he'd take a minute to sit and watch the people pass from a green Goblin bench. And often he'd pick a few out.

Tonight that woman and I will meet and make love . . .

or

I will cheer that man at the bar tonight . . .

Dirk was electrified by these little visions of human interaction. He'd certainly had enough of the animal kind. But the fantasies were foggy impressions by the time he flopped down in the chair at the kitchen table at night. There, the whispers came.

Tomorrow, they said, *you will be your own boss.*

"You're working too much," Patrick said over beers one night. "You've got nothing to spend the money you make on. That's not the way to do it, Dirk. You need to blow your pile, buddy. Get so drunk you ruin your life and start over again."

Dirk, ducking his large head toward the foam of his beer, was flooded with fantasies: asking a woman what she would like to drink; leading her through a crowd on their way to the dance floor; telling her that he was going to own his own business one day, right here in Goblin.

That's right, Dirk would think. *Any kind of business you want.*

Or maybe Dirk would melt a woman's heart with stories about the animals. Trudy . . . Alice . . . the elephants and the birds . . . how, long ago, he returned to the zoo late at night to console Eula on the loss of her baby. How he might have helped her through it.

Goblin's prized gorilla was guaranteed to turn any woman's heart to cotton.

Even his fantasies weren't safe from the zoo. From the slaughterhouse. From work.

"Maybe I'd be better for quitting one or the other," Dirk told Patrick that night. "Shake things up."

"*Mix* things up," Patrick said. "And yes. Cheers to *that*."

Often, on his rare nights out with Patrick, Dirk would excuse himself and head to the bathroom where he'd lock the door, set his beer on the sink, and stand quietly against the wall, his eyes closed, breathing deep and slow.

There he'd think of that woman again. This time he'd captivate her with his ideas, his plans, his sense of drive. No mention of the zoo. Eula. The animals. And for one glorious half minute he would be free of the feelings that pounded his body by day and the images that confused him as he slept.

Your business can be anything you want it to be, Dirk thought. *So long as it doesn't boast any tours.*

2

It was Patrick's idea to swap jobs in the first place. He'd worked as the zoo's custodian, picking up cigarette butts, maps, paper pizza plates, and empty soda-pop cans and carrying the animal shit from behind the cages to the great golden trash can at the park's north end. He also discovered that he didn't like the job very much. Half a year deep he could barely stand patrolling the grounds in the brown jumpsuit with its clever slogan across the back in white:

SOMEONE HAS TO CLEAN UP AFTER THESE GUYS!

And no matter how well he washed it, he couldn't really shake that birdshit stench that followed him home. This, coupled with the daily carving of hippo apples out of the grooves of his shoes, brought him squarely to the edge. Being spotted in this state by Sheryl Connors, his high school crush who couldn't *believe* he still lived in town and who seemed to plug her nose in defiance of his olfactory montage, pushed him over it.

"Let's trade jobs," he said to Dirk one night, also over beers. "You start cleaning up the zoo and I'll start riding the back of that truck." Dirk had been a Goblin garbageman for months. He'd cleaned Perish Park, washed the steel lids of the Goblin graves, picked up the trash along every thruway, washed the windows at the Woodruff, and once worked the same landscape crew as Goblin's most celebrated citizen, Wayne Sherman, mastermind of The Hedges.

"I've walked dogs before—" Dirk said.

But Patrick cut him off. "You won't actually be handling any animals. Just their shit."

Robin Jacobs, known to many as Goblin's biggest asshole, and also owner of the zoo, didn't care who stained their fingertips with other people's cigarette butts or who scooped elephant logs into black bags, as long as that someone showed up every day to do it. He agreed to Patrick's job-swap and just as quickly handed Dirk a brown jumpsuit.

"Ah, but you're a big one," Robin said, holding the brown fabric up to Dirk's chest. "As big as Eula, I'd say. Hope that doesn't mean you're also a big problem. Welcome to the Hardy Carroll Goblin Zoo."

Goblin Sanitation had no reservations about the switch, either, and so Patrick traded the odor of Goblin's animals for the smell of Goblin's trash. But right as it felt, there was one thing he was very wrong about. Not only would Dirk be handling the animals after all, he would very soon become the face that every Gobliner thought of when he or she recalled the Goblin Zoo. Dirk would become a celebrity there. He'd own the place. But not like he was the boss. Not *that* kind of owning. And that semantic would haunt him as darkly as the dreams of leading children down long stone hallways, walls cloaked in webs. Stone slabs so old that Dirk would wake shaking, desperate to know what sort of animals howled and laughed, boomed and bellowed, beyond them.

3

It couldn't really be stopped. Dirk working the zoo was akin to Hercules getting his shield. A mythic match. His bulking thirty-eight-year-old frame was as eye-popping for the children as the polar bears. His big mitt hands could make an entire unfolded map vanish in a single swipe. He could carry six bags of shit at once (Patrick could barely manage two) and for reasons not wholly understood by any of his co-workers or himself, Dirk had an immediate calming effect on the animals. Was it simply his size? His vibe? What exactly emanated from Dirk that soothed Eula just as she began beating her chest in despair? What unseen element brought the lions to cease roaring as he approached?

Dirk noticed the changes in behavior.

"Oh, that sort of thing happens here," Gordon McCall, one of the animal feeders, told him over lunch one day. "There's the animals that the civilians see, the animals on their best behavior, the constant flow of people passing their windows, Gobliners there to watch them eat, watch them mate. I don't care how sentient you are . . . a living thing *must* act differently when it knows it's being watched. How could it not? But there's this other side, the side that *we* get to see. When the zoo closes. When it gets dark around here and the animals crouch back into that isolation, the first minute all day they get to themselves, the first chance they get to *think* and maybe, in a way, to be the closest they can to what they were before they went and got caged. And that thing, Dirk, that state an animal can get into, is a scary thing. You don't want to approach an animal when he's there, when he's returned to that original state, where something like a man and man's authority suddenly stops meaning anything."

But none of this was what Dirk was really talking about.

"They just seem different around me," he said.

"Yeah, well, sounds like you're just catching lions being lions. Don't start thinking you have some magic power over them or you're gonna go nuts when they misbehave."

Dirk sat on the bench long after Gordon left him and replayed the way the bears lifted their heads to watch him pass or the spider monkeys hung by one arm, pointing at Dirk with the other. One night at closing time in his second week on the job, a possible explanation popped up, unasked for.

They know I'm not where I'm supposed to be. Up here—he tapped his head—*I'm caged, too.*

It was something like *a-ha*, by Dirk's standards, an epiphany. He walked toward Trudy the tiger's cage in a foggy daze, realizing for the first time how badly he wanted to free his own mind. He followed the painted footprints on the concrete, first the little bird feet in yellow, then the alligator feet in green, the white bear paws, the brown hippo toes, and Trudy's faded orange.

Passing through the wood sliding doors to the tiger habitat, he entered the incredible darkness that housed her. He had a vague sense of purpose, that meeting with Trudy just then was a meaningful thing for him to do. But just like the Goblin sky was so often rainy, and fog accumulated as easily as gnats, Dirk didn't have a clear idea of what that purpose was.

He felt along the wall for the flip switch, and Trudy's rusty cage came to life under the bright overhead light.

Wood chips and brown grass decorated the floor at the front of her cage. Dirk saw the huge tree trunk leaning against the far wall for Trudy to climb. And as he pressed his forehead to the bars, he saw the remains of her evening meal; big bones lay criss-cross over a dark purple stain in the concrete.

But Trudy wasn't visible. Not yet.

"Trudy?"

He eyed the big rock in the shadows.

She's back there, he thought.

He was about to call her name again when he saw the darkness upon the rock shift and the shape emerged of a cat much bigger than Dirk remembered. Trudy stood still at the edge of that dark-ness, the orange of her body receding into the shadow like the very first flames of a new fire.

Dirk slowly put his hand through the bars.

Trudy lifted her shoulders and hissed. But a hiss in name alone, for what escaped her throat was not the same sound made by a house cat.

"Trudy. Hello. I'm caged, too."

Now the tiger came forward, descending the rock with the agility of free thought.

Trudy went to his outstretched hand and sniffed him, once, an intake of breath that was louder than Dirk's voice.

Dirk pulled his hand from the cage. He held the bars, his fore-head still pressed to the steel. He held Trudy's gaze, too.

"How do we get out of here?" he asked her.

Then he tapped his finger to his head.

He didn't know it then, but the first few pounds of the weight of the world had been placed upon his shoulders. Still looking into the eyes of the great cat, Dirk started experiencing a restless-ness that would build within, a brewing discontent, a concept too sloppily made to speak of.

Suddenly he wanted his insides to swell up beyond the limits of his skin; swell to such a size that his body would finally split, freeing the man within.

Trudy sat before him and tilted her head at an angle that suggested she was curious as to what he was thinking.

Dirk told her, as tears welled in his eyes.

"I'm being silly," he said. "Worrying about worrying. Thinking about thinking. Wondering if I'm in the right place. You know what I think, Trudy? I think you and I are passing ships, you know, big boats in the same water. Here we are, meeting, but very soon I'll be out of this place, running my own business, married. My own boss. And when I am? I'll come back and buy you and Eula, some of the others, too. And in my house . . . there won't be any cages." He smiled as the tears rolled down his face. "I won't be here for long."

But he was wrong about that. Rather, he'd become a zoo sensation. And with each new promotion, Dirk would understand less and less about the ropes tying him in place; the cage he wanted to bust out of lowering from the rainy green Goblin sky.

4

It simply couldn't be stopped. Soon Dirk's co-workers were whispering about how odd the new guy was. Gordon wasn't the only person he'd spoken to about the animals. But after his visit to Trudy, his fellow staff noticed just how bizarre the animals *did* act around him. Dirk was big. Some might say rugged. Maybe he'd lived a hard life, a rough life, maybe he'd been to *jail*.

The gossip about the new guy reached a peak when the longtime ticket taker Don Chambers was approached by the feeder Sam Jones.

"Has he worked his spell on you yet, Don?"

"Who?"

"Dirk Rogers. The big guy. Seems everywhere he goes he brings the place to a stop."

"Really? Hadn't noticed."

"You will. The elephants watch him close."

Don thought about this.

"Sounds like he's sick," Don said, shuffling the day's tickets-to-be.

"Sick? What do you mean?"

Don peered over his glasses. "Animals don't sit still for something they're afraid of. They recoil . . . they snarl . . . they crouch. You know that. But they *watch* a man in distress. A man in a bad way. A man near the end of his rope."

"Why do they do that, Don?"

Don shrugged. "Maybe because they know there's an end to their rope, too. And they wanna know what it looks like before they reach it."

And as if the ticket booth acted as a megaphone, Don's take on Dirk was carried throughout the park and settled strong into the minds of everyone who worked there. It didn't hurt that the lumbering custodian seemed to affect the kids the same way. And Dirk, walking the zoo trails in a dull daze, performing his simple tasks in silence, wasn't entirely unaware that the children clamored for him. Somehow, through sympathy or sheer entertainment, he had become a little part of the zoo. An attraction that could be missed if he quit.

Seth Handy noticed this, too. So when the tour guide entered Robin Jacobs's office to announce he was moving to Florida, he said Dirk Rogers would make an excellent replacement. It just sort of slipped out of his mouth without any forethought.

"You know what?" Seth said, his body halfway out the door,

Robin already lifting the phone. "I'm pretty sure he'd do it for the same money he makes now, Robin. He doesn't seem to have too much upstairs."

"I'll take care of the business side of things, Seth. Good luck in the humidity."

But when Seth left his office, Robin set the phone back down. He reached over to the window and fingered the blinds apart, looking for that big, strange custodian.

The same money? Would he? The kids *did* seem to like him. In fact, one of them was hanging from Dirk's right biceps just then.

Robin tented his fingers and crossed his ankles on his desk. Seth Handy might've just saved the zoo two hundred dollars a week.

He laughed.

Dirk Rogers was promoted to tour guide that afternoon.

5

"Remember, Dirk, as tour guide you are the face of this great place. Yours is the smile these children will take with them into adulthood when they think back on the Hardy Carroll Goblin Zoo. You'll be right there next to Trudy swallowing a steak, Eula beating her chest on the grass. Some of these kids will grow up and have kids of their own. And when they're sitting around, scratching their heads, trying to figure out how to entertain their little turds, *your* face will come to mind and they'll bring those little turds to our doorstep. Do you understand?"

Dirk understood. He'd never been promoted before. It was the sort of thing you cheered at the bar.

"If you fuck up, if we discover you're no good at this, then you get fired, I fill your place, and we all move on with our lives. But do me a favor, huh?" Dirk's boyish but brute face looked like a moron's to Jacobs. "*Don't* fuck up. Don't make me look like a jerk. You do something ridiculous and I'll make sure every employer in Goblin knows something about it. It'll be hard to get a gig bagging groceries. Do you understand?"

Dirk nodded.

Jacobs felt a strange dark swirling in his belly. *Christ,* he thought. *This guy makes you feel heavy, doesn't he?*

But who cared? The kids loved him. Rumor was the animals did, too.

"Mr. Jacobs?"

"What?"

"Do I get a different jumpsuit?"

"No. Same one."

"And what do I do now?"

Jacobs smiled and rose behind his desk.

"Dirk?"

"Yes?"

"Now you get to work."

6

The tours went like this:

Children congregated up to twenty minutes before the hour. Most of the kids were between six and eleven, but Dirk would see a million strollers, too. Stoned teenagers weren't a rarity, either. It was kick, after all, hearing the animals described the way the big guy at the zoo did it.

Kids whined to their parents, swatted at bees, turned red from the sun, or huddled beneath a zoo umbrella to keep safe from the ruthless Goblin rain.

Without fail, at the onset of every tour, someone would yell, *We want Eula!*

Dirk wanted to see Eula, too, but there were so many stops on the way. And yet he got it: The tourists couldn't help pining for the big game. To see a living thing so strong it could kill accidentally, with one clumsy step. The hippos, the elephants, the rhinos, the tiger, and, the pinnacle, the massive lone gorilla at the northern peak of the tour's circle.

"Imagine," Don the ticket taker once said to Dirk, "if we had a Great Owl in here."

The smaller, less endangered birds would have to do. But as remarkable as it was to see fifty species of bird crowding a sixty-foot-high wire dome, and as beautiful as it was to hear them speak to one another in cosmic song, a bird was, after all, something you could find in your backyard. The Hardy Carroll Goblin Zoo knew the importance of the buildup. Start with something common. Work your way to the majestic. The reptiles came next. Dirk led the troupe along the green scaly footprints painted on the concrete. More than one parent felt compelled to ask, *Will they be in cages?*

Many of the younger kids wouldn't even look at the cobra at all and some of the boys, in order to impress the girls, would smush their own faces against the glass. One night Dirk had been in the reptile house when a drunk zookeeper accidentally knocked over a turtle cage. It shattered against the cement floor and Dirk realized the glass cages weren't as unbreakable as most zoo-goers thought they were. Often, directing a tour, he'd imagine the cobra breaking the glass, attaching itself to a young boy's face. Later, when the nightmares began, he did nothing to stop little boys and girls from being sucked out of line, taken in the jaws of a snake.

In his nightmares the tours continued above all things.

Just as they must in reality.

Alice, the big crocodile wading beneath the rickety wooden bridge, always got their attention. Often Dirk was tasked with tossing a duck carcass over the kids' heads, then plugging his ears for the screams as Alice's huge jaw snapped shut, severing the fowl in half.

But as he entertained, light as he appeared to others, a dark mist began to circle Dirk's feet. The nameless abject misery that wasn't with him when he woke would begin its cruel climbing of his body. What was it? Dirk never asked himself this question. To him the sensation was real, but it wasn't the sort of thing he talked about with Patrick over beers. It wasn't even the sort of thing he talked about to himself, standing silent in the bathroom of the Pudgy Duck with the doors locked, his back to the wall. Whether it was because the circles of the tour wound Dirk's soul into a knot, or because the gradation in size of the animals mirrored his budding discontent, the intensity of Dirk's internal storm built in step with that of the tour he guided. And by the time he reached the bears, that dark mist had wound itself up to his chest.

Mister Guide! Is it true that the polar bear's fur is see-through?

So often the questions were the same. And Dirk understood subconsciously that a pattern existed: the things that people were concerned with.

The animals, he thought, had ways of dealing with the burden (the *cage*) of the body.

The transparent coat for the polar bear's body; what Dirk would like to have happen to his own, freeing, by seeing, the man within. The distance between the giraffe's mind and the rest of its awkward body. The flight of the birds. The way the ostrich buried its head in the face of so much turmoil.

Oh, how the animals knew what to do when faced with the weight of existence! Dirk knew unrest. He knew confusion. He knew what it meant to *long* for something. The great mass of foggy consciousness would approach him slowly, a gray star from deep in the Goblin sky descending. It grew and it grew until not only was he blinded by it, but his body felt hot and his mouth got sticky dry with its heat. In these moments he had nowhere to run for cover (Trudy found cover in the cave-shade of that manufactured rock), and this frightened him greatly. To Dirk these questions had no shape. For all his wonderful size, his hands weren't big enough to hold these ideas up close for examination.

This was the face of the Goblin Zoo.

Parents sometimes wondered at the way the big guide trailed off—teenagers elbowed one another and said he'd *zoned out*—but the kids adored him. And really, what else mattered?

Lift me up! Lift me up! I wanna see the elephants from as high as you are!

How they laughed when Dirk crouched to their little level, when he hollered hello to the awesome gray animals dusting themselves off with their trunks, and when he picked a kid up carefully and placed his feet on the wood fence bordering the stone ditch even Trudy could never clear. It was impossible for parents not to remark how wonderful the tour guide was with the children. How much he was just like the *brochure*. For parents in desperate need of a break, Dirk was custom-made; he not only guided them competently from one exhibit to the next, but he entertained them on the way.

And he did this by being himself. Big. Lumbering. Sensitive. Somewhat knowledgeable. He was exactly what Robin Jacobs hoped he would be, what Seth Handy thought he might be, and what Patrick never would have guessed in a thousand years. Dirk was, in a Hardy Carroll Goblin Zoo kind of way, *bankable*. And nobody, least of all himself, had the smallest sense of the maelstrom swirling like breeding mosquitoes inside his chest and head.

Holding a kid up, looking for himself out at the great elephants, the mist surrounding Dirk's body and mind thickened.

What do the elephants do to cope with existence? How do they pay their respects?

Thoughts never came this lucidly, but more like soft dark clouds ... swelling then bursting ...

The elephants bury their own.

A stoner teen might've detected a head-trip at this point and pointed to the bulking guide.

It's worth the ticket for the tour, many said. *Just to watch the guide.*

And the guide, ignorant of those who were keeping tabs on him, looked deeper into the foggy dark of his thoughts.

They bury their own because, to the elephant, death is freedom. They congregate, form a circle, use their trunks like shovels, and shovel sand over their own in a hole they dug, too. They are smart animals. And they keep their eyes on the body that looks so much like themselves because they are curious to know what the end looks like. What it looks like when the cage is opened. The fence isn't the elephant's cage; it's their bodies.

Sayings and phrases, a connection of ideas that came vague and less articulate to Dirk. But the meaning was loud and clear.

Often, standing in front of the elephant exhibit, Dirk would imagine a child was lying in that elephant grave. He imagined himself in it, too, as all that sailing sand would look like Goblin rain turned a calming brown. This was an image Dirk could hold on to. The sobriety with which the elephants worked, the sound of the gravel scooped and carefully dropped overhead ... these were thoughts Dirk could manage.

Slow ... grave ... natural.

We want Eula! someone would inevitably say at this point in the tour. But Trudy was next.

He led the children along the orange paw prints painted on the concrete path. And every time they entered Trudy's habitat through the wooden sliding doors, he recalled the night he'd visited her alone.

Dirk felt a bond everlasting with the tiger. The kids saw her as some kind of entertaining monster.

Show us your teeth, Trudy! SHOW US YOUR TEETH!

There were never any dark visions or haunting fantasies when Dirk was near the tiger cage. The room itself was gloomy: thick black bars; slats of jaundiced sunlight through old windows; the many voices of many kids bouncing merrily off the concrete walls. But Dirk felt more at peace near Trudy than at any other stop on the tour.

Perhaps it was because of what was coming next. The ultimate in Dirk's tour-guide mind-screw, when the mist that had started at his ankles officially enveloped his head.

Who wants Eula?

WE DO!

Who wants Eula?

WE DOOOOOO!

Without exception, impatient zoo-goers would rush ahead to the bamboo viewing point, where, if they were lucky, they'd see the shape of a black foot stepping partially into view. A foot that looked much like a man's. But a man as big as the guide and no other.

The prize of the Hardy Carroll Goblin Zoo was at hand, and the hideous banner hanging above the path enforced this. A picture of a female gorilla ferociously frowning above the words:

ENTER IF YOU DARE! IT'S GOBLIN'S GREAT GORILLA!

The grass framing the concrete became tall weeds and trees planted to simulate the brilliant animal's natural environment. The banner was stretched between two enormous bamboo stalks, and here the path turned to dirt. Less than a hundred feet past it were a series of windows framed in bamboo, windows overlooking an expanse of small rolling hills, green with fresh grass. The bamboo was framed with spotlights, for the winter days when the sun went down too soon.

Eula was the closest thing Robin Jacobs had to a cash cow because, like a dream employee, she could be found sitting upon the most visible hilltop, pulling at the low-hanging branches from the nearest tree, looking as magisterial as the photos promised she would. Despite being inclined to entertain, Eula carried a firm dignity in the face of captivity. She was, without argument, the most accessible animal in the park.

For Dirk, Eula was the peak of all the lumbering thoughts that plagued him on the tour. As he stood behind the pack of children and looked over their heads at the gorilla, Dirk was accosted by thoughts as black as the chest she beat.

He had no choice but to let them come.

Without knowing the exact words to describe it, Dirk had long considered a man to be no more than a mind held captive in a clumsy body. But Eula had it worse. Here was a woman not only confined by the body of the beast, but by the fence of the habitat as well. To Dirk, Eula was a woman wedged so far into a clunky ape vessel that she couldn't possibly see the world the way she was meant to. The image of a brain Saran-Wrapped tight lingered in the balcony of Dirk's theatrical, touring mind. *Eula.* A living thing so close to the few freedoms of man . . . lost like a single blade of grass in a maze as confusing as Wayne Sherman's Hedges. *Eula!* So austere to the parents, so *awesome* to the kids, but she was the real horror for Dirk.

Her literal captivity was hard enough for him. But to consider the woman *inside* the gorilla, with no notion to break free, was enough to keep Dirk silent for the duration of the tour's stay at her post.

The zoo-goers just assumed he kept quiet because of how amazing she was. Eula, after all, spoke for herself.

But Dirk couldn't have said a word if he tried.

EULA!

The prize of the Goblin Zoo was, for Dirk, imprisonment. She was too close to man for comfort. She struck a nerve that vibrated into ugly song, rattling the gorilla suit she wore. And after the kids had their fill of her, Dirk knew he'd made it through the worst of it. The rest of the animals, those on the way back, were simply a formality ... even the buffalo hardly sparked a deep thought. And by the time they'd followed the little webbed feet to the penguin house, the zoo's anticlimactic finale, Dirk was on autopilot.

The cold of the penguin ice was like a fan set to cool his overheated imaginings.

Done at last, the parents would thank Dirk and the children would enthusiastically wave goodbye. It was true what Robin Jacobs said. Dirk's *was* the face of the zoo. And he wondered how many of them, those leaving the tour, would confuse his own face for Eula's, two prisoners who spent their days in the park.

After they were gone, Dirk would walk back to the front gate, ready to face another round, another pack of impatient children and their grateful parents who knew nothing of limp freedom and restraint.

Dirk Rogers guided nine of these tours every day of the week, reliving the misty cycle anew with each, peaking like clockwork at the bamboo lookout where Eula sat confined twice over.

7

"That does *not* sound good," Patrick said one night over beers.

Dirk, pulling on a bottle, raised his eyebrows. "No?"

"Anytime things get dreamy for you, I get worried. It means you've got to thinking. Know what I mean, Dirk?"

Dirk didn't know what he meant. He was telling Patrick about the zoo. Had he sounded dreamy? Had he mentioned dreams at all?

"Either way you got the better end of this deal," Patrick said. "I can't wipe the smell of Goblin garbage from my skin, no matter how many showers I take. And you . . . you're like a local celebrity these days. For crying out loud, I see your face on the maps in the trash every day." He sipped his beer. "But I suppose the grass is always greener. Or as us Gobliners say, if it wasn't raining we'd complain about how dry we were."

"What do you mean *dreamy?*"

Dirk believed it meant something.

"You sound a little burdened by your work. That's all."

But it didn't seem like that was all. Not at all.

"Hey," Patrick said. "All I'm saying is, quit the zoo or the House. One or the other. Then you'll have time to take a woman out. And *then* you'll be worried about her instead."

Dirk felt a hotness in his belly. He *wanted* a woman to worry about. He wanted to meet one very badly. Wanted to take her about town in a whirlwind of good times. He wanted to enter a bar like the City Slope with her on his arm.

He'd dress up for it. A suit maybe.

Yes.

He'd clean up well and he'd enter the City Slope with a woman on his arm and he'd take her shawl and hang it on a hook and pull out her stool and hold her hand as she sat down. Then he'd pull a black wallet out of his back pocket and finger the bills as he ordered them both martinis. *That,* he thought in a moment of what felt like supreme clarity, *is how you become your own boss.*

It has nothing to do with your job at all.

But Patrick was right. He *didn't* have a woman. And working the two jobs was doing something to him (*nightmares*). How was he supposed to meet someone when he was so bone-tired from all the tours? What made him go on this way, filling all his time, when he had more than enough money to hit the streets, hit the bars, get himself a suit, after all?

"The problem," Patrick said, "is which do you drop? They're both going pretty well for you."

This was true, too. But Dirk was thinking of dropping them both. Start over or something. Maybe head out to The Hedges and see if Wayne Sherman needed help maintaining that maze. He knew a guy who watered plants at the Woodruff. Said it was the best job he ever had.

But just then, watering the plants sounded too much like feeding the animals.

In the beginning Dirk *liked* the zoo. He walked the paw-print-painted paths in a sort of wonderment, with a genuine respect for the park. But that was gone. Or going.

What was he like before he started working the tours? He couldn't remember. It seemed he'd been leading children in circles for decades.

"You know what we ought to do?" Patrick said, leaning over the table.

"What?"

"We ought to meet us some women. Together. Next week. All we need is a plan. Let's get you to go have some fun. Shit, I used to do it all the time. It's nothing. We'll meet up after work and we'll go—"

"Let's go to the City Slope." Dirk said suddenly. He sat up straighter.

"You wanna go there? Sure. The City Slope it is. Next week. Same time."

"Next week. Same time."

It sounded so easy, the way Patrick proposed it. But it had been so hard to come to that conclusion on his own.

Dirk felt good. He flagged the waitress down and ordered the next round. The television announced that the Marauders were up ten. Dirk and Patrick drank and watched the game and drank a little more.

"Same time next week," Dirk suddenly said. Then he and Patrick cheered their beers, and the clinking of the glasses echoed until it receded into the low steady hum of the otherwise lifeless bar.

8

Long before the night he and Patrick decided to meet up again, same time next week, Dirk sat in "Captain" John Gruff's office at the Goblin Slaughterhouse. *The House*, to those who worked there.

"That'd be pretty ironic, don't you think?" Gruff asked him.

Dirk had heard that word before but didn't know for sure what it meant.

"You working the zoo and the slaughterhouse?"

He still wasn't sure.

"Yes," he answered.

Twenty minutes later he walked out of the office titled *tour guide* twice over. In fact, the duties expected of him at the slaughterhouse nearly mirrored those at the zoo. Six tours a day, Saturday and Sunday. And, oh yes, he'd be expected to chip in with cleaning all the guts and unusable parts out of the steel gutters at night. And, oh yes, he might even be asked to chip in with some of that slaughtering, too.

He didn't have to know the meaning of the word *ironic* to understand that it was a strange thing he'd done. Going out and getting a job at the House might've made sense if he needed the extra money. But Dirk lived humbly and the zoo took care of him just fine. And yet he'd gone and spoken for his Saturdays and Sundays, just as he'd spoken for the other five days of the week a couple of months before. He had no answer when he asked himself why he'd done it, other than a foggy, marshy feeling that it had something to do with freedom, yes, with releasing the prisoners in the House, playing any part that was asked of him.

Even that of killing.

Walking out of Gruff's office after the interview, Dirk rationalized the move without actually using any words. It just felt right. Like the two jobs were the same somehow and by working them both, he'd prove it.

And the immediate links weren't that difficult to find.

It was quite possible Dirk would be killing the same animals he would later feed to, say, Trudy come Monday.

The nightmares began less than two months later.

9

What with all the violence abounding (Dirk once heard two men discussing what to get their daughters for Christmas as one held a piglet down and the other removed its guts), the flow of blood as heavy as the mythic Goblin rain, and the brute force with which "Captain" Gruff ran the place, bad dreams were only a matter of time.

Maybe, if he were able to say so, Dirk would've felt a variety of relief at his second job. If death was the only real freedom from the body, then Dirk was a verified liberator. And maybe, if his thoughts were more concrete, and if he was given to philosophical discourse, the death-run-rampant in the House would have resolved itself in theories, essays, manifestos he might write as he mopped the gutters at the end of his shift. But they weren't. And he didn't. And, instead, Dirk was frightened by the very death he cleaned up.

The eyes of the dead animals looked like the eyes of tourists to Dirk. Eyes turned upward, blank, asking their guide's advice. Dirk would see similar eyes in the faces of the children he led through the horrific stone corridors of his nightmares and sometimes even at the zoo.

His boss at the House made matters more confusing.

"Death," he once told Dirk as he was handing him a mop, "is just what happens next."

Since neither man was given much to articulating philosophy, the comment hung in the air between them for some time before hitting the blood-soaked floor at their feet. Dirk did think a lot about death on the job. The skins still hanging from their hooks and the parts that didn't make it through the grate reminded him that, not only might a man stumble upon the horrific discovery of his own imprisonment, but his entrails would long be proof that he once occupied that cell.

To Dirk, the extra pieces of meat at the end of the shift spelled:

TO THINK IS TO MUTILATE

He imagined the cows might have read it, might've thought the same phrase, in the half second before the sledgehammer came down. Dirk tried to wash it away. He hosed the floor every day he worked. But the words left a stain. And as the discarded bits of flesh and face slid away from him, he often imagined his own limbs being pulled out to sea: a great intake of breath from a submerged blood-covered beast, happy to swallow another dimwit who thought life's great meaning was measurable by the number of goose bumps it gave you when you considered its girth.

Oh, how the House mocked the zoo. Oh, how Dirk felt split in two.

Mop.

Wipe.

Clean.

Kill.

Mop.

"We're a family," John Gruff once told him. "If someone else isn't available, and I need you to kill something, you do it. Right?"

Show an animal.

Kill an animal.

Feed an animal.

Kill an animal.

Show an animal.

The tours at the House were simple. Health inspectors or city employees; men looking for jobs, men looking to sell hogs.

Dirk gave them a tour of the House when they came.

Show an animal.

Kill an animal.

Kill an animal.

Show an animal.

Gruff had even worked it so Goblin Middle and Goblin High got yearly tours. "Educational," he called it, for ten bucks a head. And besides, he argued, some of those kids would be working there one day.

Kids at the zoo. Kids at the House.

And yet, despite the indefatigable horrors Dirk experienced on both jobs, despite the fact that he couldn't imagine anything more powerful than the pair of places, in the end, the dreams were simply bigger than both.

10

The night before he and Patrick met up at the City Slope, there was no sign of the rain that was on its way. Tomorrow would be a record rainfall, no small feat for Goblin. And Dirk, having swiped an unopened invitation for a party in Rolling Hills from his pillow, fell heavy on his bed with thoughts of women and dancing and a nice suit, too. But instead of dreaming of such pleasantries, he had another nightmare. And this one was darker than midnight.

11

It's a fog, really, not that different from any fog that creeps over Goblin in the early hours after (and if) the rain finally relents. It's a fog but it doesn't look like things are wet. Everything in Goblin sort of shines with an eternal slick . . . that sheen of having been finished enough times to stave off a rain that shows no mercy . . . a rain that the surrounding cities whisper to one another about and wonder to one another about and thank God they don't have to endure, too. But that luster . . . the way the benches almost glow green . . . and how the grass reflects the moonlight . . . none of these things are wet. And Dirk knows it because his brown jumpsuit doesn't feel wet when he stands up from that bench, and the grass crunches dry and hard beneath his boots, and he stands there in the mist and wonders how it ended up that he's made it here before the kids.

It's a fog, Dirk tells himself. It doesn't mean anything.

A lamppost standing tall in the dirt near the bench he's risen from shows him things. A tree branch reaches out but is cut off so cleanly at the fog's edge that, to Dirk, it looks like it belongs to no tree. It floats. So does the corner of a sign. Dirk can read,

TO TH

but nothing else and the sign may as well say only this much. He wonders if he could rip that lamppost out of the ground . . . aim it at the sign. He knows he could. He also knows no strength could ever wipe away the fog that covers the rest of that sign. But . . . he wonders . . . does he need to see the rest? Should he?

A bird enters the sphere of light so suddenly, Dirk thinks his trying to imagine the rest of the sign has created it. The sound it makes is funny to him, it almost tickles, and Dirk gasps with the pleasure of it. But this big intake of air is troubling. His lungs feel rubbery. Dirk wonders if he's let the fog in.

He holds a hand to his head and sits down again. He counts his heartbeats . . . he pays very close attention to how he breathes. He is very worried something heavy has entered his body. And then . . . the bird comes through again. This time the sound is even better . . . and it feels like for a moment Dirk's head was cocked back in a tremendous Goblin rain. Water pouring over his face and greasing his hair and running down his jumpsuit and pooling about his boots. And it's a good rain . . . the kind that grants epiphanies . . . the kind that grants peace. But then . . . the bird is gone again . . . and it takes the sound it makes with it . . . and Dirk understands that it still isn't raining and that the bench he sits on is dry as firewood and that maybe he's let more of the fog in.

He leans forward, a heavy hand held up to his chest. He has no trouble breathing. But something feels clumsy. Something feels numb. He hopes for a wild second that the sign in its entirety says,

TO THE HOSPITAL

But he doesn't think that's true.

Footsteps are coming his way down the pavement and well out of range of the light above him.

Maybe it's a doctor, Dirk thinks. *Maybe it's a man who can explain what's gotten into me.*

He waits and listens as the steps get louder, and the way they echo scares him. The echo is louder than the step. The echo is louder than the step.

What sort of creature's echo is louder than its step?

Many pictures of animals flip through Dirk's mind, and because he can see hardly anything else, the images are very well defined. Penguins and pigs. Birds and buffalo. Elephants and eels. Monkeys and—

Dirk edges forward on the bench. *Monkeys. Or something like it.*

Eula.

The name slips into every crack in his mind, fills it as if filling it with an oil that will clean it at last. But thinking that he's figured out what's coming doesn't calm him down.

Is she upset with me? he wonders. *How would Eula know to meet me here? In this fog? Has she broken free?*

The steps get closer and Dirk stares hard into the fog at something he thinks is a shape. His mind's eye imagines Eula, bulking and slow, using her hands to pull her along.

Is she injured? he worries. *She's moving too slow to make him feel any different.*

He sees a shifting in the fog. Something too small to be Eula. Something too small to be any of the animals he's—

The pictures flap rapidly through his mind.

Penguins and pigs.

Birds and buffalo.

Elephants and eels.

Monkeys and . . . men.

A child emerges from the fog. A child whose shoes, had they been inside the tiger room or the aviary, would squeak . . . would echo-bounce off the concrete walls and would return louder than the original step. A child emerges whose echo is louder than his step.

Is this where we meet for the tour? the boy asks.

Dirk stares at him for a moment. There doesn't seem to be anything strange about the boy at all.

Yes, he says. But why are you the only one here? Where are the others?

The boy looks genuinely unsure.

I haven't a clue. You are the guide, right?

Dirk rises again from the bench and wonders if he doesn't feel a little heavier than the last time he stood.

Yes, he answers. I'm the guide. I'm your guide. You can sit on the bench while we wait for the others.

What will it be like? the boy asks.

What will what be like?

The tour. The end of the tour. The animals. Will they be happy or sad?

Dirk looks around because he hears more sounds like the sound this boy made approaching. Maybe a dozen kids on their way. Maybe more. He sits back down on the bench.

The tour is going to blow your mind, Dirk says.

The boy smiles and, as he does, two fingers poke out of the boy's mouth.

What's wrong? the boy asks.

Dirk inches away from the child, not sure why, and touches his own throat. He wonders if the same thing didn't get into his mouth when he gasped before. Maybe, what with all the fog, something might've been hiding.

Dirk touches the armrest on the park bench while keeping his eye on the boy and his ear on the children approaching. The bench is still dry. More dry than it deserves to be for having been built in Goblin.

I'm just worried about us getting started, Dirk lies. I don't want us to have to rush through the tour.

That would be bad, the boy says.

Yes, Dirk agrees.

The coming steps get louder and the boy says, I want to see—

But Dirk can't quite hear what the boy wants to see. Too many steps now. Too many echoes. And the bird returns, suddenly appears, and it fills Dirk with such a sensation that he must gasp again even though he's nervous to. He gasps and falls back against the Goblin bench, giggling, the way the sound tickles him, fingers lightly on the back of his neck, the back of his throat. This time Dirk thinks for a moment that he's the boy and that the boy is his guide, telling him everything he needs to know about the birds. And it feels good. As good as the rain that isn't falling, either.

Did you say you wanted to see the birds? Dirk asks.

I said I want to see the blood, the boy answers.

And the bird leaves again, evaporating into the fog. Dirk fears he has let even more of the fog in.

There is no blood on this tour, Dirk says, clutching his own belly, feeling for what has gotten into him.

The boy looks confused.

No?

No.

How come?

There is no blood on this tour. Not on my watch.

Are we at the zoo then? the boy asks.

The echoes coming from the fog now have dark shapes to go with them.

No, Dirk answers. We are not at the zoo.

Then we are at the House. I want to see the blood.

No. We are not at the House.

The boy leans forward. The fingers in his mouth press down his lower lip and a green gas escapes him. He whispers,

Then where the fuck are you taking us?

Dirk raises his own fingers to his own teeth . . . feels a tickling in his throat . . . a man within . . .

The boy laughs.

And the echo of this laughter is louder than the laugh. And the echo of this laughter is louder than the laugh.

The shapes in the fog step through . . . twenty children more step through.

Is this where we meet to take the tour?

Is this where we meet to take the tour?

Is this where we meet to take the tour?

Dirk rises from the bench and now he knows he's heavier. Maybe it's only a pound . . . maybe it's even less . . . but he knows it's true. And all the fog in the world couldn't scare him as much as that pound or less added to his hulking frame.

The children go silent and gape at him with awe. Dirk towers above them. There are no parents here. There are no co-workers here. There are no bosses here, either.

Dirk is frightened of these children but he is frightened for them even more. He stands silent. They all do. There is no echo of footsteps. There is no fluttering of the bird's wings. And yet Dirk thinks he can hear the fog. He believes he can hear the fog breathe and he wonders if, by entering him, the fog is using him to breathe.

Dirk brings a hand to his forehead.

A little girl with remnants of the fog still clinging to her says, Are you going to guide us out of here?

Dirk looks down to her, scared.

It's your job, she says, to guide us out of here. To guide us to freedom.

And a piece of the fog she still carries with her slides up her neck and glides slowly across her cheek. For a moment her face is twisted, her features out of place.

Dirk gasps again and steps back, feeling the bench at the back of his knees.

It's your job, she says again. And now they all do. They all start telling him it's his job. Their voices are whining and impatient and Dirk recognizes this impatience very well.

They just want the tour, Dirk thinks, shrinking still. They need the tour.

And the fog passes from the girl's face and Dirk sees she is intact again. She is fine and whole. The fog just showed him something the light never could.

I need to show them freedom, Dirk thinks. I need to show them a way out. Or else they'll grow into the bodies that enslave them. They'll grow until they first reach the interior of that body-shell and are forced to live with the unbearable claustrophobia of knowledge forever.

Give us the tour! they say. GIVE US THE TOUR! GUIDE US, DIRK ROGERS! GUIDE US!

Dirk hears the fog breathe in. He is frightened for the children now. The fog wants to show him something the light never could. The fog wants to show him something the light—

Dirk steps up onto the bench. It's still dry beneath his boot, and his footing is fine. It has not rained. He is right about that and he, a Gobliner all the way, is grateful. The children watch him and wonder. The fog surrounds them like a solid curtain now, the dark cloth of the Domino Theater. Dirk reaches out and grips the lamppost. He tries to pull it toward himself. It doesn't move. He tries harder.

Incredible, a boy says.

There is an unfathomable wrenching sound as the steel of the lamppost bends and Dirk's fingers sink into it. He huffs as he works and the children have forgotten about their tour. For now.

Dirk twists the post and the sound so eclipses that of the fog breathing that he is granted an accidental reprieve from having to think of it. He thinks of the sliding steel doors of the House and he thinks of them bowing in on themselves, folding up and over again until the whole of the four doors are folded into steel squares so small he could drop them through the holes in the grate of the gutters and never have to open or close them again. He thinks of the bars on Trudy's cage and he thinks of them wrapping around one another, in and out of one another, twisting like the trees of the North Woods until the mass created is dense enough to fill the great golden trash can of the Hardy Carroll Goblin Zoo.

Dirk stops. The post is bent at close to a ninety-degree angle. He leans on it and rests.

What's wrong? a boy asks.

Dirk lifts his head and turns to the children.

I don't know how to free them without hurting them, he says.

He squeezes the post tighter but does not know it.

Maybe they don't think the same way you do, a girl says.

Dirk feels a nervous swelling in his chest. The words he has spoken and the words spoken to him by the children feel fleeting, like fluttering wings. Will he remember them? After? Already the words exchanged are vague. They drift toward the fog and there they will come to rest somewhere Dirk will never locate again.

He grips the post and bends it back up to its original position. Then he tears it down and the metal splits and he is thrown back a step onto the bench with the top half of the post in his hand.

That was unreal, a boy says. It seems to be the first words spoken by one of the kids in a long time.

Dirk steps down from the bench, lamppost in hand. The sphere of light changes with his location, showing a new part of the road they have all met. Dirk's boots make a grinding sound as they hit the pavement. He thinks of Christmas, the dirt road, but he doesn't think this is it. He walks a few feet up to the sign. He holds the light up to it.

TO THINK IS TO MUTILATE

Dirk turns back to the children. He steps through the crowd they make, toward the other side of the road. The fog splits with the light and soon Dirk sees the entrance to what looks like a cave.

There is a door. A mineshaft maybe. Something like that.

Stone walls.

The children are gathered at Dirk's knees as he steps to the door and traces the entire frame slowly with his fingertips.

It's solid stone, he says. A stone corridor.

What does that mean? a girl asks.

Dirk turns the wooden knob and the door opens inward. The light shows them six feet into the hallway and nothing more. Cold air comes out slowly, mingles with the fog, makes frost of the breathing.

It's the tour! a child exclaims.

Dirk touches his belly and hopes to God not too much fog has gotten inside him. He feels okay. He feels all right. He feels like he can do this.

He stares hard at where the light ends. There is something white there. Something sticky. Something like . . . webbing.

Follow me, he says. And the children do.

The tour begins.

12

When Dirk woke the next morning it was already raining lightly outside. Just barely. It was possible that not even all of Goblin knew it yet.

He stepped into the bathroom and stood before the mirror. The toothbrush in his mouth, he thought,

Tonight I'm going to be my own boss.

And he believed it.

Tonight was the night he and Patrick were going to the City Slope. They were going to meet some women. Dirk was going to start living a regular life. What was it Patrick said? Oh yes, they were going to "mix things up."

After brushing his teeth he opened his mouth wide before the mirror, ready lest a finger or two suddenly poked out of his throat.

Dirk dressed quickly and went to work.

13

Because he needed something to *cheer*. He needed to be able to lift his drink and say, *Because of this.*

And "going out" wasn't going to cut it. For Hell's sake, that was something he should have been doing every night. No. And it wasn't going to be "to the good fortune" he'd had so far at the zoo and the House. That idea made him sick. No way. Tonight he was going to sit down in a booth across from Patrick and Dirk was going to lift his drink and say, *Patrick! Here's to me quitting one of my jobs.*

In his pants pocket, Dirk had his two weeks' notice. Patrick would have no problem drinking to *that*. And the whole thing gave Dirk the shivers. The good kind. A quiet voice in his over-lapped mind kept saying something about the animals not think-ing the same way he does.

Something about fog, too, and guiding a tour into Hell.

14

The tours were less unbearable for the little secret Dirk had hidden in his pocket beneath his brown uniform. In fact, they were almost enjoyable. To see the faces of the kids as he showed them things and told them things they'd never learned anywhere else before . . . it was very close to amazing.

At lunch a co-worker said, "You've got a little extra *oomph* in you today, Dirk. What gives?"

Dirk wasn't about to tell him about the two weeks' notice, but he did say, "It's the tour. I feel like I've bought a ticket. I really do. I think one of the tours today will be the one I remember most . . . down the road . . . years from now. You know what I mean?"

The guy shrugged. "No. I honestly have no idea what you mean. But that's why we love you, Dirk."

Dirk hadn't thought about it before he said it but he *did* feel like a tourist. Everything even smelled different.

He finished eating and knew that half of his last day was al-ready over. It wasn't even the act of quitting so much. It was much more than that. Like he was doing something he wouldn't ordi-narily do. But that wasn't quite right. And there was something else, too. Something that jabbed a little at his brain as he was washing his hands in the bathroom. Something about the night before. Something that happened. Maybe something while he was sleeping . . .

15

The moment Dirk enters the corridor he's nervous. He's sure that his abdomen feels heavier, that his feet are more flat than even when he was standing on the bench. He starts down the hall anyway, guided by the light of the lamppost head. Every time he looks forward he feels the walls are too close, that he and the children won't be able to fit through the farthest point he can see. But once they make it there he discovers that they can.

My eyes, Dirk thinks. Something is screwing with my eyes.

There are many sounds in here. Scratching sounds. Feet on gravel. A hoarse throat perhaps. Dirk keeps thinking that it's one of the children, clawing at the walls. Trying to get out. But when he turns around he sees they are following him. That is all.

Aren't you going to tell us anything? a girl asks.

What do you want to know about?

I wanna see the blood, the girl says. I wanna take some home with me.

The children cry out with excitement but it sounds like fear, too, and Dirk looks deeper into the stone corridor, white dust and webbing everywhere.

There are other sounds, too. Scurrying sounds. Something wet ahead. Something slithering across the path just out of reach of their sphere of light. Dirk is frightened. But the fog is pressing against the closed wooden door behind them. He knows this, and going back into it would be bad. Awful maybe.

Look! a child yells.

Dirk blinks and sees something small huddled against the right wall ahead of them. He stops and holds out his arm to block the children from continuing.

What is it? a boy whispers.

He doesn't know what it is. None of them do. But it is huddled and maybe beneath a hood. It is facing the other way. Facing farther down the hall. Dirk steps forward. He can feel the heaviness of his body, he can feel the heat of his nerves as they burn, too.

He and the light are only a foot from the thing against the wall.

Are you all right? Dirk asks. His voice is strong. Thunderous almost. And things scurry ahead at the sound of it.

The thing does not move. It does not turn. It does not respond.

What is it? a girl asks.

Dirk steps toward the hooded thing.

We are going to step past you now, Dirk says. We are going to step past you and continue down the hall.

The tension is unbelievable. The light is shaky because Dirk is shaky. There are more sounds now . . . soft howls . . . metal on metal . . . dull thudding . . . and something wet sliding overhead.

Dirk looks up quick and sees a leg slide out of range. It looked like a woman's leg. A person to be sure.

This is a chicken, Dirk says to the children, pointing at the huddled thing. He's too scared to continue.

The children view it like they do the flamingos. Like they do the pigs.

Cool, a boy says.

Dirk steps past the thing and turns to look at it in the light. There seems to be no face beneath the hood. Just solid yellow skin stretched tight across a melon. Then the melon turns and Dirk sees a chicken's beak wedged into a face as putty-like as the Goblin Police.

Come on, kids, Dirk says.

They pass the huddled thing and continue down the hall. Dirk hears a swiping sound, something moving quickly behind them. A child screams then its scream is cut off.

Then . . . clucking.

Clucking.

Clucking.

Dirk knows the child was taken by the huddled thing.

He quickens the pace but it's hard. His body feels heavy. His body feels bloated. His body feels like a Goblin sky, fat with so much rain it must dump itself on an entire city at once.

He feels a hump growing in his back. He reaches for it and can feel it, yes, a hump growing in his back.

Howling ahead. Steel on steel. Grating. Clucking. The scuffle of the children's shoes on the ground, the scuffle of wet things overhead.

And now a hump growing out of his back.

How long before he can't see over his own shoulder?

16

Dirk Rogers woke every day an optimist and fell asleep despaired.

He would leave his place with vigor and return to flop upon a chair at his kitchen table, only enough energy left within him to stare at the tabletop.

But today . . . *today was supposed to be different.* Today he was quitting. Tonight he was hitting the town with Patrick.

Today the routine that haunted him had to end.

So why wasn't it ending?

Dirk, never given to fully articulating his feelings, guessed that maybe it wasn't so easy a thing to change.

"Dirk!" someone hollered. "What are you doing?"

Dirk looked down and saw he was washing his hands in the drinking fountain. At first he laughed, but really this scared him. Did he think he was still in the bathroom?

"Man," his co-worker said, smiling, "*someone* needs a vacation."

Dirk took this comment as a good omen. It sort of *righted the ship.* If it was a vacation he needed, he'd already seen to it that he was getting one. His mind must have been clouded with the anticipation of handing in his two weeks' notice.

That's all.

Dirk headed back to where the tours began. A co-worker passed him, coming from the other direction, and Dirk paused, watched the man pass, and reached over his shoulder, as if looking for a sudden hump.

Get through the next tour, he told himself. *Then put in your notice.*

But he couldn't stop thinking that the co-worker reminded him of someone called the Mixed-up Man. Someone Dirk had seen in a very bad dream.

17

*T*his is a good tour, *a boy says.* And here comes another exhibit.

Dirk thinks he hears something like footsteps coming their way, but mixed in with all the other sounds echoing off the stone walls, it's difficult to say.

He tells himself that his ears are going to hear things he doesn't want to hear . . . that the children shouldn't hear.

A figure shows ahead.

What is it? a girl asks.

A man, Dirk thinks and then says.

The man is momentarily caught between the darkness of the corridor and the light of the lamppost head. He looks dead to Dirk. Or half a man maybe. Just the front, visible half. But when he steps into the full sphere of the light, Dirk sees he is whole.

Oh my! he says. How was it?

Dirk is cautious as he responds. How was what?

The man fumbles with his hands. He seems extremely nervous. He runs in place then settles down again. He looks Dirk in the eye and then doesn't. He licks his lips and looks over his shoulder and then back past the children rapidly.

How was the prize? he says. How was the trophy?

The man wears a suit. Because it's brown it's difficult to see that it's covered in dirt and that parts are ripped open. Dirk imagines the man running alongside the stone walls, tearing his clothes apart.

I don't understand, Dirk says.

The man looks Dirk in the eye and smiles. Then his smile falls from his face and he looks down to his hands. Then back up at Dirk. He squints into the light and says, You are tourists, right?

Dirk isn't sure he wants to talk to this man anymore. But a boy behind him says, Yes.

Then you must have seen the prize.

Dirk doesn't want the kids talking to this man.

We've seen nothing but stone, he says.

The man stops moving for the first time. He is taken aback, it seems. It's hard to tell what he feels. His expressions run the gamut of emotions very fast.

Don't tell me there's just stone, he says. That would break my heart, he says. I know there must be more, he says. The brochure said so.

Dirk is silent. So are the children.

The man's face breaks into a smile again. He shows relief and slaps a hand on his knee.

You're toying with me! Good one. Now tell me . . . please . . . what was it like? I won't tell a soul.

There are so many sounds beyond him. Dirk hears something slither across the ceiling again. He looks up and sees a woman's back slip out of sight. He feels bloated. Too big. Like he's pressing against his skin, from the inside out. He looks down at his own feet and sees that, yes, his belly and chest have grown. Something has gotten into him for sure.

Tell me, the man says. I'm just starting out. You're on your way back.

There is a little gasp among the children.

We're not on our way back, Dirk tells the man. We're on our way there.

What do you mean to do, fooling with me? the man says. You are on your way back!

Dirk looks back down the hall from which they came.

What was it like? the man says. What did it look like?

Dirk says, There is nothing but fog back there.

The man cocks a thumb back where he came from. Yeah? Well, there is nothing but mist back there!

Dirk doesn't believe him. But the man believes himself. The man runs his fingers through his thinning brown hair. He looks beyond the children, then back down the hall. Dirk thinks he understands what is going on now.

I think you are mixed up, Dirk says. I think you are going the wrong way.

The children nod and nudge one another.

The man says, But I've been—

But Dirk interrupts him. You've already seen the prize.

And Dirk suddenly knows this is true.

The man pouts. He shakes his head no. Dirk wonders if he's searching his mind for what the end might have been like.

Is that right? the man asks.

I think so, Dirk tells him.

A terrible crunching sound erupts from well beyond the man. Some of the children recoil and some of them simply lift up onto their tiptoes to see what it might be. Dirk is frightened for many reasons. The sound is a familiar one, metal on muscle, metal on tissue, metal on bone. The image of a man squashed comes to mind. Squashed inside himself. Visions of pigs and cows split from head to tail come to mind, too. But what scares him most is this man. Dirk wants to ask him what he saw. But he knows that what he saw has done something to him.

As if cued, the man starts back into the darkness ahead of them. The darkness he came from. He vanishes. Dirk and the children stand still and watch. They hear shuffling, shifting, something crawling quick up the left side wall.

Then the man emerges from the darkness again.

Oh my! he says. How was it?

Even the sounds beyond him cease some. The corridor is quiet. Dirk doesn't know what to do. Then he does.

It was incredible, he answers. It was as beautiful as the brochure promised.

The man smiles. He looks like he might cry or like he's traveled so long to reach this spot in the hall and now here's this big man with all these children tell-

ing him, Yes, you have made it, yes, it was incredible, yes. The sorrow Dirk feels for this mixed-up man is bigger than the sorrow he feels for himself. He can feel the sympathy pressing against the interior of his body-shell and he worries lest it split him apart, leaving the kids with no guide for the tour.

Thank you, the man says, thank you. Maybe I will see you back at the beginning. Maybe we can talk about what we saw together. Maybe we can talk about what the end looks like. Together.

He steps forward and sticks out his hand for Dirk to shake. Nervously Dirk takes it.

Truly though? the man says. Just like the brochure?

Yes, Dirk says.

The man steps past Dirk and the children at last. He vanishes into the darkness behind them.

I hope there are many exhibits like that one, a boy says. That one made me think.

Dirk aims the half lamppost ahead.

I have a feeling, he says, there will be more.

The Mixed-up Man, a girl says. And Dirk almost tells her his name is Dirk. Then, walking again, guiding again, splitting the darkness apart with the lamppost again, he realizes she wasn't referring to him.

18

"Come on," Dirk said out loud. Some of the kids on tour looked up at him.

It was a bad sign that, on this day, a day that was supposed to be so good, he was still letting the bad in.

One kid nudged another. They snickered. After all, the big tour guide was *talking to himself.* The rain was starting to "catch up" as Gobliners said, for when the sky was clear, the rain was simply lagging behind. But this storm felt bigger than most. People were talking about floods. And here, the tour guide in a slicker looked just as stormy as the sky.

Dirk knew it had something to do with a nightmare, specifically the one he had the night before, but bad dreams were nothing new those days. In fact, Dirk was so used to them that he didn't know *what* to blame for his daily flip-book of horror visions. If pressed, Dirk, using all the power of philosophy he was capable of conjuring, would have said it was a *way out* that consumed him. Freedom from a box he didn't fully understand the dimensions of.

The children were occupied (for a few minutes anyway) and nobody noticed as the big tour guide in brown zoned out on the path. He lifted a hand to his head. Thoughts materialized slowly. Pieces of the unconscious night before.

There were stone corridors, he thought. *But there are always stone corridors.*

The children laughed at something Dirk wasn't paying attention to.

There were children, yes, but there are always children.

Dirk excavated his memory but there was nothing he hadn't seen before, nothing to make this day any darker than any other day.

Nothing you hadn't forgotten *before*, he told himself.

Was this true? Was there more to the dream he dreamed a hundred times?

"Mister Guide Man!" a child yelled, tugging on his brown pants. "You're not doing your job!"

Dirk looked down at the boy, his eyes a foggy green. "You want to see the rest? You want to see the prize?"

"Yes!" the kids cried. "Yes!"

19

*I*t's just a hall really . . . stones piled one upon the other . . . something easy to make. But Dirk can't believe how much of it there is. It seems the children have been keeping up with him for a long time now and he wonders if, when he was their age, he could have done the same. His body feels heavy. It even looks heavy and this worries him greatly. The hump on his shoulder has reached almost as high as his eyes. His feet are so large that he stumbles.

His abdomen hangs in lumps. His hands are swollen to the size of small mittens. He knows it's the fog. He knows the bird distracted him back there on the bench so the fog could get in. And now it's growing.

He lumbers on. The lamppost head continues to emit enough light to guide them.

Some of their number have been lost. There was the boy swiped by the huddled, clucking thing. Another, a little girl, touched her arm to the webbing and when Dirk tried to free her, her arm snapped off at the elbow. She ran screaming into the darkness from which they came. Another boy was taken when a trapdoor opened and long hairy legs pulled him into the floor.

Look! a boy says.

Dirk stops and holds the light to the ceiling where they see the leg of a man or a woman jutting out from the darkness.

Can I touch it? a boy asks.

No, Dirk answers.

He steps forward slowly and the leg slithers out of sight.

Dirk continues and the children follow.

The sounds have changed. There is still the echo of the children's sneakers. The echo of the children's voices. There is still the constant sound of something scurrying ahead, slithering to either side. But the scratching has been replaced entirely with the sound of steel. Not machinery. Not exactly.

Metallic echoes now.

Deformed, Dirk lumbers on. The children keep tight to him.

Something fast whisks by the pack, heading the opposite way, something large, fleshy, bloated . . .

Dirk tries to move fast but he feels fat. He feels like he is carrying the weight of at least two children now. He accidentally brushes against the wall. His arm explodes into pain and he starts bleeding immediately. He thinks the walls might be lined with burrs, something serrated. He continues by holding the lamppost in the hand of the injured arm and tries to tighten his shirt around the wound with the other.

Avoid the walls! he says. Then he realizes how fitting a phrase that is for the time.

The children take his advice and now the pack walks more in the center of the hall. Dirk is surprised that there is enough room for them to do this. The air is getting thick. Sludgy. The tunnel is hot. It's heavy on the lungs. It is heavy on the body.

Dirk hears a child wheeze. He turns to him.

Are you all right? he asks, his own face swollen to twice its original size. His voice sounds too fatty to be his own.

The boy nods yes, and his nose falls to the gravel floor. From the hole in his face, a new one, an ape's, grows in.

Dirk stares at the boy a long time. Then he looks to the rest of the children. He believes there are only two-thirds of them remaining. He doesn't know what took the others, how each in turn has vanished.

He continues.

Astonishing sounds erupt ahead. Crunching. Slithering. Swallowing. The darkness ahead takes on a darker pallor and Dirk considers stopping. It looks like something might be blocking the way. He can't tell. He lumbers forward. The darkness approaches as Dirk approaches it. It is stationary. He wonders, Is this the end? The range of light shows him that it is not.

Rather, the walls have changed.

The stone has given way to steel.

Dirk reaches cautiously and touches the new wall. The light of the lamppost head shows him that it is smooth. It is old, but it is smooth.

I think we're near the end, a boy says.

Why do you say that? Dirk asks.

I've taken the tour before.

Dirk crouches to the height of the boy, but a second tongue in the boy's mouth causes Dirk to rise again and step away from him.

What's it like? Dirk asks.

What's what like?

The end.

A little girl laughs and says, Now you sound like the Mixed-up Man.

20

Something a kid said or something Dirk saw or something too slippery to hold was driving Dirk crazy. He no longer cared about how he was supposed to be feeling. Yes, he had his notice in his pocket. Yes, he was celebrating with Patrick tonight. Yes, he should feel liberated. But now he was all twisted up again. Just like yesterday. Just like the day before yesterday and the day before that. If there was any difference at all it was that this time his thoughts were coming twice as fast. Twice as hard. Instead of the hailstorm he was used to, today's problems were big rocks that could never get through the grates of the gutters at the House and would be difficult to carry to the dumpster at the zoo. Dirk fought the onslaught nobly. He tried. He imagined how he'd look in that suit at the City Slope. He imagined a woman on his arm. But there was no stopping the way he felt.

Now you sound like the Mixed-up Man.

He thought about that two weeks' notice. He imagined days off. What he might do, where he might go. The GAG, Perish Park, the Domino. He'd relax on the lawns he once mowed. He'd walk the marble floors of every municipal building he once mopped.

It sounded nuts, Dirk guessed, but he missed the days when he picked up all the trash and threw it all away.

Dirk fingered the paper in the pocket of his brown pants and smiled.

This was his last tour, he realized. Last one for the day.

The children lolled absently, waiting for the big guide to tell them what to do next. Dirk wiped sweat and rain from his face and said, "That's it. Thank you for touring. Thank you for coming to the—"

BOOM!

The Goblin sky erupted. The tour takers ran down the path covering their heads. Dirk stood still in the rain and watched them. He heard siblings racing. He heard parents chase after them. He heard cars start and wipers start and tires squash the fresh-fallen water. A parking lot of lights turned on at once, battling the gray-green of early evening and a rain they all knew wasn't going to leave them alone.

Dirk watched it and thought,

This is what the end looks like.

And then his mind connected some loose dots.

That's it, he thought. *There was an end.*

The rain slid from the brim of his brown hood.

And I saw it.

21

Soon there is a break in the steel. Dirk holds the light near. There is a space. Two inches where the steel ends and then continues.

Cautiously Dirk extends his fingers toward it and to his surprise they slip through. He feels air. Real air.

Outside, he says.

He holds the light against the open space. He can't see far but he sees there is no fog here. He leans forward and breathes the air in. It feels good. Very good. The children mimic him. One by one they experience the air in the break. While they do so Dirk steps to the other side of the corridor and sees there is a twin. A duplicate break in the opposite wall. He sets the lamppost head down for the first time since entering and grips the two sides of steel. He tries hard to widen the space. The children think he can do it. They've seen him tear a lamppost in half. They've seen him break a little girl's arm.

But for all his might, Dirk can't bend the wall.

He leans forward and takes in another great gulp of the outside. It fills him with a renewed vigor for getting to the end. Dirk wonders if that's what the space is for. To give him enough strength, just enough, to keep him going.

He goes.

Things slither across the ceiling with more regularity now. Sometimes Dirk sees the entire back of a man. A woman's profile. Toes and fingers.

Dirk reaches another break in the steel. He and the children gulp another breath before continuing. More bodies cross the ceiling. One even comes at them on the stone floor. No arms. No head. All legs. The children step aside.

Cackles ahead. Crunching. Fire crackling, too. A third break in the steel walls comes sooner than the second did. Again Dirk and the children take a breath of the outside.

The fourth one comes so soon that only half the kids breathe it in. And Dirk now understands that some of the noises are coming from the outside. He stumbles ahead. His torso feels huge, his feet are like flat paddles, the hump on his back is making it impossible to see the children. But he knows. He knows that only ten or so were there at the last break in the steel. He knows he's lost ten or more along the way.

The fifth break comes even sooner. Then the sixth. The seventh. The eighth. There are so many symmetrical breaks in the walls now that most of the air in the corridor is from the outside and it can hardly be called a corridor anymore. But the breaks are not big enough for Dirk or the children to step through. The ninth, the tenth, the eleventh. Through the breaks Dirk sees there is a green Goblin mist . . . like the man said . . . but it is nothing like the fog. In the mist . . . in the darkness just past the mist . . . Dirk sees people. Shapes. Faces. People watching him and the children. Some snicker. Some gasp.

Dirk starts to understand what is happening. By the fourteenth space in the steel he knows it for sure.

He stops and holds the light close to what used to be a stone wall and is now only three-inch wedges of steel spaced three inches or so apart, reaching the ceiling and the floor.

We're in a cage, Dirk says.

What a twist! one of children says.

And we're being looked at, Dirk says.

He counts some fifty faces in the green mist beyond the bars. Some of the children step to the bars and grip them like little prisoners.

This is not the end, Dirk says. There's more. Follow me.

He begins to walk but the children are slow to follow. Dirk turns and sees that some of the people from the outside are at the edge of the cage, bent at the waist and whispering to the children. The children whisper back.

Don't speak to them! Dirk yells.

A woman from the outside turns to Dirk and frowns and her face slides down her head like jelly.

The children seem to be astonished by what they hear.

Don't listen to them, Dirk says.

He feels something wet touch his arm. He turns quick. A man has been licking Dirk's arm.

Come on! Dirk calls to the children.

A hand comes through the bars, reaching for Dirk. Dirk grabs it and bends the fingers back. They squish like dead fruit, like the soft pumpkin flesh of the Goblin Police.

An unbearable howl erupts from the mist and Dirk has to put his hands to his ears. He drops the lamppost as he does. His hands feel fat. His ears feel phony.

Without the light, it feels like a thousand mouths are at the bars, whispering directions.

Dirk struggles to bend at the waist—his body is unevenly bloated—but he takes hold of the lamppost again and says, This is not the end.

Then he's moving again and some of the children follow.

Dirk can't look over his shoulder but he knows only five or six are still with him now. A few remain with the people from the outside. Listening to their whispers.

Did he tell you anything? a boy asks, short on breath they are moving so fast.

I didn't let him, Dirk says.

You should have. It was interesting.

Yeah?

The boy catches up to Dirk.

Yeah. He told me that to be your own boss means something else than what people mean when they say it.

Dirk stops and turns to face the boy. What?

I told you, the boy says. It's—

But what does it mean? Dirk says.

It doesn't mean you want to be your own boss. It means you want to be the master of your own mind.

Dirk stares hard into the child's eyes. He is no longer looking at the boy at all. His eyes glaze over. What the boy said means a great deal to him.

Thank you, Dirk whispers.

He continues. The children follow.

They race through the corridor now. The air from the outside is colder. Dirk doesn't look through the bars anymore. His clumsy body doesn't concern him now. He can feel the end is close. He forgets the children are with him and then he remembers the children are with him and then he forgets. He thinks of the Mixed-up Man and he tells himself he's got to remember things. He reminds himself of everything. He reminds himself to remember. He refuses to forget the end.

He has no idea how fast or slow he's actually going. Passing bars. Metallic echoes. A boy tugs at Dirk's pants.

What is it?

Mine was different, the boy says.

They are moving so fast now.

What do you mean?

Dirk worries for a moment that he can't remember what the kid is talking about and that he should be able to.

The boy says, The whispers I heard. The things I was told.

What did they tell you? Dirk asks, running.

They told me that freedom is doing something you would never ordinarily do. Freedom is leaving the person you're used to being behind. Real freedom is doing something so dreadful that you have no choice but to turn your back on yourself. Do you understand?

Dirk wants to stop. He wants to address this child. He wants to tell him that what he heard back there was horribly wrong.

But there's no time for that. The slithering crunching crawling howling metal-on-metal metal-on-bone grinding mopped guts grates bars bending blood and fog

ENDS.

The path ends.

No more bars. No more cage.

Dirk drops the lamppost. They don't need it anymore.

They've reached the end.

And the children scream.

Dirk is confused. What he sees is beautiful. A landscape fans open before them, small withered shrubs far from one another, open space, colors so bright Dirk squints.

A boy says LOOK just as Dirk sees a costume of some kind on the ground. His eyes adjust and he sees it's a gorilla suit, unzipped, left behind.

How could you do this? a child yells.

There is a white wind. It blows through Dirk's hair and he brings a six-fingered hand to shield his eyes from it. He sees a child rendered dust by the gust.

How could you show this to us!

Dirk's eyes are open and he is trying but he can't find the children in all the white wind.

How could you! they yell.

How could you show this to us!

Dirk's eyes water from the wind. Tears run down his face. He reminds himself to remember every detail. He hears the children taken in the wind. He hears the wind above all else. And he is blinded by it. What he sees is beautiful.

Ten feet beyond the gorilla suit, crouched behind a shrub, is a naked woman looking back at him.

Eula, Dirk says. You escaped.

22

To see Dirk then, standing still as the sky unloaded, his stoic face wet with sweat and rain and tears now, too, to see him at the precise moment of comprehension, would have been enough to change any Gobliner's opinion of the face of the zoo and the House.

He stepped forward at last, his boots heavy and wet, and headed back to the tour's starting point. A sign there said:

THIS IS THE PLACE ALRIGHT!

Dirk stared at it. How many times had he seen this sign? When was the last time he read it? A profound sadness filled the infinitesimal spaces of his brain like grout. He touched the sign, as though saying goodbye to it, and headed inside.

Once there, he approached the tools. He had his end-of-the-shift duties to take care of before leaving to meet up with Patrick for the much-needed night out. He had to take some trash out. Mop up a bit. Wipe some surfaces. Clean some glass. He performed these tasks quietly, hardly thinking of them at all. The place was empty as his co-workers were either already on their way home or beyond Dirk's range of hearing. Dirk didn't speak. He kept his eye on his work. Whatever he was feeling could bloom, if he let it, into relief. He had a vague idea that he'd been through Hell and was now making the right changes. But he was worried that if he wasn't careful, the feeling could snap back at him, blossom into something blacker than the Hell he'd already been through. He had a vision of himself falling down a flight of stairs in that darkness, all mixed up and broken on the floor of Hell's cellar.

There was a little more cleaning to do, a few notes to be made in the tour log. He had to leave his uniform by the laundry. Make sure the lights were off. Wipe the muck from his boots. And . . .

And there was an animal to kill.

Yes, a job the boss had told him about this morning, at the head of the shift. Dirk hardly listened to him when he said it, knowing the job inside out. It was as if the boss could've said *Hey, Dirk,* and Dirk wouldn't have needed another word for clarification.

And wasn't that why he was quitting in the first place? Wasn't it a bad thing when your job became so routine you didn't even have to listen to the instructions your boss gave you?

One more animal. Okay.

He opened the equipment locker. At first the tools confused him. Like they were new tools. Different. Strange shapes, odd angles.

Dirk took the scythe and lumbered toward his final act. The many events from his nightmare were shrunk now to the size of a birthday present.

His mind was clean.

Sadly, the animal seemed glad to see him. They all did and they always had. Dirk approached her and crouched beside her.

"It's my last day," he told her, stroking her back. "But maybe one day we'll meet somewhere less cluttered."

The animal rested her head in the crook of Dirk's arm. He

stroked her head lightly before sliding the tool out from beneath his slicker.

The sound it made was quick. Slick. And Dirk's entire forearm was bathed in the warmth of her blood.

Then Dirk got up and headed back inside, off to take a shower.

He imagined how he'd look in his suit as he washed his hands and body.

On his way out, Dirk stepped into the office and placed his resignation on the desk. He turned the lamp on above it so the boss couldn't miss it. He stood in the doorway and looked back at the white paper for a long time.

It felt good. Man. It really did.

As far as Dirk knew, it would be the last time he ever stepped foot in the House.

23

"That's *awesome!*"

Patrick was as excited about Dirk quitting the House as Dirk thought he'd be. "That's gonna take more than one shot," he said, ordering another round from the bar.

The City Slope was just what Dirk needed. They sat at the bar, on golden stools, sinking into the ambience, feeling the music, the voices, the nightlife surrounding them. The bar was crowded. A wall-length mirror framed in soft marquee lights reflected the pair, and Dirk liked the looks of himself in a suit.

A future with many nights like this one was spread before him like a pack of playing cards. He could pick them all if he wanted to.

Dirk and Patrick cheered Goblin. They cheered the rain. They cheered everything.

"Look," Patrick said, nudging Dirk and motioning to a pair of women in the mirror. "This might be our moment."

They looked like nice ladies to Dirk. A brunette and a blonde, both wearing dresses that suggested they, too, needed a night out.

Patrick swiveled on his stool and spoke to them first.

And as he did, Dirk looked about the crowded bar, feeding off the chatter, the energy, the style. It was so simple to him just then, his elbows on the mahogany bar, so easy.

Then in the shadows of a booth he saw Robin Jacobs, his boss at the zoo. The other men with Jacobs looked like bosses, too, and Dirk smiled because the phrase he'd said so many times (*today I will be my own boss*) didn't mean what he'd thought it meant.

"Dirk," Patrick said, tapping his friend on the shoulder. "You've got to meet Laura and—"

"Janine," the blonde said.

"Janine," Patrick echoed.

Dirk turned to face her. He stood up and offered Janine his seat. Smiling, she took it.

As far as Dirk was concerned, she was the most wonderful woman in the room.

"A librarian," she said. "I know. I shouldn't be out drinking." Dirk leaned against the bar and talked to Janine with confidence, assuredness, and freedom.

"The zoo," Dirk answered. "I should be out drinking more often."

Janine said she might have seen him before. She took her teen reading groups to the zoo once a year. Dirk told her he'd have remembered her. Whether this was true or not didn't matter. It made Janine smile.

A great song came on the bar speakers. Bright harmonies. Bright words. Janine put her hand on Dirk's once as she laughed at something he said.

"Hey Dirk! Dirk!" Patrick was shouting over the music. "What did your letter say?"

Dirk looked at him inquisitively.

"The letter, your resignation, at work today. What did it say?"

Dirk blushed.

"It said: *Thank you but for now on I'm my own boss.*"

"That's it," Patrick said, slapping a hand on the bar. "Isn't Dirk the best? What a move!"

Janine liked it. Dirk liked that she did.

He ordered another round.

Soon things were bordering on blurry, but Dirk showed no outward signs of being drunk. Patrick did. He stumbled through his words and got louder with every drink. He slammed an open palm down on the bar a dozen times, accentuating everything any of them said.

Then Dirk excused himself and headed to the bathroom. Once there, he locked the door and set his drink on the sink. He gripped the sides of the sink and looked at himself in the mirror. He smiled. There was something sad, deep within him, but tonight it was distant. Tonight he thought of Janine and Patrick and Laura and the zoo and the House and all the shitty jobs he'd ever had and he smiled.

And yet, something lurked. Casually almost. There was something he wasn't thinking of. Something he maybe didn't have to think of but something that had slipped his attention either way. Like the numbers didn't add up the way they were supposed to.

He downed the rest of his drink and exited the bathroom. Back at the bar, the two women excused themselves and Janine put a flat hand on his chest as she told him she'd be back.

"These girls are *great*," Patrick said.

Dirk nodded. The girls were indeed great.

And yet something lurked.

When the women came back, Janine said, "Let's do something crazy, Dirk."

Dirk raised an eyebrow.

"What do you have in mind?"

"I don't know." She was leaning back in her stool. She was feeling as good as he was. "Let's walk through the rain. Outside, on the streets. Now. It's the most powerful rainfall we've ever had. I don't know that I wanna miss it." She touched his chest again. "Sometimes it's good to make contact with a powerful thing."

"That sounds gre—"

"Oh!" she said, cutting him off. "We could walk through Perish Park? Visit the cemetery? Goblin graves, anyone?"

It took Dirk all of a second to decide where they should go.

"I can give you a tour," he said.

Janine looked at him funny, then her eyes widened and her lips formed a perfect circle.

"Are you shitting me?" she said. "The zoo?"

"Yes."

"Dirk Rogers, that's the best idea I've ever heard. Will we get in trouble? Will you?"

It felt to Dirk like giving her a tour was the only thing he knew how to do.

"Not if we don't break anything."

Then they both laughed, images of broken animals like china plates in both their minds.

Dirk helped her put her coat on.

"Whoa!" Patrick said. "Where you guys going?"

"We'll be back," Dirk told him. Janine told Laura the same.

"You see, my friend?" Patrick said. "It's already begun."

As they were leaving, as they made their way through the solid block of Gobliners between them and the door, Dirk heard his name shouted and turned to see Robin Jacobs beside him.

"Good one, Dirk," he said.

Dirk was confused.

"What?"

"I said *good one.* You made me laugh."

Then Janine was tugging Dirk's arm and Robin Jacobs vanished into the curtain of bodies behind him.

Outside, Dirk removed his suit jacket and held it over Janine's head.

"Have you done this before?" she asked.

"No," he said.

"Are you worried?"

Dirk gripped her around the waist.

"No."

Then they were running out from the cover of the City Slope awning, running through the most impressive Goblin downpour either of them had ever made contact with.

24

"We have slickers," Dirk whispered as he unlocked the gate.

There were many trees just inside the entrance and the rain was lessened by their cover. It was incredible to Dirk how different the zoo looked, seen this way. Without the burden of his duties, the place shrank to the size of a kennel.

Just then the zoo and all the thoughts it provoked were manageable.

Dirk walked Janine to the small brick administrative building, where the slickers hung by the lockers inside.

It was dark in there and the two stifled drunk laughter as they bumped into desks, chairs, office fans.

Dirk grabbed a flashlight and two slickers. Then he fingered the blinds in Robin's office, parting them to get a look at the grounds. The rain made it hard to see any distance and Dirk recalled whispering faces in a mist.

He turned on the flashlight and led Janine outside.

They passed the information booth, no longer under the cover of the trees, and the rain attacked their slickers.

"Okay," Dirk said, "here's where it starts."

Shining his light on the aviary, Dirk headed toward it, pointing out the bird feet painted on the path. He unlocked the door and pulled the plastic aside.

"We have to be quiet," he said. "They'll be asleep."

Janine stepped through. Dirk turned his flashlight off.

Moonlight shone through the glass of the domed ceiling and colored everything a midnight blue. Dirk brought Janine to the center of the sanctuary and silently pointed out small dark shapes lining the branches. Janine heard feathers lightly rustling, and some of the sleeping birds cooed.

"Are you afraid of snakes?" he whispered.

"No."

Inside the reptile house Janine took Dirk's arm gently. He shone the light on the cages and a hundred reptilian eyes looked back.

"I think they like you," she whispered.

Then they were standing at the wood fences overlooking the bears. Rain pounded their hoods. Dirk shone his light in and out of the caves but the best he could show Janine was half a sleeping body.

"Do you have a favorite?" she asked him.

Dirk nodded.

"But she's last," he said.

He wanted to kiss her. She wanted him to. But Dirk was occupied with impressing her first. The zoo felt good to him. Simple things like the signs and arrows ... the color of the garbage cans ... the mural on the side of the Food Hut. The zoo felt friendly. No, the zoo was Dirk's *friend*.

"Trudy's next," he said.

The paw prints on the concrete were hardly visible now beneath the layer of water. Their shoes sloshed as they hurried.

Dirk pulled aside the sliding wood doors and stepped inside the tiger room. The concrete floors, the dirty windows, and Trudy's dark cage looked different in piecemeal, by the end of Dirk's beam.

"Spooky," Janine said.

"Trudy," Dirk called, stepping to her cage.

She was in the shadow made by the tree trunk and the rock shelter.

"Trudy," he said. "Come on out."

The big cat looked back at them but did not come out.

"Looks like she wants to be alone," Janine said.

Dirk thought about it. Then he turned off the light.

"Whoa," Janine said. "I don't think I've ever been in the dark in the same room as a tiger before."

"Are you scared?"

"Yes."

They both laughed. Then Dirk was holding Janine's hand, leading her back out into the rain.

They ran along a dirt path, then under a banner hung between two tall bamboo pillars. Dirk led Janine to the observation windows. Thanks to the bamboo canopy, they were sheltered here.

Dirk kissed Janine.

With his back to the exhibit, his lips upon hers, he reached out and flipped the switch for the gorilla exhibit lights.

The grassy hills behind him were flooded with illumination.

And over Dirk's shoulder, Janine saw Eula upon her favorite hill-top.

Then, squinting, Janine pulled her face from Dirk's.

"Is she sick?" she asked.

Dirk turned quickly.

Eula lay on her right side, her left arm dangling across her chest. Her strong black fingers barely touched the grass, and the rain pummeled her without mercy. A pool of deep red swallowed fresh raindrops by her neck.

But it wasn't just that she wasn't moving. There was something wrong with her color.

"With everything . . ." Janine said.

Dirk took off, leaving her behind.

She heard him unlocking a gate.

Then she saw Dirk come into view of the window. She watched him crouch and slowly lift a scythe from the wet, discolored grass.

Next to it was much of Eula's skin. Dirk lifted it with his forefinger and thumb; a man picking up a fallen costume.

Janine screamed.

"I worked at the House today. Didn't I?" Dirk looked across the hills to Janine at the window. "Didn't I quit the House today?"

Janine stepped back.

Dirk heard crunching sounds. Slithering sounds. Metallic echoes. Metal on stone. Metal on *bone*.

"I did this," he said. "I did this!"

Janine slipped into the darkness of the path. Dirk didn't see her go.

He collapsed by Eula's skinned side.

"This is not freedom," he said. "This is not escape."

Slithering sounds. Whispers from a mist. A Mixed-up Man.

Tears fell from Dirk's face to hers.

"Didn't I quit the House today? Eula? Didn't I?"

Soon the timed lights turned themselves off.

Dirk Rogers, the face of the zoo, held Eula and cried.

"What I see is beautiful," he told her in the darkness of the park.

The shock of what he'd done was bigger than the bloated lumbering body of his nightmares. And somewhere far above him, in a place higher than where the rain fell from, there was a ceiling. There were four walls, too, and a floor. Dirk knew that now.

"I quit the House today," he told her, laughing now, as the rain became one with his tears. "Isn't that wonderful? I quit the House. That's where I was, Eula. I was at the House today. All day. All . . . day . . . long . . ."

THE HEDGES

1

It was already raining hard outside and had been for an hour, so when Wayne heard a knock at his door he assumed the little girl had used one of the escape paths and wanted her money back. Or maybe she just didn't want to get wet and sick. Maybe her mother raised her well. But when he opened the front door, she stood in the gravel just beyond the porch with her hands on her hips. And she was smiling. An angry little smile. A *knowing* little smile. Like she was thinking, *I'm onto you.*

Wayne shifted his weight from one foot to the other, surprised to find himself nervous.

"I solved your puzzle," the girl said. "Unsolvable my butt."

"That's unlikely," Wayne said.

Her eyes got wide.

"Oh no, it's *not*," she said. "It is not unlikely at all, Mr. Sherman."

Wayne brought a hand up to his face. He hadn't shaved in a week and his beard was catching up to his mustache.

"Oh yeah?" he said. "What did it look like?"

The girl tapped the toe of a black dance shoe. Her hands still on her hips. Her posture suggested Wayne had done something very bad, indeed.

"I'm turning you in," she said.

These words, Wayne knew, were exactly what someone would say if they solved The Hedges.

Shit.

"Now, hang on a minute here," he said, buying time.

What he wanted to do was bring her inside, sit her down, talk her out of it. But in the end, what good would that do? If she didn't turn him in right now she was bound to tell one of her little friends at school.

Hey, Mary, I got to the end of The Hedges. You won't believe what he's got in there.

"Come on, little girl," Wayne said, smiling. His thick brown-and-gray hair hung messy about his surprised face. "Do you have to do it right now? Can't you give me a little . . . time?"

The girl looked offended. "What? So you can hide everything and make me look like a little liar?"

She's smart, Wayne thought.

"Nu-uh, mister. The Goblin Police need to know what you've been hiding out here."

Wayne felt a stab of crazy rage. He could kill her. It'd be easy. Right now. He could grab her by the throat and bash her little head against the patio till it split.

But Wayne Sherman had never hurt a person in his life. He'd never even cut the arm or head off one of his many topiary statues throughout the city.

No, he wasn't gonna hurt her. What he had to do was get the hell out of Goblin this second.

"All right, all right," Wayne said. "Do what you have to. But before you go, will you tell me how you did it?"

The girl frowned. "It wasn't *hard,* mister. I don't mean to *burst your bubbley,* but it was easy."

"Easy? Nobody's ever done it before, girl."

"Yeah, well, that's because nobody guessed you're a psycho creep."

"Hey, come on now. You're too young to understand this."

The girl just stared up at him. A growing puddle of rainwater reached the tips of her black shoes.

"Are you finished?" she asked him.

"Finished what?"

"Finished pretending it's okay what you've got in there?"

Are you finished? Wayne seemed to hear the far-off creaking of doors closing. Closure, perhaps.

But not finished yet.

The girl pointed at him. "You just stay where you are. Okay? I'm going to leave now. I'm going to get the police. I'm going to tell Mayor Blackwater. Don't make me look like a liar."

They stared at each other for a long time.

"Okay," Wayne finally said.

The little girl turned and went to her bike. Wayne watched her, already calculating how long it'd take for a girl her age to ride back into town, to tell the police what she'd found.

How much time did Wayne have exactly?

Shit.

He watched her ride off into the rain. An unseen clock seemed to start ticking.

Shit.

On any other day, he might've worried about her getting there safely. Might have even given her a ride. But the Goblin Police were very serious, indeed.

What are the odds? he thought.

But he knew the odds. Always had. He knew *everything* about The Hedges.

Seven billion, eight hundred twenty-four million, six hundred thirty-two thousand, four hundred eighty-eight to one.

The odds.

The chances of solving The Hedges.

Wayne shook his head sadly. He'd always imagined bringing the victor inside. Pulling up two chairs from the basement. Sitting down with a pitcher of lemonade. Discussing the route taken and why. Wayne wanted to *congratulate* the winner. And yet he didn't think anybody would ever do it. And he had years to back that assumption up. And he knew that, if there ever was a winner, if ever someone solved the unfathomable puzzle he'd built so long ago, he'd have to do the same thing he had to do right now.

Run.

He stepped inside and went to the kitchen. He poured himself a glass of lemonade anyway.

Shit.

He simply couldn't believe it. When he sold the girl the eight-dollar ticket three hours ago, it was sunny outside and the only thing he was worried about was whether she'd get too scared and he'd have to go retrieve her. If he'd sold a million tickets then a million ticket holders thought they'd be the one to do it. And how many times did Wayne smile and shake his head when a customer came back claiming there was no finish? No prize? No trophy?

Wayne sipped his lemonade and looked around his kitchen. It felt something like saying goodbye to an old friend. A friend who was there the day you met the girl of your dreams. The friend who first said, *You two are good together.*

He'd have to run. Right now. This second. He'd have to get a bag together. Get his things. Go.

He'd have to leave this kitchen for good. This house. This land. The Hedges.

Wayne tried to smile. A very small but loud part of himself was happy to leave The Hedges behind. To move on.

At times, it looked more like a tomb than a maze. And the weight of living next to it had taken its toll.

But Wayne knew better. Knew he was more than just *tied* to The Hedges. They marked a very powerful period of his life. When, at age thirty-six, he started living like an artist. Phase Two, he liked to call it. He hadn't only built The Hedges in a suffocating haze of sadness; the labyrinth had become Goblin's most lucrative tourist attraction by far. Aside from the two men he had fashioned topiaries of at the city gates, Wayne Sherman was slated to become Goblin's most celebrated citizen.

Wayne Sherman was as beloved a Gobliner as it got.

And all he had to do was keep the finish line secret. Forever.

He wiped the lemonade from his lips.

It'd be like getting struck by lightning twice. The chances of that little girl . . .

But he had to go. He had to leave right now.

So he started. He put himself in motion. He grabbed a bag.

And what would happen to The Hedges? Would they grow over? Would the walls of every path eventually touch in the middle? Would it swallow itself like that?

Wayne knew it would. He knew that one day it would become just a giant solid block of green. He smiled sadly at the idea of someone trying to maintain them.

He wouldn't stand a chance.

At the front door he stopped to peer outside. The rain was ridiculous. The girl couldn't be too far yet. But the police, once they got word of what was out here, wouldn't be long.

He imagined he saw blinking red and blue lights. But it was only the words on the sign itself, THE HEDGES, seen through the falling water.

He remembered painting that sign. Remembered wondering if anybody would come out.

Shit.

The Goblin Police were serious, indeed.

Wayne packed his things, wondering why he never built himself an escape path. In case the winding ways got to be too much, when the bushes simply felt too tall to conquer.

A safe way out of this maze.

2

By the time Margot reached the Goblin Police she was so wet that the receptionist thought she might have fallen into the Blackwater River.

"I have a criminal for you," Margot announced.

The receptionist, a small man of forty, tilted his head as though Margot had made a high-pitched whistle sound just out of his range. Then he saw she was serious.

"A criminal, you say?"

"You're already taking too long," she said, looking past the man to the officer behind a tall desk. The Goblin Police were easy to spot: long faces, long arms, sunglasses. And skin that looked more like putty than flesh. "He's gonna try to get away."

The officer behind the big desk lowered a sheet of paper he was reading. Seeing his features in full, Margot felt a shiver. And far in the recess of her young mind she asked herself, *Does Wayne Sherman deserve this?*

But of course he did. When the officer spoke his voice came deep and slow, like all their voices did. Margot's mom said they talked like a pitch-shifted tape recording. Margot didn't know what that meant exactly.

"What . . . is . . . it . . . little . . . girl?"

"It's the bush guy," Margot said, quickly, wanting this exchange to be over with, wanting them to be on their way already.

But the officer did not respond.

"That man who makes all the statues. The man who lives next to The Hedges."

Now other officers slowly crept into view. Some peered their heads out from around corners. Some turned around in the chairs at their desks. Margot had mistaken their gray uniforms for the paint on the walls.

"Wayne . . . Sherman . . . ?" the officer at the desk asked.

Margot had their attention. And no matter how weird the Goblin Police made her feel, she was going to be a legitimate Goblin hero by the end of this.

"Yes," she said. "I was inside The Hedges. I got to the end."

Now the other officers slowly rose from their chairs and advanced toward her; their lanky bodies moving snakelike.

Margot eyed them, waiting for them to say something. But it was clear they were waiting for more from her.

"You won't *believe* what I found out there."

3

While Margot spilled the beans to the officers at the station, Wayne was taking a little too long getting the hell out of his house.

He was in the bedroom. Sitting on the edge of his bed. Thinking.

He didn't mind leaving his things behind. He didn't mind leaving his house. Even The Hedges. But the rush of it all, the *urgency*, put a twist on things.

It was as if the little girl woke him up from a twelve-year space-out and when he looked at his hands he was stunned at how wrinkled they were.

You were young once and you built The Hedges, but you are older now and must run from them.

How quickly it happened.

Good for her, Wayne thought.

He looked around the bedroom, the weight of Time upon him. What did he really need to bring? Maybe a tent. His boots. A change of clothes. He kept some money under his bed. Five grand. He'd need that.

What proof would they have? Wayne thought. *It's the word of a nine-year-old girl. And by the time they get here, The Hedges will be empty.*

But this thought didn't comfort him. Not enough. The Goblin Police meant business. And once they were on your trail, they stuck to it. Wayne knew this because he'd had to deal with them back when he built The Hedges. The Goblin Police sucked. And now, after watching him like Great Owls, looking for a mishap, they might actually have something on him.

He stood up and went to the closet.

Maybe I don't need to bring anything at all. Maybe I just need to go.

He opened the closet.

One half was all his stuff. The flannels he wore when he trimmed The Hedges. Jeans. One cotton suit. Some button-down shirts. Boots.

The other side was all Molly's.

Molly . . .

He touched an old dress of hers. A light-blue sundress that used to hang off her body like beach sand. He took it off the rack and held it out before him at arm's length. He held it about where it would be if she were wearing it right now.

He kissed the empty space where her head would be.

"I love you, Molly."

A lump arose in his throat. He set the dress on the bed.

Back in the closet he touched a pink tank top, brown shorts, a small white dress, a blue shirt. His head felt funny. Spinny. Dizzy with Molly.

Before she died, she used to say, *Will you pick out what I'll wear today?*

Wayne loved when she asked this. And more than once she'd turn to find just a pair of underwear lying on the bed.

Wayne! she'd say, her eyes wide in mock shock. *Don't you have ideas!* Wayne would laugh and lie on the bed. He *did* have ideas. He remembered those ideas as the best he ever had.

"We gotta go," he said. It felt like all of Goblin was pressing upon him. The weight of the city that had celebrated him.

But he couldn't leave Molly's things behind. It simply wasn't the right way for things to end. They could take everything of his. But not Molly's. No way.

Shit.

Because now this could take a while.

He picked up an old green army bag from the floor of the closet and started putting her stuff inside. A long black winter coat with wolverine fur lining the hood. A lacy, button-up shirt that once drove him crazy. A small orange T-shirt with a white number on the back. Jeans Molly had altered herself. A pink sweatshirt. A black pullover. A white bra with flowers on the breasts.

But the closet clothes weren't enough.

He grabbed her jewelry box, her perfume, the magazines she last flipped through, her makeup.

Molly used to tell him to stop staring at her while she put her makeup on. But Wayne loved to do it.

You're addicted, she'd say, rolling her eyes. *You need a counselor.*

Look at her! The most beautiful woman he'd ever seen, teasing him so!

I've already gone through this, Wayne thought. *This isn't fair.*

The army bag was getting heavy. He zipped it up and brought it to the front door. Then he went back into the closet and grabbed a brown suitcase from the floor. Next to the suitcase he saw a pair of Molly's shoes. He got to his knees. There were six pairs in all including his favorite: a yellow pair of heels that somehow brought out the green in her eyes, from all the way down there.

There was a book about North American birds on the floor next to the shoes. He fit it snugly into the case. Her binoculars, too.

Her camera.

Shit.

There was an undeveloped roll inside the camera from the day before Molly died. Wayne hadn't discovered it until a week after she was gone. The roll was from a trip the two took to Lake Oslow. A day they took turns flashing the camera on their naked bodies on the beach.

Nobody, she said, *sees these.*

And every time he'd seen the camera, or thought about it, he thought how, if he developed that roll, he'd get to see her again naked one more time.

"Molly . . ."

He felt his pants getting tighter. Nothing turned him on like Molly did.

He packed the camera into the suitcase, latched it shut, and carried it to the front door.

Then he went into the hall closet and found a big duffel bag mashed into the back corner.

Then he grabbed everything.

Towels, her toothbrush, her family photo albums, underwear,

socks, sunglasses, gloves, hats, handbags, her pillow (that had stayed on her side of the bed for the twelve years since she'd died), a grocery list, receipts, her checkbook, a pair of scissors she used to clip phone numbers from the phone book, a keychain with her name on it, coats, boots, nylons, maxi pads, deodorant.

Everything.

Wayne was sweating. He was starting to work in that frenzied distant state in which he'd built The Hedges so long ago. When he did this he was a much different-looking man than the easygoing proprietor who sold that little girl an eight-dollar ticket forty billion years ago.

Big or small, all projects felt the same size to him, whether it was erecting Neal and Barbara's topiaries on their front lawn, clipping the boots of Jonathan Trachtenbroit at the city gates, or constructing The Hedges themselves.

Even packing a bag full of Molly's things was an artistic accomplishment, perhaps even more satisfying than the others.

Wayne sweated. Wayne thought. Wayne worked.

4

Margot sat in a wooden chair next to a long cold table. Her little feet didn't come close to touching the tiled floor. She leaned on one of the chair's wooden arms and it creaked and every time it creaked she mistook it for movement by one of the officers. It was mostly dark in the room and other than the slow, deep questions, her answers, and the sound of a pen to paper, the creaking was the only thing she had as proof that she was sitting in the natural world.

The officers themselves didn't help with that.

Ten of them listened very closely to what she said. Their eyes were hidden by their mirrored aviators and their mouths moved slowly side-to-side, as though chewing small models of The Hedges.

Margot tried to ignore all this. For crying out loud, they were doting on her like she was the star witness for the trial of the century!

That much she loved. That much made her smile. And yet a picture of the mustachioed man at The Hedges with the kind eyes in the clay-ish hands of the Goblin Police worried her.

A little bit.

"Polly Majors told me that Brian Bowen and Carl Nelson tried and failed. They told *her* it was impossible. They told her there was *no way* a girl could do it. They said there was no way an *adult* could do it."

Margot shook her head. There was no response from the Goblin Police. Just that pen hitting the paper. A distant clacking of a typewriter, too.

"I asked my mom what she knew about The Hedges and she said nothing. Said if you've gone there once you've seen it all. I asked her why nobody ever figured them out and she said there was nothing to figure out. That the man who runs them just wants to make it more of a mystery so more people come out. She said it was a hoax. A trick. She said she wouldn't waste eight dollars on a walk through the bushes. Boy, was *she* wrong."

The officer nearest her leaned forward, making a creaking sound of his own. But the word that came to Margot's mind was *plastic*.

Just under the brim of his gray hat she saw that his hair looked as greasy as an oil change.

"You . . . went . . . out . . . there . . . on . . . your . . . own . . . ?"

There sure was something about the way these officers said

things! Margot wanted to punch him in the face. She didn't even know why exactly. Just wanted to see how far her little fist would go in.

"Yes," she said. "I went out there alone. I had to wait for a day when Mom would be working late. But you already know *that*."

They did. They'd called Margot's mom at the Goblin Art Gallery (the GAG) and scared the pants off her when they said they had her little girl.

She was on her way.

"I don't think she'll be too angry," Margot said. "I'm practically a hero."

She folded her hands in her lap. She was going to milk this moment. These creepy men couldn't take that away from her.

"I thought he might be no good when I got my ticket because he was half asleep when he answered the door. And he was wearing pajamas of all things. When he wished me good luck, I could tell he didn't think much of me. I could tell he didn't think I'd solve his maze. I wanted to ask him why he thinks nobody ever had? I wanted to tell him my mom told me there was nothing to solve. But I was scared I might jinx myself if I said anything like that. You know what I mean? I thanked him coldly and walked across the porch to a small dirt path that takes you to the entrance. The entrance was *amaaaaaazing*."

Another officer leaned toward her, half in the light now. Margot had thought he was a filing cabinet the whole time.

"We . . . know . . . what . . . The . . . Hedges . . . look . . . like."

Margot scrunched up her face and looked around the room.

"Oh, really now? Then maybe you also know how it ends?"

She folded her arms and kept her lips closed tight.

"Please," the nearest officer said. "Tell . . . us . . . how . . . it . . . ends."

Margot thought about it. Or pretended to anyway, because there was no way she wasn't going to tell how it ended. That was the best part. *Her* part.

"All right," she said, brushing her hair back from her face. "The entrance is huge. It's the biggest doorway I've ever walked through in my life. There's an archway over the threshold that says . . ." She looked down at her feet. "I can't remember. But I remember feeling very small. It was a little frightening. But the bushes were so *green*. Dark green. I was more interested in their color than anything else. I entered and followed the first trail to the . . ." She thought about it. Used her hands. "The *right*. I followed it to the right and, *presto,* there were six or seven different ways I could go. And that sleepy Mr. Sherman sure kept his eye on those Hedges! I tell you, I forgot for a second that I was walking through bushes and branches! It was more like green walls. Like . . . it would hurt if you pushed me into one. And they were so tall! *So* tall. And that's how he does it. He distracts people with how beautiful and big it all is. He makes the place so wonderful that it's no wonder people get lost and lose their way. It was very hard to stay focused. All I wanted to do was look around. But I'm much smarter than most people. Certainly the nimrods at school. So I kept my focus anyway. Standing before those seven different paths, I told myself I was going to do it. That a *man* built this maze and that I'm as clever as any man, big or small. And if I couldn't, then maybe I'd have to wonder if Mom was right. If I couldn't find the end then I'd agree that there was no end to find."

Outside, hard rain came against the police station windows and all the officers turned to face it at once. Margot, sorry not to have their attention, even for a moment, noted how the wrinkles in their neck showed as they stretched the skin.

"Hey!" she yelled. And just as slowly they looked at her again. All together.

Then Margot glanced at the window and wondered what a powerful storm such as that one might do to faces that looked so easy to adjust.

Take off your glasses, she wanted to say. Then the thought scared her. Deeply.

"So I chose a path," she said. "And began my descent into his maze."

5

Wayne had to put his shoulder into shutting the car door. The Ford Flareside truck was loaded. All told, he'd packed eight bags and suitcases full of Molly's stuff. Every time he thought he was finished he remembered something in the basement or the kitchen or the extra bedroom and he had to go back and get it. It was hard. He did his best to hurry, to take hold of her hair straightener and shove it in the bag, but he couldn't help but stop and muse for a moment on each object.

What did she do with it? How did she use it? What did she look like when she did?

He had his raincoat on now. It was coming down hard. Almost felt ominous, or like Wayne was suddenly a part of a biblical tale. He'd lived his whole life in Goblin. His family had been around for generations, stretching all the way back to Henry (Hank) Sherman, the man who strangled Jonathan Trachtenbroit in Perish Park on Election Day. He had *roots* in Goblin. He was born in Goblin, grew up in Goblin, and became a hero in Goblin, too. From helping his father mow the lawn when he was a kid to being told by another kid she was sending the Goblin Police to his door. It'd been a long time.

He wondered if it had something to do with roots. The more roots you had, the more you had to dig up.

Inside, he sat down again on the edge of the bed and fell flat onto his back.

He stared at the ceiling fan.

He was going to leave. He had do. But he just needed one more deep breath in the room where he'd spent six years making love to the woman of his dreams. Just one more moment with it. He deserved that. One more memory of Molly.

He had time. The girl was on a bike. The Goblin Police moved like slugs.

He had time for one more. And if it turned out he didn't?

"Then you'll grab a pair of shears and cut your way out of it," he said.

It felt good, thinking like that. Shears and scenarios. Carving and cutting and cleaving a thing until it fit into the room where you wanted it to go.

Wayne closed his eyes. He remembered.

6

When Wayne met Molly he was mowing for the city. A string of baloney jobs (his résumé read like a guide to Goblin) had finally dumped him on the city's lawn, and he'd saved enough money to buy himself the small yellow house that would one day stand next to The Hedges. In those days he believed he had everything he'd ever need. His yellow house. Goblin. Marauder games. A good book. A glass of lemonade.

He didn't know it yet, but there was more to want.

He was thirty years old and had never had what one might call *an artistic urge.* Years later he'd be able to talk all about the subject, if a ticket buyer wanted to, especially when he became the city's artist in residence. But at thirty, as far as Wayne Sherman knew, he'd be mowing lawns and drinking lemonade far into old age. And this vision didn't bother him at all.

Molly never knew that the man who turned her world inside out (the man she expected at twenty-one but who didn't show up until she was thirty) would go on to become a local celebrity for erecting an incredible work of art in her honor. Molly grew up in Goblin, too, but on the opposite side of town. Ten miles from the confusing North Woods.

As far as the pair could remember, they never saw each other until the day they officially met. But both attended a play at the Domino Theater called *The Real Reason I'm Happy* when they were eleven and Molly liked to count that as the day they started dating.

Molly didn't have a routine, and the mapped-out steadiness of Wayne's daily life was a far cry from the restlessness that followed her wherever she went. Before meeting Molly, Wayne would never have been able to name something as abstract as an emotion (he didn't think like an artist, not yet), and Molly was already alphabetizing them. She could isolate moods. Could feel their effects undiluted, point them out, and remind herself that it was, after all (like any mood), temporary. Wayne wasn't aware of such things. If he was angry, he was angry. It didn't register with him that the feeling he had at any given moment could be unusual for him to have. When Molly died (seven years after they met), this inability to recognize a rare (and therefore demanding) emotion would become nearly disastrous for Wayne. But up to that point he would never have considered expressing it. This would become Molly's one complaint with Wayne during their incredible run. But she didn't approach Wayne's internal holding cell with aggression. Rather, she looked at it (while biting her nails) and thought, *Well,* something's *gotta open him up.*

As far as Wayne knew, he wasn't intentionally hiding anything. But just like Molly was able to recognize the purity of his actions, she saw how his being in the emotional dark could one day cause him trouble.

Like when his parents died. Wayne grieved in a way Molly had never seen someone grieve before. As if he were kicking drugs. As if he had volunteered for a spiritual sweat lodge, something Blackwater or Son of Blackwater might've partaken in before the Original 60 arrived in Goblin. The way Wayne locked himself in the extra bedroom of his yellow house for seven days, it wasn't hard to imagine him this way.

But Molly lured him out. Like he was lost in a crazy maze and she'd put up a sign that read, HAD ENOUGH? GO THIS WAY →

She didn't have to take him by the hand. She didn't guide him or give him the best directions. How would she know the quickest way out of someone else's grief? Rather, she simply told Wayne that a way out *existed.* And because he loved her, he believed her. Lover as teacher. Wayne clawed his way out of the swampy sludge and when he walked outside again, into an amazing emotional sunrise, Molly was there, waiting for him with a smile.

They met at a grocery store. Wayne was mowing lawns on the west side and stopped in on a break. He didn't see her until she said,

"You must really like lemonade."

He looked up to see a woman far too beautiful to be bagging groceries. Her brown hair, her green eyes, and the slope of her nose all looked too right to him, an impossible commingling of features.

"Yes," he said and said no more. But he stared at her. He couldn't stop.

And Molly liked it. She also liked that he was covered in grass. She liked that he smelled like the outdoors and that his clothes and skin were green from working.

He thanked her and he left.

That night Wayne had an incredible dream and in it the woman from the grocery store was sitting across from him at the library. He wanted to speak to her but she kept shushing him with a smile.

That night Molly had a dream, too. A dream in which Wayne came into her bedroom, covered in green grass, and satisfied her like she'd never been before.

She was shocked when Wayne came into the grocery store the next day. He'd grabbed the same items he'd picked up the day before. Molly understood that he wasn't thinking clearly. That the lawn guy wasn't here for lemonade.

"I'm Molly," she said.

"Wayne Sherman. I dreamed of you last night."

Molly blushed because she assumed Wayne's dream was similar to her own. "I dreamed of you, too," she said. "That means we have to go out."

"Outside?"

"Out on a date."

"Right now?"

"When I get off."

"When's that?"

"Right now."

Over an early dinner at Jerome's, Goblin's favorite steak house, Wayne learned that Molly owned the small west side grocery store. While Wayne told her his story, Molly looked for clues that might indicate he was full of shit, but none came. Wayne was wonderful. He spoke with sincerity and honesty. She couldn't help but think him innocent.

"What was your dream about?" she asked suddenly, biting her lower lip.

Wayne told her.

She considered it.

"So maybe you thought I was the kind of person who likes to keep things in. But as you can see, I talk a *lot.*"

When she told him her dream Wayne was stunned silent.

"That doesn't seem fair," she said. "I had the night of my life and you were being told to shut up the whole time."

The two spent three hours at Jerome's. They told each other everything.

Molly didn't know what she wanted any more than anyone else. When it came to men, she had a vague idea that one day she'd meet a great one and that all the odd stumbles prior would make sense that day.

Wayne seemed *settled down* since the day he was born. His life was without clutter. He spent his money on a nice yellow house with a great big field beside it. He was obscure (almost anonymous) in his own family. Years later, after Wayne Sherman became a household name for building The Hedges, Gobliners asked, *Where is he from?*

It was clear after their first date that there would be another. And so there was.

When Wayne came by his parents' place to tell them he met someone, his mother was shocked. She'd never seen her son this way. He sat down on the couch and excitedly described her to them. Her interests, her jokes, her store. He told his mom how he brought Molly a flower every day. Whether he got it from a yard he was working on or bought it on the way home didn't matter. How Molly put each one in a glass of water and saved all those that died. Saved them first in a box and later in a barrel.

"Well," Mom said, "if you don't get married, you're a fool."

Wayne and Molly liked the sound of that.

They decided to exchange vows at the northeast entrance to the North Woods. All the brittle black trees, winding in and out of one another, seemed to connect that day like wreaths.

Never mind the legends of the woods delivering men to madness. Never mind that no Gobliners stepped foot inside. And certainly never mind that the woods were allegedly haunted by a whispering witch who could detonate your heart with a story.

"What are we doing if we're not doing it to the death?" Molly had said.

Sixty white chairs were set up facing the entrance. A barrel of gardenia petals was spread out thickly down the aisle, a smell that would always remind those who were there of the Shermans' North Woods wedding.

Wayne wore a gray tuxedo that matched the premature color in his thick hair. He didn't quite look like the artist he was six years from becoming, but he matched well with the twisted black trees behind him. Molly's mom thought he looked almost like a woodsman. Wayne's mom never saw such a gentleman.

When Molly walked down the gardenia carpet (a member of the Goblin orchestra played a harpsichord, her favorite) a hush came about that rivaled a funeral. If someone were to tap Wayne on the shoulder, their hand might have passed through him, rendered ghostly as he was by the haunting music. Molly passed as graceful as the music that accompanied her. As magisterial as the woods she walked toward.

The two locked hands and Molly, surprising Wayne, whispered, *Please don't die before me.*

It was a phrase he'd never wash from his memory.

With a friend acting as magistrate, the couple was walked into the shadows of that entrance, prepared to speak their vows. There was joy in there, there was fear, there was humor, and there was trust.

I promise to warn you of sadness, Molly said. *To keep you from finding comfort in its arms. And though I can't ward off all evil things, I can tell you when they are near and I can help you fight them. I promise to be there when you need someone whether you know it or not. I promise to sustain this feeling we feel now forever. I promise you will never be alone. Since that day at the grocery store, neither of us will ever truly be alone. I will not promise to love you because that is something I just do. I love you.*

Wayne cleared his throat.

I promise to protect you, Wayne said. *I promise to respect you. I promise to celebrate you. But I do not say* until death do us part *because I expect we'll meet thereafter. And I do not promise to love you . . . because that is something I just do. I love you.*

There was a moment of silence. Molly's eyes swelled with tears and the water acted like a magnifying glass. A slanted beam from the sun lit her up and for one amazing moment, she looked like a spirit to Wayne. A witch perhaps, peeking out of the woods.

They exited the North Woods married.

The small crowd rose and clapped. The men nodded and the ladies wept. Everyone present knew they'd witnessed the rare bonding of true love, in which two people did not settle down, but rather settled up.

Molly would die, six years later, in her sleep, and Wayne, devastated and very close to being destroyed, intended to keep all his vows.

He'd start by planting her a bush.

7

"I want to call my mom," Margot said suddenly.

One of the officers slowly slid the phone to her. She dialed quickly.

"Mom?" she said. "Mom . . . what's it called when you're going one way and then you think you ought to go the other and then you're not sure?" She waited for the answer. Her big eyes scanned the floor. "Yes!" she hollered. *"Turned around."* She put her hand over the receiver and said to the officers, "I was turned around."

Despite her attempt at covering the phone, Mom heard her clearly. She was driving through the rain in a hurry. She didn't like the Goblin Police. Didn't like them, didn't trust them, didn't want them around.

And who *talked* like that?

Ma'am . . . we've . . . got . . . your . . . little . . . girl.

That was terrifying, What did they want her to do? Drop off a suitcase full of money? She'd moved to Goblin when she was twenty-six and Margot was just two and from the start she felt uncomfortable around the Goblin Police. Her first run-in with them was the result of a broken taillight and the encounter was so awkward and so long that she felt like she'd been tricked.

As if they were keeping her on the side of the road as part of a ritual.

And now they had her little girl.

"Honey," she said into the phone, "listen to Mommy. Don't let those officers take you into a room alone. Do you understand?"

Margot scrunched her brow. One of the officers coughed and a cloud of green mist rose to the ceiling.

"What do you mean, Mommy?" She tried to smile but it was

suddenly uncomfortable. She saw her eyes looked scared, reflected in the aviators worn by the officers.

What was Mommy talking about?

"Just tell Mommy you promise, Margot. Okay? Mommy's gonna be there soon and we can answer all their questions together."

Margot felt a lump in her throat.

Together. Together did sound better than the way it was. Alone. She'd been so excited to talk about her discovery that she hadn't thought about who she was telling it to. She knew the Goblin Police were weird, but could they also be . . . bad?

Margot scanned the room, nodding, pretending to be listening to her mom talk. A minute ago this group of officers made a great audience, but now . . . now they were changing in her eyes . . . their tall fatty bodies . . . their toilet-white flesh . . .

Margot felt like she'd done something very wrong. Like her mother knew it but she was too stupid to know it on her own. She wanted to cry.

"Promise?"

Her mother's voice came from far away. From somewhere safe.

"Yes," she finally said. "Promise. Hurry up and get here."

"Mommy's on her way."

Margot hung up the phone.

"Little . . . girl . . ." the officer before her said. "Go . . . on. What . . . happened . . . next . . . ?"

She wanted to cry. Like a tear as big as herself was inside her and she was about to explode with it.

"Next," she said, her voice trembling, "next I cracked the code. Hate to burst his bubbley, but it was easy."

8

The actual creation of The Hedges wasn't so much a blur for Wayne as it was a burst. And he remembered all of it. Every branch.

What started as a humble tribute to his dead wife became the building of a masterpiece that would change Wayne's life forever. His memories of Molly (there were thousands by the morning he tried to wake her and could not) haunted him in a very bad way. He endured an unbearable couple days of visits from friends and family. He did all the right things. He shook hands, he listened to the wonderful things people said about Molly, he cried a few times in front of them. And he was consoled often. But after everyone that was going to visit had done so, and Wayne was left alone in the little yellow house that so recently protected Molly, too, he saw he was staring continuum in the face. Timelessness without her stretched before him and he was numb with fear. Curse his good health. Curse his strong body. There were a thousand ghosts of Molly inside that house: one for every place she ever stood, sat, or lay.

So Wayne stepped outside.

I'll plant her a bush, he thought.

It was the least he could do.

Wayne drove to Mr. Paul Keller's garden/feed store. He knew Keller well, having worked every lawn in the city, and refused the deal he was offered.

"I don't mean to offend you, Paul," Wayne said, "but it's to honor someone, and a deal somehow lessens that honor."

Keller smiled. "You've always planted to the beat of your own roots, Wayne. Full price it is."

Back home, with sunlight enough to do it, Wayne dug up the

earth and put it in the ground. He stepped back and studied the single bush alone in the vast expanse of his big empty field.

Well, Molly, this is for you.

Later that afternoon, washing his hands at the sink in the bathroom, Wayne looked out the window at the bush he'd planted. He was ashamed. The meager bush was no tribute. He dried his hands.

Wayne didn't think, *I need more bushes.* No decision like that was made at all. It was simply that he had to *do* something; something with his hands, something with his body, something mindless and live and instant.

He got into his truck and headed back to town. Back to Keller's store, where his friend helped him load the truck bed with more bushes.

By the time The Hedges were one-sixteenth the size they'd end up being, people (neighbors, family, travelers driving into Goblin from the East) were already stopping by his house. Wayne was cordial enough but he was firm in turning people away. He didn't know what he was working on any more than they did and talking about it only muddied things. The pace he worked at was incredible. His thirty-seven-year-old body dripped with sweat and was burned a dark tan by a sun that was as prying as his neighbors. His money was dwindling. Everything he bought was for this *thing* in his backyard. New spades, shovels, a pickax, trowels, gloves, clippers, scissors.

Buckets for the trimmings. Buckets for the dirt.

Very soon it was as if The Hedges were building themselves.

Wayne stopped answering the phone. He stopped checking his mailbox. He stopped acknowledging anybody who stopped by. At any time of any day one could find his strong, shirtless frame out in the yard, planting his illogical syndicate of shrubs.

People thought he was losing his mind. Most were sure of it.

Wayne still wasn't thinking like an artist. *Acting* like one, yes, but there was yet to be a design; not even the idea that he was *expressing* to begin with. He just moved. Acted. Reacted. And after a time, a pattern emerged. The paths he created, paths to enable him to operate, started to make routes that made sense to him. Angles came out of other angles. Points within points. A left turn became right. A right was then left. For Wayne, it was as complex as the emotions he was dealing with. He knew of no purpose for it. No use. But the paths eerily resembled the irrational catena of thoughts a man has on any given day. After any given tragedy.

And these days weren't any days. These days were awfully close to the day Molly died and Wayne had the memory of an unwakable wife to spur him on. If Wayne *was* an artist, he'd have recognized that he was in one of the zones all artists pine for. That mindless (and therefore free) state where there *is* enough time in the day. The Hedges (not named this yet) shot from the ground like frozen steam sent skyward from green Goblin geysers. Giant leafed horses standing high on their hind legs.

Nobody could see Wayne Sherman from the road anymore when they passed by.

He was inside it now.

But to have seen Wayne Sherman operate within that mania, that green beast reaching up and up around him, to see him almost still, at peace but in motion, wedged there in its belly, savored by it, swallowed by the thorny green lips as it grew . . . would have been to witness one of the most hallowed moments in the history of Goblin.

By the time the last of the trimmings were bagged up and taken away, The Hedges stood eleven feet high and two hundred yards deep; they covered over half his land. The little bush he'd first planted to honor his dead Molly was as lost in it as the man who had planted it.

Finished, Wayne stood on his lawn, his gloved hands at his sides (the blisters stopped bleeding a third of the way through) and he smiled as big a smile as he had.

I promise to celebrate you.

The sun was just visible over the top of The Hedges.

He fell to his knees and cried so hard he thought his chest might crack. He cried for Molly and cried for the sheer spectacle of his grief, too.

Through tears, he looked up at his creation. His first moment as an artist.

I promise to protect you.

He rose at last. Whatever the beautiful block of green was, Wayne Sherman adored it.

He walked inside, took a shower, and fell asleep, dreaming of the maintenance it would take to maintain it. But rather than fear the paths overgrowing, rather than worry lest his living creation get out of hand, Wayne was happy for the work.

For in doing it, he would honor his Molly forever.

9

"If you cared to notice," Margot said without the same arrogance she'd had at the beginning of the interrogation, "the bushes were obviously trimmed from south to north. At an angle. Mr. Sherman didn't do such a good job hiding the fact that he trimmed the path to the finish line first. Whatever the prize was, it must have meant a lot to him to go and hide it so well. I just looked for where the bush ends would be a *little* bit longer. Meaning, of course, that they had been cut *first* the last time he trimmed them. I followed that path."

The Goblin Police didn't respond. Margot was alternately

scared and disappointed. How she cracked the code was supposed to be a triumphant moment for her. But these officers didn't seem to care.

She swallowed hard, tapping her fingers lightly on the arm of the wooden chair.

"Yeah, well, I was right to do so."

Margot shifted in her seat and the wooden arms creaked. She felt something she didn't want to feel; far away and deep inside her she felt bad for Wayne Sherman. Like she was tattling on a helpless kid at school.

What would these men do to The Hedges' guy if they got him?

"Is Mommy here yet?"

10

Margot had good reason to worry about Wayne Sherman's well-being. Rather than tearing out of his driveway and leaving Goblin, he was sinking deeper into his bed. Deeper into the mossy memories of Molly.

Deeper into The Hedges.

Three days after building them, Wayne was inside them, studying his unplanned work. The Hedges, he understood, could act as a refuge. A place he could go that he'd never gone with Molly. A place without her ghost.

But that day Wayne wasn't alone. Well within the bushes, he found a neighbor huddled up in a small clearing. The man, Burt, looked up at the sound of Wayne approaching.

"Oh thank *God*!" he said, rising.

"What's going on?" Wayne asked.

"I'm sorry for trespassing, Mr. Sherman," Burt said. "It just looked so . . . so *fun*. I had to see it up close. I've been in here for two days. Do you know the way out?"

"Two days?"

Burt nodded, sheepishly. "Rightfully hungry, I'd say."

Wayne stared at him a long time before laughing, and it felt like it was his first laughter in a very long time.

"Wait," he said. "You entered these bushes two days ago and you've been lost since?"

"Well, yeah."

Now Burt laughed, too.

"Yes," Wayne said. "Yes, I know the way out. Come on."

Wayne led Burt into the yellow house and fixed him some lemonade and soup. "I guess that'll teach you to trespass," Wayne said, smiling.

After eating, Burt set his drink down and cleared his throat. "You ought to charge people, Wayne."

"For what?"

Burt leaned forward, his eyes wide with intensity.

"Charge people for a *ticket,* man. A ticket to take a walk through that thing! Hell, I'm telling you! You're sitting on a gold mine out here." He leaned back in the chair. "But you better put up a map or you're gonna get a lawsuit."

Registering The Hedges as a tourist attraction was straightforward enough. But the men from city hall agreed with Burt: Wayne would have to give ticket buyers an easier way out. They couldn't risk out-of-towners telling their friends back home that they'd gotten lost in Goblin for five days. Nearly starved to death.

So Wayne carved escape hatches. Signs read:

HAD ENOUGH? GO THIS WAY >

Hidden paths that were easy to find with an arrow. Paths that would take visitors directly out of the maze.

The city approved of these additions and the deal was finalized and nobody (including Wayne) thought it would amount to much more than what it already was.

A spectacular gardening job.

But within eighteen months, The Hedges became Goblin's biggest-grossing tourist attraction and the name Wayne Sherman was on the lips of every city official. It seemed that Wayne's creation even made people forget that his ancestor strangled the beloved Jonathan Trachtenbroit.

Gobliners forgave. Billboards went up east of the city:

DO YOU THINK YOU CAN SOLVE . . . THE HEDGES?

DO YOU KNOW WHERE YOU'RE GOING? THE HEDGES

18 MILES TO THE HEDGES—DON'T GET LOST!

WHAT'S HIDDEN INSIDE?

Even the city officials didn't know the answer to this last one.

And while Wayne hadn't set out to bring business into his hometown, it was all a kind of fun for him. A distraction and an honor at once. Soon every hotel in Goblin sported glossy pamphlets describing The Hedges. The Woodruff hung a full-color poster in the lobby. Wayne got a four-page spread in *What to Do in Goblin,* including a photo of himself, bearded, with his arms crossed, smiling as the wind blew his thick hair and the tops of the breathtaking bush maze behind him.

The Hedges were an unfathomable success.

It was only a matter of time before the city asked him if he'd be interested in other topiary projects. Two big ones, for starters, Goblin luminaries to frame the city gates at the south highway entrance into town. Branch edifices of George Carroll and Jonathan Trachtenbroit. Wayne smiled at the thought of someone seeing a Sherman trimming Trachtenbroit's neck, but he agreed and was paid a lot of money for the job. Immediately following, he got calls from the city's upper crust: Neal Nash hired him to fashion him and his wife, Barbara, for the same fee the city gave him. And soon after that, *everybody* was asking Wayne Sherman if he'd please come over and immortalize them with shrubbery. Blue-collar workers from the Transistor Planet, Goblin Games, Goblin's Magic. It didn't matter to Wayne if you were loaded or broke, you could afford a Sherman. It was all in the name of Molly, after all, and what did money mean to a person who was robbed of her life in her sleep?

Once Wayne's photo graced the cover of *The Goblin Post* he was invited to too many dinners to attend. Socialites tried to pair him up with single women. Business offers were made.

Wayne Sherman had become a household name. A celebrated artist.

And by then, Wayne *was* thinking like an artist.

Phase Two of Wayne's life was sitting firmly upon him.

And Molly never left his thoughts.

The more he worked on The Hedges, the more he felt he was keeping her alive. He refused, almost amiably, to "get over her" like so many people suggested he do. The way Wayne saw it, there was nothing to get over. Molly was it for him. Did people expect him to *pretend* time could heal a wound that size? If God came to his door and said, *Wayne, listen . . . this is why I took Molly from you . . .*

Wayne would have guided Him along the front porch, thanked Him for coming, and asked Him, *Would you like to try a turn at The Hedges? Can you guess what's inside?*

Molly wasn't a bump, a hurdle, a hill. There was nothing to get over.

Molly was the end for Wayne. The end of Phase One. The finish line.

11

"After a while," Margot said. "The paths practically *told* me which way to go."

It seemed to her that the officers were getting impatient. She'd seen this sort of restlessness in her mom whenever she tried to tell her all the gossip from school. The way the closest questioning officer arched his back. How two in the back looked across the room to each other. How an officer to her left started tapping his pale fingers, slowly, like rubber erasers on a desk. She was going to have to get to the end soon. This wasn't fun anymore.

"Actually, it was pretty neat," she said, talking more the more scared she got. "But I wasn't about to tell that man that. It was neat because, after following the trimming, you started to see that the route you took was the easiest one to take. Where the turns weren't as sharp and the ground was easy on your feet. After a while it seemed like there was no decision to make. Like the man cut the grass to take you a certain way."

Margot was too young to understand this but, approaching The Hedges from an emotional standpoint was the right way to do it. The usual visitor saw The Hedges as a big puzzle to play with for an hour or two, but Margot tuned in to the fastidious care the man who sold her the ticket had put into it. She felt something else in there, too. Something like sadness.

"Because the deeper I got, the darker the paths. That's another thing. By then the tops of the bushes almost met. It was scary but I was *not* scared. In fact, the bushes acted as cover when it started raining. And so then I started thinking . . . wouldn't sleepy Mr. Sherman want to keep his prize covered? Safe from the rain? Well . . . *I* was safe from the rain and so I knew I was on the right path. It rains more in Goblin than anywhere else in the world! He wouldn't let his prize get soggy. It was very clear to me that he cared a lot about it.

"And then the bushes *really* started connecting overhead and I walked through total darkness for a very long time. I felt my way along the bush walls. Scratched up my fingers. Look." She showed them. "I knew I was close to solving Mr. Sherman's puzzle when I walked into one of those walls and fell back on the path. But when I searched the walls for a door . . . there wasn't one! There was no way out. And I *knew* I wasn't supposed to turn around. I got angry about it for a second. I started to think maybe Mom was right. Maybe the end of The Hedges was nothing but darkness. Some prize that would be, huh? I was ready to give that pajama man a piece of my mind. I thought that if I just had a little light I'd be able to figure it out. And that's when I realized that I was there." She snapped her fingers. "I was *at* the finish line. I just couldn't *see* what the prize was."

Wayne Sherman was right: Margot was a smart girl. She started shaking the bushes in the dark. She'd run to one, grab thorny branches, and upset them as best as could. Then she ran to the next wall and did the same. She shook until she wished she had the strength of a woman and not that of a little girl.

"Break apart, Got dammit!" she yelled. *"Break apart!"*

And about when she thought she'd done all she could, a little light came through from above. Not enough to see anything yet, but enough to encourage her to keep going. Then she ran from one side of the dark corridor to the other, throwing her small body against them.

"For the love of God! Show me the prize!"

Back and forth. Back and forth.

The gap widened. More light came down.

She could see her hands . . . her shoes . . . the ground . . . dirt. She also saw the corner of a glass case.

She stopped.

The prize *had* to be in that glass case. She ran to it and put her face against it but there were simply too many shadows still. She couldn't see all the way in.

Out of breath, she got back to work. Shaking the bushes. Shaking the walls. When her fingertips started bleeding she didn't cry out.

She was so close to solving The Hedges . . . so close to telling everyone she knew . . .

Shake!

Back and forth. Back and forth.

Shake!

She screamed as she pulled, pressing her dark dance shoe against the wet wall.

She could do it.

She couldn't.

She could do it.

She couldn't.

She could—

CrrrrrrAAAAAACK!

The roof split open.

Margot stumbled back and fell on her ass. The branches above pointed to the sky. Sunlight flooded the cove that undoubtedly marked the finish line of The Hedges.

Margot got to her feet and didn't think to cover her head despite the rain.

"And I saw it," Margot told the Goblin Police, her shoes dangling above the cold tiled floor. Her eyes got wet. As though she'd seen something with more than enough meaning to move her. "At the very end of The Hedges is—"

"It's . . . the . . . wife," the closest officer said. Then he raised a pale hand, signaling the others.

Margot's face scrunched up with confusion. She waved her hands, too.

"His wife?" she said. In the reflection of the officer's aviators she saw how small she looked in the big police chair. "That's the stupidest thing I've ever heard. His *wife?* What does that even mean? No. It was most certainly *not* his wife."

The Goblin Police did not move. Even the ones who had half risen to go arrest Wayne Sherman for keeping his dead wife in a bush maze behind his house.

"What . . . was . . . it . . . then?"

Margot smiled. Despite the fear she felt, despite the nagging worry about what would happen to Wayne Sherman, this was, after all, her moment.

"It's the key to the city, guys," she said. "Wayne Sherman hid the key to the city in The Hedges."

Then the officers were up and moving, faster than Margot thought they could. So fast, in fact, that she hardly understood what was happening as two of them grabbed her by her arms and carried her out of the room, into the hall, and toward their cruisers that sat purring like big cats under the unfathomable falling rain.

12

Wayne sat up quickly in bed. How long had he been thinking? Didn't he know by now that thoughts like these were impossible to stop?

Shit.

There might be an officer outside right now, his puttylike hand extended, about to knock on the front door of the yellow house by The Hedges.

He finally got off the bed, walked to the bathroom, and splashed some cold water on his face.

"Bring it with you," he said to his reflection. "Don't let them have it."

Wayne walked outside and the rain came so hard that it was as if Goblin itself were telling him,

Take it, but it won't be easy.

And yet, it had been so easy to take in the first place.

After burying Molly in her grocery store apron (Molly was prouder of that store than anything else in her life), Wayne avoided all attempts at conversation by friends and family and went straight to the Greasy Glass. Located deep in the shadows of the GAG, the Glass was the kind of place where the very artists who got their work displayed across the street might have tossed back six or seven drinks. Or more. Wayne drank more. Ten, eleven, who could tell by the time he exited one of Goblin's most obscure dive bars and found himself pissing in the bushes behind The Milky Way.

The irony of finding himself drunk and publicly urinating by the city's adult movie theater immediately following the burial of a person so pure was not lost on him and so he laughed. Not the happy kind, as the single guffaw came out like a groan, laughter chopped in half perhaps, and he spotted something made of wood between the branches beyond his boots.

Wayne didn't stop (couldn't stop) pissing as he knelt to the dirt and reached with one hand into the gnarled bushes for what every Gobliner born and bred would have recognized as the key to the city.

After staring at it for a long time, too long, long enough for the Goblin Police to have spotted him and arrested him had they driven by, Wayne pocketed the key, zipped up, and stood with his back to the outside brick wall of The Milky Way for as long as it took to get sober.

He didn't dare take the key out of his pocket during this time but he touched it, through the fabric of his funeral pants, and thought,

The spirit of a city, the ghosts that make it go. It's no coincidence that you found this today, buddy. Molly goes into the earth and the key to the city goes into your pocket.

A talisman. An omen. The long-lost key to the city that the more spiritual set claimed belonged in city hall. An old wives' tale. A silly little myth. Whenever the key wasn't in city hall, they said, Goblin's ghosts ran rampant. History was all over the place at once.

Bad things happened.

Some mediums even said the key attracted ghosts.

Wayne liked this idea. Liked the possibility of Molly's return. He brought it home.

And the day he finished The Hedges, he no longer feared who might look in the cellar of his yellow house, who might chance pick up a book about Son of Blackwater and Colonel Wes Farraline and the contract signed in sand, who might open said book and discover, in there, what Wayne Sherman had found, grieving, in an alley.

The Hedges became something of a beacon that day, the shining signal Wayne sent to Molly, *Come back, come back to me, come to the key to the city like the crackpots say you will.*

He kept it behind glass at the finish line.

And now, taking the gravel path about a hundred yards from his house, along the outer edge of the big green box, Wayne approached his maintenance shed. Inside he took hold of his ax.

In case of emergency . . .

Wayne smiled. The little girl solving The Hedges certainly constituted an emergency. The Goblin Police would come for the key. And Wayne could get to it much faster if he entered through the escape hatch nearest the toolshed. So ax in hand, he ducked some low-hanging branches and entered The Hedges from the side. He could see that the top cover had been broken open long before he reached the finish line.

Rain came down heavy in there, coursing in off the arched branches above. He pulled his hood back, letting that water rush over him, letting Goblin's history and his own history wash over him, too. Setting the ax down, he looked at the wooden key.

He wiped rain from his face and lifted the ax again.

With one good swing the glass protecting the key to the city exploded into a thousand sharp triangles, all falling to his boots in the dirt. Wayne climbed onto the wood base and reached down for the key.

"We gotta go," he said.

Putting the key in the chest pocket of his parka, Wayne jumped the two feet back to the ground, crushing glass beneath his boots.

Then he exited The Hedges. Once outside it, he turned to face his accidental masterpiece.

"Phase One," he said. "Poor lover. Phase Two: artist in residence." Then he tapped the key in his pocket to be sure it was still there. "Phase Three: on the run."

Then, giving The Hedges a smile only the oldest of friends could share, Wayne Sherman ran.

13

Are you fucking kidding me?

Margot's mom Shelly was panicking. The police station was empty. Not one officer was there to tell her where her daughter was. Where they took her.

We . . . have . . . your . . . little . . . girl.

She screamed in the empty station, and the flat echo of its return told her how futile it was.

Where could they have gone? What had the officer said on the phone?

We . . . have . . . your . . . little—

No, no. After that. A place. A city landmark.

The zoo?

Perish Park?

The North Woods?

Come on, she thought, *come on come on come on.*

She took a deep breath. The craziest rain she'd ever seen was pounding against the station windows. The empty chairs and burring desk fans gave the place the feel of having been left in haste.

She went through it again.

We . . . have . . . your . . . little . . . girl. She . . . found . . . something . . . in . . .

in . . .

in . . .

the ZOO!

NO!

She punched a pencil holder, knocking the contents on the registration desk.

"Fuck Goblin!"

How could they do this? How could they take her daughter somewhere without telling her? That had to be illegal. Right? They knew she was on her way! There wasn't even a sign taped to the door. What kind of police station would *do* something like that?

The worst kind, Shelly. A big bad wolf of a station that doesn't give a fuck what's legal or not. A scaly underwater monster kind that takes little girls and—

STOP IT!

Just stop.

But it was too late. Terrible visions spread before her mind's eye like a color chart for a morgue. Margot in a squad car. Margot strung up in a tree. Margot buried alive. They could *touch* her. And what could Shelly do about it? *File a report?* She saw complete panic coming up over a hill. This was as bad as when Margot swore that one day she was going to ride her bike alone out to The Hedges.

"*The Hedges!*"

Yes.

Shelly tore out of the station. The rain hit her like the long clayish fingers of the Goblin Police, trying to keep her back.

In her car again, she peeled out of the lot and headed northeast.

The Hedges. That corny fucking place with no real finish line. That lame-ass tourist attraction.

"Fuck Goblin," she said again. "*Fuck it!*"

And then, "Well, I don't have to worry about getting pulled over now. They're all too busy with *my little girl!*"

14

The officer that followed Margot through The Hedges looked very angry when they got to the finish line and found nothing but broken glass. Margot, for her part, felt something like relief. The whole experience was turning on her. The Goblin Police were more than simply creepy to her now. They were scaring her. None of the officers said a word the whole drive over, and every now and then one would breathe real heavy like he was working to do it. Staring straight ahead (his fat white hands gripping the wheel), the driver didn't turn his head once.

Not even when a car almost clipped them on the right. Not when a woman darted out of their way on a street corner. Not when a dog ran across the road.

So he'd been hiding the key to the city. Margot didn't know much about that other than some kooky parents said the key to the city belonged in city hall, and that Goblin was in danger of being "unbalanced" without it there. It was the kind of thing people blamed things on.

You got fired? Well, if the key to the city was still in city hall . . .

A murder on Farraline Street? Has Mayor Blackwater found the key to the city yet?

So Wayne Sherman had it. But did this make him . . . bad? Margot couldn't make up her mind. As she led the officers along the triumphant route, she was alternately proud of being the one person the police could count on to guide them to the finish line, and anxious that she shouldn't be alone with Goblin Police at all, let alone in a maze. Their lumbering, heavy steps trailed close behind the whole way, and some of them made noises she'd never really heard before. And the deeper she took them, the more she felt the *size* of The Hedges. The truth was, she felt less and less safe by the turn. And by the time they hit the once dark passage where the bushes met overhead she was shaking. She recalled her mother's words:

Promise Mom, okay? You won't go in a room alone with them?

Yes, Mom, but is a pitch-black corner of a maze okay?

She wanted to cry. She did, a little bit, her back to the officers. She heard cracking sounds behind her, but she didn't think it was boots on sticks. Sounded more like bones resetting, skin stretching, a living transformation.

When they got to the end, she had to turn and face them. They looked just like they had in the station. Still wore their sunglasses. Still looked uncomfortable in their own skin.

Or maybe they didn't. Hard to say.

"Did . . . he . . . know . . . we . . . were . . . coming?"

The same pitch-shifted voice. A tape slowed down. The kind of voice teenagers said sounded like Satan.

Margot swallowed. Had she forgotten to mention that Wayne knew they were coming back at the station?

"Yes," she managed to say. "But I told him to stay put. I swear."

There was silence. Then the officer removed his glasses.

15

At about the time the officers following Margot discovered the key had been carried away, Wayne was crossing the Goblin city limit, heading south. He passed between the pair of leviathan topiaries he'd erected himself and imagined them growing over, till the two city luminaries looked covered in hair and tumors. He drove the speed limit. Soft music came through the truck's small speakers and he tried very hard to ignore the fact that a little girl had changed his life; that the Goblin Police couldn't be far behind.

As far as he could tell, he was driving through one of the worst rainfalls in the history of the city. As a lifelong Gobliner, this comforted him. He felt sheltered, under cover, hidden. And with the speedometer at a steady fifty-five and all headlights working, he believed he was going to make it.

The spinning lights in his rearview mirror told him he might not.

Wayne was six, perhaps seven, car lengths over the border when he pulled to the side of the road, his wipers feeble against what fell from the sky.

In the mirror he saw the cruiser door open. It had gotten dark since Wayne pocketed the key to the city and he wondered, now, how much time he'd spent thinking, sitting in his truck, after he left The Hedges. When had night come? By what meek announcement?

Tap tap.

The officer was bending toward the window, signaling for Wayne to roll it down. The rain seemed to be doing something to his face.

Wayne rolled the window down. Halfway. The rain came in, spraying the arm of his raincoat.

"Wayne . . . Sherman?"

Yes, I'm Mr. Sherman, and there used to be a Mrs. Sherman, too, but something horrible happened and I couldn't wake her one morning. I found the key to the city after her funeral, and I kept it rather than turning it in to you guys. Kept it because I heard it sets the ghosts of Goblin free.

"Was I speeding, Officer?"

Wayne Sherman was a Goblin celebrity. A statue of himself might be standing next to Carroll and Trachtenbroit one day. Maybe the man just wanted an autograph.

"Get . . . out . . . of . . . the . . . car . . . Mr. . . . . Sherman . . ."

Wayne looked ahead, up the road, into the rainfall, farther from Goblin.

"Mr. Sherman?"

Wayne turned to the officer slowly. "I'm about fifty feet outside Goblin, Officer. Isn't this out of your jurisdiction?"

The officer rose to his full height and put his hand to a black stick at his belt.

Wayne thought of Molly.

The officer pulled the stick out of the loop. He lifted and let it fall to his palm. Lift. Thump. Lift. Thump.

"What's . . . in . . . your . . . pocket . . . Mr. . . . . Sherman . . . ?"

Wayne didn't look down to his chest, but felt the bulge there. The key to the city.

The officer swung the stick, shattering the glass. Wayne reached into the rain and grabbed the officer's head with both hands. He brought it down hard. He saw the glass sink into the officer's skin like it was pudding. The officer brought his hands to his face and screamed, and it sounded like whales to Wayne, the unfathomably deep voice of something huge, hidden, submerged.

Wayne gripped the steering wheel and slammed his foot on the gas. He had an idea. More like a directive. Something he suddenly had to do.

It was the way the officer sounded as he reached to the new holes in his face. The way the rain came down harder than it ever had. It was the way The Hedges had become so popular, too, and it was the motor behind Goblin. The shadowy engine that ran things. The dark corners that existed in the middle of the street by day.

He had to hide the key to the city. Hide it again. Hide it in a place where no Goblin officer could ever find it.

He tore off from the side of the road then over the grass divider into the northbound lane.

He was going back to Goblin.

He blazed up the highway, pushing the old red truck beyond its stable capabilities. The engine resisted. He had a rain-blurred memory of the officer stumbling back to his car. But Wayne had a good head start.

When the speedometer reached ninety-five, the entire truck was shaking.

16

When Shelly got to The Hedges, she could tell the police had been there. She pulled in fast (the gravel like mud from all the rain; holy *shit* this rain). She left the lights on, the car running, and ran up to the porch of the little yellow house. The door was open, swinging a little from the wind. When she walked inside she almost tripped over a chair that had been turned over. It was dark inside. She felt along the wall for the lights and found them.

"Holy motherfucker," she said.

The place was destroyed. She didn't know one thing about the man who ran The Hedges, but she was pretty sure he didn't live like this.

Everything that could be turned over was.

Okay, she thought. *They didn't find what they were looking for. They left. Where'd they go, Shelly?*

In that moment, Goblin felt infinite. And the cold of infinity settled in her chest.

She hadn't passed any police cars on the way here. Or had she? The rain was thick. Easily one could have been going the other way, its lights off. Yes, Margot could've passed ten feet from her, mother and daughter side by side for a blink in time, then gone again to . . . wherever they were going.

Shelly started to cry. Not the type of tears that stopped her from moving, though.

She searched some of the fallen objects, broken shards, the man's life in slices.

When she found a visitors' log on the ground, the tears came a little harder. The last name listed was written in a handwriting she knew very well.

MARGOT

And then, next to it,

The girl who will solve your Hedges.

Shelly smiled despite the tears. Despite the fear. Kneeling now amid Wayne Sherman's life, she brought the log close to her face and yelped when she saw a note addressed to herself.

Mommy . . . we're going to the North Woods.

It was written fast. A desperate little scratch. Shelly could tell. Shelly knew. Like her little girl was in all the trouble Shelly feared she might be.

The North Woods?

Why did her daughter have to *sneak* a note to her?

But she knew why.

Margot was a smart girl—*thank* God Margot was a smart girl. She knew Mommy would figure out to come here, and so she left a note because she was *smart* and could recognize when she might be in trouble.

Margot was in trouble.

Shelly ran from the house and got back in her car. She tore out of the gravel lot.

The North Woods.

They had a head start on her. But how much? And there was no way the police were going to take Margot *into* the woods. That was as silly as suggesting, say, that the key to the city was found.

Nobody went into the North Woods. Nobody. And if someone was planning on dragging a little girl into *those* woods, why . . . why . . .

"Why, she'd have to sneak a note to Mom to tell her."

Margot!

17

Wayne was heading to the North Woods. The officer with the glass in his putty face radioed it in. Margot heard the call. The wounded officer had been following Sherman through town. Thought he might be heading to the woods. Something about Sherman and mazes.

He said that Sherman was in serious . . . fucking . . . trouble.

Margot heard that, too.

The other officers, gathered in the living room of the little yellow house, moved fast to the door.

"I have to use the bathroom," Margot said.

She couldn't shake the image of the officer's eyes when he'd taken off his glasses in The Hedges. They looked like cartoon eyes to her. As if they'd been drawn on his putty flesh. Like there was no way they could blink. Big with black irises. Staring down at her like a drawing hanging in a bad place.

"Hurry . . ." an officer by the door said. Thank God all their glasses were on again. Thank God she didn't have to try to make sense of what she'd seen in The Hedges.

Margot walked slowly to the bathroom. On the way, she saw the visitors' log on the ground. She took it with her, wrote Mommy a note, and left it where she'd found it on her way out.

"Where are we going?" she asked the officer waiting for her.

She knew from the radio call that they were going to the North Woods. But she wanted to hear him say it.

He didn't say it. Instead he grabbed her by the wrist so hard that she thought the skin there had somehow melted, been squished, fallen in. But when she looked at her wrist she saw that it was his fingers that had morphed, not hers.

Margot tried to pull away but the Goblin officer dragged her down the porch steps to a waiting cruiser.

Margot didn't want to go to the North Woods. It took a lot to scare her, a girl capable of solving The Hedges on her own, but the legend of the witch in the North Woods had always gotten to her.

"She has no teeth," Margot said as she was shoved into the car. "And so when she whispers, she spits on you. And then you're infected, then you've got the bad stuff in you, too."

But the officer didn't respond. And looking out the window, Margot realized that the car was moving faster than any car she'd ever been inside of.

Speeding.

Dangerously speeding.

Toward a witch with no teeth.

18

Wayne still had a good lead when he reached the northwest entrance. He parked the truck and left all Molly's things inside.

"Sorry," he said, genuinely wanting to carry it all with him.

But he carried only the key.

And he believed he had an advantage on the police in here; he had a history with mazelike trails. As long as they didn't bring that little girl with them.

When the first cruiser pulled into the open grassy area where Wayne's car still ran, Wayne was deep in the woods, well past the place he and Molly exchanged vows so long ago.

The key to the city banged against his heart in his chest pocket.

19

Margot asked, "What are you going to do to him if you catch him?"

The officer looked to the rearview mirror and Margot was sure, absolutely *sure* that his face was about to change, that it was all going to drip from his skull, showing her what the Goblin Police really looked like under all that putty.

It didn't happen, but Margot was as scared as if it had.

20

Wayne couldn't help but compare the North Woods to The Hedges. The likeness was remarkable. Distantly, far from the immediacy of running through the woods, he wondered if there was a connection there, as a Gobliner, having tried but failed to create an impenetrable maze of his own.

The girl proved The Hedges were no match for this.

He felt for the key at his pocket, found it still there, and continued. Deeper.

He believed he must have lost the officer tailing him already. In a place like this, one turn could do the trick. One decision. But Wayne was a long way from slowing down.

By then, the bark blended in with the night. Wayne's eyes had adjusted but only so far. The trunks seemed to grow out of the ground as he approached, insane life sprouting before him. Like ten thousand black bushmasters turned to stone. It smelled fresh in there, but fresh like fresh meat. Or fresh like the air just before a sea-storm hits. The thick odor of animal fear and self-preservation. Deer, squirrels, wolverines, wolves, and Great Owls sensing, perhaps, an inevitable wave of violence.

If the police caught him, that was.

Or perhaps the life in the woods, or the woods themselves, sensed the key he carried.

Old wives' tales.

Perhaps. But Wayne himself had held on to it, *wanting* to believe it could rattle the ghosts of Goblin, turn the city inside out, destabilize the place. Mayor Blackwater spoke of finding it one day, but Wayne didn't know whether the man meant it or not.

An unexpected thought struck him then: Had Wayne hidden the key as a fuck-you to Goblin? Did he want the city to be unstable because it was here that Molly died in her sleep?

Wayne, in the midst of his trouble, felt proud. He *had* built something that he could at least compare to these incredible woods, one of the hallmarks of the very city he'd repudiated by hiding its key. He wished he had come through them before. He wished he could stop and study them.

He heard movement behind him and believed it was the officer with the shards of glass in his face. It was impossible to consider that the officer had taken the same turns Wayne had, so many by now, and yet that's what Wayne considered.

He touched the key once more and thought,

You thought it was hidden well before? Try to find it in this place . . .

21

When the car carrying Margot reached the northwest entrance, she saw a second cruiser running with its lights on. The caravan that had gone from The Hedges to the North Woods had four cars of its own, and when they parked alongside Wayne's packed truck it looked like a midnight corral. The rain and subsequent fog gave the headlights a depth Margot didn't want to look into.

The entrance to the North Woods was lit up and Margot tried to slink deeper into the seat.

But the Goblin Police did not seem afraid.

The officers were out of their cars, standing before the entrance. Their tall silhouettes made shadows on the trees.

Margot watched as three officers searched Wayne Sherman's car. The guilt she felt for having led them here was unbearable. She saw an officer wipe his finger along the broken glass of the driver's-side window. She watched him suck his finger . . . tasting it . . . and she could handle it no longer.

She got out of the cruiser and entered the dark rain.

"I can figure these out," she said suddenly. "I can find him for you."

The officers turned slowly toward her, their faces visible in the glow of the headlights.

They looked different.

At first Margot thought it was the lights alone. Then she saw.

The officers had taken off their glasses. All of them. So many unnatural eyes looked upon her.

One of them opened his mouth and a voice deeper than the running engines spoke to her. Commanded her.

"Show . . . us . . ."

Margot's heart was *racing*. The rain, the woods, the night, the police. She tried to breathe steady like Mom tried to do, but there was just too much to fear. Tears blurred her vision. The officer who spoke walked awkwardly toward her. She didn't see him. She was holding her head in her hands, her eyes toward her wet shoes. She didn't know how close he had come. When he spoke, when he said, "Show...us...now..." she could feel his breath and Margot screamed. Then the officer's chin fell to the dirt.

"What..." Margot began, pointing at the fallen feature. The rain pooled in it already.

The officer grabbed her arm with violence.

"Yes!" Margot said. "I'll show you! I'll show you right now!"

The officer pulled her from the wet ground and thrust her ahead, toward the entrance. She stumbled forward and could hear the men following. She wasn't thinking. Not like she normally would. Trembling, shaking, she entered the woods and stepped past the spot where the man who built The Hedges once exchanged vows with his wife. She crossed through the light that the cars created and stepped into the darkness of the woods. She didn't have to listen hard to know the police were following her lead. They sounded like a pack of animals. Impatient...clumsy... hungry...

She had no idea where Wayne Sherman was and had no idea how to find him.

But she had a plan, a terribly flimsy plan, something to satiate the monstrous entities behind her.

For a time.

She would have to invent something equally insubstantial when that time was up.

She led the officers deeper into the woods.

22

Deeper into the woods.

Wayne forged on. Breathing hard now.

So many of the trails went uphill when you were so

sure they were heading down. Wayne's legs were on fire. The shifts in elevation. The ups and downs. He wasn't used to it. The Hedges were flat, built on an open lawn. But the North Woods grew out of mad land.

He thought of Chief Blackwater and the settlers who hid in these woods. Wayne was no expert on Goblin history, but he knew that Blackwater claimed all of Goblin was *bad land.* As the key banged against his chest, he thought of Blackwater, Son of Blackwater, Farraline and Carroll, and the Original 60 settlers. He thought of the owls and the witch and all the stories young Gobliners learn before they're old enough to know better.

He gripped the key through the parka.

Running, hiding, he felt suddenly as if it was his duty to keep the key hidden. That Goblin was nothing without its ghosts. That to return the thing to city hall would somehow be returning the entire soul of the city itself.

Wayne continued. Deeper.

The rain came through the web of treetops in volumes. The slow burning in his legs was getting to be too much. He was talking to the key now, but it didn't sound like talking. Half words and mumbles obscuring the snapping of twigs that somehow continued behind him.

I'm not letting them have it, he thought. As if somehow the key and Molly were one. Both the spirit of Goblin.

Another snapping stick behind him. Was it the same officer? Many officers?

His eyes hurt from focusing on the darkness. The muscles in his neck tensed. It was as if he were rebuilding The Hedges, experiencing the unbearable effort once again.

The woods seemed to close in on him. The trails got tighter. More branches, too many branches, reached for him as he passed. They cut into his parka sleeves and drew blood from his arms.

One even cut the pocket at his chest and Wayne caught the key without looking as it fell.

The key to the city.

The spirit of Goblin.

Wayne was in deep.

23

*Y*ou're like a den mother, Margot told herself. *You're leading a bunch of Girl Scouts on a nature walk through a very interesting wood.*

She knew the story of the North Woods. Every kid in Goblin did. She knew about the whispering witch who could make your heart explode. She knew about the indigenous chief driven mad. And yet the thing she was most afraid of was with her already.

You told them you could find him, she told herself calmly. *So . . . pretend to find him.*

She couldn't bring herself to turn around, to look at the Goblin Police in the North Woods. Instead she led silently.

They need you, she reminded herself. But for how long?

She made decisions quickly, giving the appearance that she knew where she was going. And the pride of solving The Hedges carried her.

But the North Woods had no finish line. No stationary key behind glass. Wayne Sherman must have been moving, too.

She thought of him, Wayne, as he was when she bought her ticket.

How scared he must be.

There was no denying the fact that this was all her fault. She'd started the whole thing. She'd—

A hand planted itself on her shoulder. She jumped in the darkness.

"How . . . close . . . are . . . we . . . ?"

Margot didn't turn around. Couldn't bear seeing those cartoonish, unblinking eyes.

"We're close," she said. "I can smell the grass on him."

Could they tell? Could they tell she was lying?

24

If Wayne hadn't been driven by losing the police, his body would have collapsed. It would have been difficult to walk this far without a worry in the world. The sounds of somebody following him continued.

"Molly," he huffed, "remember how we both dreamed of each other the night we first saw each other?"

He started to laugh.

The whole thing, The Hedges, running from the Goblin Police, real love . . . it was all so . . . *funny* to him then.

Snap!

Someone behind him still.

Snap! Snap!

"Remember how—"

Snap! Snap!

Wayne stopped. Whatever it was, wasn't going away.

He turned to face it.

Blackness.

Wayne squinted, searching for movement. He knelt, needing the rest.

"Molly," he said. "What do you think it is? The police? Or . . ."

It was closer now; the sound of branches pulled aside, the crackle of sticks and dead leaves.

Wayne rose again.

Memories of Molly circled through his mind like a wheel of fortune on fire.

He breathed deep.

Then whatever was trailing him stopped.

He thought he could make something out, a shape, life, a hundred feet from where he stood, rooted like a gnarled tree or an eleven-foot-high bush wall of a maze.

"Hello," Wayne said.

It was a woman.

She stepped out from behind a tree and Wayne realized she was much closer than he'd thought. A trick of the eyes. A trick of the North Woods.

He also realized he still had the key to the city in his hand.

Before she reached him, Wayne understood it was Molly. There was no question in his mind, his eye, his heart. She was naked just the way she was at Lake Oslow, the day they took photos, the roll of film he never developed. The roll of film that sat packed in a bag in his truck outside these very woods.

"Molly," he said, smiling, trying to almost flirt with the impossible vision. "I can't tell you how long I've wanted to see you this way."

Then the tears rolled down his face like Goblin rain.

The Hedges . . . a tribute to Molly . . . and now the North Woods . . . and Molly's ghost to greet him.

He gripped the key to the city.

Molly sat down on a stump Wayne hadn't seen was there. Her naked legs glowed in the darkness. She gestured for Wayne to come to her.

"If I'd have known it was you," he said, "I never would've kept walking deeper. You know that, right?"

She looked up at him with the same eyes that she used to look at him with across their small yellow house by a big empty field.

She held out a smooth hand and Wayne took it. He knelt beside her, one knee in the dirt, holding her hand in his, their eyes locked as tightly as the lids of one of those great Goblin graves.

"Molly—" Wayne started.

But Molly leaned closer to whisper something in his ear.

25

The noises (over her shoulder, at her heels) had swelled to a symphony of high-pitched giggles, garbled grunts, half words, heavy breathing, and the horrible sound of rubber being torn apart. Whatever Margot was leading through the woods no longer looked like it did when they'd entered.

She knew this without looking.

She had visions of poor Wayne Sherman dying at the hands of these officers; the soft-spoken proprietor who asked her to give him a minute forty thousand years ago.

It's the wife, she remembered the officer saying.

But it wasn't his wife. It was the key to the city. And yet, was there a connection there? Did the key to Goblin somehow represent his wife? Or something like that?

Oh, what had she done? She thought she was sooooo smart. Sooooo brave. Soooo heroic. And now she was just a little mean girl. She wanted so badly to find Wayne Sherman and tell him, *I hope I accomplish something as great as The Hedges when I grow up.*

"Are . . . we . . . close . . . ?"

The voice no longer resembled the voices from the station, from Wayne's yellow house, from the entrance to the woods.

Margot took a deep breath. She heard something like bones snapping behind her. She felt something like wet fur against the back of her neck.

She didn't scream.

But she ran.

She ran deep into the blackness of the path and quickly climbed one of the trunks of the brittle trees. It curved up and outward and up again, until she didn't know if she was climbing up or down. She climbed fast, scraping her little legs on the way, and stopped where the trunk met another from an equally gnarled tree.

Her heartbeat was in her throat.

She could hear the officers approaching. The muffled, atonal voices grew louder and danced with the wind in the woods. She didn't want to see them, she didn't want to see them, she didn't want to—

"Little . . . girl . . . ?"

They were standing at the foot of the tree.

"Are . . . we . . . going . . . to . . . have . . . to . . . get . . . you . . . out . . . of . . . that . . . tree . . . ?"

Margot closed her eyes tight.

Oh my God, oh my God, oh my God, oh my God, oh my God, oh my God, oh my God!

She edged farther up the trunk and as she did, she felt something beside her.

Feathers, her mind told her.

She did not scream.

But she opened her eyes to look at it.

The darkness beside her started to move. Margot remained silent as a head turned to face her, an animal, two red dots in all this wet darkness.

She knew what it was.

A Great Owl.

"Here . . . we . . . come . . ." an officer said below.

In the blackness, the eyes of the owl were like candles. Margot followed them and, looking over the trunk, saw the faces that had been following her.

She caught her breath short.

It wasn't a group of Goblin officers looking up at the tree, not anymore.

Margot covered her eyes but it was too late, and she took with her the huge donkey teeth jutting from gray gums, the eyes four times larger than her own, the balding scalps . . .

Margot covered her eyes again and shuddered.

"Where . . . is . . . she . . . ?"

The words were something like prison bars sliding open to Margot. News that Wayne Sherman would be fine. *Relief.*

They hadn't seen her.

They thought they saw something in the tree, she told herself. *And the owl made them think it was only an owl.*

The officers started to move on. The sound of bones snapping, gibberish, and slobbering clay lips grew faint.

But they called out for her down the path. In a direction Margot hadn't been yet. A direction Margot wouldn't go.

She waited.

She waited.

She waited.

Then she could wait no more.

"Thank you," she whispered to the owl.

Then she worked her way down the rough wet trunk. When her black dance shoes touched the dirt, she thought,

Now . . . reverse it all.

The officers couldn't have known that Margot's method through the North Woods was more simple than that of The Hedges. With the winding of the paths it would have been hard to say what direction they were going. They weren't paying attention to her. They were looking for Wayne Sherman.

But Margot had simply made a right every chance she had.

Margot hoped they would get lost in the woods forever. Go mad like the indigenous chief. Stumbling into one another until they died of starvation.

She just hoped they wouldn't find Wayne Sherman before then.

She ran.

She silently thanked the Great Owl again.

She prayed for Wayne Sherman.

26

The story Molly whispered to Wayne was incredible. The words didn't just evoke images but *conjured* them out of the dirt he knelt upon. Huge ideas explained in a language so graceful Wayne didn't even know he was nodding until his neck started to hurt from it.

Molly continued to whisper.

Wayne's eyes were closed. He listened, his hand in hers. There was no reason to worry . . . no reason to run . . .

She whispered . . . and the story she told was a story Wayne had been waiting to hear for twelve years. A story that explained death and loss and loneliness. A story that gave good reasons for each. The frenzy in which he had built The Hedges was clear to him now . . .

Molly continued to whisper.

The voice was like medicine for twelve years of pain. Twelve years of sadness, frustration, rebellion, anger, hate—

Wayne suddenly felt something like a hiccup in his chest.

Molly held his hand tighter. She continued to whisper.

Wayne felt a tightening in the muscles of his chest, something pressing down on his shoulders. He was cold now. The rain felt colder, too.

He gasped, trying not to interrupt the story, the whispering in his ear. But he couldn't help it, something was happening, his fingers and toes, hands and feet . . .

"Molly," he said. "Stop."

The woods got darker. The trees, it seemed, were trying to strangle something out of him.

Now it was happening to his ankles and his wrists, his lower legs and forearms. He could feel it, could feel the blood *receding*.

Retreating.

Going home.

Molly continued to whisper but her words were confusing now. Absurd images with no meaning, phrases from a children's television show.

Wayne felt a heaviness in his chest. Like it was bloating. Like he was being pumped with vinegar.

It hurt.

He opened his eyes.

"Molly?"

He couldn't bring his head up to look at her. Could barely move his neck at all.

He tried to pull away but the hand held tighter. It hurt. It all hurt. He writhed in the dirt, still tied to Molly by his hand. A hand he had volunteered . . .

There were no words in the story now. Only swirling whites and grays, the look of the Goblin sky before it rained.

Wayne screamed with what breath he had. His veins were dry; a series of empty paths, with nobody there to maintain them.

He thought of The Hedges as he opened his other hand and dropped the key to the city.

It fell to the forest floor.

And everything, all the pain, stopped so suddenly that Wayne barely noticed as Molly gasped.

On all fours now, catching his breath, he saw the key beneath him. Then he saw the hand that reached for it and understood that it was not Molly who had been whispering to him at all.

The eight-fingered hand moved fast. But Wayne saw the wrinkles, the warts, the dried blood.

When he looked up, the witch was gone, and only the darkness of the North Woods remained seated on the stump.

Wayne rose again. He felt along his chest, his legs, his groin, his face, making sure it was all still there, still working, still alive.

Then, understanding vaguely that the key to the city had been stolen by the witch of the North Woods, Wayne Sherman smiled. Goblin might fancy him the master of the maze, but there was nobody who knew the impossible passages of undying pain like the woman he'd just encountered.

Wayne laughed. In the distance he heard what sounded like a bowstring, men yelling. He saw a flash of light.

He remained still, wondering what the fate of Goblin might be with its key in the hands of a witch.

He waited.

He waited.

He waited.

Until he could wait no more. Then he quietly started to make his way back, having left himself a trail of breadcrumbs in the form of right turns, and only right turns, all the way into the black nether heart of the North Woods.

And the closer he got to the exit, the more he thought of the places a man could go, a man whose car was already packed, a man who had already accomplished everything he could in a place that no longer held him.

27

When Margot exited the woods, her mother put her hands to her mouth and cried out with painful relief. She had been waiting, scared, parked next to the idling police cruisers for a long time. The northwest entrance was lit like a pumpkin. She knew better than to go inside. A dead Mommy wouldn't help Margot at all.

"Mommy!" Margot yelled.

They embraced in the lights of the cruiser.

"What did they do to you? What did they do!"

"It's okay. I'm okay. I tricked them. I lost them in there."

Shelly studied the scrapes on Margot's arms and legs. The fear in her daughter's eyes. The confidence there, too. Then she carried Margot to the car and put her in the passenger seat.

"We're leaving Goblin, Margot. We're leaving Goblin for good."

Shelly pulled the car away from the cruisers.

It took them twenty minutes to reach the city's southern border.

As they passed between giant topiaries framing the city gates, Margot thought of Wayne Sherman.

Was he okay?

She thought of The Hedges and how she didn't care that the kids at school would never know that she solved them.

"Good riddance," Shelly said as they crossed the city limit.

Margot told herself that Wayne probably made it out okay. After all, he built The Hedges.

If there was anybody that could find his way out of a maze . . .

EPÍLOGUE: MAKE YOURSELF AT HOME

Bone white and trembling, fearing for his life, Tom checked the address again: 726 Rolling Hills Drive. It said so right above the arched doorway. It was twelve fourteen. How half an hour had passed within the city was lost on him but he wasn't thinking of numbers just then. He was thinking of white eyes floating in the back of his truck. He was thinking of a timeless, angry voice that had spoken but one word:

Drive.

He had sixteen minutes of hope left. Sixteen minutes that might see him handing over that very box and whatever it was that came with it. He'd been instructed to destroy the contents of the box once that time was up.

Tom didn't want to go near the box.

Please, Mr. Crawford, he thought. *Answer your door.*

He rang the bell.

There was an awning over the front door, or rather, a layer of stone that followed the arch and jutted out, protecting Tom from the merciless downpour.

He rang the bell again. Heard it ring out and echo within.

"Come on," he said. "Answer the door."

But no one did.

He looked back to the truck parked in the winding, cobblestone drive. More specifically to the closed door that Tom didn't want to open.

Had he imagined it all? Did a crouched figure *really* tell him to drive? And if so . . . was the figure out of the box? In it? Could it come and go as it pleased? Come and go, in and out of a crate nailed two hundred times over?

He rang the bell again. He banged on the door.

"Mr. Crawford! Hello! Delivery!"

Still no answer.

Stepping out from the cover of the awning, stepping onto the wood chips of a pristine landscape job, he brought his nose to the glass of a wide window. He could make out a staircase. A table near the front door. Hardly more than that.

It looked like nobody was home.

"Shit."

He looked back at the truck again, idling, steam rising from the tailpipe, creating curtains for that locked back door.

Just leave it here, he thought.

Then he thought of Jerry and how he'd explain this.

Never mind the money, Jerry. I decided not to follow those directions after all. Yeah. The box spoke to me, Jerry.

It *did* say something. Didn't it? And what would work protocol have to say about *that*?

Through the glass he saw no sign of life.

IF RECIPIENT IS NOT HOME (OR DOES NOT ANSWER THE DOOR) BETWEEN 12 AND 12:30 OR IF DRIVER MISSES THIS WINDOW OF TIME, DESTROY CONTENTS OF BOX.

Tom could almost still hear the doorbell echoing through the house. Wind chimes played in a cave. Could Dean Crawford hear it, too? Was he bundled up somewhere inside?

He wanted it destroyed the whole time.

Tom tried to shake this idea as quickly as it came.

But it was hard. The way truth is hard to deny, no matter what someone wants to believe.

2

He tried the door handle.

And the door opened.

"Mr. Crawford?"

He glanced over his shoulder, the truck looking like a beast to him. Blocking the way to the street. Telling him to enter the house. Nowhere else to go.

"Delivery, Mr. Crawford!"

He pushed the door open farther. He reached inside, searching for a foyer light.

"Mr. Crawford?"

His voice echoed like the bell had moments before. He finally took a step and when his boot touched the foyer floor it struck Tom that he was officially breaking into a client's home.

It was cold inside. It felt like nobody was home.

Tom took the flashlight from his coat pocket, flipped it on, and brought merciful light to the house.

He walked in, deeper, until the foyer became a large carpeted room with couches and a television as big as Tom's truck.

There was no one in the room and it really *felt* like there was no one in the room. As if no one had been home for weeks.

Through the living room, Tom came to the kitchen. Then to

a large room with a fireplace and what looked like rugs made from actual animal hides.

"Crawford?" he called.

He came to a closed dark door. Even under his meager beam he could tell the wood was strong. The knob turned easily and he pushed it open slowly, shining the light inside. It was a study or a library. The kind of room Tom had never had in a house of his own. His beam traced a tall bookshelf that covered the wall to his left, then settled on a table edge, an idle lamp, a paperweight, and—

"What the fuck are you doing?"

And the man sitting at that desk, too.

Tom leapt back.

"Mr. Crawford?"

The man had a shotgun pointed at Tom's chest.

"Did you destroy the contents of the box?"

"No, Mr. Crawford, I . . ." He raised his hands to show he had no weapon of his own. "I'm too scared to go near it. The box . . . the box *spoke to me.*"

"My God, man," Crawford said. "What have we done?"

A metallic squawk shook the room and Tom turned to the study door. He knew that particular sound better than anybody else in Goblin could know it.

The back door to the truck had just slid open.

Forcefully.

"How well do you know your history?" Crawford asked, the gun still trained on Tom's chest. Crawford was sweating bad. The look in his eye suggested this was the end of a much more complex tragedy.

"My first kiss was in Goblin," Tom said, arms still raised.

"Not *your* history," Crawford barked. *"Goblin's."* He chuckled and shook his head. "But that's how it always is here, isn't it? People mistaking their own stories as adding up to one big one."

"Mr. Crawford," Tom began. "Who is that coming through your house?"

Crawford grunted.

"Would you believe me if I told you it was a corpse?" he said. "Would you believe me if I told you that what you hear in the kitchen now are the cold dead feet of a native long since double-crossed by the treacherous white men who forced him and his kind out?"

Tom was shaking. He lowered his arms and stepped deeper into the study. Crawford held the gun on the open door.

"Are you . . . talking about . . . Chief Blackwater?" Tom asked.

Crawford snorted surprise. "So you *do* know your history."

"I . . . I kissed that girl . . . by the . . . Blackwater River . . ."

Crawford fired the gun into the empty space of the open door. Tom cried out.

"Not Blackwater," Crawford said, cocking the gun again. "By God, the chief's body was never found. But his son . . ."

"Why did you order this box?" Tom asked fast. His voice shook. Crawford didn't hesitate in answering.

"We went too far, is why. We wanted too much. When I saw your truck pull up I changed my mind. Can you blame me?"

Eyes appeared in the study doorway.

"Hello," Dean Crawford said. "Son of Blackwater. Back to gain retribution for Wes Farraline's signature in sand?"

Crawford fired again.

A bullet tore a purple hole in the dead man's chest, but the corpse advanced.

"Do *not* come any closer!" Crawford cried out.

But the silhouette advanced. Crawford gasped. It looked nothing like a native, after all. This wasn't Chief Blackwater, Son of Blackwater, or anybody related to Mayor Blackwater, at all.

It's a ghost, Crawford thought. *It's what Chief Blackwater warned his tribe about. It's what drives Goblin mad.*

Crawford fired again.

The thing was at the desk, an arm's reach from the gun.

"You were here before any man stepped foot in Goblin," Crawford said, his voice shaking. "You're what makes Goblin—"

Something moved with such swiftness that Tom thought a bird had flown into the study. When he heard the CRAAAAAACK beside him, he knew it was Dean Crawford's skull.

Crushed like a pumpkin, Tom thought, as the gun fell to the desk and the man fell to the floor. And in the hand of the dark silhouette was what it had taken from Crawford's head.

The brains, the eyes, the ooze all shone in the moonlight through the study window.

The shape turned to face him.

"I'm not a Gobliner!" Tom cried out. He wasn't exactly sure why this was the right thing to say, but he believed it was.

He was a forty-four-year-old delivery driver who hadn't been to Goblin since he kissed a girl thirty billion years ago and he didn't want to die like this. The pressure . . . the violence . . . his mind in the hands of history.

What had Tom delivered to Goblin tonight? Was it . . . misery? Pain? Crime? Corruption?

Was it the kind of *bad* that can be felt by anyone near enough to feel it? The kind that spreads? Was it irrevocable . . . unflagging . . . *driven?* Tom thought of the map of Goblin he had stuffed in the glove compartment. He saw it now as if under a sheet . . . lumpy and not easily defined. As if the trees in Perish Park and all the streets had been robbed of their color, stolen by whatever infamy he'd brought with him. Something as living and unliving as the rain. All the great topiaries, that place The Hedges, the Blackwater River . . . they'd all lost their color, their vitality, their peace.

The West Fields. The North Woods. The Woodruff. Transistor Planet. The Milky Way. Goblin's Magic. Goblin Games.

What other black calamities had occurred, this night, this rainy, rainy night?

"I'm not a Gobliner!" he repeated, holding out both hands as the silhouette reached for him.

Then it had Tom by the collar and it dragged him from the study. Through room after room, kitchen and foyer, until the sky unloaded upon Tom once again.

What had Tom delivered tonight? Was it . . . loneliness? Fear? Gluttony?

Ambition? Confusion? Loss?

Tom cried out for it all to stop, but it was useless. The unfathomably strong hand that held him, the dead fingers, firm shadows, couldn't be lifted from his body with a dolly.

Soon Tom felt the metal of the truck against his back. Outside, under the moon, the thing was no easier to see.

Tom had to close his eyes.

"Drive," it said and Tom opened his eyes slowly, confused and scared, as he wanted to know, *needed* to know, if the impossibility who pinned him to the truck meant what Tom thought it did.

"Drive," Tom echoed.

The thing opened the passenger-side door and threw Tom across to the wheel. Tom bashed his head on the window and when he removed his hands from his head he saw it was climbing up into the cabin.

"Drive."

Tom started the truck.

He put it in reverse and backed out of the cobblestone drive, reentering the Goblin neighborhood of Rolling Hills, where a party still raged in the distance.

Tom drove. But he didn't drive south; he didn't drive back

home to where he could have been eating pizza and drinking beers.

He headed toward the party. The party first.

Because Tom knew what the silhouette wanted and what it meant when it said drive.

Tom headed toward the lights and loud voices, where he knew the shadow beside him would find others like Dean Crawford, men and women who (deservedly or not) would face their darkest hour tonight, this night, the night Tom delivered scorched history, *pre*-history, to the city of Goblin.

And after the party? After the party they would drive onto the dirt thruway called Christmas (a name Tom remembered from childhood), heading deeper into the city, where many more Gobliners juggled their fears, their lives, their history, unaware that a bigger story was traveling fast toward them.

And as the rain smacked the windshield, as the truck swallowed the muddy road, Tom wondered about the people he'd see crushed tonight, killed like Dean Crawford was, the people whose stories were as dark as this violent sky, the people who, stitched together, made up this gorgeous handbag of hysteria, the people who, despite the horrors that came with it, all called the same place home.

Goblin.

ACKNOWLEDGMENTS

Del Rey Books . . . thank you for inviting more people into the city of *Goblin*. I hope it rained sufficiently on all.

Paul Miller and Earthling Publications . . . thank you for putting out the initial limited edition of *Goblin*. Thrill of a lifetime.

Ryan Lewis, Candace Lake, Wayne Alexander, and Kristin Nelson . . . this was the book that brought us all together: the first I sent to Wayne. Thank you for the whirlwind that has followed.

Allison . . . shall we move to Goblin? Raise Weimaraners in the West Fields? Vizslas, too?

And Dave Simmer . . . remember when you asked for a book and I sent you one called *Goblin*? I'm gonna keep thanking you forever.

ABOUT THE AUTHOR

JOSH MALERMAN is a *New York Times* bestselling author and one of two singer-songwriters for the rock band the High Strung. His debut novel, *Bird Box,* is the inspiration for the hit Netflix film of the same name. His other novels include *Unbury Carol, Inspection, A House at the Bottom of a Lake,* and *Malorie,* the sequel to *Bird Box.* Malerman lives in Michigan with his fiancée, the artist-musician Allison Laakko.

joshmalerman.com

Facebook.com/JoshMalerman

Twitter: @JoshMalerman

Instagram: @joshmalerman

ABOUT THE TYPE

This book was set in Requiem, a typeface designed by the Hoefler Type Foundry. It is a modern typeface inspired by inscriptional capitals in Ludovico Vicentino degli Arrighi's 1523 writing manual, *Il modo de temperare le penne*. An original lowercase, a set of figures, and an italic in the chancery style that Arrighi (fl. 1522) helped popularize were created to make this adaptation of a classical design into a complete font family.